THE
REPLACEMENT
WIFE

Also by Darby Kane

Pretty Little Wife

THE
REPLACEMENT
WIFE

A Novel

DARBY KANE

wm

WILLIAM MORROW

An Imprint of HarperCollins*Publishers*

F
KAN

THE REPLACEMENT WIFE. Copyright © 2021 by HelenKay Dimon. All rights reserved. Printed in the United States of America. No part of this book may be used or reproduced in any manner whatsoever without written permission except in the case of brief quotations embodied in critical articles and reviews. For information, address HarperCollins Publishers, 195 Broadway, New York, NY 10007.

HarperCollins books may be purchased for educational, business, or sales promotional use. For information, please email the Special Markets Department at SPsales@harpercollins.com.

FIRST EDITION

Designed by Diahann Sturge

Library of Congress Cataloging-in-Publication Data has been applied for.

ISBN 978-0-06-311780-8 (paperback)
ISBN 978-0-06-320541-3 (international edition)
ISBN 978-0-06-311968-0 (hardcover library edition)

21 22 23 24 25 LSC 10 9 8 7 6 5 4 3 2 1

For my dad, who missed seeing this one released to the world

THE
REPLACEMENT
WIFE

Chapter One

So much planning went into a scheme like this. It was all about matching the timing to the perfect set of circumstances. Once the details of how and when became clear, most of the other pieces would fall into place. The components mattered as much as the whole. Picking the right moment to move in. Not being too obvious or excited. Not giving anything away until the last second . . . then savoring the fear and panic.

Years, months, weeks. Those were timeline questions and not really relevant. The stinging attack would happen when it was supposed to happen. One little push and the plan would start rolling until it accelerated, racing down the right path, the one purposely set.

Saying the right thing. Doing the right thing. Taking control in an explosion of power.

But, for now, it was a matter of knowing when to hold back and when to leap. Developing a stillness that let the body melt into place, blend into the background.

Now? Or what about now? Is it time yet? Satisfaction waited just out of reach. One stretch too far.

Unlike so many things that happened in life—buying a house, switching jobs—this was not the kind of thing to plot out with strict deadlines. But just winging it didn't work either. In or out. Commit or don't. Give into the need.

Not today, but soon. Very soon . . .

Chapter Two

Another family dinner. This one on a random Thursday evening in mid-September. Same kitchen. Same table with the wobbly leg. Same people. One husband. One seven-year-old boy who hated anything that wasn't a chicken nugget.

One brother-in-law who might be a killer.

Not a *that was a horrible accident* type of killer either. No. A person who killed over and over, targeting and wiping out the women closest to him.

Elisa Wright looked across the table, over the pile of mashed potatoes and stack of homemade dinner rolls, at Josh. She couldn't shake the now familiar anxious churning. With every forkful of food, every joke, every smile he gifted them, the word *murderer* flashed in her mind.

She closed her eyes but the bright kitchen lights wouldn't blink out. The truth gnawed and pricked at her. Exploded in her head and shot through her while she assessed and dissected every word he said, looking for clues.

The big problem? She was the only one who questioned him.

Everyone loved Josh. He was attractive, but not too much.

Successful, but not too much. With brown eyes and brown hair that curled at the ends, he looked like an older version of that cute guy in your college history class who faded into memory long before he messaged you on social media two decades later with an overly familiar and slightly inappropriate greeting.

Charming, great at conversation, and really unlucky in love. The description fit Josh. That and, if her instincts were right, so did killer.

On the surface, he loved hard and grieved the loss of love even harder. He was not a guy who liked being alone. He craved stability and a relationship. He never gave off a playboy vibe. He'd spent most nights and weekends during the last seven months at their house, where Elisa fed and mothered him. Cleaned up after him and laughed with him.

Now, after years of knowing him, she feared him. Questioned every move and every explanation.

Josh knocked on the table right next to her hand. "Hey, sis."

She jerked back at the mental interruption but didn't say a word.

Nathan, secure in his place in the world and enraptured by his uncle's antics, as usual, snorted. "She's not really your sister."

"Close enough," Josh said with a wink.

Fair because she'd considered Josh family from the day they met nine years ago. She'd been dating Harris, his brother, and heard all about Josh's love of hiking and the years he spent spinning out of control. Harris basically raised Josh. Only seven years separated them, but the number didn't reflect the reality of sleepless nights and rounds of money worries that had haunted Harris as he'd done all he could to save and support Josh all those years ago.

That made them close, more like father and son in some ways. The idea used to fill her with pride. She'd listened to the stories and could imagine her brilliant husband balancing his dreams and the hard work of veterinary school with raising a flailing brother still haunted by the unexpected loss of their parents.

She'd spent years admiring Harris for shouldering more than his share growing up. As an only child, she'd been more than a little envious of the brothers' tight relationship. Now she wanted Josh out of her house. Out of their lives. Gone and forgotten.

She felt Harris's fingers settle over hers. He rubbed his thumb along the back of her hand in that reassuring-husband way she loved. The gentle touch still had the power to calm the nerves jumping around inside her.

"You okay?" he asked in a low voice.

How did she tell him that his beloved baby brother scared the hell out of her?

She couldn't and that problem created an unpassable divide between them. He hadn't picked up on her pulling away, but she was and she couldn't seem to stop it. She vowed to figure out a solution before her marriage imploded. She just needed time and evidence . . . and some sign that the husband she adored would believe her. That he'd take her side against blood.

The breath she'd been holding came out on a shaky exhale.

She concentrated, trying to force a lightness she didn't feel into her voice as she glanced at her son with an exaggerated eyebrow lift. "I'm cranky because someone woke up before six and wanted to play outside."

"It was raining." Nathan practically whined the response, as if any rational person would prefer splashing around in muddy driveway puddles to sleep.

Harris laughed. "And that's good?"

Nathan smiled back. "Yes!"

"Interesting you didn't know about the family's early morning activities." Josh put down his wineglass and reached for another dinner roll as he glanced at Harris. "Where were you?"

Mindless conversation. She could do this. "He was still asleep."

"Story of your life. Right, Elisa?" Josh leaned in close to Nathan as if they were sharing an uncle-nephew joke.

She tried to keep her expression neutral but feared it came off more like a grimace. "Something like that."

"Uh, nothing like that, actually," Harris joked. He gave her hand a squeeze before picking up his fork and heading back in for another piece of steak.

When would this dinner from hell end? She couldn't force down another bite. Hoping Josh would choke didn't seem to be working either.

While she was forcing things, she forced a smile, this one for Harris. He was the hardest worker she knew. He'd built a practice and opened up not one but two locations of his emergency vet hospital in just a few years, way ahead of schedule.

It wasn't Harris's fault his brother was a psychopath.

"Okay, but . . ." Nathan stopped to chew and swallow when his father sent him *that* look. As soon as the chicken cleared his throat he was shifting around in his chair, practically bouncing with excitement. His gaze flipped to Josh. "Wanna watch a movie with me tomorrow night? *Doolittle?*"

"Again?" Harris cringed but Nathan was too busy staring at his uncle to notice.

No, no, no. She didn't want Josh in her house, at her table, or near her son any more than necessary to keep family calm.

Before she could invent a lame excuse, Josh shook his head. "Any other time, yes, but I have to take a pass on tomorrow." When Nathan's face dropped, Josh squeezed his shoulder. "Later, during the weekend. Okay?"

Nathan shrugged. "Fine."

"You'll survive a Friday night with just your boring parents for company," Harris said in his most convincing dad voice.

Nathan dropped one leg until his foot inched toward the floor, suggesting he was ready to move to the next thing on his agenda. "May I be excused?" he asked as he stared at his tablet on the kitchen counter. The one loaded with his video games he was allowed to play after dinner.

Harris nodded. "Take your plate to the sink and you can go."

Nathan jumped down, dropping a nugget on the floor as he went. He whipped around his chair. Knocked into it. Basically made as much noise and as much of a scene as possible.

"No running in the house!" The same words she spent half her life shouting ever since Nathan learned to walk.

The adults watched Nathan set the plate on the very edge

of the counter, just far in enough not to immediately fall. Then he was off. Made a beeline for the tablet, grabbed it, and hummed his way into the small television room off the kitchen.

Josh laughed as he followed the scene then his smile fell as he turned back to the table. "Speaking of tomorrow . . ."

"Were we?" Harris asked in his usual joking manner as he continued eating his dinner.

"I want to explain why I can't come over and—"

"It's fine," Elisa rushed out. Better than fine. Whatever his conflict was it saved her hours of panicked pacing as she tried to think of a way out of the visit. "Nathan can go one night without seeing you."

Something about the way she said the phrase made Harris glance at her.

Josh plowed ahead. "I have a date."

The scrambling fight for the right words stopped in Elisa's brain. She went from a mental frenzy of wanting Josh out of her house to blank. And it wasn't just her. Harris's stunned expression mirrored the confusion running through her.

After more than the usual amount of hesitation, Harris slowly lowered his fork to his plate. Nothing else moved. "A date? Really?"

The breath had punched out of her but now it was back along with a full dose of rage. *"What?"*

"Is the idea of a woman agreeing to go out with me that shocking?" Josh said, clearly amused by the joint stunned reaction.

"Well, with the . . ." Harris shot her another quick glance before looking at Josh again. "It's just a surprise."

Screw that. This was not a time to verbally tiptoe, so Elisa didn't. "You can't."

"Of course I can," Josh said.

She tried to remain calm. Not blurt out accusations or question him. She didn't have the evidence for that yet. But . . . come on. "Okay, but should you?"

"I know it seems sudden, but we've been going out for a while. I kept it quiet until I was sure the relationship was going somewhere. I'd like you to meet her now." Josh leaned back in his chair. "I was thinking maybe this weekend."

Elisa preferred never. "Not possible."

She'd spent two days trying to wrap her mind around the idea the man she thought she knew, someone she viewed as family, who meant everything to Harris and Nathan, lacked a heart, a soul . . . a conscience. Now he was trying to shove her into the position of accepting his twisted life choices.

Josh frowned at her. "Is next week better?"

She was trying to hold it together, but *he had to be kidding.*

"What's going on?" Josh's frown deepened. "Why are you both looking at me with such weird expressions?"

Elisa shoved her chair back, ignored the way the legs dragged against the hardwood floor, making that annoying screeching sound, and stood up. "We're not meeting her."

Harris reached toward her but didn't actually touch her. "Elisa."

"Why not?" Josh asked at the same time.

He had the nerve to sound surprised, as if this whole discussion wasn't obscene. As if what he suggested wasn't shocking and horrible. "You've been dating this person—"

"Rachel."

Elisa didn't want to know this new woman. Not even her name.

Before she could explain that—shout and scream it at Josh—Harris jumped in. "I think the point is the timing."

No. Wrong. "Not just that, but it doesn't help."

Josh's gaze traveled from Elisa to Harris, not showing one ounce of understanding. "What are you two talking about?"

She really wanted to punch him. "What about your missing fiancée?"

Chapter Three

Josh held up both hands in some sort of mock surrender. "Wait a second."

Elisa was done with waiting. No more keeping quiet, thinking about it, trying to avoid it. They needed to hit this topic head-on. "You can't possibly think this is okay."

"Elisa, please." Harris sighed the same way he did when Nathan asked the same question for the tenth time. "The situation is . . . delicate."

Sounded like her usually brilliant husband was having trouble with simple words tonight. "'Delicate'? Really?"

Stress pulled at the edges of Harris's mouth. "Is 'difficult' a better word?"

She sat down hard in her chair again. "Neither is big enough, but whatever. You explain it to him."

Harris stared at Elisa for a few charged seconds before turning to his brother. A guy who was either clueless or pretending to be. Both options made him a hollow shell of a man.

Harris took his time moving his plate away from the edge

of the table and making room to rest his elbows there. "Abby has only been gone seven months."

No, not like that. Elisa couldn't let the word *gone* sit there as if it were remotely accurate. The word failed to speak to the gravity of the situation. "She's not just *gone*."

Harris blew out an exaggerated breath full of frustration. "Okay, why don't you pick the words I should use?"

If that was a challenge, she accepted. She looked at Josh. "Abby is missing. Your fiancée, the supposed love of your life, has disappeared."

Josh shook his head. "No."

She couldn't believe he wanted to fight about this simple point. "Yes."

"We've talked about this. Talked so much that I can't stand to have another conversation about it." The color drained from Josh's face as he spoke.

It. Not *her*, *it.* Elisa hated him. "Try one more time."

Josh blew out a long breath before starting. "Abby ran away. She left me. Came close to abandoning me at the altar but, lucky for me, decided not to wait that long and subject me to the full level of embarrassment she clearly craved."

Ah, yes. The familiar refrain of Josh as victim. Elisa had bought into that nonsense for most of the time she'd known him. Not anymore.

He created drama. He had outbursts. Most days he usually did what everyone did—went to work, paid his bills, hung out with friends and family. But there were times, when he claimed to be pushed or wrongly targeted, that he came out verbally swinging. He'd explode into road rage if a driver dared to cut him off. He'd become obsessed with payback if anyone made him feel unworthy.

If she was right, he killed the women in his life only to turn around and complain about being alone. Talk about a sick, circular mess.

"You make it sound like Abby left willingly." Elisa couldn't believe he thought he could sell that, but the pleading in his eyes suggested he did.

"Exactly!"

Elisa watched him, looking for any signs of lying. His hands shook and the vacant stare highlighted his shock at being challenged. But he was forgetting one small detail . . . "I still don't understand how you know it was Abby's choice to leave."

Elisa feared he could speak with authority on the subject of Abby's leaving because he was the one who made her disappear. That Abby was dead and buried somewhere and only Josh could lead them to her. Elisa would bet everything she owned that horrifying result was true.

"Where is this coming from?" Josh morphed into anger, as if he had a right to be furious at her for raising the issue. "We discussed this situation months ago and resolved it. Now you're bringing it up again?"

Elisa ran right into a wall of guilt. She'd messed up. She'd been in a terrible place in her own life and accepted his half answers back then. Didn't ask enough questions. She owed it to Abby to do better now. "She's still missing, Josh. She hasn't made contact or popped up somewhere."

Josh visibly wrestled with his control. He clenched his

jaw as he spoke. "She left with her car and her purse. I took that as a sign she wanted to end things with me."

"With you, not me." And that was the point. The one thing Elisa couldn't manufacture an excuse to explain. "No one has seen or heard from her since. Not me. Not her other friends. Not people she worked with. Not the people she owed projects to."

Abby Greene disappeared from the planet seven months ago. Thirty-one and vibrant and in the middle of investigating ways to set up an art studio. Not someone looking to end her life or move away—the two alternatives the police offered months ago, back when they pretended to listen and care.

Elisa had met Abby at a book club and introduced her to Josh. That meant she'd basically walked Abby to her death. The guilt at having assisted in the whole sick process clogged Elisa's throat until she choked on it.

"Maybe she wanted a fresh start." Josh rolled his eyes. "Come on. You're looking for extreme solutions when the most obvious one—she wanted to move on—is staring right at you."

"Let's keep from getting defensive, okay?" Harris asked. "She's trying to figure this out. We all are."

Elisa appreciated the spousal support but had to wonder if it was conditional. Could she go too far, say the wrong thing, and then get body-slammed in the fallout?

But she could focus on what her husband *might* say or do later. She had Josh's attention now. "I'm the one who reported her missing. Abby, the woman you told us you couldn't live without. I've gone over the last few months in my head and you have never, not once, made a serious attempt to find her."

"Because she dumped me!" This time Josh yelled the response.

"She disappeared!"

"Okay, stop. Both of you." Harris took a quick glance into the other room, but Nathan sat with his headphones on and his gaze locked on his tablet. Oblivious.

Elisa looked at Nathan bent over and laughing at whatever he was watching. "Right. No one wants him to know his almost-aunt could be dead."

"What the fuck, Elisa? This is some sort of unhinged fantasy. You were fine last week when we had lunch, but now I'm a monster?" Josh threw down his napkin in true dramatic style and stood up.

"Don't go off on her," Harris warned. "And no one used the word 'monster.'"

Elisa thought it fit, but she kept that to herself.

"Abby left me. I'm allowed to be pissed about being dumped without any explanation. I get to move on." Josh exhaled one more time as if he'd reached his limit. "Is it possible, just hear me out, that this is a medication issue for you?"

"Hey!" Harris smacked his hand against the table. "Don't go there."

Unhinged. Crazy. Lost it. Harris might act outraged now, but she'd heard the two of them whisper about her. They talked as if she were fragile. Couched the concerns in terms like *she's not herself* that sounded benign but carried a harsh judgment.

She'd been clawing her way out of a tunnel, not sharing

even a hint of her darkest moments with them for fear they'd slap a label on her or shove a bottle of pills in her hand. But Josh's behavior was the issue now. Not her. Not the last year. Not her personal demons.

"How long?" she asked in the most dignified voice she could muster.

Confusion washed over Josh's face. "What?"

"How long have you been seeing the newest one?" Because that mattered. When she weighed all the facts about how he really felt about Abby and his indifference to her disappearance, timing could be the key.

"The way you phrased that—"

Her patience expired. "Answer me."

"Elisa." Harris's voice had a slight edge this time. "Maybe we could take the emotion down a notch or two. It's bad enough when he explodes. We don't need both of you in outrage mode."

Not possible. She'd been keyed up and unraveling for months but she finally felt more herself. More in control, and she could no longer shut down her fear about what had happened to Abby. Her mind raced with it. It clenched and clawed at her.

Exactly one man could end the anxious thumping inside her. All he had to do was tell the truth.

"Abby is my friend." Elisa refused to use the past tense. "No one is questioning her disappearance except me." She looked at Harris as she delivered the explanation he should already understand, then turned to Josh. "So, how long did you wait before getting a new girlfriend?"

The answer was going to piss her off. She could feel the pressure ramping up inside her. See his gaze dart to Harris as if he'd find an ally there.

Josh didn't answer for a few seconds. When he did, his voice was clipped and sharp. "I'm not doing this with you."

Killer.

She tried to maintain her control as anger and unease bounced around inside her. Her mind sorted through every detail, every scrap of information she'd collected from memories and computer searches since the serious doubts about Josh settled in two days ago. She refused to let this go. She would find Abby even if she had to fight the men at this table—and destroy one of them—to do it.

"I'm sure it's only been a week or so of informal dating." Harris said the words slowly, as if he was weighing them as he spoke. He stared at Josh. "Right?"

That was the man she loved. The one she married. He didn't just accept things. He asked questions. The way he was looking at Josh now, Harris expected a real answer.

Welcome to the club. She joined in the staring. "Well?"

Josh looked back and forth from Harris to Elisa. "You two know you're not my parents, right?"

"No." Harris shook his head. "Let's not do that shit. She's asking a legitimate question. Just answer her."

Josh didn't say a word to that. More than a minute crept by as he looked up at the ceiling then around the table. He drew it out until Elisa almost lunged across the table to squeeze the answer out of him.

"Three months," he said in a flat tone.

"Months? Really?" Harris's expression morphed until the shock was clear to see. "You went that long without saying anything to me?"

Josh. The man was garbage. His fiancée disappeared and he never searched for her, never questioned it. He just moved on. Found another woman and slipped right into a new relationship.

"Abby left me, Elisa." Josh leaned forward as a pleading note moved into his voice. "We were weeks away from being married. We were in the final planning stages. Then I get home from work one day and her clothes were gone, along with four thousand dollars from our wedding account." He slumped back into the chair. "She stuck me with the mess and the bills. So, forgive me if I didn't mourn her betrayal long enough to make you happy."

Not a hint of worry. Elisa knew she carried that alone. "But did you mourn her at all?"

"Why would I?" He scoffed. "And when exactly did I become the bad guy in this situation?"

"Look, this is a tough subject." Harris had flipped back into mediator mode. He was a problem-solver. He kept his voice low and soothing.

Other times, fine. With Nathan, sure. Now? She hated it. "Don't do that."

Josh nodded. "I agree with Elisa. We don't need you to play the role of peacemaker."

"Are you sure? Because it sure feels like it," Harris asked, clearly exasperated that the two people closest to him wouldn't just let him fix things for them.

Josh ignored the dig and looked at Elisa. "I know she was your friend and you're hurt. She abandoned both of us. And when she did it." He winced. "I mean, the timing. She left a few months after you—"

No, no, no. "Don't."

The rumbling started in her ears. She could hear the noise and waited for a muffled darkness to close over her.

Eleven months. That's how long it had been since that awful day.

Something in Josh's eyes softened. He looked less hunted. Sounded less defensive. "You were at a low spot. You'd been through one of the worst things imaginable. You needed her and—"

"Stop talking." Elisa refused to be his excuse for ducking this conversation. Her life, what happened to her back then, the anxiety she had to wade through every day just to get up and function, was not the point. They were talking about Abby. "Where is she?"

He sighed. "I honestly don't know."

The words tumbled out of him so easily, but she no longer believed him. "Maybe you should figure that out before you move on to a new woman."

A cool disdain radiated off Josh. "Maybe you shouldn't judge me."

Too late. "It's hard not to since you're thirty-five and already have a dead wife and a missing fiancée."

Two women—gone. And no one seemed to care but her.

Chapter Four

The dinner ended quickly after that. While Elisa handled the dishes and cleaned up the kitchen, Josh made excuses to leave early. After a truncated visit with Nathan that still managed to include an in-depth discussion about which was the best superhero, Josh shot out the door without sparing her another glance.

Harris acted slightly better. They watched television for a short time before he declared it was time for bed. He took over Nathan's nighttime routine, which included what felt like a hundred reminders about brushing his teeth and reading a favorite book.

She was pretty sure Harris drew the whole process out as long as possible. She'd showered. He'd showered then gone downstairs and fidgeted around. Relief flowed through her when she finally heard him come back upstairs.

A few minutes later he appeared in their bedroom doorway wearing lounge pants, a T-shirt, and his dark-rimmed glasses. He walked by her without taking the usual opportunity to touch her through her nightgown or kiss her bare shoulder along the thin strap.

He let out a dramatic exhale as he sat down on his side of the bed. "We've had better dinner parties."

He'd retired his contact lenses for the night but clearly not his sarcasm.

She squeezed a dollop of moisturizer out of the tube she kept by the bed and rubbed her hands together. She kept rubbing long after the cream disappeared into her skin. "This isn't funny."

"You unloading on my brother?" He leaned back against a stack of pillows and crossed his legs in front of him. "No, it isn't."

The words carried a slap but he delivered them in an almost bored tone. She had no idea what that meant, but they sure as hell weren't just going to climb into bed and read or go to sleep after that. "Are you kidding right now?"

"I don't understand what happened. Josh comes over all the time. He watches Nathan. He eats with us. The two of you joke around." Harris shook his head. "When did everything change? Why the sudden interrogation?"

She couldn't tell him the truth. Not until she knew more. Irrational or not, she blamed Josh for adding this new, unwanted dimension to her marriage—secret keeping. "He didn't wait before moving on. He barely blinked at her disappearance."

He frowned. "You can't believe Josh did something to Abby."

Elisa couldn't think about anything else.

Words rushed up her throat but she tamped them down. She had to tread carefully. They'd built a life based on trust, love, and respect. To her, those weren't empty words read during their vows. Taking a shot at Josh, someone so important to Harris, invited the kind of turbulence she strained to keep out of her marriage.

She settled on a shadow of the truth. "I don't know what to believe when it comes to Abby."

That was the problem. Her heart ached at the thought of Josh being someone other than the man she'd loved as a brother for years. But her brain screamed with the need to know the truth. Harris and Josh were so close. They talked about everything, but she wouldn't let her mind wander to the possibility that Harris might know more than he pretended about Abby's disappearance.

"You brought up Candace's death," Harris pointed out. "That was a low blow."

Candace, Josh's first wife. They'd been married for five and a half years when she died. After a few rounds of whispering and creative gossiping, everyone in town deemed her death a tragic accident. Everyone, including Elisa.

"Not many men have a history that includes two dead women," she said, trying to be delicate but clear.

Elisa was thirty-seven. She'd lost her mom to cancer and grieved that loss. She never knew her dad, but she had a husband and she couldn't imagine a life without him. Josh lost two great loves and . . . nothing. He moved on, never looking back.

"Abby isn't dead." Harris exhaled as if struggling to gain his composure before settling in for a long speech. "And Candace's death was an accident. A tragic mix of too much white wine, wet feet from the pool, and a narrow staircase."

"Right." She knew the details. Josh's wife, Candace, fell and hit her head. One of those horrible things that never happen . . . except if Josh was involved.

"Then why bring up Candace's death at all?"

"I don't know." But she did. The coincidence of two women Josh loved disappearing from his life proved too strong to ignore.

Harris continued his list as if it absolved Josh. "Candace's family loved Josh and believed him. The police called it a terrible tragedy. The medical examiner said it was an accident."

She didn't need the play-by-play and, honestly, hearing it now from Harris it sounded a bit forced. She'd been there for all of it. A few reporters doubted and tried to change the story, but the claims fizzled and the case was closed. Some portion of Candace's estate went to Josh. He sold the house almost immediately, insisting he could never live in a place he now associated with such a devastating loss, and pocketed a large sum of cash.

"Yes, the Packards were very supportive." Elisa remembered Candace's parents and brother and how hard they grieved for the only daughter of the family.

Candace descended from local royalty. A gift from her grandfather, Al Packard, allowed her to buy them the house Josh always dreamed of. It sat nestled in the trees in coveted

Northside Bryn Mawr, about twenty minutes from Philadelphia on the Main Line. A large Nantucket-style home with blue shingles and a massive in-ground heated pool.

"Everyone was, Elisa. Including you."

The story of Candace's shocking death had been splashed all over the news, but Elisa heard it directly from Josh the night it happened. She sat in a plastic waiting room chair and held his hand as he broke down at the hospital. A detective, now retired and the father of Josh's closest friend, walked Harris through procedures and questions while Josh rotated through bouts of crying and stoicism. She tried to remember the detective's name. Barnes or Burroughs. Something like that.

Through all the chaos and the in-and-out of law enforcement and medical workers, the story never wavered. Josh had heard a cry from the kitchen and ran into the house to find Candace at the bottom of the back stairs in a pool of blood. He tried to revive her as he waited for the ambulance, but she never woke up.

He made the decision to take her off life support four days later. Dead at thirty-two.

Elisa never doubted it. Not a single piece . . . until two days ago. "Some people wouldn't believe one guy could be that unlucky."

"Do you?" Harris shifted to face her head-on. "Elisa?"

Not anymore. "I don't know."

"Josh wouldn't hurt a woman. Or anyone." Harris scoffed. "You know that."

Did she? Desperation clawed at her. The need to believe him swamped her, but her brain kept shouting *no*.

Harris shifted on the bed, moving closer. "Hey, what's going on with you?"

Pain burst inside her head. She'd tried so hard to keep her questions locked inside, not give a hint of her doubts to Harris. Not yet.

"Abby wouldn't leave without telling me." That was only part of the story, but it was a big part. They were close, like sisters. They talked every day, and Abby never gave a hint about leaving.

But that last month . . . something had changed. Abby had stopped talking about wedding preparations. Their conversations over coffee turned shallower. They centered on Nathan or nonsense things. Nothing about Josh or about Abby's concerns about getting married.

"Are you really so sure about Abby?" He shifted again until he sat on her side of the bed and his hand skimmed over the robe covering her thigh. "She was . . . flighty? Free-spirited? I don't know the right words, actually. But she was always late for things. She forgot to come to a dinner once because she got caught up in a design she was making."

He wasn't wrong. Where Candace had been all business and talked about corporate expansion and other subjects that held little interest for Elisa, Abby was far less constrained by schedules and plans. She saw the world in a different way, through colors and light. She talked about how she could waste the entire day trying to put a feeling on the page or trying to find the right shade of yellow. She sometimes got an idea for some design and spent hours locked in the studio she rented, losing all track of time.

None of that meant she ran away from Josh. "Being forget-ful or getting lost in her work is different from going missing."

He shook his head. "Look, I was disappointed, too. You cared about her."

There was that damned past tense she avoided at all costs. "*Care.* I care about her."

"I thought Abby was good for Josh. She could defuse his anger and redirect his frustration. With her, he had control and focus. He didn't obsess about stupid things." Harris closed his eyes as if he'd gotten stuck reliving those times. When he opened them again he looked clear-eyed and ready to argue. "He can be exhausting and, frankly, immature. He's much better than he used to be, but maybe Abby had enough. The police thought this was a simple case of a grown adult wanting a different life. Happens all the time."

That sounded like gibberish to Elisa. "Has this 'wanting a different life' thing happened to anyone else we know?"

His mouth flattened into a thin line. "No."

Adults, even irresponsible ones, checked in with someone. "Why hasn't she called me? Why is her phone disconnected? Why not leave a note so I wouldn't worry?"

He shrugged. "She's probably embarrassed or worried you're angry with her."

More guilt slammed into her, but she pushed it away. Kept treading just to keep breathing. "That's ridiculous."

"I doubt it's even dawned on her that you could be stand-ing here, spinning wild thoughts about her being abducted or kidnapped."

Wild thoughts. As if women didn't get abducted every single day. As if partner abuse wasn't a thing. "That sort of horrible stuff actually does happen."

"Not to anyone we know. That's Friday-night-true-crime-show stuff."

"What if—"

"No, look." He took her hand. "I know Josh took a shot at you and brought up the one thing you don't want to talk about. He shouldn't have, but you have to admit the timing of when Abby left might be part of the problem here. It could color your thoughts now."

The timing. Abby had disappeared months after that awful day. Elisa fought the usual rush of memories. Scenes flashed in her mind. The blood. That gasp.

Pain in her chest ramped up, built and tightened until it wrapped around her in a suffocating hold. She dropped Harris's hand and pressed her palm against the side of her head. Then to her throat, fighting off the wave of feverish heat that poured through her. "No."

Tension swept through the room. "Elisa."

"I'm fine. This isn't about that day. This is about Abby and Josh." Her hands shook and her knees kept buckling as if her weight was suddenly too much to carry.

She tried to lean into the side of the mattress as she reached down. Air refused to fill her lungs. She dragged in breath after breath, hearing the ragged edge as she struggled to regain control.

Her fingers fumbled against a knob on the nightstand drawer. She yanked and pulled until it opened. The lockbox sat right there.

"Elisa . . ."

Her head snapped up and she saw the sadness in his eyes. "Please don't judge me."

He glanced at her hand, then to the unopened box. "I'm not, but I do worry."

That she'd finally lost it. He didn't say the words, but they hung in the silence between them.

She crashed through the anxiety by focusing on Abby. On what happened to her. On why she left and couldn't check in.

"I worry about Abby." Elisa had said the words so many times, out loud and in her head, that they felt small. Not nearly as all-consuming as missing her felt.

"She's fine. Probably sitting in a café on the West Coast drinking coffee."

So casual. So unconcerned. She tried to imagine feeling that cavalier about a woman's safety. "That feels so dismissive."

Harris's shoulders fell a little and his smile looked a bit more forced. "Trust me."

"I do." But the trust no longer extended to Josh, and that was the problem.

Chapter Five

The doubts—always there but until that moment only lingering in the back of her mind and never pushing to the forefront—started two days ago with a laptop computer. One Elisa had never seen before. Small and seemingly neutral. A *thing* used for work and email . . . but it turned out to provide potential clues to unraveling everything.

She hadn't been snooping that day. Not really. She'd been at Josh's home hunting for, of all things, a vacuum cleaner. Thinking it had been months since a woman lived in his house, she'd hired a service to come in and give it a thorough cleaning. Then silly worries set in. Did he have cleaning supplies and extra garbage bags? Had he picked up the clutter? Did he have any embarrassing bachelor things that shouldn't be on display for company?

Call it a mother's instinct, but she knew there would be mess. A high likelihood of underwear on the floor or some male nonsense. She didn't want the people sent by the service to get stuck picking up his clothes.

She found the laptop tucked away in the back of Josh's

downstairs closet. Behind a box of little-used and faded Christmas decorations. Under a duffel bag stuffed with paperbacks Abby had picked up at the used bookstore. She loved to go in and search the shelves for mysteries and romances. She joked about being more of a book collector than a reader, and she took that collecting seriously.

Finding out Abby's things still had a place in Josh's home didn't make sense. He claimed she'd run off, so why keep them? Why hide them . . . ?

Elisa had spied a familiar well-worn college sweatshirt. RISD, RHODE ISLAND SCHOOL OF DESIGN. Abby's favorite piece of clothing, what she wore around the house on cold days. A valued possession, but she hadn't taken it with her. No, she'd used it to wrap up and hide the laptop she'd also left behind.

That's exactly how Elisa smuggled it out of Josh's closet—bundled up and hidden. She knew Josh and how much he hated being questioned about anything, so she kept "the find" quiet. He'd twist this around and blame her for snooping. Totally divert attention away from the real question about why he had Abby's things and not her.

Stumbling over the laptop led to two days of teeth-clenching frustration. Every spare moment, every time she was alone, and when Nathan and Harris went to sleep, Elisa tried to figure out the password. She'd searched every memory, every photo and scrap of anything she had from Abby, looking for a clue. Elisa even did Internet searches to figure out Abby's former addresses and the mascot from her high school, and nothing worked.

This morning Elisa thought of one more possibility. She opened the laptop and stared at the password screen. She sat on the love seat in the small sitting room connected to her bedroom.

After last night's familial explosion, she didn't want to wait for a better time to investigate. She'd dropped Nathan off at school and circled back home, skipping her usual coffee stop. The need to open the laptop and peek inside, to find some clue as to Abby's disappearance, drove Elisa.

She thought about the sequence and finally stopped debating and typed. 05182004. The date Abby's twin sister died.

Abby had claimed she knew the exact minute it happened. It was as if someone reached inside her and ripped her middle right out. Sliced through her with jagged blades. A sudden shock of intense pain drove her to her knees and kept her there, gasping and struggling to breathe while her sister collapsed on the school's running track outside. Dead at fifteen.

The cause, a previously undetected heart defect. The result, a loss Abby described as so intense, so shattering, that years later a stray memory would shake her until even her teeth hurt, then throw her into a violent rage, only to leave her empty, shuddering and hiccupping from tears.

The worst day of Abby's life. That's what she'd called it and why Elisa skipped over using the numbers as a possible password. It would be a date to forget, not remember.

Elisa stared at her fingers as they hovered over the keys. The thin gold band she never took off blinked back at her. She could walk away right now, hand the laptop over and hope it led the police in the right direction. Not be responsible for either condemning Josh or exonerating him. But eleven months ago her sense of stability had been shattered, her control obliterated. She wanted both back. That started now, with this. With Abby.

05182004 . . . worked. Finally.

Yes!

Elisa searched and scrolled. There weren't a lot of saved files. No photos and the Internet hadn't been set up. But Abby kept business files, like Excel spreadsheets, on there and what looked like a draft proposal for a small business loan. Those pieces connected her to the area and suggested she wanted to put down more roots here, not take off on some wild excursion.

It could be a lead. A snippet that convinced the police to actively investigate. Then she saw it. The folder marked "unlucky." She had to reenter the password to access it. A file of saved screenshot messages popped up on the screen. Pieces of what looked like an ongoing chat between Abby and some unknown person that started with a dire warning.

Elisa read the initial message twice before the words sunk in.

CONCERNED: your fiancée isn't who you think he is
ABBY: Who is this?
CONCERNED: someone who knows the truth
ABBY: Fuck off.

Warnings. About Josh.

Tension yanked and pulled at Elisa as she sat there. Until she knew for sure what was in every message, she might still be wrong. Her life could go on, bumpy but normal. She wouldn't have to test Harris's loyalty to her versus his brother.

She shifted on the couch, letting her foot fall to the floor before tucking it up under her again. She rubbed the back of her neck, trying to ease the constant tightness she felt there. Only that last line of the message—so Abby that Elisa could almost hear her voice as she said the words—eased the anxious gnawing inside her.

Fuck off. That was Abby's favorite phrase. Half the time she said it just to say it, no heat behind the words at all. Once, a woman sitting next to them at a coffee shop kept eavesdropping. She finally leaned over and gave Abby a little speech about how using profanity showed a lack of intelligence. The woman was sixty-something and Abby told her to fuck off, too.

Elisa needed to know how this saved conversation ended. She'd fill in the rest after she knew the punch line to the messages, no matter how horrible it might be. She tapped the arrow-down key, watching blurred lines of black ink whiz by, incomprehensible and temporarily mysterious, and landed on the final one.

CONCERNED: let me help you
ABBY: It's too late. I think he's going to kill me.

"Elisa?"

She jerked at the sound of Josh's unexpected voice. Her hard gasp of surprise touched off a coughing fit. The word *caught* screamed in her head as she struggled to regain her composure.

Her instinct was to drop the laptop. Throw it aside, hide it. But Josh could see her. He stood in the doorway to her bedroom, her private sanctuary, and watched every move she made.

His eyes narrowed. "What are you doing?"

Too late.

Chapter Six

Random questions bombarded Elisa's brain. Did Josh recognize the laptop? Could he read the panic in her eyes? She tried to mentally sort through each thought as she closed the laptop with shaky hands.

She had to swallow twice before any words came out. "Don't sneak up on me."

That was a house rule. The need to repeat it took some of the edge off the panic flowing through her. She welcomed being pissed off because it gave her something else to think about.

She couldn't tolerate people showing up without warning . . . or surprises . . . or anyone invading her space. He knew better, which made her wonder if scaring her was a way to get revenge for her questioning him. For her daring to ask a question about his missing fiancée.

"Right." He shook his head. "Sorry."

She noticed for the first time that he held two takeout cups.

"I felt bad about how we left things last night and I brought you coffee as sort of an . . . I don't know . . ." He shrugged. "Lame peace offering, I guess."

He wore a navy suit and looked like he'd just stepped out of a business meeting and into her bedroom. If he was waiting for her to say something, well, she couldn't. Not then. Not anything coherent. Adrenaline pumped through her. She could feel it race around, pinging from here to there, scorching her nerves.

People liked to wax on about what they would do in a dangerous situation, if their fight-or-flight instinct would kick in. She knew from experience she didn't possess an innate ability to quickly assess and decide. Her body's first option was to shut down . . . or it had been. But maybe not anymore. Maybe a person could panic, fail, and change their trained behavior because instead of physically and emotionally folding, this time energy coursed through her. It gave her power and wiped out the blinding fear, if only for a little while.

"May I come in?" He hadn't crossed the threshold and actually entered her space. "I really would like to talk, just for a minute."

She forced her fingers to wrap around the edge of the laptop and moved it to the cushion next to her. She stood up, trying not to draw any attention to it. It wasn't odd for her to be on a laptop or working in her bedroom. This was all normal . . . or as normal as her life got these days.

His gaze dropped to the computer and stayed there for a few seconds before returning to her face. "I didn't mean to mess up your workflow."

He showed up, surprised her, and now lingered. His actions were the very definition of interrupting someone's work-flow. But she was intrigued and the fluttering sensation had moved back down from her throat to her stomach, so she could handle this impromptu meeting. She *would* handle it.

A tense silence surrounded them. Her usual move would be to rush in and say something to ease the discomfort. That's what she did. She fixed things. She tried to make life easier for the people she cared about. But she didn't have an interest in taking that road this time. He came, blustered right into her room, so it was up to him to carry the conversation.

"I know you're worried about Abby," he said. "We don't agree on who she was at the end, but I'd like for us to get around this."

This. Elisa wasn't sure if the word referred to their fight or to Abby. "Okay."

"Needless to say, I was pissed when she left me. Even before that, she'd started questioning me and everything I did or said. Judging me. Telling me to calm down, which I hate."

All of that sounded like motive to Elisa. It was also new information. Josh never talked about issues in the relationship. He certainly never offered that information to the police. He'd presented as if they were super happy and Abby being gone was a total shock.

Elisa had mentally dissected every conversation, every lunch date, every text exchange of funny memes and Abby never gave a hint either. She got quieter and stopped showing any excitement for wedding things. Elisa had chalked the change up to wedding jitters, but now she knew better. Abby's change in tone, in personality, signaled the slow unraveling of whatever Abby and Josh shared.

"Remembering how tense the relationship got near the end infuriates me because I was willing to stick it out. She wasn't. That's why I said what I did at dinner last night." He took a step forward and handed a coffee to Elisa.

"Thanks." She grabbed the cup, tightening her grip until the plastic top popped off and she had to push it down again.

His gaze traveled from her hands to her face. "I'm sure you're sorry for the things you said to me, too."

Not even a little, but it was interesting that he'd skipped from apologizing *to* her and decided to apologize *for* her instead. As far as she could tell, he didn't really need her for this conversation.

"She dumped me and it stung." He shook his head. "Saying it doesn't make it any easier. It's still painful."

She'd bet having a new girlfriend slip right into Abby's place helped heal his broken heart.

"Well, my point is that I didn't want any reminders of her or our time together." He looked at his feet as he shifted his weight back and forth. "I packed up her stuff and put it in storage."

More unexpected news. "When?"

"The weekend after she left. When I realized leaving amounted to more than the usual argument and she wasn't coming back." His voice filled with *how dare she* indignation.

She really wanted to throw the coffee at him. "You only waited days? But she could have come back. You didn't want to know why she was gone or if something made her leave?"

"The reasons didn't matter. They still don't." He stared at her for a few seconds before spewing again. "Look, she made the choice, not me. Once she did, fine. I was done with her."

He sounded less mature than Nathan, and she could at least bribe him with a Popsicle most days. "You wrote her off so quickly and never looked back."

"I don't want to do this with you today. That's not why I'm here." He reached into his jacket pocket and brought out a key. It was on a chain and connected to what looked like some sort of security card. "Maybe looking in the storage unit will give you some clue as to where she is. You can contact her, just leave me out of it."

The key and card dangled in front of her as he gave her permission . . . as if she needed that. A note with an address and number for the storage unit slowly turned on the end of the chain.

A thought popped into her mind. If he put Abby's things in storage, then why had he hidden the bag and laptop in his closet, places Abby wouldn't have kept them? She almost asked. Almost let it slip that she'd been rummaging in there, but no. He was keeping secrets, so could she.

"What she did to me sucked, but leaving you without a word was also shitty." He shrugged. "I want you to find peace with this. I don't want it to nag at you or for it to mess up our relationship. I think of you as a sister. Always have. It would be really terrible if Abby destroyed that, too."

Elisa didn't have a response to that, so she held out her hand and he dropped the keychain in it.

"Great." He shot her a megawatt smile. "I need to get back to work, but maybe this weekend we can get together?"

"Maybe," she said, trying to sound as noncommittal as possible.

"Okay." He nodded. "Good."

He clearly thought they'd made up and she'd move on. That she'd shut up and just take his word that her friend abandoned her life for no good reason. Never mind that with one woman in his life dead and another missing, "finding peace" was not really an option.

She waited until he headed for the hall before asking the glaring question he'd ignored. "Why would Abby leave anything at your house if she planned to walk out on you forever? Why not just pack up all of her things and take them with her?"

He slowly turned and faced her again. His expression didn't give anything away. She thought she saw a hint of anger, but he quickly covered it.

After a few seconds of staring he answered her in a flat voice. "I don't know, Elisa. You'll have to ask her."

"I wish I could."

Chapter Seven

Elisa managed to spend all of Saturday morning running around without accomplishing much other than picking up the downstairs and cleaning the kitchen. A feat of sorts when living with a husband who liked to kick off his shoes as he walked in the door and a son who left piles of stuff in every room he entered, but not exactly what she had planned for her few hours without either of them in the house.

Still, today was off to a better start than yesterday. She'd held on to that chain with the storage key Josh had given her until it pressed an indentation into her palm. Now it sat safely under a pile of never-worn bracelets in her jewelry box.

The need to read through the rest of the messages on Abby's laptop pulled at her. She'd gotten through half before life intruded. She would have finished once everyone went to bed, but Nathan picked last night to have sleep issues. Now, those messages and any secrets they held would need to wait. Today was a family day.

She'd promised and she intended to deliver, even if it meant going to a very loud restaurant with an indoor playroom for kids. She loved that Nathan could burn off a lot of energy but dealing with all the shouting and noise was an emotional fight for her. She preferred quiet—always.

Before picking up Nathan and Harris and heading for Nathan's first choice for eating and drinking, she stopped at hers—The Coffee Café. Harris had texted four times while she stood in line. The texts included increasingly ragged pleas for coffee. Each time he changed the size of his drink until the most recent text where he suggested just getting him two cups. So, that's how his day was going.

She chuckled at her normally unruffled husband sounding so harried. Then an odd sensation pricked her. A rumbling that started in her brain and made her flush warm. Someone was watching her. No surprise there. The line to order tended to merge with the pickup line in the tiny shop. The general mood was one of uncaffeinated annoyance, so how dare she be amused.

She glanced up and saw a woman staring at her. She had a vague memory of the redhead but couldn't place the time or situation. The woman had bundled up in a raincoat that fit the gloomy gray day. The sunglasses didn't match, but maybe she was going for mysterious.

Elisa grabbed her cups and breezed by an older gentleman standing behind her. The redhead didn't return Elisa's smile as she headed for the door.

Elisa didn't think about anything but the lunch ahead of her when she pulled into the vet clinic parking lot in Ardmore ten minutes later. She balanced the cupholder on one arm as she shut the car door. Her keys jangled. People milled around the outside of the clinic, tense and some visibly upset, probably waiting for news of their sick pets.

She gave them a been-there sympathetic smile, because she had been, then glanced up at the windows on either side of the clinic door. The reflection caught her off guard. Raincoat. Auburn hair. She spun around, expecting to see the woman from the café standing behind her, but only a lot full of parked cars greeted her.

Where did she go? Then the voice in her head asked a second question . . . *Was she ever really there?*

A heaviness settled in Elisa's chest. Her mood morphed from bright to wary. That woman . . . She couldn't just disappear; she *had* been there. Standing. Staring. Waiting . . . for something.

Elisa's gaze bounced around the parking lot. People walked from their cars into the gym a few doors down from the clinic. A steady line of traffic circled the lanes looking for open spots. At least seeing the woman here explained why she looked familiar. They probably lived in the same town and their paths had likely crossed before. It was the only reasonable explanation. She didn't have room in her life for one more unreasonable occurrence.

Putting the woman out of her mind, refusing to let that sinking feeling inside her overwhelm the rest of the day, Elisa walked into the clinic. She said hello and waved to the reception staff as she made her way back to Harris's office.

Down the hall, past the room with barking dogs and the rush of technicians moving pets around for tests, she arrived at the door marked HARRISON WRIGHT, VMD. So official.

So impressive. Even after almost nine years of marriage seeing his full name spelled out like that still made her heart do a little flip.

They'd carved out this path together. It existed mainly in the suburbs just outside Philadelphia, and that insular existence suited her. From their house in Villanova, to the clinics in Ardmore and Paoli, the area consisted of miles of neighborhoods filled with trees and soccer fields. Corner restaurants. Lush green lawns. Historic stone homes mingling with new developments. Barbecues at home. A school for Nathan that was small enough for her to know all of the teachers and most of the parents of the kids in Nathan's grade.

Her life now didn't bear any resemblance to the one-bedroom apartment she'd lived in with her mom, growing up in Ohio. Just the two of them. Then, never enough food or anything else. Now, abundance that carried with it a certain level of guilt for being so lucky.

Elisa knocked once on Harris's door before opening it . . . and almost dropped the coffee tray. He sat at his desk looking a bit ruffled from his early morning shift. His expression didn't say much, but the vibe of the room was off. And she knew why. Josh stood there with his palm on the lower back of the woman next to him.

The infamous new girlfriend?

Elisa glanced at Harris. He threw her a *sorry* half smile but didn't say a word.

Leave it to Josh to ignore her concerns, to pretend they didn't fight about this meeting two nights ago, and just show up with this new woman anyway.

"Hi, I'm Rachel." The woman extended her hand then laughed when she looked at Elisa's hands, filled with coffee cups and a purse and keys. "Oh, sorry."

She was pretty. Stunning, even. Tall and slim with long brown hair. She wore a floral dress, jean jacket, and motorcycle boots, and managed to pull off the look without any trouble. Perfect face. Perfect nose. Sweet smile.

The whole moment was awkward as hell.

"Rachel, this is my sister-in-law, Elisa." Josh smiled at both women. "Harris's wife."

Killer. The word refused to leave Elisa's head.

Harris cleared his throat as he stood up. He was over six feet and in command of the room, so the move grabbed everyone's attention. "Josh and Rachel came by to say hello."

"Hmmm." That's all Elisa could think to say. Screaming a warning at this woman to run and run far seemed like too much drama for an initial meeting. It would keep her safe, sure, but Harris wasn't ready to hear the warnings. Elisa doubted Rachel was either.

The way she looked at Josh, all soft and in love. Elisa had seen that look before. Josh's first wife, Candace, had it. Abby had it. Now this new one . . .

Shit.

Candace had died at thirty-two. Abby disappeared at thirty-one. That suggested the women in Josh's life had an expiration date. This one—Rachel—looked a little younger, so she might have time to wise up and escape before anything bad happened to her.

Elisa had thought of Josh as a baby brother from the

minute they met. Josh immediately accepted her back then. She didn't have a sibling and she'd been drawn to Harris and Josh's connection. Both frustrated by how defensive Harris could be when Josh messed up and delighted by their easy rapport. The way Harris interacted with Josh gave her a peek into how he might behave as a father—dependable, loving, and rock solid.

She'd also liked Josh for Josh. They joked and argued. Years later, she'd watch him play soccer in the yard with Nathan. She'd viewed him as a great uncle and brother, someone she could depend on. Now she had to fight the urge to buy this Rachel woman self-defense lessons and a plane ticket to anywhere but here.

Harris walked around the desk and took his coffee cup from Elisa's hand. He leaned in to give her a kiss. She heard his whispered "I'm sorry" before he leaned back again.

"I know this is a surprise." Josh delivered the understatement without apology.

"Yes." A surprise because how could he think this was okay?

"You could say that," Harris said right after her.

Rachel frowned. "Wait, what?"

Josh waved off her concerns. "It's fine."

No . . . Elisa tried not to use her son as an excuse to get out of parties she didn't want to attend and work events that left her bored, but she used him now. The timing seemed right because she didn't want to drag Rachel into the middle of this. None of what was happening now was her fault. "It's just that we promised Nathan, our son, we'd pick him up from his friend's house and take him for lunch to this place where he likes to play games."

Rachel sharply inhaled. "I'm so sorry." She glanced at Josh. "You said they knew we were coming."

Josh made a humming sound. "Did I?"

Jackass. Elisa spent years mentally emphasizing Josh's best features and trying not to dwell on his faults. Now the negatives were all she could see. "It's fine, Rachel. I promise."

"I didn't want to meet your family in an unexpected rush." Rachel frowned at Josh, treating him to a *wait until we get home* expression. "That's not fair to me or them."

Josh shrugged. "You heard Elisa. This isn't a big deal."

Not what she said, but Elisa decided not to dwell on that.

Rachel treated him to an eye roll. "To you it's not, but I wanted to make a good impression."

"You did," Elisa said, trying to reassure the poor woman.

Elisa didn't want to get to know Rachel and she certainly didn't want to like another unlucky woman in Josh's life, but it might be too late. Any woman who knew how to handle Josh, was unwilling to just accept his bullshit, had Elisa's immediate approval.

"We like you just fine." Harris leaned against his desk and took a sip of coffee. He eyed Josh over the rim. "My brother, however, could use a kick in the—"

"Tomorrow," Elisa blurted out before she could stop herself or come up with a better plan.

"What?" Rachel asked.

Harris looked even more confused. Much more of that raised-eyebrow thing and he'd end up with a killer headache.

Too late to back down now, but Elisa really, really wanted to. Instead, she plastered a big fake smile on her face and issued a formal invitation. "Come over to our house for brunch tomorrow."

Rachel shot Elisa a half smile. "Are you sure?"

"Of course she is," Josh said.

He really was missing the point. Elisa tried to help him find it. "I invited her, not you."

Josh laughed, but after a while no one joined in his amusement. He glanced at Harris for assistance.

"Don't look at me." Harris shook his head. "You created this mess."

Elisa loved that answer. Josh did cause all of this. Maybe tomorrow, on her own turf, she could force him to clean it up.

Chapter Eight

Thanks for not losing it with Josh today." Harris made the comment as he unbuttoned his shirt and threw it on the chair by the window.

She sat on the edge of the bed brushing her hair and wondering how and when he would broach the subject. They'd spent all day and evening with Nathan, listening to endless chatter and rounds of singing. Now at night, alone in their bedroom, Harris circled back.

He wasn't an avoider. She thought avoidance came in handy at times, but not tonight. She plunged in. "I did. On the inside."

"He's—"

"A child." Possibly a murderer, but she needed to collect more evidence on that. Those laptop messages from Concerned gave her a new place to start.

"My brother," Harris said at the same time.

No yelling. Harris rarely yelled or even raised his voice. His work involved emergencies and delivering difficult news. Between that stress and the pressure of running a business it wouldn't be a surprise to see his frustration turn to explosion, but it never happened. He possessed a wealth of self-control. When he walked in the door each night, even when he was on call, he did so as a father and husband. The rest fell away.

All those stories from friends about difficult husbands and warnings in magazines about men being shitty had kept her noncommittal dating streak alive and scared her away from serious relationships for years. Then she met Harris through a colleague at the hospital where she used to work. The woman lived next to Harris when he was single and she made the introduction. That led to a ten-month courtship that ended with a white dress in Las Vegas and Josh as the witness.

Elisa shifted around to face him. "I don't want to fight."

She made the announcement because she didn't have any resources left. She felt depleted and empty. Pummeled by all the questions in her mind and exhausted by the need to steer away from them to give her family a good day.

His gaze slipped down to the gap in her robe and her bare skin underneath before inching back up to look at her face again. "Hard agree."

She understood his amused tone because she understood him. He liked peace. Craved it. He grew up in a volatile household. Not violent, but loud. His parents drank and fought and then drank again. Harris described them as careening from problem to problem, pretending they were fine all while insisting their children be perfect to shore up the public façade.

All that fighting, all the drinking, culminated in a car accident that killed them both and injured the innocent, unsuspecting driver they hit. Harris had been twenty-three, and left to sort out the family finances and struggle with a sixteen-year-old, emotionally messed up Josh.

When the worst happened, Harris doubled down, asserting more self-control and ratcheting up his determination to have a stable, successful life. Elisa understood how the tragedy shaped him. She also hated that he'd been forced to be so responsible for so long.

"I don't want to think about Abby tonight." The words slipped out, but Elisa meant them.

"Yeah, about that." He sighed as he sat down on the arm of the chair he used as a makeshift closet. "I hope it's possible for you not to dwell, but I kind of doubt it."

Dwell struck her the wrong way. "You have to admit her disappearance doesn't make sense."

He tapped his fingers together. "I know you think that, but—"

"Fine." Nope, they would not fight. She would not let Josh mentally slink into the bedroom with them. "Maybe spending a little time with Rachel will make me feel better. She seemed nice. Not intimidated by Josh. Maybe a bit young, but I'm almost six years younger than you and no one squawked about that."

"Five years and four months, but who's counting." Harris laughed. "And the cause-and-effect loop you're drawing is a little fuzzy."

Because it was nonsense. A stall tactic. But she did have one legitimate non-Josh question to ask him. "Does a redhead work for you?"

For a few seconds Harris just sat there, looking at her.

"Well?" she asked as she took out her moisturizer and smoothed a dollop on her legs, then on her arms.

He watched every move. "We're changing subjects?"

She nodded. "We are."

"Okay, so . . ." He cleared his throat. "Is there a specific redhead we're talking about?"

"Tall with shoulder-length auburn hair. Deep red. Pretty." Elisa tried to remember her face, anything specific, but she couldn't call up a picture in her mind.

Harris groaned. "Is this a test of some sort?"

She stopped shifting around. "Huh?"

"You're sitting there, probably naked under that robe, and making your skin all shiny and smooth while asking about some random woman? This feels like a test."

She hadn't even noticed. "Pretend it's not."

"Honestly? I'm having some trouble concentrating right now."

She loved the way he lightened difficult situations by highlighting something funny or absurd. It was this dry tone that some mistook for seriousness. She knew better, but her question about the woman was real and actually didn't have anything to do with him.

"But, no on the redhead." He made a face but added, "I don't think so."

"*Think?*"

"Come on. I don't notice a woman's hair." His mouth dropped open as if he realized a potential husbandly error that could ruin the rest of his evening. "Except yours, of course. Yours is beautiful."

"Uh-huh." She untucked the covers from under the pillow and folded them down. "What color is my hair?"

"See, I knew there would be a test." He shot her a smile that suggested he thought he'd won something. "And the right answer is chestnut brown."

"Listen to you with the fancy color description."

He took her mind off the darkness. She'd come through the worst months of her life—some people, like her former therapist, insisted she was still going through them—but his smile, his laugh, the way he would say the right thing and make her feel less tense, worked like being thrown into the light.

"Okay, being honest here," he said as he held up his hand. "I saw the box in the bathroom the last time you colored it. Then I got sidetracked, trying to figure out if I'd ever really seen a chestnut."

"You're making me sorry I asked." But she wasn't. In those few seconds of messy thinking he'd made her forget that anything bad could ever happen to them.

"So, why did you?" he asked.

Right. The redhead. "I saw this woman today while getting coffee, then again in the parking lot at the clinic."

"Maybe one of her pets is an ongoing patient at the clinic?" He stood up and opened the drawer to his dresser. Turned his back to her as he grabbed a clean T-shirt.

That made sense. "Possible."

He glanced up in the mirror above the dresser and stared at her reflection. "Did something happen with this woman?"

"No."

He turned around to face her again. His eyes narrowed with what looked like concern. "Really?"

She didn't mean to give him another reason to worry, but she clearly had. "Do you think I fought a stranger over coffee?"

His features softened again. "I wrestled with a cat suffering from explosive diarrhea today, so even if you did, I still win."

She refused to ask for any details. "Poor baby."

"Me or the cat?"

"Don't be ridiculous. The cat." She moved back to lean against the wall of pillows stacked on the bed.

"No." He shook his head. "It has a loving family. We're not adopting it."

He spent a lot of time insisting they not become *that* vet family. The kind with nineteen pets. She disagreed.

"Of course not. We already have two cats." An unreasonably small number, in her view. They had some land. They could handle more. "Fuzz and Buzz would be appalled at the idea of having to share."

"Those names." He groaned. "Never let a four-year-old name the pets."

"Lesson learned."

"Right . . . " He made the word last for five syllables, as if he knew what was coming next, because he probably did. It was a popular refrain in their house.

"And the next pet will be a dog. Named by me." She'd long ago sided with Nathan on the need for a dog . . . or three.

Harris rolled his eyes. "So, this woman . . ."

She admired his deft change of subject. "It's fine. I'm sure it was nothing." She wasn't even sure why she brought it up except that the woman had looked familiar.

"Was there a point when you thought it was something?" When she shook her head, he kept going. "The whole story about seeing her sounds oddly mysterious."

Yeah, that's what Elisa was thinking.

Chapter Nine

The house smelled like bacon.

The last thing Elisa wanted to deal with today was a family brunch, but she'd issued the invitation, so she was stuck. She'd spent the morning getting everything together. Muffins made. Frittata in the oven. Husband outside tackling overly energetic son.

The last one made her smile. She stood at the sink, drinking coffee as she watched Nathan spike the football then dance around in a circle in the backyard. Harris laughed so hard he doubled over.

The house had filled her with joy from the moment they bought it. They'd lived a little farther out from the city before Candace died. With Josh emotionally reeling, Harris's business growing, and Nathan becoming ever more mobile and curious, they'd chosen to move closer to Philadelphia but still have land, thinking more family would be better. That was three years ago.

The battle over housing style began immediately after they put the "for sale" sign in the yard. She'd wanted easy. A one-story, completely renovated modern home. They bought a three-story, historically significant—which she now knew meant *in need of serious repair and upgrading*—white Federal-style home with an impressive wraparound porch. A true money pit.

Having grown up in one-bedroom apartments, this property with its outdoor patios and outbuildings struck her as overindulgent. They had a carriage house she'd converted into an office she never actually used because she preferred to work upstairs in the space off the bedroom. But Harris was a history buff. The idea of a *historically significant* home appealed to him. He was happy, so she was happy.

Her smile faded as soon as Josh joined Nathan and Harris in the yard. The game of fake keep-away where Nathan managed to outflank his towering father and uncle usually gave her a warming sense of calm. Today, no. Nothing about Josh calmed her these days.

"Nathan is adorable," Rachel said as she joined Elisa at the kitchen window.

"And loud." He started screaming with his usual level of deafening sports enthusiasm before Elisa finished the description. "See?"

Elisa poured Rachel a cup of coffee. She'd arrived with Josh a half hour ago. The strained small talk since then had given Elisa a headache. She'd sighed with relief when Harris finally suggested "the men" enjoy some outside time to burn off a bit of Nathan's energy.

"You ever think about having children?" Elisa asked.

"Never." Rachel laughed. "That sounded abrupt. What I

meant was that it's not on my radar yet. There are other things I want to accomplish first."

Elisa still wasn't sure exactly how old Rachel was. "You have time."

"Is there anything I can do to help with the food?" Rachel asked over the rim of the mug as she took a drink.

"It's all done. We have about twenty minutes until we're ready to eat."

Josh already had escorted Rachel around the house. That left more small talk . . . or the *big* talk. But Elisa didn't feel grounded and ready to launch into the necessary *be careful because Josh could kill you* discussion right now.

"Do you need to be in the kitchen, or could we walk around the property?" Rachel asked. "You know, just get some air."

"You're asking the right person. If you go with Harris you'll get a twenty-minute explanation about how you're standing on land where George Washington and the Continental Army camped on the way to Valley Forge."

Rachel winced. "That's a lot of information for a Sunday morning."

"Oh, that's only his opening speech. He can tell you all about the weapons and the battles. American history is his passion, and he loves to share what he's learned."

Rachel's eyes widened in mock horror. "Dear God."

"Exactly." Yeah, only two brief meetings and Elisa already liked Rachel. She wanted to dislike the woman who stepped in as Abby's quick replacement, but the timing was Josh's fault, not Rachel's.

Elisa pointed her mug in the general direction of the back

door. "We'll sneak out and sweep around the yard, thus avoiding any chance of being pulled into that game."

Rachel laughed as she followed Elisa. "Thank you."

They walked in comfortable silence for a few minutes. The sun beamed down, counteracting the slight chill in the air. Winter would roll in soon enough. Elisa intended to enjoy the rich colors of the fall mums spread around the yard in large pots for as long as possible.

While they sipped coffee, they moved along the fence outlining the property and cut through the lush lawn shaded by trees with leaves just on the cusp of changing color. From a good sixty feet away she could still hear Nathan's squealing laugh.

Elisa mentally tested conversation topics before finally leaping in. "I should probably know this but what do you do for a living? Are you in the energy field, like Josh?"

"I like how you tried to make his job sound interesting." Rachel smiled as she sat down on the bench at the entrance to the raised-bed garden, walled off in an attempt to confuse at least some of the wildlife in the area and give the vegetables a fighting chance. "Like he owns an oil company or something."

"That was by accident, I assure you." Elisa thought back to how excited Josh was when he took the financial analyst job a few years ago. "Assessing power line projects and the feasibility of—"

Rachel let out a fake snore. "I just can't."

Talking about Josh didn't appeal to Elisa at all. She'd much rather talk about Rachel, who seemed charming and funny . . . and should have the chance to live a nice, long life. "It's a stable job and he seems to like it."

"I asked about it when we first met and his bottom line was 'it keeps the lights on' and I appreciated the practical nature of that." Rachel crossed one leg over the other and tipped her head back, inhaling.

She seemed relaxed, so Elisa used the moment to segue into something more interesting—a subject only tangentially related to her potentially homicidal brother-in-law. "Where did you two meet?"

Rachel's head dropped back down and she looked at Elisa again. "Dueling work conferences. He was at one and I was at another in the same hotel."

Elisa realized Rachel never answered the job question. "What did you say you did for a living?"

"I didn't."

"Okay." That was odd. Elisa couldn't think of a reason to hide the information.

"Human resources." Rachel treated Elisa to an I-know-you're-fishing-for-information-about-me glance. "I give seminars and workshops."

Elisa used to work in a hospital finance office, putting her accounting degree to work. Not all of her human resources dealings had been positive. She found the process hit-or-miss, depending on who you talked to, and everyone tried to talk with the one person who managed to get things done. "Workshops on what exactly?"

"Consulting on everything from hiring practices to workplace safety issues. I basically go into companies, assess problem areas, and set up plans for improvement."

That sounded vague but Elisa figured most of Rachel's

work came with a confidentiality agreement. "Knowing what I know about the business world that sounds like a full-time job."

"It requires more tact than I can muster most days." Rachel shook her head. "The travel is the exhausting part. I end up living out of hotel rooms."

A dizziness hit Elisa out of nowhere. She leaned back harder into the bench to keep the spinning sensation to a minimum. "That's my nightmare."

Rachel took a long sip of coffee before responding. "You don't like traveling?"

Round and round. "I don't leave a twenty-mile radius."

Rachel laughed but when Elisa didn't join in, Rachel slowly lowered her coffee mug to her lap. "Wait, really?"

"Don't ask." Not something Elisa intended to talk about today or with anyone but Harris. Trauma found ways of sneaking in, pushing past her defenses; she didn't need to make things worse by throwing open the door and inviting it in.

"Well, the point is I met Josh, we talked, started hanging out." As Rachel spoke her hand sliced through the air. Fingers moving. "Now we're dating."

Elisa concentrated on the words. She watched Rachel's hand flip around. Didn't let her mind wander any further than right there. "That's a lot to happen in a few months, especially with you being in and out on trips."

Rachel shrugged. "Well, we actually met a year ago."

The spinning stopped. Elisa thought her breathing might have hiccupped a bit, too. "What?"

Rachel kept on talking with her hands as she looked around

the yard and spilled the details Josh had held back. "We were friends, then more . . ." She glanced over at Elisa and her smile disappeared. "Are you okay?"

No. Not at all. Elisa tried to stay focused while questions and timelines pinged in her head. "You know about Abby, right? His missing fiancée."

"Of course." But Rachel's frown only deepened.

"Then you can see why I'm confused about the timing, about when you started as Josh's girlfriend and when Abby ended." Though Elisa now suspected Josh dated both women at the same time, which introduced a whole new reason why Josh might want to be rid of Abby.

"I . . . uh . . ." Rachel set her mug on the bench between them. "I never met Abby."

"That wasn't my point." Elisa assumed that was obvious. Josh hid the timing and potential overlap. He knew cheating provided a potential motive. Rachel had to know. The police should care about this.

Elisa heard the footsteps first then Josh's voice broke into the conversation. "Everything okay over here?"

Chapter Ten

Josh probably thought she'd cower or feel bad about snooping. Nope. Elisa plowed right ahead. "You lied."

He stood there, hovering over them dressed in jeans and a baseball-style shirt. "About what?"

So comfortable. So sure of himself even when caught. Deflection. He was a master at it. Elisa wanted to scream. "You two have been together for a year."

"Okay, wait." Rachel shifted as she winced. "Maybe this isn't the right time for this conversation."

Elisa didn't even spare Rachel a glance. All of her focus stayed on Josh. "We're ignoring enough difficult topics right now, let's go ahead and tackle this one."

Josh continued to stand there, all relaxed as he passed the football back and forth between his hands. "Why are we talking about this?"

He acted as if the courtship, the engagement, the buildup to the wedding with Abby never happened. He'd flipped this mental off switch and moved on.

Elisa stood up, still holding her mug. "You said you met

Rachel after Abby left. Months after. That you've only been dating Rachel for three months."

The only show that he understood the seriousness of the topic was his slight frown. "You're confusing the concepts of dating and meeting."

Always her. Never him. Elisa was done with his deflection. "Am I? Please enlighten me."

The last of his practiced indifference slid away. "Why should I? This is none of your fucking business."

If he was done tiptoeing through family time, so was she. "Abby, my friend who is missing, is none of my business?"

Rachel stood up between them. "Maybe we should—"

Josh pushed Rachel to the side and stepped in until he trapped Elisa between his body and the bench behind her. "I don't know what's going on with you lately, but I'm sick of being your target. You need to fix whatever bullshit is happening in your head."

She refused to be afraid of him. He was the one who'd pushed this showdown with his half answers and lame excuses. "Excuse me?"

Rachel tugged on his sleeve. "Josh . . ."

"No more pretending you're fine, Elisa. You're not." Color flooded his face as he crowded in closer. "All of a sudden you're digging around in my personal life. Judging, making snide comments, doubting me. Stop."

The edge of the bench pressed into the back of Elisa's calf. She tightened her double-fisted grip on the mug. "I'm asking a simple question about dating timing. You're the one who's getting defensive."

"You don't see me crawling all over your life." The anger left his face. An I'm-about-to-be-an-asshole expression took its place. "I mean, you're not exactly stable right now, Elisa. You know that, right? Please tell me you get that."

This time Rachel shoved and pushed at his arm. "Josh, stop."

The wall of fury inside Elisa started to crumble. She'd never been great with confrontation. She faked her way through it because that was the only way to survive and being a mom didn't give her much of a choice, but having to hold that pretense in her own house quickly drained her energy. "You're trying to change the subject."

"This conversation is over." He turned to leave.

Elisa caught him by the arm. "Not this time."

"Hey!" Harris's voice rang out as he jogged toward them with Nathan close behind. "What's going on?"

Josh shook his head. "Your wife—"

"Stop." Elisa issued the warning then fought to drain the anger from her voice to talk to Nathan. "We'll be right over, honey. Go back and play."

Being seven, Nathan had his own ideas. He ran up to the group.

Josh stopped him before he could get to Elisa. Wrapped an arm around him. "Hey, buddy."

The sight of Nathan leaning against Josh tore something loose in Elisa. "Nathan, come here."

Her voice had this high-pitched note of panic in it. She also could hear the slight wobble in it.

Nathan looked at her. "Why are you yelling at Uncle Josh?"

"I'm not." Tension pounded around them, threatening to

double her over, but Elisa forced a half smile for her son's benefit. "We're just hungry. Go inside and wash your hands then we'll eat."

"You know what?" Rachel tapped Nathan on the shoulder until he looked up at her. "I need to do that, too, but I don't know where the bathroom is. Can you show me?"

"Yes!" Nathan started running toward the house. "Here."

Elisa could feel the shaking start inside her. It rattled in her head and made her knees buckle. She grabbed onto the back of the bench and nodded at Rachel. "Thanks."

Harris waited until Rachel left and Nathan was out of earshot to plunge ahead. "Well? What's with the shouting?"

Elisa tightened her grip on the bench as she watched Josh. "You cheated on Abby with Rachel."

"*What?*" Harris sounded stunned at the accusation.

Josh just shook his head. "Jesus, Elisa. You are so determined to find me guilty of something."

Her body felt like it was coming apart. The strength seeped out of her muscles and the fuzziness in her head made it hard to think . . . to breathe.

He sounded reasonable. Held it together. But he didn't deny the accusation.

She punched through the fog that descended on her from the inside out. "Instead of giving speeches, answer me. Is it true? Did you cheat on Abby?"

Josh sighed. "You know something, Elisa? Maybe this, your paranoia, is about you and not me."

"Whoa." Harris stepped in front of Elisa to confront his brother. "That's enough."

"No. Let him say it. We've both been holding back. Talk." Elisa dropped the mug in the grass and grabbed onto the back of Harris's shirt. She tried to move out from behind him but Harris continued to shield her.

"Maybe you and Abby weren't really that close. Ever think of that?" Josh shifted to the side and kept his unblinking gaze on Elisa. "She left and didn't tell you because you were a family obligation to her, not a friend. You met her first but, really, you were forced together because you dated brothers and that's it."

Harris held up a hand and pushed Josh back. "What the hell is wrong with you?"

Josh shook his head. "Me? Ask your wife. She's the one who's not okay."

Elisa could see the tension snap across Harris's shoulders. Barely controlled fury thrummed off him.

"Stop talking," Harris warned.

Josh scoffed at Harris's words then walked away. He took one more shot as he left. "You know I'm right. She's not okay."

Elisa tried to ignore the personal attack and focus on the bigger picture—he never denied cheating.

A TENSE MEAL with limited talking apart from Nathan's confusing explanation about the right way to spike a football led to a quiet afternoon and evening. Harris barely said a word. He didn't yell, but he didn't vow support for her either. He played with Nathan, got him ready for bed, then started his usual nighttime routine.

The silence crackled with energy. She waited for the tension to explode or for her body to break down. Josh's comments about her not being okay . . . they hit too close.

She'd been battling insecurities and fears. With her life in free fall, she'd been unable to handle another emotional blow, so she lapped up every explanation Josh offered about Abby back then. The police thought everything was fine. People who didn't know Abby referred to her "artsy" personality. Elisa bought in because then she didn't have to think about the horrible alternatives.

She'd been on pain medicine back when Abby disappeared and when she stopped taking it, some of the haze cleared. Anger had hit her first. A sense that Abby should have checked in. That she was being selfish and uncaring in not making contact. Then Elisa found that laptop. She realized that Abby hadn't just picked up the things that mattered to her and headed for somewhere more fun.

Everything had changed now. Guilt flooded through Elisa for being angry for so long. All that time blaming Abby when Elisa realized she was the one who had failed the friendship. That quickly Elisa's anger switched focus from Abby to Josh. Doubts bubbled and grew.

Elisa was obsessed with knowing the truth.

Focusing on finding Abby gave her a purpose. After months of dragging her body out of bed and pretending to be fine, searching for an answer made her feel productive again. It eased the dull ache inside her. The sensation of not being happy or sad. She just lingered in the middle. In the nothingness.

As the hours passed, she welcomed the dimming of the lights and the television being shut off. Instead of rushing to join Harris in bed and possibly ratcheting up the fury and frustration flowing through her with another round of arguments that would leave her unsettled, she peeked into Nathan's bedroom. He lay with his arms thrown wide and his head half off his pillow.

Their black cat, Fuzz, sat on the windowsill, surveying the yard. Only his tail flickered when she entered the room. Buzz, the tabby, was nowhere to be seen, which probably meant he was asleep under Nathan's bed, as usual.

She sat down on the edge of the mattress and brushed Nathan's wild hair off his forehead. The night-light in the corner cast ragged shadows on the walls. The star decals on the ceiling gave off a slight yellow glow. She could see his face in the dim light. Reveled in how a day of adult snapping and silent treatment hadn't stolen his ability to relax and dream.

After a few minutes, one eye opened. "Mommy?"

Only half awake he drifted from the *Mom* he had started calling her because he said he was big now, to the *Mommy* she preferred. He had to grow up, sure, but she didn't have to love every part of the process.

She rubbed her hand over his leg through the blanket. "Go to sleep, baby."

Instead, he flipped to his back. His eye drifted shut but he spoke anyway. "Why don't you like Rachel?"

The words slammed into Elisa.

"Why do you think that?" she asked in a louder voice than she planned.

"Uncle Josh said you don't like her because you're jealous." The words came out slurred and sleepy.

Of course. Josh. The jackass.

She thought about dropping the topic and letting Nathan sleep, but . . . "When did he say this?"

"I like Rachel."

Not really the answer she wanted, but interrogating a half-awake kid wasn't okay with her. Him drifting off and being unlikely to remember the talk didn't make engaging in rapid-fire questions any better.

She sighed. "So do I."

"Uncle Josh and Rachel are going to take me camping . . ." His words drifted off at the end, but then he added one more thing before returning to his heavy breathing. "He promised. Just the three of us."

Over her dead body.

Chapter Eleven

Crazy. Insane. Deranged.

The words mattered. Pick one too weak and no one listened. That lack of a spark threatened the plan. Pick one too strong and everyone got defensive. Ran around, trying to prove a negative. That shifted the focus off where it needed to be.

The goal was to slide into a sweet spot in the middle. The place that wasn't *too* anything. A careful drop. Suggest a subtle unraveling—something uncontrolled but stoppable with the right intervention. Therapists. Rest. Medication. Put the spotlight there and keep it there with worried trolling.

After that, denials and justifications—promises of being fine—will sound hollow. Defuse arguments by attacking, all under the guise of being helpful. Sow doubt and everything will fall into place.

This could result in serious collateral damage, but so what? This wasn't the time to baby a conscience.

Play the scene right and escape notice . . . and blame. Then? Problem neutralized.

Chapter Twelve

Elisa knew avoiding the issue would only make it fester. She had questions and Josh needed to provide some answers, preferably without the dramatics. Sure, he was pissed. Harris was pissed. No one seemed to care that she was pissed, but she was. So, time for a private chat. A difficult but necessary one.

The morning after the most awkward brunch in family history, she took the R5 and headed for Josh's office, hoping to catch him off guard. He worked in the iconic PECO Building in Center City. It was known both for the colors and messages that lit up the top, and the monthly tours of its environmentally progressive "green" roof.

She hadn't been in the city in so long. For almost a year she'd confined her life to a tight square of miles. She traveled from home to Nathan's school, sometimes to Harris's work, and back home again. Except for a few detours, those mostly for food and doctor visits, she leashed herself to the house. A safe area she could control.

She'd hyperventilated before leaving today. She'd had to

force her body to calm down once she heard how loudly she was breathing on the train. Now, she concentrated on staying focused on Josh. Just Josh. Not on the street or how close she was to the hospital where she used to work, or the people buzzing by on the sidewalk. Nothing but inhaling and exhaling, mentally batting back the white noise that threatened to drown her.

She could not panic.

Focus on good memories. That was the answer. Like a date with Harris before they were engaged. That sometimes, but not always, could drag her mind to another place. To a safer one where her heartbeat didn't whoosh in her ears.

She loved Center City Philadelphia and used to convince Harris to come in for an activity or meal every weekend before they had Nathan. An outdoor concert or movie. The museum. An art show.

Parenthood decreased her downtime to almost zero. The incident eleven months ago stole the rest.

The plan today was to get in and out. She'd just called Josh and asked him to come down for coffee at the place a few doors away from his office building. That saved her from having to talk to a bunch of people or maneuver her way on an elevator. The idea of being trapped in a little box did nothing to calm her jumping nerves.

She crossed the street and glanced up at the glass entry doors to the building. People passed her on the sidewalk. More than one helpfully reminded her that she could stand somewhere else.

The one thing she loved about Philadelphia was the way

people just said what they were thinking. No filter. The other thing was the colorful and inventive ways they told you that you were an asshole for being in the way.

She inched away from the street and wound her way across competing lines of pedestrian traffic. Having her back against a solid wall would give her a sense of control, so she wanted to get there. She tried to slow her breathing. A man slammed into her shoulder, knocking her sideways. She glared at the back of his head for a few seconds before turning around again.

A woman walked toward her. An off-white coat cinched at her waist. Tall and sure. Pretty and dressed to impress.

The same redhead.

"Hey!" Elisa pushed past the couple in front of her, trying to get to the woman. Just as she broke free of the people marching around her, the redhead took a sharp turn. She pushed inside Josh's building and kept moving. Elisa picked up the pace, determined to follow the unknown woman who kept showing up.

She ran right into Josh. She put up her hands or she would have slammed into his chest. Seeing him ranked second in the surprises that had greeted her so far.

Half out of breath and squirming to get a better view, she looked around his shoulders. "Did you see that woman?"

It was a ridiculous question. Men and women mingled everywhere. The streets were filled with people, some in business attire and others in comfortable clothes. None of them was the *right* redhead.

"Elisa? What are you doing here?" But he didn't wait for an answer. He took her arm in a gentle hold and pulled her away from the main traffic area of the sidewalk. They moved until they could turn a corner and get out of the fray.

She drew in a big breath when she finally leaned against a wall. "Who was that redhead?"

His concerned frown deepened. "Who are you talking about?"

"She was right there." She peeked over his shoulder one more time, but it didn't help. The redhead was long gone. "You passed her in the doorway to your building."

Right? He had to have passed her. She went in. He came out. They worked together, or at least in the same building. The idea made sense a second ago. Now it sounded ridiculous as she thought it all through.

He rested a hand on the wall by her head. "Elisa, I'm really worried about you."

No . . . this wasn't about her. She was there about Abby . . . then this redhead . . .

His voice droned on. "You rarely leave the house. You've become paranoid. You finally ventured a bit out of the tight area you've confined yourself to and it's to come see me? That doesn't make sense."

His words finally penetrated the mental fog billowing up around her. "No. That's not—"

"Rather than concentrating on getting better you're obsessing about me." His voice stayed low, almost soothing. "Conjuring up conspiracies and apparently seeing things."

None of that was true. She wouldn't let it be true. The street started to spin around her. She shifted her head to the side and dizziness whirled through her.

Somehow, she managed to get words out. "I am trying to find Abby."

No . . . wait. That's not why she came today. She was there to talk about their fight. Then the redhead appeared.

"Abby is gone, Elisa," Josh said.

"That's what I'm afraid of." Dead. Missing. Kidnapped. Hurt. All of those remained possibilities and no one had come up with a reason for her to think otherwise.

"Look, I know what it's like to have a huge, life-altering shock." His words didn't match his concerned and caring tone.

Why did the buildings keep jumping? She had to close her eyes to keep the rolling sensation from moving through her.

A panic attack? *Not now.*

He leaned in closer. "You stumble around, looking for anything to grab on to."

"Stop." She tried to push him away. Still, he hovered.

Spinning. Spinning. She closed her eyes to shut it out.

This time he sighed at her. "For whatever reason, probably because I'm safe, my life has become your focus."

He wasn't safe. That was the problem. He was a giant question mark.

The headache. The infernal looping. She put a hand to her head in a desperate attempt to hold it steady. All the moving and shifting was making her sick. "You're twisting this around."

"I'm trying to be clear." He put a hand on his hip and studied her. "I'm starting a life with Rachel and you're not going to rush in and ruin it by spouting off deranged theories."

Deranged. He thought she was mentally ill. That she hadn't moved on or gotten better. "How dare you talk to me like this?"

He pushed away from the wall and stood straight again. "Go back to therapy, Elisa. Get help and do it before you destroy something that matters to you."

All hints of lightness and worry had disappeared from his voice. He sounded flat and angry now. He was threatening her. Maybe not explicitly, but she sensed it. The warnings broke through the dizziness and the muffled words shouting in her brain.

"Harris. Nathan. Your entire cozy life," he continued. "You could lose it in a second."

She shook her head and a wave of nausea washed over her. She breathed through her nose in a vain attempt to keep it together.

"Gaslighting isn't going to work." But her voice sounded weak and breathy. Pulsing with pain.

"What am I supposed to think? You're running around. You're seeing women who aren't there." He put a hand between them as he reeled off her perceived failures. "You're scaring the hell out of your husband and son."

"That's not true." She couldn't move her head . . . or her legs. She balanced all of her weight against that wall.

Groggy. That was the best way to describe the lethargy weighing her down. She went from angry to useless. Her muscles rebelled and her thoughts felt muddled.

"I love you like a sister, so I'm not going to tell Harris that you came here today to confront me."

She lifted a hand to grab onto his suit jacket, but her fingers slid against the cloth and fell again.

What the hell was wrong with her?

"I came here to talk with you." She spit the words out, but she no longer remembered how she'd got there or why she'd tried.

"You're skulking around on the sidewalk. Spying and, frankly, looking and sounding out of control." He frowned. "Are you drugged?"

"No." She meant to shout but she could do little more than mouth the word. She rubbed a hand over her face, tried to force life back into her body.

"This is not normal behavior. It's the kind of behavior that could change your life." He shook his head. "Harris and Nathan need stability."

They were all that mattered to her. "You actually think my husband and son would pick you over me?"

His expression was blank, unreadable.

"You're a monster." She believed that with every part of her.

"One of us needs help, and it's not me." He glanced at his watch as if he'd already wasted too much time on her. "I'd hate to think about what would happen if people started questioning your ability to take care of Nathan."

Her fingers grabbed onto the wall. Her nails scratched against the cool stucco. "Go to hell."

"Get help." He stared at her. "Before it's too late."

Chapter Thirteen

The trip had been a huge mistake.

Elisa gulped in breaths and fought back angry tears during the ride home. Josh's accusations echoed in her head and her hands shook. So little of the trip registered. Twice someone sat next to her then got up and moved. Scenery swept by the window in a blur. The thumping of the train banged in her head until every part of her ached and it hurt to open her eyes.

What felt like hours later, she got to the house. She stumbled and fought her body until she was back inside. Her raincoat slipped off her shoulders and down her arms. Her hair, which she'd tied back in a ponytail, fell in chunks around her face.

She sunk down, right there in the foyer. Her purse slid to the floor and her back pressed against the front door.

What am I going to tell Harris?

The question repeated in her brain. Part of her hated that he was always her first concern. She'd gone to college, worked as an accountant then a finance director at the hospital. Had responsibilities. Fought hard to make sure she could always support herself. Now, her life was about him . . . and Nathan. Their needs. Helping them succeed. How much she loved them.

The phone in her pocket kept buzzing. It matched the high-pitched ringing in her ears that refused to shut off. She let her head fall back against the door they'd spent months choosing because it had to be perfect. Because if everything looked perfect then no one would notice her falling apart.

The doorbell binged and she let out a scream. When the knocking started, a second scream rumbled up her throat and caught there.

What did Josh do? Who did he tell?

"Mrs. Wright?" The muffled question penetrated the door. Elisa. Her name was Elisa.

She covered her ears with her hands and began to rock back and forth. Something was happening to her, like a slow dissolving. The control she'd fought so hard to maintain slipped away. She could feel it, lunge for it, but not grab it.

"Mrs. Wright?" Sounds of shuffling followed the second callout. "I know you're there. We need to talk with you."

We . . .

The noise crescendoed in her head. A cacophony of screeches and words shook her. She tried to block the sound. Counted backward from ten then tried a second time.

Then silence. The riot of banging and ringing ended. All the words bombarding her brain stopped. Still, she sat there. Quiet and waiting. It could have been hours or minutes.

She'd never experienced a panic attack like that and didn't want a repeat, so she fought on. She struggled to normalize her breathing. In for three . . . out for three.

"Okay." She said the word out loud as a test to see if her voice still bobbled.

Her thoughts tumbled and churned. None of them made sense except for one—Nathan. What time was it? At some point she had to get in a car and pick him up.

"Right." She felt around for her cell phone but kept her eyes closed. "I can do this."

Her internal clock said it wasn't that much past noon, but what if it was? She couldn't be late. She had to be the responsible, happy mom in the carpool line.

With her fingers wrapped around the cell, she took one last deep breath and opened her eyes, ready to check the time and get moving again.

Rachel stood right in front of her.

Chapter Fourteen

Elisa's scream bounced off the walls. She slammed her back against the door and tried to get leverage, but the bottom of her heels slipped on the hardwood floor.

"What are you doing here?" Elisa wasn't sure if she asked the question more than once or if it just kept repeating in her head.

"Okay." Rachel held up both hands as she squatted down, pushed in closer. "It's okay."

Her voice, so low and soothing, only intensified Elisa's panic. Pale with drawn features, Rachel looked two seconds away from calling an ambulance.

"No." Elisa didn't even know what she was saying no to, but it sounded right.

Rachel nodded. "You're okay."

But she wasn't. Her home, the one place she could relax and set up rules that kept her safe—her refuge—had turned out to be like everywhere else. A danger zone.

"I'm not sick." What Elisa really meant was *I'm not crazy.* People threw the word around when they meant silly or ridiculous, but it applied here. She truly worried she was having a breakdown. Nothing sounded right or felt right. The constant urge to throw up battled with the need to curl into a ball and sleep in the darkness.

"You're under stress, that's all." Rachel took the cell phone out of Elisa's hand. "We should get you somewhere—"

"No!" Not a hospital or facility. Elisa didn't want to leave her house. Right now, she didn't want to leave the floor.

"Tea." Rachel shifted position until her hand rested under Elisa's arm. "Something warm to drink. Then, maybe, some sweatpants and a blanket."

That sounded so good, but . . . "Nathan?"

"Josh told me he stays after school on Mondays for some sort of tumbling and running class, yes?"

Elisa could only nod.

"Good. You've got hours, then. It's not even one." Rachel stood up and lifted Elisa up with her. "We'll sit and relax for a bit."

Elisa tried to push away and stand on her own, but her body rebelled. Her muscles relaxed and she fell into Rachel, who somehow managed to handle both of their weight. Up off the floor, Elisa glanced down and saw a piece of paper under the corner of her forgotten purse.

"Wait." But she didn't have the strength to bend over and fetch it.

Rachel grabbed it. A business card. She read from it. "'Ashburn and Tanaka. Private Investigators.'"

"Right. Them." The people calling and knocking. Elisa took the card and shoved it in her pocket. Not that she needed a reminder. She knew exactly who they were and what they wanted.

"Did you hire them?" Rachel asked.

"No."

Rachel didn't ask another question. She steered Elisa toward the couch. Took her coat the rest of the way off and eased her down onto the cushions. Elisa didn't say a word during the process. It had been so long since anyone had taken care of her.

Her mother had died years before Nathan was born, from ovarian cancer that ran wild through her body while she waited to qualify for health insurance at work. Now, a woman Elisa barely knew guided her back from the brink.

Elisa snuggled into the pillows stacked behind her and watched Rachel rummage around the kitchen, opening doors in search of tea. She found it and kept on working. For the first time, Elisa realized Rachel was wearing workout clothes, as if she'd stopped in after a run or on the way back from the gym.

"I really am okay, you know." Elisa didn't believe the words as she said them, but she was relieved her voice sounded stronger. Surer.

"You've had a shitty few days." Rachel returned to the couch with two mugs of steaming tea.

She sat down with her legs tucked up under her and faced Elisa. She put one of the mugs on the coffee table in front of Elisa. "I didn't mean to scare you when I came in."

Elisa's mind started to focus again and one question popped into her head, begging for an answer. "How *did* you get in?"

"Josh's keys. Back door." Rachel took a sip of her tea. "I grabbed them without really thinking. He couldn't find his sunglasses and I figured it would be better for me to come and look than for him to do it."

Did that explain? Elisa didn't think so but in her current state couldn't be sure. The panic attack had her reeling and confused.

Rachel winced. "I should have called first. He said you're always here, so I knocked. When you didn't answer I went around back to look in the yard."

"Okay. That makes sense." But the ease with which Rachel had entered the house put Elisa on edge. She knew some people thought the drop-in was fine. Elisa was not one of those people and needed to set visitation boundaries. Making that clear would be more effective once she could stand up without falling down again.

"I heard the doorbell and looked in the window. That's when I saw you sitting in the foyer." Rachel blew out a long breath. "I thought you'd passed out or something."

Elisa glanced at the windows lining the far side of the wall then turned toward the door. Rachel would not have had a clear view, which allowed Elisa to make things up. "I fell."

Rachel sighed. "I think we both know you didn't."

So much for that. "Right."

Elisa closed her eyes and sank deeper into the pillows fluffed up behind her. Her initial reaction was distrust, to question Rachel's motives and story. Elisa forced her mind in another direction. Rachel wasn't Josh.

Now Elisa had to think of a polite way to tell Rachel she

could leave. Elisa craved a long bath and a clear head. She'd almost been sucked under today. The world spun and her vision flickered. She hadn't suffered a deep mental fog like this for a long time.

Rachel cleared her throat. "Look, I know—"

Elisa's eyes shot open again. "What?"

Rachel just sat there. She put her mug on the coffee table but didn't force a conversation. She sat there, looking comfortable in the silence.

"I didn't mean to snap at you," Elisa said and truly meant it.

"I snuck into your house and scared the crap out of you." Rachel looked amused as she shrugged. "I earned a shout or two."

Elisa really did like Rachel. She had a caring smile and seemed strong and decent. That didn't mean she could survive Josh, and Elisa couldn't come up with the right words to make Rachel understand that . . . yet. "Still, you've been nothing but kind, and every time we meet I seem to be on the verge of screaming."

"It's fine."

Something about the way she said it made Elisa freeze. "Is it?"

Rachel stared at the family photo over the fireplace. "Elisa, I know about the shooting."

Chapter Fifteen

The shooting.

Eleven months and eight days ago. Elisa could add in the hours and minutes if she wanted to, but she didn't. The *incident*—how she tried to think of it because it sounded more academic than real—already took up too much space in her head. She wasn't going to give it more.

"Josh told you." Because of course he had. It made sense. It would be the kind of thing you'd warn a new girlfriend about before she met the family, on the off chance it would come up.

Don't talk about the hospital shooting.

"He provided some details, and I remembered others from the news." Rachel reached for her tea again and seemed to relax on her side of the couch. "I admit I did a computer search to find the rest."

"I don't blame you." Elisa didn't. She'd planned to do some background checking on Rachel, just to be safe, but the days kept blowing up in emotionally unexpected ways.

"We don't have to talk about what happened to you," Rachel said in a near-whisper.

Good, because Elisa never talked about it. Some of her closest friends had shied away, clearly afraid of saying the wrong thing. Others gave her space and she never closed the gap again.

Sure, she talked at first with a therapist she didn't want because going over the pieces of what happened that day kept the wound open and exposed. Elisa also talked with Harris, but she'd purposely downplayed the details. The first weeks after had been this careful dance. She felt fragile, and he treated her like she might shatter at any moment. Only Nathan carried on, keeping his life focused on what he needed. As it should be.

Elisa inhaled nice and deep. At some point the incident should be a distant memory that no longer filled her with dread, but not yet. Reliving those terrifying moments created stark visions, ones that refused to fade.

"I worked at a hospital in Philadelphia, handling expenses and procurement." Elisa hated how that part of her life was in the past, but it was. "Right out front of the building on weekdays there was this coffee cart. It had the best muffins."

"What kind?"

Elisa appreciated the question because it let her stall and hold back the worst of it for a few more minutes. "Weirdly, cranberry. Usually not my favorite, but they were so good. A little sweet and a little tart." Elisa exhaled again, trying to gather the energy to keep talking. "Every day I had either a small salad and muffin or yogurt for lunch, and I always got it there."

Rachel smiled but didn't say anything else.

"Then one day—" Elisa's voice broke. She heard the snap deep inside and felt it twist through her whole body. She brought her legs up until her feet were flat against the cushions and she could balance her mug between her knees in front of her. "Maxine Webber, my boss, joined me for lunch. We were outside, talking about nothing really. Nothing work related. She was excited for her grandson's second birthday and complaining about the outdated kitchen her husband insisted was fine as is, without renovation."

Elisa tried to relax but her muscles kept seizing up on her. "Her husband was a contractor and could do the work, but Maxine wanted to hire someone so that it would actually get done. She said her husband didn't want to be on call once they got home, so nothing of theirs ever got fixed or updated."

Without closing her eyes Elisa could see Maxine, a tall black woman. Slim and focused. She didn't take any shit and some of the people who worked for her hated that. They met her with a bit of a *how dare she* attitude, which was bullshit.

Maxine was Philadelphia born and raised. Stayed there for college and worked her way up and into administration at the hospital. Elisa liked her, respected her. And eleven months and eight days ago Elisa held Maxine as her blood ran onto the sidewalk.

"A former coworker named Keith, a guy who was fired for being lazy and late and, according to some reports, inappropriately handsy, showed up with a gun." Elisa could see him, too. That smile on his face as he rounded the cart, walked up to the two of them on the sidewalk. The *"You're dead"* whisper right before he raised the gun. "His plan was to shoot his way through the building to get to Maxine, but she was outside, so . . ."

"He didn't have to work that hard." Rachel reached out a hand and rested it on Elisa's leg through the blanket. "You're lucky to be alive."

Yeah, lucky. "He shot and people scattered. Except me. I froze. I stood there, watching him switch his aim. I heard this muffled noise and then he was flat on the sidewalk. Hector, the man who ran the food cart, tackled Keith and his next shot went wide."

The memories crashed over her. People running. Wheels screeching as some cars stopped and others raced away. All of the screaming. The blood seeping through Maxine's jacket. Small gasps as she fought for her final breaths.

Elisa had stood there, watching but not really seeing it. None of it registered. Her body froze. Then she'd glanced down and saw Maxine's face. The tears and then the blood seeping out of her chest wound.

Elisa broke out of the nightmare vision long enough to rub her upper arm. Touching the area brought a hint of pain, but she thought it was more of a memory of the pain. "I didn't realize that last bullet fired grazed me until the ambulance came."

"Damn, Elisa."

"I finally dropped to my knees and tried to help Maxine. I remember I kept shouting for someone to call for the ambulance, which they'd already done." Elisa blew out a haggard breath. "But I was too late. All I could do was hold her while she died."

Rachel picked up Elisa's mug and handed it to her. "You made sure she wasn't alone in her final moments. I'm sure that means something to her family."

Elisa wrapped her fingers around it, craving the heat inside. "Yeah."

That's what the therapist had said. And Maxine's husband. And Harris. They all meant well, but it brought very little solace. Being the one still alive left Elisa unbalanced and clawing through a mountain of anxiety.

"So, I left my job and now I hate to leave my house." An abbreviated version of the horrors that still haunted her, including being snuck up on and loud banging noises, but Elisa could tell from the concerned expression on Rachel's face that she understood.

Even talking about it sucked the energy out of Elisa. She took a sip of tea, but it didn't crack the icy coolness flowing through her.

"Is that why you have the office here?" Rachel hitched her thumb in the general direction of the backyard. "You work from home?"

"A few months ago I started doing some freelance accounting work for a few businesses in the area." Elisa worked part-time and set her own hours, which was all she could handle right now. "Harris thought creating the office would help."

"Help with what?"

Making his wife whole again. But instead of saying that, she laughed. "I don't know. Give me a place to go, I guess. He thought the act of getting up and leaving the house would be helpful."

"You've had a hell of a time."

Rachel didn't apologize or get all tongue-tied, trying to find the right words when there weren't any. She didn't rush to make things better. Elisa was grateful. So many people had said *I'm sorry* to her since the incident that the words didn't have any meaning anymore. Maxine was dead, not her. Maxine deserved the love, not her.

"And it's still not over." Elisa reached into her pocket and took out the business card. "The hospital did an internal review of its practices and cleared itself of any wrongdoing, of course. An attorney for Maxine's family disagrees and hired these investigators to determine what, if anything, could have been done differently."

Some of the color returned to Rachel's cheeks. "Oh . . ."

Not the reaction Elisa expected. "Did you think the investigators were for something else?"

"Honestly? I thought you hired them to investigate Abby's leaving."

Disappearance. Elisa silently corrected Rachel because she didn't want to normalize losing Abby, even in her mind.

"I've never talked to the investigative team in the hospital case." Elisa had ignored the calls, but she read the business card now. "Martin Ashburn and Shelby Tanaka."

"Why not meet with them?"

"Talking means reliving it and . . ." Elisa shook her head because it sounded silly, as if she'd never escaped those minutes on the sidewalk. Answering questions couldn't possibly make it bigger or worse in her head. "I don't know."

"You told *me* about what happened."

And nothing surprised Elisa more. "You must have that kind of face."

"I guess." Rachel stared into her mug for a few seconds before facing Elisa again. "May I offer a suggestion?" She waited for Elisa to nod before continuing. "Fight back."

"Meaning?"

"You're spending a lot of time thinking about Abby." Rachel held up a hand when Elisa started to talk. "Which I understand, and I think you should do. She was your friend."

Elisa thought about what Josh had said to her about Abby's relationship with her as being convenient and nothing more. "*Is* and yes."

"Hell, I'll help you track her down or look for clues, or whatever, but your timing might be off. Maybe doing all of that right now is a way of avoiding the shooting, which doesn't sound healthy."

That was not the first time Elisa had heard that explanation. "Now you sound like Josh."

"I'm not sure you mean that as a good thing, but I'm serious." Rachel looked like she was struggling to find the right words. "Talk to the PIs. Get your life back. Feel more solid and then tackle the Abby issue."

But the waiting . . . "What if she's in danger and waiting makes things worse? What if I wait too long and miss the opportunity to help?"

"You can't help her if no one will listen to you."

"You don't think they're listening?" Elisa didn't bother defining *they* because Rachel had to know she meant Harris, Josh, and possibly the police, all people who saw her as damaged.

"Right now? No. I think you're making it too easy for them to discredit you."

Chapter Sixteen

Elisa felt better by the time Rachel left an hour later. More in control. More stable. Less likely to shatter into a million pieces.

She dumped the mugs with the cold tea in the sink and re-clipped her hair in a ponytail. She craved normalcy but wasn't sure what that even was anymore. But Rachel's comments stuck. She needed to be okay if she wanted people to listen to her about Abby. It was too easy for Josh—or anyone—to write off her concerns as being part of past trauma.

Reliving those moments today . . . her breathing still hadn't returned to normal. Putting Josh and their fight out of her head, and what Harris would say when he found out, and he would, proved to be a challenge. She'd take a step and a stray sentence would wiggle its way into her head. She'd remember the look on Josh's face. The way he insisted *she* was the one who could be a danger.

She'd never let that happen. Nathan and Harris meant everything to her. She'd protect them, no matter what it took.

In her mind, that meant shielding them from Josh and whatever he had planned for Rachel. But first, Abby. Elisa decided to go to the storage locker tomorrow. Today, she needed to finish reading the messages on the laptop. Getting a few minutes here and there to sneak away and read through some wasn't efficient. She needed a full, uninterrupted read.

She walked upstairs and headed for her bedroom and the laptop. The idea of changing into lounge clothes tempted her, but she still had to pick up Nathan. Play the role so that people at his school would be less likely to believe whatever nonsense Josh told them. She'd defeat rumors by being visible and fine. Put together and smiling. The perfect vet's wife and mom.

A few seconds later, the cursor blinked at her as she reread the first message again. The next few consisted of this Concerned person trying to get Abby's attention and Abby saying "fuck off" in different ways. But Abby didn't block or ignore the unknown sender. She repeatedly told Concerned to stop hiding behind an anonymous name and she clearly kept reading. So did Elisa.

CONCERNED: it's easy to ignore what I'm saying because he's taking you out for nice dinners and being attentive but what happens when he stops acting like this?
ABBY: That's what men do. They court you then get tired. Lazy bastards.

Abby's tone started out almost amused, but only at first. A few days into the ongoing conversation Concerned's tactics changed. The points became more targeted and the information much more specific.

ABBY: Tell me who you are. Maybe we can meet.

CONCERNED: he's going to kill you too
ABBY: Tell me who you are. Maybe we can meet.
CONCERNED: you aren't taking this seriously
ABBY: What are you talking about now?
CONCERNED: his first wife

After that, it looked like Abby didn't answer a few attempts by Concerned to get her attention. Then Abby came back and, for the first time, initiated contact. Elisa assumed that meant Abby had been thinking. Something compelled her to circle back and ask for more.

ABBY: Candace died in a fall on the stairs. It was an accident.
CONCERNED: there was a bathroom downstairs on the other side of the kitchen so why would she go up the narrow back staircase she hated?

Good question. Elisa had known Candace. She was driven and business focused, much more so than Josh. She made him more accountable. More of a grown-up.

Candace had been raised with money and influence. Her family expected her to succeed. She slid in and out of that world with ease, insisting that as a biracial woman she didn't fit into any box. Black people saw her as too white. White people whispered about Candace being "too street." Those whispers were quiet and careful but not hard to overhear.

No one dared ask outright if Candace belonged on the Main Line or in the fancy boutiques. People knew her family. A generation ago her grandfather had used a family recipe to introduce a candy bar to the world. Now the company was an empire. One overt racist remark and her family's influence would take over. Deals would dry up. Event invitations would stop.

Candace talked about the discomfort of being accepted for her bank account, but insisted if people were going to judge her that way, then she was going to use all of her ammunition to keep them in line. She joked about it being the benefit of coming from "candy money."

ABBY: The police said what happened to Candace was an accident.
CONCERNED: it was made to look like one
ABBY: Leave me alone.

Elisa thought about all the police involvement in Candace's death. That detective, definitely Burroughs. Detective Burroughs. He was the father of Josh's friend, helped Josh and Harris navigate all of it. She remembered meetings at the kitchen table where the men combed through files and photographs.

CONCERNED: are you ready to read the police report about Candace's death? look at the photos?
ABBY: Stop.
CONCERNED: too much blood for a simple accident

ABBY: I'll show these messages to Josh.

CONCERNED: you won't show them to anyone–you can't trust josh and you don't want to endanger anyone by involving them and making them josh's target

That was the second time Elisa had read the subtle threat voiced by Concerned. The one that warned Abby to stay quiet and not share the messages. Ever since Elisa read the first message she'd wondered why Abby hadn't talked about all of this. Probably because of Elisa's mental state post-shooting, which was even less solid than now. Possibly because Josh was her brother-in-law and Abby wanted to protect her. But also because Concerned made it clear sharing was not safe for the people Abby cared about, and Elisa knew that included her.

Elisa didn't get it. She didn't know who Concerned could be. One of Candace's family members or someone in law enforcement? And why lie? The police report should support Josh, but Elisa could feel Concerned trying to convince and turn Abby. The tension jumped off the page as the tone grew more terse and the messages more frequent. The desperation was tough to miss.

Elisa kept scrolling, even though she knew that, in a way, reading along invited Concerned into her house.

CONCERNED: candace wasn't his first

ABBY: What does that mean?

CONCERNED: ask him about Lauren

Elisa stared at the screen. *Who's Lauren?*

Chapter Seventeen

Elisa was still up in the bedroom rereading all of the saved messages and not one step closer to figuring out the identity of Concerned when she heard the front door shut and pounding footsteps as Nathan raced through the first floor. He was talking about something and it sounded like frogs, so she stayed where she was on the love seat.

She'd called the police to talk with Detective Burroughs, but he'd retired. That meant talking with the detective she'd talked to about Abby before, but he was out for the day. She doubted he'd return her message, or he would with a *case is closed* curt response about Abby. Another wall. More questions and no answers.

A few minutes later Harris stepped into the bedroom. He wore a frown and the sleeves of his dress shirt were rolled up as if he went from work right to—

He stared at her. "Anything you want to tell me about today?"

The Josh showdown. She knew despite his statement about not telling Harris that he would run right to his big brother and tattle. He had that *you're losing it* speech locked and ready to go. No doubt he wanted Harris to hear it, too.

She dropped the laptop on the cushion beside her and stood up. "I know you're angry."

"Not angry, but all you had to do was call me to help out."

Okay, that didn't make any sense. "What?"

He unbuttoned his shirt, revealing a white tee underneath. "To pick up Nathan."

"Oh my God." Her hand flew to her mouth right as a wall of motherly guilt crashed down on her. She'd forgotten all about her son and getting him from school. What the hell was that? "I lost track of time."

"The school called you. I called you." He took the oxford shirt off and threw it on the end of the bed. "Hell, I thought something happened to you." His gaze traveled over her. "Are you okay?"

That wasn't her biggest concern at the moment. "Is Nathan okay?"

"Of course." Harris snorted. "He's probably rummaging through the kitchen, looking for something to eat because, and I quote, 'I'm so hungry my stomach is shrinking.'"

She could hear Nathan's voice, complete with sighing, as he delivered his little speech.

"I told him we had apples at home, and he informed me that apples didn't stop hunger. For the record, he's probably not going to be a nutritionist when he grows up." Harris shook his head. "Be happy you missed it. It was a very dramatic car ride."

Normally she liked the amused banter and Nathan stories,

but not now. She'd been so focused on Josh and the laptop . . . time had drifted. She must have sat in the same place for hours, but how was that even possible?

Maybe Josh was right. Maybe she was losing it.

She had to get to Nathan and hold him. Make sure he was fine. "Let me—"

"Hey." Harris was in front of her in two steps. "Elisa, what's going on?"

His face filled with concern. The mixture of confused and sad and worried was hard to miss. No matter how much she wanted to fall into him and forget everything—to go back before the shooting and start over, be able to warn every person she cared about of the horrors and confusion to come and steer them out of them—that wasn't possible.

How did she forget Nathan? She'd been so clear about needing to pick him up. She even talked about the time with Rachel. Then there was this Lauren person. The theories and questions raced around in Elisa's head.

Wait . . . calls? No one had called her.

She looked back at the couch. "Where's my phone?"

Harris rubbed his hands up and down her arms. "Slow down for a second."

"I can't. I have to—"

"You forgot me," Nathan announced.

She looked around Harris to see Nathan standing in the bedroom doorway, holding what looked like a hastily put together stack of peanut butter and crackers.

More guilt. This time it threatened to suffocate her.

She went over to him and crouched down in front of him so she could see his face. "I'm sorry, honey. I got busy and—"

Harris put a hand on Nathan's shoulder and gave it a squeeze. "And she asked me to come get you, which I did. Problem solved."

Nathan didn't look convinced as crumbs fell to the floor from the cracker sandwich in his hand. "Alec's mom called and you didn't pick up."

Great. Now Alec's annoying mom knew their business.

"I'm not sure where my phone is." That wasn't a lie. Elisa thought she'd brought it upstairs with her but she didn't see it.

Nathan shrugged. "It's okay."

It really wasn't. Yeah, he'd forget, but she wouldn't. Not for a long time. That's how motherhood worked for her, a constant mental scorecard of the ways she'd messed up. Harris took everything in stride. She obsessed.

But today was a first. She didn't miss important meetings concerning Nathan or forget to pick him up. Despite the emotional whirlwind of the last year, she'd tried to stay on track where he was concerned. If she could only hold it together for ten minutes a day, those ten minutes belonged to him.

Nathan tipped his head back and looked up at his dad. "Can I play my game?"

"Finish the snack then wash your hands."

Nathan nodded and zoomed out of the room. She didn't even bother to tell him to slow down this time.

"Were you working?"

Harris's voice pulled her back into the moment. She turned

to him. He looked tired from a long day and a bit harried, likely from having to leave the clinic early and grab Nathan. He didn't mind doing transportation duty, but he usually had a heads-up first so he could rearrange his schedule.

She stood up and studied his expression, wondering if Josh had called and what the school said about her absence in the carpool lane. "I lost track of time."

"That's really it?"

No, that wasn't even close to being *it*. "Who's Lauren?"

The question slipped out, but she didn't regret it. She intended to talk to him about Lauren this evening, regardless of what mess Josh caused or how exhausted Harris was from his day.

Harris's mouth dropped open but he didn't answer. The lack of a response wasn't like him at all. He didn't hesitate or make up stories; at least, she thought that was true. These days she didn't know what to believe, but the stark look on her husband's face suggested something horrible was coming.

"Harris?" She'd run out of energy and tact. "Lauren. Josh. Spill now."

He blinked a few times. "How do you know about Lauren?"

That didn't sound good. Elisa's curiosity grew. "No spinning. Who is she?"

Harris glanced at the door, likely to make sure little ears weren't waiting out there in the hallway. Nathan couldn't keep a secret to save his soul, but it looked like Harris could and she didn't like that revelation at all.

Harris finally faced her. "Lauren was Josh's wife."

Chapter Eighteen

Wife. *Wife. Wifewifewifewife.* Elisa ran the words through her mind a few times. They still didn't make sense.

"Josh was married to a woman named Lauren?" *Please say no.* She couldn't tolerate any more secrets.

Harris gave her a slow nod. "Yeah."

The even bigger question. *Was? And when?*

Harris closed his eyes for a few seconds before opening them again. Still, he didn't answer.

"What exactly are you saying, Harris? Or trying really hard not to say?" He seemed to be dancing and avoiding and otherwise not acting like the man she knew at all.

"Candace actually was Josh's second wife. He was married once before, when he was much younger." Harris exhaled. "To Lauren."

They'd never talked about anyone named Lauren. Harris and Josh never told her about this other wife. She'd never seen a photo or heard a friend say the name. Josh's now-not-first-wife Candace didn't mention Lauren. Abby didn't mention her. All of that suggested no one knew about this marriage outside of a very tight group, which might consist only of two.

Sounded like Lauren wasn't just another of Josh's wives. She was a Wright family secret.

Elisa tried to stay calm when she wanted to stomp around and throw things. "Where is Lauren now?" Dread filled Elisa but she had to ask the question anyway. A part of her even guessed the answer before he said it.

"Lauren is dead." Harris hesitated as if waiting for an explosion before starting to talk again. "But the answer to what you really want to know . . . it was an accident."

Elisa's hands went numb. All of her did. "Another accident? Another dead wife."

"No, listen. I know how it looks and sounds, but no." Harris held up both hands as he walked toward her. He stopped before he touched her.

"Who the hell keeps a dead wife secret?" She felt her family imploding. Everything she knew, all the truths she held on to and depended on, was false.

He shook his head. "It's not that simple."

"It is. You both lied. You did it without blinking and without any sign of remorse." Pain, confusion, and fury moved through her. The sensations combined until her insides trembled.

"I wanted to tell you so—"

"Save it." She couldn't hear that right now. "And it's not just about telling me. Lauren's name should have come up after Candace died. Did the police know about a mysterious first wife? Did they ask questions?"

Harris just stood there, not saying a word. Not defending or explaining.

Then it hit her. The friend. The friend's connected father. "Did Detective Burroughs know about Lauren?" She could tell the answer by looking at Harris's strained expression. "Oh my God. The detective knew and ignored the death or hid it?"

"Not 'hid.' He looked into it and said it wasn't relevant to Candace's death."

"What does that even mean?" He made it sound as if Lauren and Candace were interchangeable, and that made Elisa choke down the bile rising in her throat.

"Exactly what it sounds like." Harris's hands came up again but he still didn't try to touch her. "Lauren's death was an accident, but the detective knew how two dead wives would look for Josh. That people would jump to the wrong conclusions."

She stared at his open palms before her gaze moved to his face. "You mean that Josh liked to kill women."

"You know that's not true."

"Do I?"

"The detective investigated and compared cases." Harris dropped his hands. "He didn't bury the truth. He looked into it then downplayed a previous incident, knowing it would taint the investigation."

He sounded so rational.

She hated that. "But the press? Candace's parents? Why didn't other people raise questions? Lauren's accident isn't a secret, right? So, how did this stay out of the press?" How did Harris not tell her back then or any day since?

"Everyone agreed Candace's death was an accident. The press celebrated her life, kept the focus there, as her family wanted."

"That sounds too easy. Like special treatment. Like the good old boy network ran wild." Two women dead and no one took five minutes to discuss the parallels. She wanted to sit down and rewind every conversation they'd ever had. If Harris could lie about this, keep this from her, what else didn't she know? "You never gave me a chance to understand. Nine years together and you never said a word. You never mentioned Lauren. You and Josh wrote her off as if she didn't exist."

Now she knew it was possible not to feel anything. To stand there, not knowing how your muscles continued to hold you up, feeling hollow and empty. She listed to one side and part of her hoped the world would go dark and the conversation would end.

Harris shook his head. "Josh was young and it messed him up."

"'It'? Talk about dismissive. Come on, Harris." He was better than this . . . he had to be.

He nodded. "Yes, you're right. I mean Lauren's death. That was my bad wording, not Josh's."

Not his fault. Josh wasn't to blame. That was the underlying message she picked up and it wasn't the first time. "So she died and he just happened to be there? That's a popular refrain in his life."

"Okay." Harris's arms dropped to his sides. "That's not fair."

Fair? He couldn't possibly understand what that word meant or he wouldn't use it. The dead women had a right to talk about fairness. Elisa thought she did as the person shut out from this huge family secret. Not Josh, and not Harris on Josh's behalf.

"Explain it to me. Make me understand why you—both of you—have lied to me for years." She doubted he could justify a lapse this profound but, for the sake of their marriage, she really wanted him to try.

"I didn't lie. I—"

Wrong tactic. "Really?" Her legs finally gave out and she sat down on the edge of the bed. "This is the type of lame excuse Nathan might try and he's seven."

Harris looked like he was going to say something then his mouth slammed shut. A few seconds later he started nodding. "You're right."

"I know I am."

"I fucked up. I was being protective and convinced myself it wasn't my secret to tell, which is bullshit, I know." He sat next to her, still smart enough to give her some space, but their thighs did touch. "He'd been pretty messed up before he lost Lauren."

She groaned because none of this explained another dead woman in Josh's past. "I know this part. He lost his way and only wanted to hang out with loser friends and smoke pot in someone's basement. Shoplifted. Didn't work or go to school."

She didn't want to feel sorry for Josh or hear about his stumbles. Her concern was for Lauren . . . and Candace and Abby, and possibly, Rachel. "I'm waiting for the dead wife part."

"Lauren went to school part-time. She worked as a waitress to pay her way, and that's where they met. At that restaurant."

He sat forward with his elbows balanced on his knees and his gaze locked on some random spot on the floor. "After a couple months they ran away and got married. He didn't tell me because he knew I would try to talk him out of it. He was nineteen. She was, too, and also kind of lonely. She had her mom but no one else."

"No one?" That might explain why no one ever spoke up for Lauren.

"No siblings or grandparents around to help, and her mom held on a bit tight. Suffocated her. I'm not a therapist but Lauren's mom seemed to resent the choices she'd made and the life she had, and all of that fell on Lauren." He lifted his head. "Lauren's need to get out and Josh's need to find stability likely pushed them together. They had time to get to know each other and see but were rushing it, as if whatever they felt for each other would vanish if they didn't jump on it."

Young. In love. Elisa got it. Now she wanted to hear the rest. All the stalling made her patience short-circuit. "Harris, please."

"Give me a second." He shot her a side glance. "Her death isn't an easy thing to talk about."

"You never have, so I guess not."

He sat up straight again but didn't look at her. "They'd been married a little less than a year. Both were in college." His halting voice spoke to how difficult it was for him to talk about this. "We all went on a camping trip. Lauren and Josh. Me and Patricia. A woman I was, um, dating."

Another secret. Elisa thought she knew all of the names of

his former girlfriends. Apparently not. "We'll circle back to this never-before-mentioned Patricia. Keep going."

"Everything was fine. The first night went great. We hiked and camped out by the fire." A slight smile came and went. "The next night Josh came to our tent. It was about two in the morning. He was yelling and said he'd gotten up to go to the bathroom and Lauren was gone."

The word echoed through Elisa. "Gone?"

"He went looking and found her . . ." Harris closed his eyes and rubbed a hand over his forehead. "She was in the lake. The police said she knocked her head and either fell into the water or was out of it and wandered down there."

Knocked her head? "That sounds ridiculous."

She reached out and put a hand on his. The move was less about comforting him and more about getting him to look at her.

When he finally did his mouth had fallen into a flat line. "You weren't there."

"But you were." She couldn't get over that fact. He'd gone to bed and Lauren was alive. Hours later—dead. Did he really not question what happened in between?

"I'm telling you it was an accident. Josh was—"

"Inconsolable." She thought back to the way he fell apart at the hospital as he listened to the news about Candace, apparently his second wife and not his first. Now Elisa knew he'd had practice grieving a dead wife.

"Yeah, I've seen the act." She stood up because right then she didn't want to be near Harris. The idea that he didn't question that story or wonder when a second of Josh's wives died just a few years later . . . her mind refused to process all of it.

"It wasn't an act, Elisa."

There was snap to his voice that sent her temper spiking. "You don't get to be pissed off, Harris. You hid all of this from me."

He sighed as he took her hand and looked up at her from the bed. "I did and I'm sorry. Look, I know it sounds terrible. Two women."

"That's a lot of bad luck." An unbelievable amount.

"But he's my brother. Hell, I helped raise him. I couldn't imagine him hurting anyone, let alone his wife and—"

"No." She wasn't ready to be appeased or to forgive. For God's sake, two dead wives. That was not the kind of information he could skip over then excuse.

"Why not tell me?" she asked because she couldn't come up with a single rational explanation for his leaving out this huge bit of family history.

"That whole thing, that night and the days after, was so fucking terrible." He held her hand in both of his. Traced his finger over her palm. "Seeing her messed me up. Seeing her floating . . ."

Elisa didn't want to know that part. No more death talk because she couldn't handle it. "But why hide the truth from me?"

"When Lauren died, I worried Josh would fall apart." Harris stood up, never breaking his hold on Elisa. "I was desperate. I got him to a therapist. She said after our parents' deaths Josh might not be able to handle what happened to

Lauren, so I got him to talk with her. I tried to bring up her death, but he didn't want to discuss Lauren with me. After a while it got easier for me not to try."

"You erased her. Both of you did." Elisa realized she didn't even know Lauren's last name.

"No, never that."

"Harris, you have to see how this sounds fantastical. His first wife dies during a hiking trip. His second dies on the stairs in their house. His fiancée, who should have been wife number three, disappears." All those women and no one—not even the police—seemed to care. Detective Burroughs, the one detective who should have stepped up and spoken for Candace and pushed for more information on Lauren, was too busy protecting Josh to get justice for either woman. Elisa had no idea why local police didn't care about the repetitive losses, but she intended to ask, this time armed with more background information. "Do you really not see why I'm upset?"

"That's the other reason I didn't tell you, especially after Candace. I didn't want you to find out about Josh's history, about Lauren, then draw comparisons that weren't fair to him."

To Josh. Not to her. Not to Lauren or Candace. Harris's main concern was always all about protecting Josh. Harris did it without thinking and had trained her to act the same way and never question Josh's actions.

"Lauren wandered away at night and ended up dead in the water," Elisa said, repeating the story, which made even less sense to her the second time she mentally dissected it.

"I know how it sounds. I really do, but you weren't there."

She heard the pain in his voice, and her instinct to say and do things to make this better kicked in. She had to fight to ignore it, that integral part of her. "You're smarter than this, Harris. With anyone else, you'd ask questions."

"But he's not just anyone." Harris dropped her hand and started pacing the space between the bed and sitting room. "I can't see him doing . . . he wouldn't do it."

"What else don't I know?"

Harris shook his head. "Nothing. I promise."

For the first time in their marriage she didn't believe him.

PATRICIA SUMMERS. THAT was the name Harris had given her. The woman he dated and never talked about. The one who was with him when the unthinkable happened to Lauren . . . to Josh.

Well, back then it was unthinkable. Now, having the women in Josh's life die might be the expected thing since it happened so damned often.

Elisa didn't want to be this person. The kind who snooped and researched, but the choices the men in her life had made drove her to it. She didn't know who to trust or what to think. After an entire marriage of putting her husband's needs first, of doting on him, she'd lost the ability to see things clearly.

She'd searched Harris's social media accounts for followers named Patricia and nothing. He told her that Patricia was in veterinary school with him at the University of Pennsylvania. That should make it easier to find her since Penn was the only veterinary school that awarded a VMD rather than a DVM degree.

Elisa looked for alumni named Patricia. Searched for "Patricia" and "VMD" and didn't get any matches that could have been her. Another lie? More omissions? She had no idea.

The only thing that she knew for certain was that the trail of dead and missing women leading to Josh had just gotten one body longer.

Chapter Nineteen

A confusing night gave way to an exhausted morning. Elisa shuffled around the kitchen in her gray and white pinstripe pajamas. She poured a cup of coffee and set the pot down but didn't realize how hard she slammed it on the stand until she heard a cracking sound.

"You broke it. You broke it." Nathan made the words into a song as he sat at the kitchen table, playing with a dinosaur he'd built.

"Nathan, please."

He sang louder and added a thumping sound as he smacked his spoon against the wooden table. "Broken, broken, broken."

She reached over his head and grabbed the spoon. "That's enough."

She didn't notice her hands were shaking until she set the spoon on the counter. Flexing her fingers a few times eased the trembling but didn't eliminate it. A deep fog had settled over her, and she couldn't break through it. Words sounded either too loud or completely muffled. A headache pounded through her until it felt like her skull was breaking apart.

She'd tried drinking tea and practicing her breathing exercises before Nathan ran downstairs. She'd sat in a calm, quiet space . . . blah, blah, blah. None of it worked, so she switched to coffee. Anxiety rushed and whirled through her. She'd twice realized she was biting her thumbnail while her thoughts drifted and had to force herself to stop.

She hadn't been okay for a long time, but the anxiety had intensified since that blowup with Josh outside his office building yesterday. Another panic attack waited on the far edge of her mind. She could feel it lurking out there. Building, gaining strength. She feared a second round might pull her under. Steal her breath and leave her shaking and unable to stand again.

Nathan couldn't see any of that. She needed to be strong for him. She also needed answers. Abby, Lauren, and even doubts about Candace's accident on the stairs had wormed their way into her head.

She heard an odd shaking sound. Like uncooked beans in a tin.

Nathan stopped singing but now he used the table as a drum and he was holding . . . something. He shook it like a maraca. Then she saw it. A white bottle.

Pills.

Oh my God. "Nathan, no!"

He froze with his arm in the air.

"Give those to me." This wasn't the time for subtle. She made a grab for the bottle, but he dropped his arm at the same time and she missed.

Nathan frowned at her, looking confused and heartbroken

in the way only a kid with hurt feelings could be at the same time. "What did I do?"

Harris picked that moment to walk into the kitchen. He'd stayed home this morning, hung around when this one time she'd wanted him to get to the office.

He glanced at Nathan and shot across the kitchen. He had the pill bottle out of Nathan's hand within seconds.

Nathan shoved away from the table. Angry tears came next.

She guessed he was more stunned or embarrassed than anything, but she hugged him from behind. "It's okay."

"It is not." The fury in Harris's voice suggested he wasn't in the mood to be questioned. "Where did you get this bottle?"

Nathan hiccupped and swallowed deep breaths. "The table."

Harris's gaze switched to her. "Why are these out? What the hell were you thinking?"

She looked at the label. The pain pills she'd gotten after the shooting. She'd stopped taking them but never threw the bottle away. She still took medicine for anxiety and had ever since the shooting. They had a special lock safe in her night-stand drawer. That's where she kept the bottles specifically so that Nathan couldn't accidentally find them.

"I don't . . ." She'd agreed to stop taking them more than a month ago and felt proud that she could refrain. "I thought . . ."

"You told me you weren't taking those." Anger still ran through his voice. "You promised."

"I did stop." She'd fought an internal battle over those pills. She wanted to take them. They helped her drift away. How much she needed them, how quickly she'd reached for them, had panicked her. Panicked Harris. So, she stopped using them. The anxiety meds were a different story. "That bottle should be upstairs. Locked away."

"Then what happened?"

Nathan shrank with each word Harris shouted. "Dad?"

She understood the tentative tone. Harris rarely raised his voice, so when he did the entire household's mood plummeted and the tension rose to catastrophic levels. Even now, with her mind spinning and her memories fizzy and out of focus, Harris's anger penetrated.

"I must have brought them down." But she didn't remember doing that at all. There wouldn't be a reason for her to do that.

"Why?" Harris demanded to know.

She had no idea. There was no explanation that made sense.

"Daddy?"

Something about the pleading tone of Nathan's voice, probably how young and vulnerable he sounded, got through to Harris. His shoulders relaxed and the tight lines at the corners of his mouth eased. "It's okay. Yeah, it's fine."

His rough voice sure didn't sound fine.

"I made a mistake, honey. Daddy is right to be upset." She looked across the table at Harris, willing him to calm down. "But he's upset at me, not you."

Harris held her gaze for a few seconds before looking at Nathan. "Go upstairs and get dressed."

Nathan looked down at his bowl of half-eaten cereal but didn't argue. "Okay."

"Hey, buddy?" Harris waited for Nathan to look at him. "This is your mom's bottle and you shouldn't have it. Leave it alone in the future, okay?"

"Why?"

"It's grown-up stuff."

Nathan smiled but his eyes remained watery. "Okay."

Elisa watched the scene as if she weren't a part of it. Then Harris looked at her, anger banked but just barely.

"He's gone, so explain." That was it. A few words, and more of a demand, and then he stopped talking.

"I don't know."

"What kind of answer is that?" He stood across the table from her, looking ready to argue this point to death. "This shit is dangerous for him."

An intense punch of anger hit her, pushing out the threatening abyss. "Don't talk to me like I'm a child. I mean, do you really think I don't know that?"

But he was on a roll. "We have a system. We have rules about meds."

Jesus. She got it. She screwed up. "I know, Harris."

"We agreed you wouldn't take these anymore." He rattled the pills in the bottle. "They made you feel cloudy."

They made her forget, and some days she welcomed that sensation. "I haven't."

"Then . . ." He exhaled, clearly trying to calm his anger. "Do you need a different anxiety prescription? Maybe another appointment with the doctor—"

"No . . . I don't know." *Oh, hell*. It wasn't as if she had a right to be furious about his reaction. If he left a vitamin on the counter she'd lectured him about how curious Nathan was these days. "I'm just tired."

Her mind kept telling her she deserved this interrogation,

but she could not handle one more thing. Not when she'd spent the entire night wondering about Lauren and this surprise girlfriend in Harris's past.

He frowned at her. "Come on. That's your excuse?"

Right. He worked hard. She *used* to work hard, but now she struggled to concentrate long enough to get a few hours of work in each workday. He never complained, but he had to begrudge her being in bed when he left for work some days . . . even if she was there because she *couldn't* get up.

"Say it." She'd tried to get him to admit it before today, thinking it was bad for their marriage for him to think it—for it to fester—and not yell about it.

"What?" He rolled his eyes. "Oh, God. Not this again. This is not a battle about your work hours."

"I stayed up trying to figure out why my brother-in-law has two dead wives, why my husband kept secrets from me, and how much Patricia whatever-her-name-was meant to you." There. Done. All the sorry pieces dropped between them and now it was up to him.

"You care about Patricia?" He rubbed his forehead. "What the fuck, Elisa? I married you, not her."

That really wasn't the point.

"Where is she? I did a computer search and couldn't find her." She hadn't meant to admit that last part, but in all the back-and-forth bluster it slipped out.

He grabbed onto the back of the chair in front of him. "Are you kidding me?"

"Did she drop out of vet school?" Was she another lie he was using to cover up something far worse and more sinister about what happened that night at the lake? That question had settled in her brain around four this morning and refused to leave it again.

His grip on the chair tightened until his knuckles turned white. "After seeing Lauren and trying to help me revive her, Patricia decided she wanted to go to med school, not vet school."

Oh . . . The explanation made sense. But so had Candace's fall and Abby's need for space, and Elisa didn't believe either of those stories now.

"The fact that I have to explain an old girlfriend to you . . . someone who means nothing to me . . ." He visibly gained control. His stance changed and the tightness across his cheeks seemed to ease. "I get that I messed up. I should have told you about Lauren. At the least, I should have made Josh tell you, but this is paranoid bullshit."

"I'm not paranoid. I am not crazy." But she was shouting.

Through the fog and the arguing, the distrust and the confusion, she feared she was falling apart. Slowly but definitely losing her ability to ferret out what was real and what was some horrifying spin her mind added.

"Elisa."

No. No to the sad, sympathetic voice. Not until she made him understand. Even then, no.

"Josh's love life is not normal. No one has two wives die by accident and a fiancée go missing. Not unless he's the subject of a television crime show." She walked around the table and laid her palm flat against Harris's chest, let his steady heartbeat relax her. "Please tell me you understand that."

"I just want you to be okay."

He believed Josh, but he worried about her. There was only one way to interpret that. He believed she was the one who was out of line.

Losing it. He didn't say the words, but she heard them.

Chapter Twenty

They met for coffee. Elisa wasn't in the mood or the right mindset to leave the house. She wanted to hide out, snuggle in a blanket on her favorite, overstuffed chair. Not think. Not worry. Not slowly lose her mind. She felt like this loose compilation of parts and that at any minute a piece of her could fall off, break down, or unravel.

Trying to focus on Abby's messages with the unidentified stranger didn't ease the tension that now coursed through her nonstop. Her anxiety medication took the edge off, dulled the pain that sometimes weighed down every limb and every muscle, leaving her flat and even less able to handle anything negative. Her usual self-calming routine of tea-and-sit-outside-in-the-sun did nothing to stop her mind from snaking through topic after topic.

She'd been almost frantic with the need to do *something* . . . but she didn't know what that something was. Then Rachel called. She'd suggested a coffee break and Elisa headed for the car with the keys in her hand before her brain could reboot and scream *no*.

As Elisa waited in line for her latte and muffin, she mentally planned her early exit. For months she'd entertained the idea of leaving her house for social engagements but only in theory, not in reality. During that time, she'd made every excuse and canceled almost every get-together until her friends finally stopped asking.

That's why she was so determined to see this informal date through. She needed to get back on track . . . to figure out what *normal* was supposed to be, then get there.

Elisa shifted her bag to hang over her arm and balanced her mug and plate in her hands as she walked over and joined Rachel at a table. She'd picked one toward the back of the café, which Elisa appreciated. No need to be on display. She hadn't done the small-talk thing in a while and hoped the skills were only rusty and not gone.

Rachel jumped in first. "This was a nice surprise."

Elisa had to laugh at that. "You're the one who issued the invitation."

"Yeah, but I didn't think you'd say yes." Rachel had settled on coffee and was in the process of adding three sugar packets to her mug. "You told me you prefer to be at home."

Huh. Elisa didn't remember spilling that fact, but the way Rachel said it, it didn't sound pathetic, so Elisa nodded. "But I'm weak when it comes to offers of coffee."

"I like this . . ." Rachel ripped off a piece of her pastry. "Whatever it is."

"A raspberry something."

Rachel visibly swallowed. "Can I be honest?"

"That sounds better than the alternative." And scary. It

was one of those conversation starters that clicked Elisa's senses to high alert.

"Well, I know how tense things are between you and Josh. I worried that tension would spill over to me."

Elisa felt her body relax, easing off the automatic fight-or-flight stance that now kicked in at the mention of Josh. "He thinks I'm being disloyal when I ask about Abby."

"Are you?" Rachel's serious expression morphed into a smile. "I'm kidding."

Uh . . . "You scared me there for a second."

"No, listen. You're asking questions that should be asked about Abby." Rachel flicked another sugar packet in the air before ripping it open and pouring part of the contents into her coffee. "He's defensive, and I get why, but he's still out of line."

Not even Harris had admitted that. But Rachel, an almost stranger, was giving the benefit of the doubt and Elisa appreciated that. Still, she treaded carefully, not sure how in love Rachel already was with Josh. "Does it worry you that Josh isn't the one asking the questions about a woman he was going to marry?"

Rachel shrugged as she took a sip of what had to be the sweetest coffee in Pennsylvania. "He's talked with the police about Abby. He told me they insist there's no evidence that anything happened to her."

Yeah, Elisa had heard that, too. "There's no evidence it didn't."

Rachel sat back, nursing the mug in both hands on her lap. "What do you think is going on?"

This felt like a trap. Elisa toyed with the idea of telling her

theory—that they had a fight and Josh . . . did something—
but she ran the risk of Rachel running back and telling him.
Elisa could only imagine the implosion after that. Harris already looked at her with pity. She couldn't handle it if that
expression turned to hate and shame.

"I don't know," Elisa said instead.

"You're dodging the question."

Yes, absolutely. "Is there any part of you that—"

"Thinks my boyfriend will kill me in my sleep?" Rachel
asked in an amused voice.

"Well, when you put it that way . . ."

"My guess is Josh and Abby had a good relationship." Rachel swirled the coffee around in her mug. "Fun and fairly positive for both of them. But then it got serious, and the wedding
got closer. They started fighting then one day Abby looked at
the guy she was about to tie herself to for life and nothing felt
right."

"Possibly."

"I've heard she was a bit free-spirited, so the idea of marriage might have spooked her," Rachel suggested.

That seemed to be the party line even though it didn't explain Abby's choice to run away without saying a word. Then
there was the *two dead wives* problem, an issue Rachel might
not even know about, so Elisa tried to tiptoe around the topic.
"His history with problematic relationships goes deeper than
just Abby."

"That's the most diplomatic way I've ever heard of saying
his first wife died in a freak accident."

Wives. Plural.

"Has he talked with you about . . ." Elisa's mind clicked off. She had no idea how to broach the subject of a secret dead wife.

"What?"

Elisa wasn't quite ready to ruin Rachel's mood or issue an ominous warning. She just didn't have enough information to support her concerns about Josh. What she had looked pretty bad, or she thought so. The police didn't even blink at a guy with dead women littered throughout his history . . . or they didn't know everything. She wasn't sure what that Detective Burroughs hid in an attempt to save *poor* Josh from being embarrassed after Candace's accident.

Elisa went with the benign. "I just miss Abby."

Rachel hummed as she took another sip. "That's not what you were going to say."

"I'm sure Josh is pissed off at me." It counted as a conversation pivot, of sorts. Elisa knew the answer but tested anyway.

"He's . . . confused. He views you as a sister and can't understand why you don't believe him about Abby." Rachel shook her head. "Look, I get it."

"That makes one of us."

All the amusement left Rachel's face. She slid the mug onto the table and sat there, as if whatever she planned to say took some effort.

A minute or two ticked by before Rachel started talking again. "My sister died when I was a kid."

Elisa jerked and almost dropped her coffee. "Oh, wow. Rachel, I'm so sorry."

"Do you have any siblings?"

Elisa wished she did. She often wondered if they made a mistake, not giving Nathan a sister or brother. "No. I'm an only child raised by a single mom."

Rachel looked around the bustling café. No one sat close, and no one seemed to be listening in. The guy with the laptop a few tables away glared at his screen but kept typing.

"Well, it was a long time ago. I was the youngest and clearly not the favorite," she said.

"I doubt that's how your mother viewed it." It seemed like the right response. Elisa had exactly zero personal experience with siblings. Harris rarely talked about their dad except to make clear he blamed his father's drinking for their mother's death. His comments about his mother made her sound perfect, almost saintly, which Elisa chalked up to the expected aftermath of the unexpected death. But no chatter about favorite sons.

"Not all parents are you, Elisa."

Elisa decided to take that as a compliment.

"It's just that . . ." Rachel played with the handle of the mug, slipping her fingertips over the gentle curve of the ceramic surface. "Losing a child destroyed my mother. It was as if she only had so much room in her heart and mind, and her first kid's memory ate up all of it."

Elisa couldn't figure out the right way to respond. "I can't imagine how unbearable that kind of loss must be."

"Unfortunately, I can." Rachel continued to trace her finger over that mug handle. "My mom breathed in the ache. Wallowed in it. She was this shell, shuffling around without any energy. If anyone dared to be too happy or too excited about something, she'd berate them for not rolling around in the loss with her. For her, grieving was a full-time occupation. Her sole personality trait."

Elisa could hear . . . what was it, jealousy? Contempt? "That's awful."

"She called me by the wrong name to drive home that I was an unworthy substitute. She didn't go to my events because seeing all those parents and kids happy highlighted her pain." Rachel shook her head. "I remember one birthday where she sat and cried because the party wasn't celebrating the *right* child."

Elisa wanted to fix this, make it better for Rachel, but she could tell from the staccato way Rachel delivered her words that the anger and pain wrapped around her conflicted feelings for her mother. The feelings were too ingrained for Rachel to let go.

"You paid the price." That sort of upbringing sounded so horrible to Elisa. She didn't have much growing up, but she had her mom and never doubted her love. Her heart ached for how much both Rachel and her mom had missed. "Grief does terrible things to people."

Rachel pulled her hand away from her mug. "Apparently."

Elisa wasn't sure what to ask next, but she tried. "Are you close with her now?"

"No. She and Dad got divorced. He was the one who held the family together and then he stopped trying." Rachel glanced at the ceiling for a few seconds before facing Elisa again. "I guess what I'm saying is I get messed-up family dynamics. I understand loss and how it can wipe out everything else."

"I really am sorry."

"And I know the position you're in sucks." Rachel winced. "But if you can, maybe, hold back a little. I'll work on Josh."

A pretty big jump in topic but Elisa went with it. "How?"

"Get him to appreciate your side and be more open about the days before Abby left so you can put the pieces together." Rachel's warm smile reappeared. "And in the meantime, forget him. I'll help you search or whatever you're doing, so that the two of you don't end up arguing again."

That sounded simple, but . . . "What happens if you find out something about Josh that scares you?"

"I'll leave him. That's not a hard question for me, Elisa. I have limits."

Those limits depended on her getting away before Josh launched whatever plans he had for her. Belaboring that point probably amounted to a waste of time right now. Rachel brimmed with confidence. Some of it not likely realistic because Josh had significant height and weight advantages on her.

But Elisa did find the offer of assistance interesting. If they found something incriminating and Rachel was *right there* to see it, it could save Rachel's life. And it didn't hurt to have a witness. "Any chance you're in the mood to check out a storage locker with me?"

Rachel laughed. "I have no idea what that means, but I thought you'd never ask."

Chapter Twenty-One

Unit 357.

Elisa headed down the walkway with Rachel by her side. They hadn't said much since leaving the café. Rachel looked like she was on a mission, dressed in black boots, a long black skirt, and a black turtleneck. Elisa's less dramatic jeans and oversize sweater fit in with a quick trip to a space lined with blue storage unit doors.

They got to the right unit and Elisa unlocked it. The second she lifted the pseudo garage door she froze.

Nothing. The temperature-controlled room was completely empty.

Rachel walked inside and spun around. "I don't get it."

Without breaking the threshold, Elisa scanned the space, taking in every wall and every corner. There wasn't so much as a dropped receipt or dusty footprint in there. "Me either."

"Not to question your idea of fun but this is kind of anticlimactic," Rachel said from the center of the five-by-ten room as she turned back to face Elisa. "What's supposed to be in here?"

"Abby's things."

"Wait, what?" Rachel's shoulders fell and her bag slipped down her arm. "She left. Why wouldn't she have taken her stuff with her?"

Excellent question. "I asked Josh something similar, but he didn't have an answer."

Rachel stood there, not moving. "Josh knows about this?"

"He rented the unit and gave me the keychain." Elisa tightened her hand around it now.

"I'm so confused." Rachel shook her head. "What exactly did he say was in here?"

"He didn't." Which confirmed to Elisa that this was some sort of mind game. Gaslighting. A move meant to make her question the conversation and send her spinning. "He suggested I might find answers to my questions in here."

"If Abby rented the unit and it's now empty, I get it. She unloaded it. But Josh . . ."

Rachel sounded as frustrated and lost as Elisa felt. Why do something so obvious? Josh could have skipped mentioning the storage unit and prevented the spotlight from shining so brightly on him.

The empty space didn't end the inquiry. Not for Elisa. "There's a manager on duty. Maybe that person will have answers."

"That would be nice."

Rachel stood there while Elisa relocked the door then accompanied her through the maze of hallways that mirrored each other. Elisa spotted the security cameras. Noted how clean the place was and how hard it would be to unload a unit's contents quickly. The hallways, while larger than normal hallways, didn't make it easy for carts and carriers to move in and out without being noticed.

On the bottom floor, across from the main doorway into the building, a twenty-something guy sat in a glass-walled office eating a hoagie. Elisa could smell the mix of ham and onions and for some reason it made her stomach turn over.

She slid the chain with the key and card in the small open space at the bottom of the window separating her from what purported to be the manager's office. "There's a problem with the unit."

The man dropped his sandwich with a sigh and wiped his hands on his pants. "Like what?"

"There's nothing in it."

He frowned at her. "Did you clean it out already?"

Rachel shoved her way in next to Elisa in front of the glass. "You don't think she'd remember that?"

"Right." He tore a brown paper towel off the roll sitting on the counter. He wiped his hands for another twenty seconds before finally turning to the computer. "Give me a sec."

He typed then fed the key into a card reader machine of some sort then typed again. Elisa almost reached through that little hole in the glass and grabbed the screen.

"Do you have a written rental agreement of some sort?" Rachel asked, clearly exasperated with just standing there.

After a quick glance at her watch, Elisa worried she'd messed up. It was before noon on a weekday. Her schedule was flexible because she set it. She didn't know where Rachel had to be and when but hanging out at a storage facility couldn't have been on her agenda.

She leaned over and whispered to Rachel, "Do you need to get back to work?"

Rachel shook her head. "I'm good."

"Elisa Wright," the man behind the glass announced.

Elisa didn't remember giving her name. "Excuse me?"

"That's the name. Elisa Wright rented the unit." The man looked up. His gaze traveled between Elisa and Rachel. "Do you know her?"

What the hell? "I am her."

"Okay, then." The guy shrugged. "There you go."

"No . . ." Elisa thought her head might explode from frustration. "I didn't rent it."

He turned the monitor around. "Is this a copy of your license?"

There it was on his screen. Her face. Her license.

"Yes . . . but . . . I didn't . . ." She honestly had no idea what to say or what argument to make. She knew she'd never been here. "I've never seen this place."

"Uh-huh." He turned the monitor back to face him and continued to type. "Looks like paperwork was done online."

This guy suddenly had all the answers. Except the big one—who faked the paperwork to make it look like she rented the space? There was one obvious answer. The only one, really. Josh. But that didn't answer anything. He had handed her the keychain. If he wanted to set her up, this was an odd way to do it.

"When?" Elisa asked, almost afraid to hear the answer.

"Probably a few days ago. It's a new agreement."

Not possible. Josh acted like he'd rented the unit months ago. Not that long after Abby disappeared.

Rachel put her hand on Elisa's arm and gave it a little squeeze before turning her attention to the guy in front of them. "About that agreement?"

The guy started humming. He looked at the screen and punched a few more keys. Then he headed for the file cabinet and searched through the folders in there. Finally, he returned to his seat behind the window. "It's not here. Probably isn't in the system yet."

He didn't seem surprised and, strangely enough, neither was Elisa. She should have guessed it wouldn't be that easy to ferret this out. "Of course not."

"How did the person pay for the rental?" Rachel asked.

He snorted and pointed toward Elisa. "Ask her yourself."

Before Elisa could shout about how none of this had anything to do with her, Rachel responded. "Humor me."

The guy went back to his computer, but not before treating them to an eye roll. "Six months. Paid in advance." He glanced at Elisa. "You'll get a notice about renewal."

Nothing made a lot of sense to Elisa at the moment. "What's the address of the person who rented this?"

"Ma'am, where do you live? I mean, come on."

She really wanted to shoo the guy out of the tiny, locked room and take over the search. She tried to hold on to her fake smile, a last bit of control, instead. "Is it in the file?"

The guy just frowned at them. "I don't understand what's wrong."

"Please look," Rachel said in a voice that didn't sound like it was a request.

Maybe it was all the prodding but he capitulated and read

along until he found the information. "Right here. Old Gulph Road in Villanova."

Her address. The dizziness hit Elisa a second after the realization.

Rachel looked at her. "Yes?"

Elisa nodded. "Yes."

The guy slapped a flyer down on the counter. "If you want to move your things there's a location closer to you."

"It's not my unit." Elisa rubbed her forehead. She could feel the fog descending. A subtle *what if* panic shook through her.

No. She did not rent the unit. Josh did. He told her he did. Her mind wasn't flipping that around. It actually happened.

"Ah, okay." Rachel put a hand on Elisa's lower back. "Any chance we could look at the security tapes?"

"The machine tapes over the video every five days," he said.

Of course it did, but Elisa would make it work. "Okay, can I see the available days?"

The guy snorted again. This time a lot louder. "Of course not."

The phone rang and he turned away. Elisa knew that was the end of the discussion and didn't even try to get more information.

They walked away but Rachel waited until they were some distance from the counter to talk again. "What's going on?"

If a reasonable explanation existed, it eluded Elisa. No Abby. No items. Someone named Concerned out there walking around with information she needed. "I have no idea."

Chapter Twenty-Two

Elisa dropped off Rachel at her car by the café and then drove home. Her hands flexed on the wheel and her mind blurred with stray thoughts. The desperate need to put together all the random pieces she'd discovered into a clear, shining puzzle nearly overwhelmed her.

By the time she pulled into the driveway she was exhausted and dizzy, craving sleep and quiet. She feared this was the new normal. For months now the air had carried this strange sort of heaviness. It pushed her down and held her there. Made every step labored and every breath a dying gasp.

She used to think that when the darkness came all she had to do was put on a serene front and not react outwardly while she shrank on the inside. She'd convinced herself those short moments of pain and confusion were fleeting and unusual. That she could survive if she stopped being so weak. If she wanted it enough, was strong enough, worked hard enough, and persevered through it.

The longer the soul-sucking streak continued, the more a

terrifying thought haunted her. Maybe the years where she functioned and slept and didn't feel crushed into the ground by questions and problems were a fantasy. A period of aberration. It could be moments of lucidity—now rare—were the outliers before the final blow.

She was just so sick of feeling *not right*. Off. Hazy and alone. She missed Abby. She wanted to know who Concerned was so they could talk and figure out what happened.

She really wanted to think of something other than dead wives and conflicting stories. Harris and Josh laughed and joked and played with Nathan. Watching those moments used to bring her so much joy but now left her feeling hollowed out and flat.

She'd taken a break from therapy because she'd been convinced that reliving the shooting over and over made everything worse. That therapy trapped her in a death spiral. But losing her family and her footing was the ultimate hit. Therapy, the one thing she'd insisted she didn't need, might actually be what could save her . . . or maybe the therapist would tell her to leave the Abby issue alone. That was something Elisa couldn't do.

She went into the house. She'd barely shut the front door behind her before she saw him. Josh stood in the middle of the family room. Staring at her.

She backed right into the closed door. "What are you doing here?"

His gaze bounced down to her hands. That's when she realized she had wrapped her fingers around the house key and held it out like a weapon.

He lifted both palms, but his blank expression didn't change. "I was trying not to scare you."

He certainly failed on that. "By coming in while I wasn't here?"

"Sorry. It seemed like an emergency."

Yeah, he was always sorry. "I'm getting tired of people sneaking up on me in my own house."

"What are you talking about?" he asked.

"You and your girlfriend need to text first."

"Since when?"

Elisa forced her muscles to relax and eased away from the door. A lecture on the appropriate times to use the spare key could wait. She needed both Rachel and Josh to hear that one, but she still didn't get his unexplained appearance. Even if Rachel called to tell him about the storage unit, he couldn't have gotten here from Center City in time to beat her home.

"Always. Why aren't you at the office?" Suddenly every-one shared her flexible hours, and she didn't like that one bit. People dropping in unannounced was one of her least favorite things, regardless if she was working.

"I needed to talk with you," he said.

About Abby? About the empty storage locker? About dead wives and someone going by the name Concerned who knew secret details about his past? Elisa needed answers to all of that and knew she wouldn't get them from him.

A tiny voice told her to hold on to the keys just in case, but she dropped them in the bowl by the door anyway. Next came her coat. She hung it in the hall closet, trying to keep up the pretense of this all being normal.

By the time she stepped into the family room her control had returned . . . what little she had these days. Panic no longer clogged her throat and the trembling in her hands was no longer obvious and visible. It continued to run through her, but she vowed not to let it show.

She sat on the armrest of the couch and stared at him. Those limited movements took so much out of her. Energy drained away and her mind clouded. She couldn't remember where they were in the conversation. Did he owe an explanation or had she not asked the right question?

He sat in the chair right across from her. He wrung his hands together and looked at the floor. When he finally glanced up, it was to stare at the family portrait hanging above the fireplace. The photo where they had to bribe a then-four-year-old Nathan with the promise of a trip to the park to get him to look at the camera.

As if he read her mind, Josh nodded toward the portrait. "I can't believe how young he is there. Sometimes I wonder if he even remembers Candace."

Dead wife number two. At this rate, Nathan would have memories of a lot of missing or dead women in Uncle Josh's life and no explanation about why they were gone. "We look through photos sometimes, and I tell him about Candace," Elisa said.

"He never asks me about her." Josh shrugged. "Like, when we're driving or eating or anything."

She didn't understand the strange walk down memory lane. Especially from a guy who liked to pretend the past didn't exist.

"Josh, why are you here? I don't think a visit in the middle of the workday has anything to do with your nephew." It felt extreme, as if he knew he had to get to her quickly.

"Lauren. My actual first wife."

So, not the storage unit. She guessed he didn't know she'd been there. Rachel hadn't gotten to him yet.

"Ah, yes. The big lie." In a regular week it would be the only thing on her mind. This week it counted as only one horror of many.

He made a small strangled sound. "It's my fault, not Harris's."

She knew that wasn't an admission because Josh didn't take responsibility for anything. Still, with her brain muddled and her trust at an all-time low, she decided to clarify. "What is?"

"Hiding it from you. Never talking about it."

"Why don't you?" Harris's answer didn't satisfy her. She doubted Josh's would either.

He shook his head and generally treated her to the *woe is me* dramatic victim act. "I was a different guy back then."

Not as far as she could tell, but she stayed quiet.

After a few seconds, he blew out a long breath and continued, "I was getting my life back together, but still doing stupid shit. Still blaming Harris for not fixing the impossible."

"He was in vet school."

"And excelling." Josh leaned back into the chair cushion. "He's smart and had friends and had managed to keep moving forward despite everything. I was jealous and hurting. Did stupid things. Had a temper I couldn't control. Came out fighting and yelling when I felt cornered."

That last part was still a problem for him. "But then you met Lauren."

He lowered his head again and smiled. "She was so driven and sweet. She lived with her mom, who had worked her butt off to give Lauren stability. Lauren was loyal and hardworking, always trying to use the lessons her mom taught her."

Elisa noticed there was no mention of love. No outward show of being upset at losing her. "I know what it's like to be raised by a single mom."

"Exactly." Josh leaned forward. "You're an only child and so was Lauren. There are a lot of commonalities. I think you would have loved her."

"I never got the chance, did I?"

Some of his enthusiasm faded. "Marrying young was really hard. We struggled and fought, but I had turned things around. I was in school and we had student housing as part of this work program she was on."

Ten minutes into this one-sided conversation and Elisa understood what he'd gotten out of this short, top-secret marriage. She wasn't so clear on what poor Lauren won, other than an immature husband with an inability to control his emotions.

Elisa did a not-so-subtle glance at her watch. She refused to leave Nathan stranded a second time. "Josh . . ."

"Right. Right. Right." He got up and moved to stand behind the chair. "We'd gone camping for the weekend. It was really late, or early, I guess. Well before sunrise." He gripped the back of the chair, crushing the cushion in his fists. "A noise woke me up. Actually, it kept happening. I'd hear leaves rustling or what I thought sounded like a tree branch break. I'd gotten up three times to check and realized the whole tent-in-the-wilderness thing wasn't for me."

She decided to push this along. "But this time the noise was different."

He nodded. "I ignored it at first, but then I realized Lauren wasn't in the tent and went to look for her. I was sure she was going to the bathroom. No big deal."

He didn't say anything for a few minutes. She didn't do anything to fill the silence or make this easier for him. Not this time.

"It was so dark. The trees blocked any light from the night sky coming through. The grass and mud sloped down to the edge of the lake, where just enough moonlight reflected there." The life seemed to drain out of him and he slumped, balancing heavily on the chair. "That's where she was. Facedown in the water."

He stood straight again and started walking around in a haphazard zigzag. To the fireplace then behind the chair again. Over toward the kitchen then back to face her.

All the jerky shifts made her dizzy.

"The police think she tripped and fell or smacked her head on a branch and then fell into the water. That she likely was unconscious when she went in," he said.

"Was there water in her lungs?" That's something Elisa had looked up. It was a way to tell if Lauren had been dead before she went into the water.

"What?" He frowned. "I don't remember anything but screaming for Harris and the two of us dragging Lauren out of the water and . . ."

He stopped there. She could see the tears and hear the hitch in his breathing. "And?"

"Nothing. I don't know." He dropped back into the chair. "It was so painful. After all the police questions and the investigation I didn't want to talk about it with Harris or this therapist he sent me to. No one."

"But you didn't just stop talking about her. It's as if you erased her from your memory."

"Not that."

No, exactly that. He moved on. He appeared to excel at it. "You convinced Harris to hide Lauren's death—her existence—from me."

"It wasn't like that, I swear." He dropped his head between his hands and kept it there for a few seconds. "You of all people have to understand."

This should be interesting. "Why?"

"You know what it's like to have something horrific happen and just want to block it."

The shooting. All that blood. The scene flashed in her mind. Instead of driving up her anxiety, this time she used the horrible reminder to fuel her. "She was your wife. Family."

"I know. I never should have asked Harris not to talk about her." He sounded contrite, but there was no way to tell how real his emotions were at this point.

She figured the tone reflected his frustration at getting caught. "I can't believe he didn't."

"He probably convinced himself I'd go back to being the selfish, destructive kid if he did."

That sounded like Harris. In the past she might have

accepted the excuse, thinking Harris knew best. But lately she had the growing feeling that she'd forgiven a lot, made Harris into a saint and avoided real-life issues.

"You're a grown-up now," she said.

"I am and I'm sorry."

A buzzing sound broke into the conversation.

His gaze switched to her phone and where she'd placed it on the ottoman they used as a coffee table. "What's that?"

A countdown to getting him out of the house. "My alarm. It's a reminder to get moving to pick up Nathan."

"Because you forgot him yesterday."

Her defenses rose at the unexpected shot. "Isn't Harris chatty?"

"Shit, I'm sorry." Josh shook his head. "Please, Elisa. I'm lashing out."

"Like you did outside of your office." No matter how much she tried she couldn't block the memory of his voice as he'd hurled accusations at her.

"It's a defense mechanism."

Habit. It was a habit bred from years of escaping accountability. He got away with everything. If you dared to question him, he'd unload and make you feel guilt for even trying.

He stood up. "I know you have to go, but I need to know we're back on track."

Was that a question? If so, before she could come up with a deflecting response, he stepped around the table and hugged her.

Finally he lifted his head. "I'm so relieved."

She was pretty sure she'd missed his big apology. "Because you told me about Lauren?"

"Because we're good again."

She stood there, looking at his confident, almost smug smile, and knew the one thing he didn't. They weren't good or fine or anything close.

Chapter Twenty-Three

The last thing Elisa wanted to do after her crappy morning was climb into a car and pick up her high-energy son, but she did. She spent the entire car ride on the way to the school thinking about her driver's license and when it was out of her possession. Never. Not really.

She remembered losing track of her phone for a few hours back when Harris and the school were calling for her. Someone could have gone into her wallet, looking for her license, but the list of possible candidates was short and too scary to think about. Josh. Harris. Rachel. Unless someone grabbed her license and took a photo while she ordered coffee or sat at a school or work meeting, the list ended there.

She tried not to think about Abby or Josh or anything else but staying calm as she drove to the school. Seeing her son's happy little face helped push out her lingering frustration.

"Hi!" He practically chirped out the word as he climbed into his booster seat in the back.

He carried the usual post-school armload of assorted things. His backpack, which had to be empty since he held a binder, a notebook, and his lunch box. He'd slung his sweat-shirt over his shoulder and threw it all on the seat next to him.

"How was your day?" She braced for the answer because it usually came at her at record speed.

"Evan is a bully, but I ignored him and did my running in gym." He waved to a group of friends still waiting for pickup on the sidewalk with the teacher. "My sandwich got wet, but I ate it anyway."

"How did—"

"Do you think Uncle Josh is coming over this weekend? He said he'd help me build a birdhouse and Dad could watch."

She hoped not, but with her luck, yes. "Maybe."

"What about Rachel?"

That got Elisa's attention. "Do you want Rachel to come over?"

"Yeah, she's nice." He continued to stare out the window. "She liked my shirt."

"Which one?"

"The green one." He reached his leg out and tapped his foot against the vent in the back of the front seat armrest. "Can I have a snack?"

"Apples and breakfast bars are in the holder in front of you." She tapped the front passenger seat.

"It's not breakfast," he said two seconds before he ripped into the box of bars.

She glanced at him in the rearview mirror, sending one of those *mom* looks he said he knew meant business. "Careful, please."

She eased out from the circular driveway in front of the

school. Other cars waited in the line behind her and a few
parents and care providers who didn't mind going last parked
in the lot across the street. She gave the lot a quick look . . .
then did a double take.

There she was. The redhead. Again.

They looked at each other for a second, then the woman
put her head down and got into a sleek sedan in the front row.

"Oh, hell no," Elisa whispered.

"You can't say that word." Nathan's scolding came out over
a mouthful of granola bar. "Whoa!"

A car horn honked as she cut left through the line and
drove into the parking lot instead of leaving the school, as the
pickup rules stated. Screw the rules. She refused to keep doing this—whatever *this* was—with this woman.

Nathan yelped with excitement as if he were enjoying a
roller-coaster ride. A woman in an oncoming car did a different kind of yelling, but her car windows were up. Elisa
waved, but she knew she'd get a call or letter from the school
about this later. Right now, she didn't care.

Going too fast, she turned into the parking lot and pulled
perpendicular behind the redhead's car, blocking her exit.
"There."

"Mom!"

She opened her door but stopped to point a finger at Nathan. "Do not even think of leaving that seat. I will be right
back."

"Who is she?"

Elisa closed the door on Nathan's question and walked over
to the driver's side of the sedan. The redhead didn't make eye

contact. She had her phone in her hand and faced forward. A few people watched them and the two teachers helping with pickup kept sneaking glances in Elisa's direction.

She ignored all of it. Her heart thudded in her chest and she had to breathe deep to drag in air around the clog in her throat, but she stood her ground. Once she locked her car doors, trapping Nathan where he was, her sole focus was on the mysterious redhead.

She lifted her hand and saw how it shook. *Not now.* She silently begged her body to hold on until she figured this out. If this woman was stalking her or Harris, she wanted to know now.

Using the side of her fist, she knocked on the window. "You can pretend all you want, but I'm not leaving until you tell me who you are."

People lingered, taking a comically long time to get in their cars and adjust their kids' seat belts. They probably thought . . . hell, who cared what they thought.

The standoff lasted about two minutes but felt like hours. The redhead finally rolled down her window. "Move your car."

Yeah, that was not going to happen. "Why are you following me?"

"Everyone can see you're the one blocking my car." The woman held out her hand to the people pretending to be bustling around them. "You nearly hit another car getting into the lot."

"So, you did see me, then."

The woman sighed. "You should tend to your son like a good mother."

Elisa knew that was true. She also guessed Nathan would race home and tell Harris all about Mommy's scary driving. A boy who just turned seven could be counted on for that sort of tattling. In that moment, standing right next to the woman she'd feared was nothing more than a hallucination, none of that mattered.

Elisa pulled out her phone, which had only reappeared in her purse this morning after being missing and not locatable even with the fancy app she had to find it, and snapped a picture of the redhead. A side view, but it was something.

The woman gasped. "What the hell are you doing?"

"Last chance." She stuffed the phone back in her jacket pocket. "Who are you and why do you keep popping up in my life?"

She didn't say anything. She gnawed on her lip but sat quietly shaking her head.

Elisa took a good long look . . . and, yeah, she still had no idea who this woman was. Pretty. Thirtyish. Dressed in an expensive-looking pantsuit. The kind that would fit in at an office.

"Do you really think I can't track you down with this photo?" Elisa had no idea if she could or not, but better to be bold.

"Meredith," the redhead said in a whisper.

Still not helpful. "Meredith who?"

"Meredith Grange."

That really didn't help either and now Nathan was tugging at his seat belt, so Elisa was almost out of time to get this done. "Why are you following me, Meredith Grange?"

"I'm not."

"I swear I will call the police."

Meredith snorted. "And tell them what? You're the one acting like a psycho."

Elisa hated how people threw that word around, but this didn't strike her as the right time for a lesson in decency and the seriousness of mental health issues. "I can start yelling. The people here know me. Do they know you? Do you have a kid who goes here, or do you just happen to be hanging around a school? You should know that sort of thing makes parents twitchy."

The moms would likely think she caught Harris's mistress or some awful thing, but Elisa would bet they'd support her over this Meredith.

"Fine." Meredith turned off her car but didn't say anything else.

Elisa took a quick glance at Nathan and saw him fiddling with a breakfast bar box he'd opened but not trying to escape. "And?"

Meredith sighed. "I'm Josh's girlfriend."

Chapter Twenty-Four

Josh.

The man literally had women tucked away everywhere. Some dead. Some alive. Some missing. Elisa needed a scorecard because keeping track was becoming somewhat daunting.

"Josh's girlfriend." Elisa repeated the words Meredith just said, but they didn't make any more sense in her own voice.

"Right. Now I need to go."

"That's not happening." With the window opened, Elisa rested her hands on the frame and leaned in a bit closer. "Explain."

"You don't have the right—"

"I've seen you outside of my husband's office. At Josh's office. My son's school and the place where I get coffee. Unless you want me to file stalking charges, Meredith Grange, license plate number K51 588K, you will tell me what you're talking about." Elisa was done. Through the bouts of anxiety and shame, frustration and fear, she emerged, maybe only for a second or two, but she'd had enough.

Meredith sighed. "My office is near Josh's. It's not odd to find me there."

"Tell me more about the girlfriend part." Elisa had lots of questions. Too many. "For how long?"

"About eighteen months."

Eighteen . . . what the hell? "What?"

Meredith glanced around, not making eye contact with any of the other people openly gawking now. "I need to go."

Elisa's fingers tightened on the door. "Absolutely not."

She was in it now. She didn't want to be the mom who bribed her son not to tell his father things, and Nathan would tell. He was a good-natured kid who loved to talk. He would share and share until Harris's head exploded.

Meredith's hands slid off the steering wheel. "We started seeing each other when he was with Abby."

"You had an affair." The clearer they were about timing and other details, the less chance for Josh to wiggle out of this.

"It was casual at first but became more. Then when Abby left I thought . . ." Meredith shook her head but didn't continue.

She really didn't have to. Elisa was pretty sure she knew what Meredith thought, but she asked anyway. Again, clarity was key on this subject. "What?"

"At first I was upset he started dating this Rachel woman, but now I don't know what to think."

Okay, that's not quite the answer Elisa expected. "I don't understand."

Meredith turned her head and stared right at Elisa. "Where is Abby?"

The question Elisa asked herself about a thousand times a day. "I don't know. Do you?"

"That's the point. He complained about her and wanted out of the engagement, then she was gone and . . ." Meredith straightened her arms, almost bracing her body as she sat straight in her seat. "I thought we'd be together. I thought a lot of things, so I guess I just need to know she's okay."

That made two of them. "But why follow me?"

"I've been watching you and your husband. Following Josh and this new woman."

That sounded scary. "Stalking us."

"I'm trying to get answers. Put all the details together. Watch all of you, hoping what happened will make sense." Her gaze dropped to the steering wheel. "See, I pushed Josh. Gave him an ultimatum. I told him to . . ."

Oh, God. Not what Elisa wanted to hear, but what she needed to hear. This was the kind of information she could take with her to the police and beg them to open the case again. "What?"

Meredith shook her head. "I need to know he didn't follow through and do anything to Abby."

The sordid story started forming in Elisa's mind. The police would need details. "Like what?"

Meredith started the car again. "I'm going to leave now."

No, no, no. For the first time in weeks she had to be close to a breakthrough. She'd come this far and now someone else was expressing doubts about the official story regarding Abby's disappearance. Someone who knew Josh and his lies on an intimate level.

She turned the record function of her phone on. "Did Josh specifically say he was going to do something to Abby?"

Meredith tried to push Elisa's hands off her car. "No, and please get away from me."

"Not until—"

Meredith laid on her horn.

"Stop!" Elisa shot back. But it was a good play. In her position, Elisa would have done the same thing.

They had everyone's attention now. Teachers and parents. Even a few kids pointed. Nathan stared wide-eyed from his car seat. Elisa turned off her phone, knowing any recording would be useless now.

Meredith lifted her hand but kept it hovering over the horn. "Please get back in your car."

Elisa didn't want to hear the blaring sound again. "Fine, but can we meet and talk about this?"

"No." Meredith rolled up the window.

"But—" Elisa stepped back right before her fingers got caught. She stood there, staring at Meredith, but she'd turned up the radio and shifted into reverse.

Elisa knew she wouldn't get any more. She didn't even understand what she had learned, except that Josh had cheated on Abby, and Meredith, the woman he cheated with, thought he'd done something to Abby. None of that could be good . . . it also might mean trouble for Rachel.

Elisa jogged back to her car and got in. She sat there as her chest rose and fell on frantic breaths. It took another minute before she could remember how to turn on the car and move it out of Meredith's way.

The second she had a few inches of room, Meredith reversed. She pulled out of the space with tires squealing and ignored the yells and head shaking as she pulled out of the lot and straight into the pickup line traffic without looking.

"Who was that?" Nathan asked.

"No one." All she wanted to do was shake Josh. Sit him down and force him to tell the truth. No stalling or obfuscation. Just the truth. For once. "You don't need to worry about that."

Nathan treated her to a *humpf* sound. "She seemed mad."

No kidding. "She was concerned about something. I'll talk with your dad about it."

Elisa could almost hear the click in her head. She'd been analyzing and dissecting but couldn't figure out the identity of the person who'd tried to warn Abby with those messages. Concerned.

Now she wondered if she'd stumbled upon the answer.

Chapter Twenty-Five

D ad!" Nathan got all excited when he saw Harris's car in the driveway. He practically bounced and ran to get to the door to say hello.

He'd always been like that with Harris. Her friends would complain about how little their partners chipped in when the kids were babies. Not Harris. He loved being a dad and did his share of diapers, baths, and feedings, even when his post-work exhaustion had him ready to drop. In return, Daddy meant everything to Nathan.

Elisa loved the relationship. Except for today. Today it meant Nathan would likely tattle before she could come up with a reasonable way of bringing up all the mess she'd uncovered over the last few days.

"Hey, buddy," Harris said right as he caught Nathan in a big welcome-home hug.

She leaned over their bodies and gave Harris a quick kiss. "You're early."

"Josh said they were coming for dinner, so I decided to be a good husband and come home and help." He glanced over his shoulder at the grocery bags on the counter. "Even grabbed a few things on my way."

Sweet except for the dinner guests part. That was news and not the great kind. "Josh and Rachel are coming here?"

Harris's smile fell. "Yeah, didn't you guys talk about that today?"

"No." She had been too busy trying to assess Josh. Josh had been too busy pretending everything was fine.

Nathan stood between them and shook the nearly empty box of breakfast bars. "What about the lady from school?"

That had to be a record.

"What lady?" Harris looked from Nathan to her.

So much for having a few minutes to think before jumping in. With that option gone, Elisa touched Nathan's hair. "Go wash up and—"

"Mom trapped the lady in her car."

Harris let out a nervous laugh. "She did what?"

"Drove right into her." Nathan's little arms flailed as he acted out steering the car. "*Vroom.* Flying across the road. People were honking. Addison's mom looked really mad."

"Okay, that's enough." Elisa put a hand on Nathan's shoulder and turned him toward the den. "Go play your game while I fill Daddy in."

Nathan let out a dramatic sigh. "Parent time."

That worked for her. "Yes, exactly. Go."

Harris watched Nathan leave then turned back to her. His gaze toured all over her. "Were you in an accident? Are you okay?"

"No." And, yes . . .

"Then what the hell is he talking about?" Harris's voice ticked up in volume and tightened a bit. Gone was the friendly, low-stress greeting from when they first walked in the door.

"The redhead."

"What redhead?" He shook his head. "Wait, the one you saw at my office."

Elisa wished it had only been once. She could ignore once.

"I've seen her everywhere." She took off her coat and draped it over a chair. "Your office. The coffee place. Josh's office. And now at Nathan's school."

"Stop for a second." That fast he flipped from welcoming to on-the-verge-of-lecturing. "When were you at Josh's office?"

Well, shit. "Does that matter?"

A muscle in Harris's cheek flexed. "You can barely leave the house. We never even go out to dinner but yet you're driving into Center City to see Josh? You bet your ass it matters."

Okay, he had a point, but not now. "Harris, please."

He threw his hands in the air and took a step back from her. "Jesus, Elisa. I'm trying here."

Trying . . . ? "What does that mean?"

He frowned at her. "You're dealing with a lot, and I get that. But all of a sudden you don't trust Josh. You're taking trips during the day and not telling me. You're driving recklessly with Nathan in the car."

"That's not true." Not totally. Certainly not how she'd describe what had been happening.

"Now there's some woman."

"It's all the same woman." She mentally searched for a simple way to explain all of this. It sounded odd and unreal, and the last thing she needed was to give him a reason to think she'd lost it. He already wanted her back in therapy. He talked about new meds. He was worried, but she needed support right now, not problem-solving aimed at her mental health.

"Help me understand this," he said, using his favorite start to a really difficult topic. "Nathan was in the car and you, what, drove around after this woman then confronted her?"

"She was at his school and I stopped her from leaving."

His eyes widened. "Is that what the school is going to tell me?"

She really wanted to shove at him until he *listened* to what she wanted to say. "Do you plan on checking up on me?"

"Do I need to?"

The heat in their voices escalated. So did the volume.

She inhaled, trying to summon some control. They needed to talk about this, and if she was being fair, he had every right to be confused and worried. But not this second. "This woman keeps showing up. She turned up at the school, watching me. Should I have let her go without insisting she tell me why?"

"Maybe . . . could she just have a kid at Nathan's school?"

"She was at Josh's office building." That information only made him tense up again, so Elisa put her hands on his forearms. "Listen to me."

"Go ahead."

He was trying even though he wanted to lecture and raise his voice and insist on having the conversation he wanted to have. They'd been married long enough for her to see the signs. She could also see him fighting those impulses.

She squeezed his arms, needing to feel him there and sturdy and with her. "I didn't know if she was following me or you. If she had something to do with . . ."

"What?"

"You."

He stared at her. She could see the second he got her reference.

"Did you think I was having an affair?" He sounded stunned at the idea.

The rush of relief she felt when she heard the distaste in his voice left her a little embarrassed. She rubbed her thumb over the skin peeking out from his rolled-up shirtsleeve. Anything to soothe him. "I thought it was possible."

"It's not," he blurted out. "I am not cheating. You're scaring the shit out of me, but I'm not going anywhere. I need you to understand that. I love you, and I am right here."

"I know." She rested her head against his chest for a second. Soaked in that feeling of comfort because she knew she was going to need it after she dropped the rest of what she'd found out. "She was dating Josh."

He tensed and held her away from him. "What?"

She couldn't back down. "The redhead."

"When?"

"At the same time as Abby. Maybe Rachel, too. There was definite overlap." How much wasn't completely clear because the timelines were a bit fuzzy in Rachel's mind.

Harris shook his head as if she'd confused him. "I don't understand."

She boiled it down to the simplest point. "Your brother has a serious problem with women."

Dead and alive.

Chapter Twenty-Six

Josh walked into the house a second later. "Hello."

"I need to start bolting the doors from the inside," Elisa whispered. But she meant it.

Josh kissed her on the cheek and handed Harris a bottle of wine. "What's going on? Did I come too early?"

"I didn't know you were coming at all." She'd been thinking tonight called for pizza. A break from cooking and cleaning up, but now that wasn't going to happen. She got to end her shitty day by pretending not to be annoyed.

Josh frowned at her. "We talked about this today."

"Dinner?" She didn't remember and wasn't convinced the conversation actually happened. Josh seemed to be engaging in some sort of gaslighting campaign. Give her keys to a storage unit . . . and then make sure it was empty. Send an ex, possibly current, secret girlfriend to follow her and poke around in her life.

"You don't remember?" Josh asked.

Her defenses immediately rose. She didn't because it never happened.

She refused to play whatever game this was. "Where's Rachel?"

"She's driving separately. She had some work stuff to finish up."

Elisa thought that might have been the first time anyone really talked about Rachel's work, except for her nosy questions when they first met. She knew Rachel had a job and gave workshops, but this was the first time she couldn't rush to a Wright family event due to a work commitment.

But Rachel wasn't the woman Elisa wanted to discuss. "I met Meredith today."

Josh's expression didn't hint at any recognition. "Who?"

She pulled her cell phone out of her pocket and held up the photo she'd taken. "Meredith Grange."

Harris shook his head. "Never seen her before."

"Me either. But it looks like . . ." Josh's eyes narrowed. "Is she trying to get away from you in that photo?"

Elisa refused to be derailed. Not on this. Not when the response was so important. "You know each other."

"We might work in the same building. Lots of people do." Josh walked around them toward the living area. "Why mention her? Is she a new neighbor or something?"

Looked like he planned to fight this to the end. He probably hoped she'd be exhausted by his wordplay or desperate to keep the peace. That would be a miscalculation on his part.

"She's your girlfriend." Elisa almost made a face. Something about using that word in conjunction with Josh made her queasy.

Josh froze in the middle of sitting down. "Is this a joke?"

"No." She couldn't believe he was going to deny . . . well, maybe she could. He spent a lot of time tiptoeing through the truth these days.

Josh stayed on his feet but didn't come any closer. "What's going on?"

"Elisa has seen this woman, a redhead, at a bunch of places, including Nathan's school," Harris said as he put his hand on her back and guided her into the living area and closer to Josh.

"Oh!" Josh smiled. "Is this the woman you thought you saw outside of my office?"

Thought? She knew. Elisa suspected they both did. "Why are you pretending you don't know her?"

"I'm not pretending." Josh said the words nice and slow, as if she were the one who had trouble keeping up and he needed to help her.

Harris stopped in the center of the room. "Why would she say the two of you had an affair while you were with Abby?"

All amusement disappeared from Josh's face. He looked downright ticked off now. "That's ridiculous."

The act didn't work with her this time. In the past he got indignant and she rushed to make it all better. Without her playing her family role, his came off as shaky and less convincing. "Is it?"

"Of course." Josh swore under his breath. "I didn't cheat on Abby."

Elisa wasn't in the mood for a new scene with Josh-as-victim, so she kept pushing. "So, you're standing there, saying you don't know this Meredith person?"

"Not that I can remember." Josh glanced into the den where Nathan sat in a chair with his back to them and earphones on. "Someone is messing with you."

Yeah, and Elisa guessed it was him. "She drives a black—"

"Elisa, no," Josh snapped at her. "I had nothing to do with this."

"Okay, easy," Harris said. "She's just asking questions."

"Questions that make no sense." And Josh's firm tone suggested she stop.

The doorbell interrupted Elisa's response.

"That's Rachel," Josh said.

Without a welcome, the door opened and Rachel peeked in. She came inside, carrying a bakery box, and pivoted around them to place it on the kitchen counter. "Oh, good. Are you telling Josh about what happened at the storage unit?"

Forget bolt locks. They needed an alarm system. Maybe that way people would stop waltzing in and out of her house, though Elisa doubted it.

"Storage?" Harris asked. "I feel like I've missed something."

"Hello, by the way." Rachel came and kissed Josh before facing the rest of the group. "Elisa and I went to the storage place, but it was empty. And there was this weird thing with the storage unit being in her name instead of Josh's, as she expected." She nodded over her shoulder. "That's double-crust apple pie. Josh said it's Harris's favorite."

"You should see your expression. What's wrong?" Josh asked Harris.

Harris shook his head. "I don't even know where to start."

Elisa took responsibility for that. They'd been talking

about Meredith. Now they were talking about the storage unit. Neither issue was resolved or even fleshed out. Elisa didn't blame him for being confused. Hell, she was confused.

She also didn't know if she should mention Meredith and the affair in front of Rachel. She might get furious, and had every right to, but Nathan could overhear. That scenario invited nightmares and questions . . . Elisa didn't want any part of that. Plus, she had to admit the fooling around might not be her business. It was up to Josh to figure out when to stop lying and disclose the affair. Now, in her house, wasn't the right time.

"We should concentrate on food," Elisa said, hoping to change the subject to literally anything else.

Josh shook his head. "Let's clear up this issue first. I put the stuff Abby left behind in storage then switched the unit to Elisa's name when I gave her the key."

"Oh, okay." Rachel slid her arm through Josh's and tugged him into her side. "That makes sense."

It really didn't. Not to Elisa. The timing was all wrong. The name change was unnecessary and apparently top secret since he never told her. "How did you get my license? It's on file there."

Josh shrugged. "You gave it to me and I took a picture."

Did not happen. Whatever last little bit of hope she had for Josh being the unluckiest man on earth and getting sucked into a relationship mess he didn't create died. He was an active participant in this . . . and Elisa vowed to figure out what *this* was.

Josh stood right there in the middle of her family room and

lied. Didn't even blink while making these things up. "When did you supposedly do this?"

"When we talked about the unit," Josh said.

"The date, Josh." Elisa hoped pinning him down on details would trip him up.

He shrugged. "Not that long ago."

She now had a long list of *never happened* items bouncing around her head when it came to Josh. "So, who cleaned it out?"

Josh snuck a peek at Harris before answering. "Uh . . . I guess you did."

Planting more doubt. Making her sound unhinged and losing it. Blaming her appeared to be the sole focus of this impromptu dinner they'd never talked about. Elisa saw it all so clearly now. "No, I didn't. I hadn't been there before going with Rachel."

Before she could fire another question at him, Harris stepped in. "What was in the unit?"

"Personal things. A few boxes. A duffel. Some clothes and books." Josh ticked off the list before lowering his voice and adding the rest. "Not exactly high-end items."

He strategically left out the laptop sitting on the couch in her bedroom right now. Elisa wasn't sure what that meant. "None of it was in the unit when we unlocked it."

"Someone stole the contents?" Harris sounded skeptical. "How could they?"

"They really couldn't. Did you ask the guy on duty about the items?" Josh asked.

"He wasn't helpful." Elisa didn't know what to make of Josh's helpful suggestions. He should just tell the truth . . . for once.

"Okay, wait a minute." Harris took a step back and glanced into the den. Nathan hadn't moved. "We're talking about a bunch of different topics and not really resolving anything."

Elisa still held her cell in her hand and it started to buzz. She recognized the name because someone from the office showed up via message, or sometimes personal visit, every few days—Ashburn and Tanaka. The private investigators searching for information about the shooting. She couldn't handle that on top of everything else and declined the call.

That was one problem too many. A dark weight fell on her. All she wanted was to curl up in bed and blink away the rest of this day.

"It's fine," Elisa said, barely remembering the subject of the conversation.

Harris looked at her. "What is?"

"Well, no." Rachel snorted. "It's not okay that someone took Abby's things. Josh paid for security. The storage place should have to answer or reimburse you or something."

They all started talking then. Josh said something about the storage company's liability and Harris disagreed. Rachel talked about a shirt.

Elisa had enough. "I can't do this."

The cell buzzed in her hand again. A few seconds later the voicemail notification dinged. That one might suffer the same fate as the others—deleted without review.

"First, the storage surprise, then I had a run-in with a woman at the school." She exhaled, trying to focus on one thing and failing. "Let's just say it's been a long day."

"What woman?" Rachel asked.

Elisa ignored the question. She was ignoring a lot right now, so adding one more thing wasn't a problem. "Nathan was asking about both of you."

Josh smiled and it looked genuine. "He's deep in video play."

Elisa hoped that was true. The idea of Nathan coming in and overhearing this mishmash of nonsense didn't make her happy.

"Okay." Rachel visibly tightened her grip on Josh. "Let's give Harris and Elisa a minute and we'll go say hello to Nathan."

Rachel didn't give Josh an opportunity to agree or disagree. The two of them wandered into the den. Nathan shouted his hello and then the nonstop chatter restarted.

Elisa tried to watch the welcome but Harris stepped in front of her. "Are you okay?"

"No." Why lie? She clearly wasn't fine. She hadn't been fine in a long time. With each day she grew more distracted and confused. More convinced Josh couldn't be trusted.

Lingering in the background, underneath all of that and the facts she was so sure of, was a thread of panic. The very real fear she'd had a break of some sort. Paranoia. Distrust. Frustration. Anxiety. They all whirled around in her head as she fought to catch up and stay clear.

He wrapped his arms around her and pulled her in tight for a hug. "Tell me what I can do."

She let her body fall against his as she delivered the bad news. "I just need you to trust me because I think things are going to get bad."

"I don't even know what you're talking about."

And that's what scared her the most. She was alone in this.

Chapter Twenty-Seven

Just when Elisa thought a family gathering couldn't get any more squirm inducing, dinner came along and proved her wrong. Tonight's feast included baked chicken, green beans, and a heap of deflection. She'd gone out of her way not to mention Meredith. Josh acted like a concerned brother-in-law. Nathan talked about horses. Elisa had no idea what Harris did during dinner because she'd tried very hard not to glance up from her plate.

Hours later, Josh and Rachel finally left. Harris finished up the nighttime rituals with Nathan and was tucking him in. She sat on her bed, looking forward to sending Harris and Nathan off to school and work tomorrow and having a moment alone to think.

This time last year she didn't doubt her own mind. She knew what she saw and heard. She didn't panic. Work pissed her off, but that was the nature of work. They were planning for Abby and Josh to get married.

One bullet and she'd been teetering ever since.

Call it survivor's guilt or PTSD or whatever other term

might fit. It spiked her thinking and made her question her emotions and reactions. She craved stability but didn't know what that looked like or felt like these days. She settled for existing. For getting through without crumbling.

The secret about Lauren, a previously unknown first wife. Abby's disappearance. Questions about Candace's fall on the stairs. The existence of Concerned. The redhead Elisa now knew as Meredith. The pieces spun and jumbled in her mind. Elisa tried to separate them out and concentrate on what she knew to be true, but those lines got fuzzier every day.

Harris walked through the bedroom, taking off his shirt as he walked. "Have you seen my dark blue sweater? I want to wear it to work tomorrow."

He had nine dark blue sweaters, but the answer was the same for all of them. She managed not to yell in response, which she thought showed a lot of self-control. "Either folded and on a shelf in your closet or in the special laundry bag for sweaters."

Special bag. The one she kept in the closet in the sitting room off the bedroom so the contents wouldn't get mixed in with regular laundry. The same closet where she put Abby's possessions because she knew Harris wouldn't go hunting.

Shit.

She shot off the bed. "I'll look—"

Harris stepped into the doorway separating the two parts of the primary bedroom suite, holding the RISD sweatshirt. Abby's prized and faded sweatshirt.

He frowned. "What's this?"

"It's—"

He answered his own question. "Abby's."

The man didn't know where she kept his sweaters but he recognized his brother's fiancée's shirt. *Great.*

"She wore it all the time. Josh used to give her crap about never washing it." Harris continued to hold it in front of him. "Why do you have it?"

Because I snooped through your brother's house didn't seem like the right response. "I found it at Josh's house."

"When?"

She tried to stall because the *right* way to walk him through this refused to come to her. "What?"

Harris disappeared for a second then came back into view, now holding Abby's missing duffel bag by the strap. "And this?"

"I can explain." But she didn't. She stood there, rubbing her hand up and down the outside of her thigh. Building up friction with her robe but not getting a single spark of creativity when it came to launching into this explanation.

"This is the stuff that was in the storage locker—the one you never mentioned to me until tonight, by the way. The same one you insisted was empty."

The room tilted. She grabbed onto the edge of the dresser to keep from floundering around. "It was empty. Rachel was there. She saw it, too."

"On this visit, maybe."

He thought she'd moved the items then blamed Josh. Forget that doing so made zero sense. That's where his mind had jumped. He all but said the words and tagged her as the "bad guy" in this scenario.

"No, you don't get it." She risked a few steps. Standing in front of him, she slipped the sweatshirt out of his fingers and threw it on the end of the bed. "I found the shirt in Josh's house like a week ago. The days are blurring together, but it's why I started asking all those questions that made him angry and defensive. I didn't even know about the storage locker then."

"Wait." Harris shook his head. "When were you in his house and why were you searching?"

"It's not like that." When Harris started to interrupt, Elisa talked over him. "The point is he'd hidden Abby's things. That tipped me off that there was a problem. I started searching for her. Doing Internet searches. Asking him about her. I even called the police and asked if she'd used her bank account and—"

"What?"

The conversation now was as awkward as she'd anticipated. There wasn't a good way of accusing a relative of killing the women he supposedly loved. "The detective wasn't inclined to answer my question. Not the guy you used to know, Burroughs. He retired. This was a new one."

Harris just stared at her.

She figured she better get it all out. "I realized while I was on the phone that I'd been so lost in my own mess that I wasn't looking for Abby or asking the right questions about where she could be and why."

"You decided Josh was guilty of something then went looking for evidence to prove it?" Harris sounded stunned. "Do you hear how that sounds?"

She refused to feel guilty. She didn't do anything wrong. She didn't go looking for ways to doubt Josh, but her actions put her under a microscope and left her feeling sneaky and raw. "I was trying to find the vacuum cleaner and found those things instead."

His eyebrow lifted. "Excuse me?"

The dad voice. She hated when he turned that on her. "I'm serious."

"You never said anything about any of this. And calling the police? That could lead to trouble."

Interesting. "How? Josh lied. About having another wife. About this Meredith woman."

Harris groaned as he dropped the duffel. "Jesus, Elisa. You're getting—"

"Do not say paranoid." Too defensive, but still.

"What word do you want me to use?"

Fine. She'd spell it out. "Two dead wives, one of whom was a complete secret. A missing girlfriend. Another mystery woman who says she's in a relationship with him . . . Can you not hear how unreal this sounds? You have to admit it's too much to be a coincidence."

"Did you tell the detective about Lauren?"

His question stopped her. The words spinning in her brain fell away. "Not yet, but why is that your concern?"

"I was just asking." Some of the heat had run out of his voice. "And Josh said he didn't know the redhead, so take her out of this."

"You don't get to subtract women. Her name is Meredith." Elisa hoped that was the woman's real name because she planned to do a bunch of computer searches to find out more about her.

He put his hands on his hips, ready to plunge ahead with the lecture that he clearly had waiting and ready to go. "She's not an ex or current or whatever."

He just believed Josh. Full stop. No questions.

She no longer had that luxury. "That's not what she said."

"Am I supposed to believe her?"

"You could try believing me." Seemed simple to Elisa.

He exhaled, sounding exhausted and annoyed. "Tell me what you want me to do here. Josh got into trouble years ago, but not with women and he's not that guy anymore."

"Would Lauren's mother agree with that?"

Harris glared at her but kept talking. "He can be a jerk sometimes. He doesn't like to be challenged, but do you really think he's churning through women? Killing some. Burying others."

She gathered up her robe and bunched it in her fist. "Who said 'burying'?"

"You know what I mean."

"Imagine you're me for a second." She closed the gap between them and put a hand on his chest. She had to make him understand before her questions and his quick defense of Josh tore their marriage apart. "You find out about a secret wife."

He shook his head. "That was my fault for not telling you."

"Your friend is missing and no one is asking questions." When he tried to interrupt her again, she kept talking. "And now a woman is appearing wherever you go and she says she, too, has a connection to Josh."

Another deep exhale. "I'd think something was going on."

Maybe they were inching closer to an understanding that didn't rely on the idea of her being unhinged. "'Something'?"

"He's not that guy, Elisa. Even you didn't think so until a few days ago. But with no evidence and without any warning, you expect me to put aside years of knowing him, of working with him, of trying to be a good role model, and believe he's a guy who hurts women? That he's been doing all of this in front of me and I didn't see it. Didn't stop him."

His love for his brother and all those years of playing pseudo-father were getting in the way of the truth. "No one is questioning you or all you did for him. This is about Josh and the things he hides, even from you."

Harris stood there, watching her. For almost a minute he didn't speak. When he did the strain still lingered in his voice. "Do you understand you're the only one who's seeing this, worrying about any of this?"

Unhinged. That's the way he saw her. He wasn't ready or willing to dissect Josh. She could only assume he found it easy to analyze her and find her lacking.

She dropped her hand and stepped back, putting a bit of air between them. "I guess I am."

"I just want you to be okay."

He kept saying that. She no longer believed it.

Chapter Twenty-Eight

Spinning, spinning, spinning. That's what happened when a person got too nosy. Push and someone would push back. Seemed like common sense, but apparently not.

But maybe the game had gone too far. Planting hints about mental instability sounded easy enough. Seeing things. Forgetting things. Acting odd. Coming undone. But when the target came wrapped in a problematic package the distance between sowing doubt and going over the edge shrank to almost nothing.

A destabilizing campaign was a delicate thing that demanded a lot of attention. Make the speaker's words irrelevant, yes. But one step too far and the focus shifted to rehabilitation—helping and shoring up—the target. That, too, put the emphasis in the wrong place. Got people curious, and that was only a short walk away from nosy.

The trap. The plan. One more time. It was all so close now. Sisters, by marriage or birth, were overrated.

Chapter Twenty-Nine

Elisa needed another look at Josh's house.

She dropped Nathan off the next morning and waited until Josh and Harris were at work. She debated what level of covert skulking to use. She had a key to his house and knew the alarm code. She could park in the driveway and walk right in, and no one would blink. She'd met the neighbors. Her stopping by to see Josh or handle something for him wouldn't be unusual. But that option ran the risk of someone mentioning seeing her . . . then everything would explode. Josh would demand to know why she was at the house. Harris would be furious.

No, the right answer was to ditch the car three streets over, park in front of a random house, and sneak into Josh's place through the back. Don't be seen. Don't raise questions.

Heart pounding and brain fogged, that's exactly what she did. She snuck in, silently paying him back for all the unexpected drop-ins lately.

She glanced at her watch. The plan was a quick in-and-out. Search whatever she could search, trace every step Abby might have made in her last days, and get the hell out.

The chance she'd missed something the first time loomed over her. Some note, some scrap of paper or receipt, might explain where she was or, more importantly, why she wasn't still here. Abby leaving personal things behind made zero sense. Even if Josh had taken the duffel and the sweatshirt, why keep them for months? If he wanted to run her in circles, the duffel would do that. What was with the laptop? That held incriminating information. The kind a smart man would hide or at least erase.

She stood at the bottom of the steps and glanced upstairs, thinking the bedrooms might hold the answers. But, too obvious. Where would Abby hide something she didn't want Josh to find . . . the laundry room? To this day, he sent out everything, including the non-dry cleaning items, to be handled. He knew how to use the washer and dryer. Harris confirmed their mom taught Josh those basic skills, but he liked having someone else take care of things.

Elisa wanted to kick her own butt for playing along with his practiced incompetence about everyday chores. Hiring a cleaner for him. Making dinners. Being there . . . she resented all of it now.

She slipped into the small room off the kitchen. He had detergent, which struck her as a new addition. Then she saw the nightgown. Rachel. Elisa didn't know if Rachel had moved in, and didn't want to ask.

Elisa opened cabinet drawers and searched through a few

boxes stacked in the corner. She flipped through old photographs and . . . her head shot up at the unexpected noise.

Shit. Shit. Shit.

She had trouble hearing over the racing of blood in her ears. She double-checked her watch. She hadn't lost track of time. It was the middle of the afternoon on a weekday and she heard voices.

She vowed to jump out if she recognized Meredith's voice. Catch Josh in the act after being forced to hear him lie yesterday. But the female voice belonged to Rachel. Rachel and Josh, here. At home. Just on the other side of the wall.

Caught. Elisa couldn't get caught.

She didn't move, and she tried to slow her breathing. Anything to become smaller and less visible. To not be heard. She could hear the rustling of what sounded like bags. Lunch, maybe? But this was a long way for Josh to go to eat during the day.

"Her expression was priceless," Rachel said.

"That was all you." Josh sounded as if he was moving around the kitchen, opening drawers and cabinets. "You're the one who came up with the storage locker idea."

"Because you want to destabilize her, make Harris question her," Rachel said.

"And I'm succeeding."

Rachel laughed. "Honestly, it shouldn't be that easy to rent a locker in someone else's name."

"Who knew it was? Taking a photo of her driver's license sure came in handy."

Part of Elisa wanted to storm out, have some sort of cartoon *ah-ha!* moment, but she knew the right strategy was to hunker down. She'd learned more in the last ten seconds than she had in days of Internet searching for Abby.

The two of them—Rachel and Josh—working together to drive her to the edge. The idea was horrifying but real. The two of them trying to minimize her, make her concerns sound irrelevant.

Elisa's mind buzzed with what she now knew and had her jumping to conclusions. Rachel had been on the scene when Josh was still with Abby. Abby might have been in the way. He could have just broken off the engagement, but Elisa had seen enough true crime specials to know a certain type of man handled these situations in a very different way. A deadly one.

Rachel's voice broke the silence. "I know she's been poking around in your life—"

"Our lives," Josh corrected in a firm voice.

"Yes, ours. But I do feel bad about messing with her. She's been through a lot."

"Look, I love her, so I know." He spoke louder as a rattling that could be cubes dropping from the icemaker filled the room. "The goal here is to get her to admit she needs help. Harris has to step up. This thing where she kicks around the house, hiding and refusing to take part in life, must stop. She can't go on like that."

Elisa strained to listen to the conversation without moving. Concentrating on that let her forget the problem of how to get out of here without being seen.

"What you really want is for her to stop coming after you," Rachel said.

He laughed. "That, too."

"You're not worried that this scheme will backfire on you? Harris might not forgive you for messing with her."

Josh scoffed. "Between me and her, who do you think he'll believe?"

That was the harsh truth Elisa didn't want to face. In her worst moments over the last few days, her mind wandered to Harris . . . to how much he knew. To how much he might be willing to forgive when it came to Josh.

Harris had glossed over Lauren's shocking death. Agreed with Josh not to talk about her. Worked with a detective to bury the information when Josh's second wife also died in an "accident." And now his lame talk about wanting her to be okay. She feared that really meant he wanted her to be quiet.

Silverware clanked. "What's this Meredith thing?"

Elisa pushed out all the negative thoughts and silently thanked Rachel for asking the right question.

"That's exactly what I'm saying. Elisa needs help. She's not dwelling in reality."

Rachel made a humming sound. "Right."

Deflated. That's the word that rushed through Elisa's mind. That's how she felt. Josh deflected and Rachel let him do it. All of Rachel's allegiance and loyalty stayed with him, a man she had to realize at this point likely was a killer. The only question for Elisa was if Rachel was also an accomplice.

"How much time do you have before you need to be back at work?" The tone in Josh's voice changed. No more anger. No amusement.

"Lucky for you, my big presentation isn't until tomorrow

afternoon. I was thinking of hanging around the house until I have to be there after lunch."

"That gives us plenty of time. Let's go upstairs," Josh said.

Yeah, go. Elisa saw her chance to sneak out. What she could or would do with the information she overheard she didn't know. But she now understood Rachel couldn't be trusted. Whatever Josh's plan was, Rachel was a willing participant in it.

Elisa heard footsteps and whispering. The noise grew quieter until, for the first time since she heard them come in, she could relax. Not the whole way but enough to drag in a few rough breaths and try to bring her heartbeat back under control.

She let out one last shaky breath and opened the door, half expecting Rachel to be standing there. Luckily, no.

Elisa went to the back door and stopped before turning the knob. Josh's bedroom was on the back side of the house. If he looked out the window . . . yeah, leave by the front door. She'd be extra careful and so quiet.

She tiptoed through the first floor. She could hear footsteps and the soft mumble of voices. She kept moving. She almost got there when she saw that damn closet. One last look. She might have missed something last time because seeing the duffel bag in there a few days ago and her brain had run off on a tangent. She hadn't searched around for more.

She cringed as the closet door made a creaking sound. *One minute.* She started the countdown as a voice in her head screamed for her to go. She aimed the light on her phone into the dark space.

A few boxes lined the wall. The vacuum set off to the side.

Everything was neat and organized. Nothing was thrown in there or tucked behind anything. The space looked totally different from how she remembered it.

"What the hell?" She whispered the question as she fought to put together what the cleaned-out space meant.

She backed out of the closet and shut the door. When she turned around, Rachel stood there. Right on the bottom step.

Elisa drew in a deep breath as she forced herself not to scream.

"Rachel . . ." The name came out in a strained sound that barely rose to the level of a whisper.

"Hon, did you find the nightgown?" Josh shouted from upstairs in an amused voice, but he didn't appear. "Not that you'll need it."

Rachel looked at the front door. "Go."

Elisa could only shake her head in confusion.

Rachel leaned in closer. "I'm an ally. No matter what you hear or what you think you heard, don't forget that."

Elisa was too busy running to think anything.

Chapter Thirty

I'm an ally. Rachel's words ran through Elisa's mind. She couldn't kick them out.

The next day passed without incident, mostly because Elisa stayed at home and pretended to work. She spent all day on the computer. Instead of assessing the books of a jewelry store as part of an informal audit in a divorce case, she searched the women in Josh's life. And searched.

Now she knew more about Lauren. An only child. Parents divorced when she was young then Dad was out of the picture. The circumstances reminded Elisa a bit of her own upbringing, except that her biological father had never been in the picture. Mom had insisted on that, and since her father was married to someone else, he agreed.

She found a funeral announcement for Lauren's mother, Allyson. There was a lovely poem someone had written about a mother's love. Not a whole lot of information or names of relatives to track down, except for a note in the comments section. The person wrote that it was smart to leave "them" out of the obituary and another person agreed. Elisa had no idea what that meant or the significance of "them" but she'd dig more to find out.

As to Lauren, from what Elisa could see, a quick police investigation confirmed the accident during the camping trip. It highlighted her head injury. The only additional news was the picture from an article of Harris and Josh standing side by side. A much younger Josh inconsolable and leaning on Harris. The photo summed up their entire relationship.

Meredith was tougher to track down. She didn't have much of a social media presence. Elisa found a business profile belonging to a woman named Meredith Grange who had worked in condo sales at a new waterfront building along the Schuylkill close to Josh's office, but not much else. No photo. Just the name and after that, nothing. It was almost as if she'd changed her last name or moved away, neither of which made sense with the story she told.

Then there was Rachel. That went nowhere because when Elisa started typing she realized she didn't know Rachel's last name or the name of the business she worked for.

But all of that happened hours ago. Elisa didn't want to think about the women or Josh or anything else for one more minute tonight. After a long day, bent over a laptop, her back hurt. Harris came home from work as if their fights and the harsh words that passed between them had never happened. He walked in the door, changed, played with Nathan, then talked about office gossip at dinner. He never mentioned Meredith or the storage unit. That was the evening. To her it felt strained and fake, but he didn't show any discomfort.

A day of nothing. A night of nothing. Lots of pretending in between. That's what her life had become.

She closed her eyes as she eased back into the pillows. Harris slept facing her on the bed. He'd fallen asleep while she fake-read a magazine over bouts of dizziness that came and went without warning. Giving up, she reached over and turned off the light.

She drifted. Just as she'd fall asleep, she'd jerk awake again. She thought she heard a knocking sound, which wasn't unusual in an old house. The third time it happened, she lifted up on an elbow and looked around the cool, dark room. She could only describe the feeling as . . . wrongness.

Energy buzzed through her as she tried to figure out what noise had kept dragging her out of sleep. Before they went to bed Harris locked the doors because that's what he did. But still . . .

She pushed the covers back and got up. The second her feet hit the floor her head started to spin. She grabbed onto the headboard, shaking the bed and knocking her cell to the carpet.

Harris didn't move.

Water. She needed something for the sudden pounding in her head. Instead of going into the bathroom, she headed for the hall. With each step the floor grew colder.

"What is happening?" She whispered the question under her breath so as not to wake Harris.

Opening the door, she stepped into the hallway and the equivalent of a freezer. A breeze actually blew from one side of the house to the other. The furnace must have died. Not unexpected in an older house, but not the way she wanted to spend the night.

She was about to call for Harris to get up when she saw the window at the end of the hallway. It was old fashioned and opened almost like a small door from the side instead of sliding up and down. It was open and the wind billowed in, sending the sheer curtain flying through the air. They were headed into fall. Warm days were giving way to very chilly nights. She'd put blankets on the beds and switched out the screens for the storm windows.

The window should be closed and locked. The fact it wasn't probably explained the banging, but not the reason for the window being in this condition.

She took a few steps, trying to ignore the squeaking places where the old hardwood floor moaned. Her bare feet tapped against the chilled floor. She listened for any other noises but didn't hear anything above the usual shifts and creaks.

Nathan.

She ran into his room. Didn't breathe again until she saw him sprawled there, taking up every inch of mattress on his small bed.

"Oh, thank God." She didn't realize she was panting until she leaned against the doorjamb, gulping in air. She put a hand over her mouth to keep from waking him up. Seeing her there, all frazzled and ready to hug the crap out of him, would scare him. She didn't want that . . . but she was tempted.

Once her vision stopped blurring and her heartbeat settled, she conducted a quick scan of the bed. Fuzz and Buzz cuddled next to him. Neither lifted a head to greet her. Little did they know they'd missed a chance for a nighttime escape through that hall window.

The room looked as picked up as a kid's room could look. She stepped over a block village he'd built then half knocked over with his remote-controlled monster truck and checked the lock on his window. This one worked fine.

Cold air still poured in the house. Rushing down the hall she beat back the panic that rose up, trying to overrun her. It got as far as her throat and stuck there. She slammed the window shut and locked it. She wiggled the metal fitting a few times to see if it—maybe, somehow—had come loose, but no. If anything, it stuck a bit and she needed to give it a good shove to close the window.

The logical explanation for the window issue was seven years old and asleep a few doors down the hall. More than once he'd opened windows on the second floor so he could drop things out of them. The screens generally blocked him and caused tantrums that ranged from low-key to apocalyptic.

Nathan got some sort of rush from dropping different things and figuring out which one would land first. Harris joked about their budding physicist. She'd thought Nathan had moved on and forgotten about the windows, but maybe not.

A thought kept nudging into her head. The one about how the window had not been open hours earlier when the house wound down. Even if she'd somehow missed the chill or the blowing curtain, Harris would have noticed. Surely at least one of them had their head far enough into the parenting game to prevent a safety lapse.

She glanced into the yard. The motion sensors would sometimes flood the yard with light, but not now. The usual lights on the porch and at the door to the separate home office burned. A few other solar lights outlined a path around the grass and small waterfall feature Harris had installed. The night plunged the rest of the yard into shadows.

She thought about going downstairs, but the coolness seemed to be centered around the window and nowhere else. Her mind went back to Nathan. To a horrifying vision of what could have happened.

She slipped into his room and stared at him again, amazed at how trusting he looked. She shut his door and slid down with her back against it. Anyone coming in would have to go through her. The rest of the world seemed to be falling apart, but she would keep him safe.

Just a few minutes. She'd sit and watch . . . not think about the window or why it was open. The problem is that with everything else going on, she didn't even feel comfortable asking Harris if he'd opened it for some reason. Perhaps he'd realized the storm window didn't fit correctly or he'd been fixing something.

Those answers sounded reasonable. But if he didn't touch the window it became one more reason for him to believe she was losing her mind. To decide that she'd opened it. That she'd made up the story about it being open. Argue that she saw something that wasn't there.

Yeah, asking Harris might be objectively reasonable but little in her life was turning out to *actually* be reasonable these days.

Chapter Thirty-One

Elisa didn't realize an hour had passed until she lifted her head and spied the clock next to Nathan's bed. She stood up, ignoring the ache in her lower back and the way her knee felt funny, and approached him. A bare foot hung out from under the covers and his arms were spread out at his sides. She opened the door and the cats abandoned him, likely in favor of food.

He slept with the comfort of feeling safe and secure. She'd fought hard for that. Envied it a bit. Mostly she worried about what his life would look like if Josh really had done something wrong, as she suspected, and then got caught.

Nathan would forever be the killer's nephew. She hated that for him . . . but not enough to cover for Josh. She'd rather move and change names than let Josh continue to hurt women.

She tucked him back in bed and gave him a kiss before heading downstairs. She made tea, careful not to clang glasses or make any other noise. The tea box promised she'd drink a warm cup and fall off to sleep, but she doubted it.

She glanced across the kitchen and into the family room.

The cats had traded Nathan's bed for the couch and snuggled there together. Her laptop also sat there. She'd sent the saved file with the messages between Abby and Concerned to herself. Also saved it in three other places and made a copy and put it in their safety deposit box at the bank. Just in case Abby's laptop disappeared without warning.

With the way things had been going, she needed a fail-safe system with multiple backups. If Josh really did kill women who crossed him, then she couldn't be too careful.

She retrieved the computer and opened the file. She skipped the first few pages because she'd read them about forty times. She'd read the entire file over and over, but concentrated on the beginning, thinking that's where the clues about Concerned's identity were mostly likely to be.

This time, she skipped to the middle. Read a few emails then paged ahead again. She stopped on an exchange that made the blood drain from her head.

ABBY: But why get engaged to these women if he only ended up hurting them? He could just date and never get serious.
CONCERNED: he likes the kill
ABBY: Fuck off.

Exactly two days passed without a word then Abby initiated contact again. Concerned responded almost immediately.

ABBY: He's not a serial killer.
CONCERNED: no but he gets bored and when he does he ends the relationship by removing the woman—permanently

ABBY: I don't get it.

CONCERNED: he gets so much attention, so much love and support, when the women die–then he can be the good guy who loves hard and has had very bad luck

ABBY: That's ridiculous.

CONCERNED: maybe but he will kill you to keep feeding his addiction to the spotlight

The words flashed in her mind. Elisa took a long sip of tea, hoping to drown them all out. Concerned issued the warning and Abby disappeared a month later.

Ten completely awake minutes later Elisa knew sleep wasn't going to happen tonight. Her mind refused to shut off. She could see the blood. Imagine Abby's body, broken and still. Buried. Burned. Forgotten.

Actually, not forgotten. Elisa wouldn't let that happen.

The personal items and the messages on the laptop, all those Internet searches that led nowhere, and Meredith. Elisa had uncovered pieces that didn't quite fit together. Unearthed secrets that pointed to more danger. She needed to keep digging. Hunt for answers and then get those answers in front of law enforcement before her entire life blew apart.

It had been more than a week since she found Abby's duffel bag and cracked her computer password and Elisa could feel the clock ticking down in her head. Every step she had taken so far had put her farther away from finding her emotional footing again. Doubts threatened to drown her. Things she knew to be true got hazier the more Josh hammered on her being wrong.

She needed help. Rachel had offered, but after the conversation Elisa overheard . . . no way. Rachel might claim to be an ally but she'd sounded all too willing to join Josh's gaslighting campaign when she didn't know anyone was listening.

Harris had made his position clear—Josh first, always.

That left her. Only her.

Well, maybe not just her. The one thing she'd been avoiding might be the one way to get the answers she needed.

Maybe she wasn't alone after all.

Chapter Thirty-Two

By the time Elisa dropped Nathan off at school later that morning, she knew she had one more lead she needed to follow. Maybe not so much a lead as an instinct. She'd been assuming that Rachel could end up another one of Josh's victims. That one day soon she'd get a call about Rachel tripping off a cliff while hiking or "accidentally" falling out of her office window. Some nonsense that should once again point the suspicion at Josh and make it impossible for him to slither away . . . though he likely would.

A bit of eavesdropping had skewed Elisa's perspective. She'd spent her entire life trying not to get dragged into other people's mess. To recognize and honor boundaries. The one time she snuck into a place she shouldn't have been and overheard a conversation not meant for her, everything changed. Now instead of viewing Rachel as someone to protect, Elisa saw her as a potential adversary. Rachel certainly had made it sound like she'd not only teamed up with Josh, but that she'd found new ways to make Elisa's life difficult.

Lesson learned. Wariness fully engaged.

But the mistrust ran deeper than a few harsh words in Josh's kitchen. Elisa still didn't know anything about this woman who'd popped up and taken a seat at the family dinner table without really being asked. The only way to look into Rachel was to know more about her. Even if she burned through the morning doing it.

With Nathan and Harris out of the house, Elisa had gotten the laptop out. She'd tried looking up the license plate number on Rachel's car. That sounded easier in theory than it was in practice. The guy at the DMV refused to tell her anything, which was probably a good response for a government agency. Privacy and all that.

With that option closed, Elisa expected to find a "free" website that would give her the basic information, like the name and address for the car registration or license, which hopefully would belong to Rachel. All she found were paid sites, and she didn't trust those.

Trailing Rachel to her office seemed like a dramatic alternative, but the only decent one . . . but so far, nothing. Elisa thought ahead and picked up a rental car, leaving hers in the rental lot for now. The idea was to make Rachel spotting her less likely, but that didn't seem all that necessary since Rachel didn't really go anywhere.

She'd mentioned having a big presentation this afternoon. Elisa rushed around to get to Josh's house before Rachel left for it. Right after Elisa parked down the street, she spotted Rachel, dressed impeccably, as usual, in a black dress and heels, leaving the house. Instead of heading to an office, she went straight to a coffee shop, and not the one close to Josh's house. Miles out and seemingly inconvenient to most obvious convention spaces and office parks.

Rachel looked at her phone and read off her laptop. She didn't talk to anyone or even write down a note. She sat there . . . for more than an hour.

When Rachel finally got up and gathered her things, Elisa was ready. She didn't think she knew anyone who lived in the neighborhood, but with her luck she probably did, so she'd slouched down in the car seat to prevent ruining her covert operation. But now they were on the road, Rachel driving and Elisa a safe distance behind.

Whatever Rachel was going to do, she needed to do it. All Elisa needed was a business name. She'd take it from there, or hand the information to someone who would know how to spin that into more.

Rachel drove another few miles, getting farther away from Philadelphia and deeper into the suburbs, and turned into a motel parking lot. Not a fancy hotel with convention space. Literally, a one-level motel with tiny rooms and peeling beige paint. Kind of a dump.

Elisa parked across the street at a fast food burger place and watched. When Rachel fiddled with her rearview mirror, Elisa ducked. She counted to ten, then ten again. With her heart pounding, and half expecting Rachel to appear at the car window, Elisa sat up again, but Rachel wasn't looming there.

Rachel hadn't even left the car, but she did now. Got out, taking her bag and computer. With keys in her hand, she approached room 9, opened the door, and slipped inside.

What the hell?

She had Josh's house and wherever she lived. Her office. Yet, Rachel was staying in a motel? Elisa couldn't find any logic in it. Having learned a few confusing and random things, Elisa wanted to know more.

She'd pushed her luck right to the edge, but went a few more inches. Feet, actually. She started the car and drove across the street to the motel. Parked as far as possible from room 9. Sat there with the car running, debating if she should get out and take a closer look or just take off.

Rachel always seemed to show up where she shouldn't be, but this time Elisa was the one stuck out there without a reasonable excuse. The last thing she needed was to be accused of stalking Rachel.

She got out of the car anyway.

Adrenaline pumped through Elisa hard enough to rattle her teeth. She didn't blink as she watched for Rachel's door to open. Elisa silently begged the universe to be on her side just this once, as she maneuvered around the car Rachel parked right in front of the door under the big LOBBY sign. Elisa glanced inside the car and saw the tag hanging from the rear-view mirror. A parking pass. If it was for the motel that definitely meant Rachel was staying here . . . but why?

In three broad steps Elisa was at the lobby door. She opened it and lurched inside. She was out of breath with her nerves spun up by the time she looked up at the room in front of her.

The lobby was a small room with a desk at the far end. The amenities consisted of a computer and a television. There was a chair and grass-green carpeting. The inside basically matched the rundown look of the outside of the building.

The woman sitting behind the desk frowned. She looked to be in her forties with curly black hair. She wore a guarded expression. "What are you doing?"

"Sorry." Elisa could only imagine how ridiculous she looked. "I need some information."

The woman's frown deepened. "Okay."

"The person in room nine . . . what's her name?"

The woman made an odd noise. "I can't tell you that. It would be against the rules."

She didn't sound very firm in that position, so Elisa took a risk. "What if I gave you a hundred dollars?"

The frown disappeared. "Cash?"

She'd clearly played this game before. That made one of them. "Yes."

The woman held out her hand and Elisa rushed over to fill it with twenties. There was probably a smart way to do this to ensure she got the information she paid for, but Elisa needed to move fast. She was way out of her depth, and the longer she lingered the greater the chance Rachel would show up.

"So?" Elisa asked.

The woman hit a few keys on the computer in front of her. "Jane Dickson."

Who the hell was that?

"She paid cash for three weeks. She's been here for more than two. Hasn't made any local or long-distance calls and spends most evenings somewhere else."

Elisa wondered if that last bit was actually on the monitor. "Do you have a copy of her license or anything like that?"

"Doubt it. If we do, it's in the safe and I don't know the combination."

Of course not. "Anything else?" When the woman stayed silent, Elisa tried again. "If I gave you another hundred would you have more information for me?"

"No."

"Okay. Thanks." Elisa didn't run to the car, but she didn't walk either.

She unlocked her car and almost dove in. Just as she started it, the door to room 9 opened. Panic bounced around the inside of the vehicle. It was so thick, Elisa almost choked on it.

She ducked, hoping she'd dropped out of sight on time. Equally hoping the car door wouldn't open next to her. When she heard a door open and shut, she tried to gauge the distance. It sounded like the lobby door, but who could be sure?

Elisa didn't wait. She put the car in reverse as she sat up. She pulled into a break in the traffic, trying not to draw attention. She made it onto the road before she looked in the rearview mirror and saw Rachel step out of the lobby door and stand in the parking lot.

Elisa didn't think Rachel saw her, but it didn't matter. Elisa had come for specific answers and ended up with more questions. Somehow she knew even less about Rachel than when the day started.

Chapter Thirty-Three

Elisa had avoided their calls and visits, letters and emails. Now she stood at the door to the office of Ashburn and Tanaka, the private investigators, and tried to get her brain to signal her hand to turn the doorknob.

Three minutes later—she knew how much time had passed because she felt every second tick down inside her—she heard footsteps on the other side of the door before it opened. A woman stood there. She wore a navy pantsuit with what looked like a regular cotton T-shirt underneath. She was one of those women whose age was difficult to peg. Probably fortyish, with long black hair.

"There's a camera right there." The woman pointed toward the far wall. "While it comes with the job to see people mill around out here, you're starting to make my assistant really nervous."

"Sorry."

Elisa meant to bolt. Just take off down the hall and get to the elevator or the stairs, whichever came first, but her legs refused to move. This new habit of being locked in her body made life impossible. Her brain would whir to life, spinning with panicked scenarios, but her body froze. This new "normal" had started with the shooting and crept up on her numerous times since when her anxiety spiked.

"We can talk out here, but you might be more comfortable inside," the woman said.

"Do you know who I am?" It was a silly question. Of course she didn't.

"You're Elisa Wright." The woman smiled. "I'm Shelby Tanaka."

One of the names on the business card. Not what Elisa expected but she didn't know why other than she'd seen one too many television shows where the private investigator was a fifty-year-old alcoholic white guy. She'd never met a real-life investigator, male or female, Asian or not.

"You've been looking for me," Elisa said, stating the obvious.

Shelby didn't force contact. She closed the door, giving them privacy in the empty hallway, and leaned against the wall. "I know our repeated contacts can be annoying, but we really do just want to talk with you."

"About?"

"Maxine Webber."

That part was not a surprise. "I mean, I know you're asking about the shooting and what happened to her, but why?"

Shelby folded her hands together in front of her. "There's a question about your former employer's liability for the shooting. Questions about what the hospital knew or should have known and when, and what safety measures should have been put in place to protect Maxine and everyone else who works there."

She spoke so clearly, So matter-of-fact. No judgment. No pressure. The lyrical sound of Shelby's voice lulled Elisa into believing this whole mess might just be okay. . . . or almost did. "Maxine was killed on the sidewalk outside of the office."

"I know. I also know the hospital fought your worker's compensation claim and lost."

She probably knew way more than Elisa did about the business, people, and building where she worked for years. Which left the obvious question. "Is this because the hospital wants me to sign some sort of agreement?"

"No."

"I got a letter . . ." Which Elisa had ignored, so she couldn't quote it.

"I don't work for the hospital."

A relief. Elisa couldn't add *battling her former employer* to her list of things to handle right now. She was barely surviving and accomplishing the most basic tasks. "Then what do you want with me?"

Elisa expected stalling, but Shelby dove right into a real answer. "Mostly workplace atmosphere information. We need to know what, if anything, Maxine said or did before the shooting that might be relevant. That includes outside, earlier that day, and in the days before. If Keith had made threats before being fired. The work environment. Hostility, concerns, that sort of thing."

"I thought you were a detective agency." Elisa assumed

investigators got involved in divorce cases and gathering evidence about adultery and, maybe, doing a bit of background. This sounded bigger, more thorough. More like part of a bigger team effort. Legal stuff. "Is the hospital being sued?"

Shelby didn't blink. "We were hired by Maxine's family, but there are limits on what I can say about legal strategy."

"Yet, you expect me to talk and spill everything."

"Honestly? It's going to happen eventually. We can do it this way or a lawyer might schedule your deposition in the future. You could get a notice to appear in court." Shelby shrugged. "Talking to me should be less stressful."

That phrase, the emphasis on *stress*, made Elisa wonder what exactly Shelby knew about her life since the shooting. "Okay, I get it."

"I know this is sensitive—"

"Understatement," Elisa shot back then immediately regretted the burst of emotion. Shelby had played this conversation so cool. Elisa wanted to mirror that quality. "Sorry."

"There's no need to apologize, but I would like you to come in." Shelby nodded toward the closed office door. "We can sit down and talk. This will be very informal. I promise."

Sounded serious to Elisa. "Uh-huh."

"If anything makes you uncomfortable we can stop, or find a way to work around it."

"I had no intention of ever speaking to you." This whole conversation brimmed with understatement, that comment being the most understated of all. Elisa had gotten good at hiding and had planned to stick with that strategy.

Shelby nodded. "That's the impression we got."

"'We'?"

"The Ashburn of Ashburn and Tanaka is Martin Ashburn, my partner."

Interesting. "Husband?"

"Ex-husband's uncle, actually." She rolled her eyes. "It's a long story."

Even more interesting. "Sounds it."

Shelby laughed. "If you come inside, I'll tell you all about it."

As icebreakers went, that was a tempting one. And Elisa had showed up today for a very specific reason. A personal one. "I actually have a deal for you."

Shelby stopped in the middle of shifting toward the door. "I'm listening."

"It's about this." Elisa took out Abby's laptop. "I need help tracking where the messages came from. I've tried. Even followed directions on this video I found online, but I didn't get anywhere. But it's not just this. It's other things."

"Such as?"

"Investigating people. An Internet search can only get me so far." Following Rachel had turned out to be scary and potentially dangerous, so she was ready to seek out some expertise. "You help me and, in return, I stop trying to avoid you."

Now the other woman just looked confused.

Elisa didn't blame her. Nothing about this situation felt or sounded right. Very little could drag Elisa out of the safety of her house and away from her kitchen and yard, but this topic did.

"You'd be paid, of course." Elisa didn't stammer around. She plunged right in just as Shelby had done. "I think my brother-in-law is a killer and that he knows I think he is one and is trying to drive me over the edge before I can unravel his secrets. Make me doubt my own mind."

Shelby's eyes widened a bit but there was no other outward sign of surprise or confusion. "Ah. Well, then. It sounds like we have a lot to discuss."

"I'm serious."

"Ms. Wright—"

"Elisa."

"Elisa." Shelby put her hand on the doorknob and waited. "We've been tasked with doing background on the shooting, the individuals involved, and the hospital. We've looked into everyone's situation."

Elisa could hear a hint of an underlying message but she didn't quite get it. "Meaning?"

"I know a lot about your family. Your brother-in-law's history is . . ." Shelby looked like she was searching for the right word. "Let's say fascinating."

Fascinating? More like deadly, suspicious, and terrifying. "Then we should talk."

Shelby opened the door and gestured for Elisa to go inside first. "After you."

Chapter Thirty-Four

Elisa couldn't mess up Nathan's pickup a second time in a week. She'd caused enough trouble by confronting Meredith on school grounds the other day. As expected, that move touched off a whisper campaign. More than one parent who barely knew her suddenly took an interest in her life and asked how she was doing. She and Harris had gotten a call from the school and a note from a teacher about driving safety. Honestly, it was all a bit much.

More than one divorcing couple had used the school as a battleground to fight over three hours of visitation time on a Friday or a random holiday. Elisa drove a little fast and everyone had a theory. Okay . . . maybe it was a bit more than a speed issue, but the point was she didn't need more nonsense in her life.

Thanks to a slide through an *it was yellow a minute ago* stoplight, she arrived at the school in time. Barely. She was the second-to-last car in the pickup line. Only the mom with five kids, three of them under three, and a husband who'd just gotten caught stealing money at work pulled in behind her.

Glancing in the rearview mirror and thinking about that poor woman's life made Elisa feel guilty about how miserable she'd been. She never felt like she had the right to be sad or anxious. She should just stop it. She'd mentioned that more than once in therapy and her now former therapist explained that wasn't how mental health worked. Every snide or unthinking comment Josh made could get her wound up and feeling shitty all over again.

She pulled up to the teacher and assistant running today's pickup and rolled down the passenger side window. Right as she did, she realized she didn't see Nathan. "Is he still inside?"

The teacher and assistant looked at each other with confused expressions. "He left with his uncle right as school ended."

No, no, no. "What?"

"Josh Wright. He's on the approved list." The teacher said each word nice and slow, as if she needed to be clear for Elisa to understand.

Josh. A mix of anger and panic tumbled through Elisa. She swallowed a scream and fought not to break into desperate, wailing tears.

"He also had your text," the assistant said in a rushed sentence.

Okay, wait. Elisa inhaled a few times. "A text?"

The assistant nodded. "The one you sent to him, saying you'd be late and asking him to step in for you."

Never happened.

The assistant glanced at the car behind Elisa. "I saw it and checked your approval list, so everything should be fine."

It absolutely wasn't.

"He's definitely on the list," the teacher added. "He's picked up Nathan before without incident."

Elisa wanted them not to stop talking for a second so she could think. So that she could figure out how to stop her hands, and whole body, from shaking. "Yes, but—"

"The list. Yes." The assistant kept doing that annoying nodding thing. "He's on it. We double-checked."

"I know about the damn list. Okay?" Elisa shouted to get them to shut up but got an entirely different reaction.

The assistant's face fell.

The teacher wore that *displeased teacher* look that every student everywhere dreaded. "Ms. Wright—"

"I know." Elisa tried to rein her emotions back in and find enough control to get through this conversation. "Forget it. Sorry."

The assistant shot Elisa an unconvincing smile. "Nathan seemed very excited to see his uncle."

"Of course he did." With only a quick look in her side mirror, Elisa pulled away from the curb. Tires squealed and the few people waiting around and talking at cars stared at her. Again.

She wanted to slam on the gas and race home. Yell and swear and brutally chastise herself for not editing that stupid list. But she held it together. She needed to hold it together.

A reasonable explanation. That's what she needed. Her first call to Josh went to voicemail. Then the second. When his recorded voice came on the line a third time, she knocked her cell off the stand, sending it flying to the passenger's side of the front seat.

An anguished mix of pain and terror gripped her. "Please don't hurt my baby."

She made the usual fifteen-minute drive home in about five. Treated every stop sign as optional. By the time she finally pulled into the driveway and slammed on the brakes, her mind was wild with horrible possibilities. The sure way to hurt her—to make her stop searching and be quiet—was to threaten Nathan.

Without bothering to shut the car door or grab her bag, she ran into the house. Her heart slammed against her chest and her breath rushed out of her.

She threw open the door, letting it bounce open as she started yelling. "Nathan!"

No response.

She heard voices, possibly a television. She could see something dark and crumpled sitting in the distance on the kitchen counter. None of it really registered, and none of it mattered until she saw Nathan.

"Nathan? Where are you?" She hesitated at the bottom of the stairs and headed for the kitchen instead.

She'd almost broken into a dead run when the back door opened and there he was. That cute little face. Smiling as he ate . . . something. "Nathan!"

"Hi, Mom."

That's all he got out. She dropped to her knees and grabbed

him. He'd gotten taller, so he actually leaned over her, but she didn't care. She wrapped him up in a smothering, your-mom-needs-a-moment-to-calm-her-paralyzing-fear hug.

He made a squeaking sound. The whining started a second later. "That's kind of tight."

"Sorry." She wanted to bundle him up and run, but she forced a smile and eased up a bit on the hold enough to touch his hair. "I missed you."

He made a you're-kidding face. "I was at school."

"There you two are," Josh said as he walked in from the backyard without his suit jacket, which explained what was sitting on the counter. He carried his cell and wore a carefree look that said *no big deal*.

"Josh." Her voice shook. She wanted to beat the shit out of him. Pummel him and keep doing it. Only her refusal to lose it in front of Nathan saved Josh.

She stood up but continued to hold on to Nathan. He squirmed and chewed but generally tolerated her.

Nathan threw his head back and looked up. "Uncle Josh picked me up today."

"I heard." The shake grew more pronounced, but Nathan didn't seem to notice.

The smirk on Josh's face suggested he did.

One of the cats brushed against her leg. She didn't look down to see which one. No way was she breaking eye contact with Josh. "Nathan, have you fed Fuzz and Buzz?"

"The second he got home." Josh winked at Nathan. "He's very responsible."

"Right." And her temper rumbled and fought, waiting to burst out. "You can go back outside and play."

"Okay," Nathan said in his usual cheerful voice. "You coming, Uncle Josh?"

She answered for him. "He'll be out in a few minutes."

Nathan didn't wait for any more adult talk or questions. He leaned down to pet the cats then escaped into the backyard again.

Elisa stood there, watching him go. She started a mental countdown, trying not to blow up at Josh. He wanted a reaction. The gaslighting and pushing suggested he craved the opportunity to see her crumble. Every move he made was carefully planned and calculated to throw her off balance.

She would not give him the satisfaction of losing it. Of letting him be the stable one. Nathan deserved better. *She* deserved better.

"Why did you show up at Nathan's school today?" She asked mostly to see what ridiculous excuse he'd offer.

He had the nerve to frown at her. "You asked me to."

More lying. More gaslighting. "I didn't."

He tapped on his phone and then turned it toward her. "Your text."

She took his cell and read the message. *I have a problem at a client's office. Could you pick up Nathan? If not, I'll call Harris.*

She'd never seen that. She wouldn't send that. Months ago when life was different and she viewed Josh as a brother, yes, but not now. She didn't trust him to feed Fuzz and Buzz on time, let alone to be with Nathan for hours without her.

She didn't think he'd ever hurt Nathan, but she couldn't

take the risk. She had zero trust. Not in herself or in others right now. And if she was right, he'd killed before. At the very least, he could easily bad-mouth her or do something to make Nathan angry with her. She refused to let Josh unleash that kind of destruction in her life.

"How did you do it?" she asked, knowing she sounded paranoid. But he knew the truth about that text. "Let me see the phone number attached to that text. Is it really mine or did you just put my name on someone else's number?"

He walked around the kitchen island to the sink and washed his hands. "What are you talking about?"

She guessed she was right. "I didn't send that."

He turned around and sighed at her. "Elisa."

The way he said her name sounded just like Harris. All exasperated and concerned. She didn't buy any of it.

"There's no one else here, Josh." She threw out an arm. "You can tone down the performance. There aren't any witnesses to appreciate it."

"Wow." He swore under his breath. "You really are losing it."

Crazy. Unraveling. Unhinged. The words he didn't say lingered right there. At least now she knew he was going to ride this out. Insist this was about her, not him. Use this ginned-up example as one more piece of evidence that she was not okay.

"You think that's an appropriate thing to say to someone who's suffering from a mental health breakdown?" she asked.

"I think it's time for you to admit this whole thing—all the stuff about seeing people and investigating Abby—is about destroying me, and I don't know why. I love you and think of you like a sister."

"Lucky me."

He exhaled. "I'm trying here, Elisa."

She would not crumple at his feet. She took out her phone and showed him the screen. "You know how I know that text isn't from me? See? No message to you."

"Did you delete it?" he asked.

He had a ready response for any question or fact she sent his way. That made sense since, for decades, he'd mastered the art of shirking responsibility for everything. It was hard to compete with entrenched self-denial.

"There was nothing to delete." Truth existed. She held on to it, not letting her mind wander or doubt, even though a tiny voice in her head pulled her in that direction.

He shrugged. "Maybe you accidently re-sent an older message? That would explain the mix-up."

More deflecting. He made the situation he created her fault. Her mistake.

She would not bend. "No."

"Well, the how and why don't really matter. It all worked out fine." He grabbed an apple out of the bowl on the counter. "And I like to spend time with Nathan, so we're good."

"There's no response."

He frowned. "What?"

One tiny piece. That's all it took to trip him up. For someone so practiced in the art of gaslighting he lacked follow-through. Always had. Always would.

"That text you received?" She meant the fake one he created about picking up Nathan. "You got that but didn't text me back."

"That's not—"

"I looked at your phone, remember? It's not there." She watched his fingers clench and unclench around that apple. "So, I wonder how I was supposed to know you could get Nathan and I didn't need to call Harris."

He didn't say anything for a few seconds then he set the apple down on the counter. "You know I love Nathan."

"Just as you loved Abby and Candace and Lauren."

His eyebrow lifted. He looked more amused than pissed off. "Are you making an accusation?"

It was her turn to shrug. "Just having a conversation."

"You know if you can't be here for Nathan I will be. Forever. That's a promise."

No, *that* was a threat. Elisa heard it loud and clear. "Lucky for Nathan, I'm not going anywhere."

Josh smiled. "Let's hope not."

Chapter Thirty-Five

Elisa held it together for the rest of the day. Josh lingered, hanging out and playing with Nathan until Harris came home. Instead of staying for dinner, Josh excused himself, saying he had a date with Rachel. But Elisa knew the subject of the conversation when Josh asked Harris to walk him out to the car and they stood in the driveway talking for almost twenty minutes—her.

Josh's plotting, laying the groundwork for whatever he planned to do to her, had switched to full speed. He no longer dropped subtle hints. He'd moved to full-scale warfare.

The ongoing emotional battle made her sick. She'd been dizzy and nauseated for days. It took her longer than usual to crawl out of bed. She couldn't focus. At almost all times she felt two seconds away from blowing apart or crashing to the floor.

Her former therapist had explained how depression could manifest with physical issues. Sometimes headaches and flu-like symptoms were really Elisa's body's way of begging her to stay down. The first step to shutting off completely.

Not today.

Plastering a fake smile on her face and marching through her usual day was not helping, but she couldn't let Harris see the reality. That would play right into Josh's evil hands. So, she stood there, washing dishes and humming. Pretending she was fine. Her life was fine. Her marriage was fine.

It was all bullshit.

"Do you need help?" Harris asked as he walked back into the kitchen after playing with Nathan and getting him started on his nighttime routine.

"I'm good."

He leaned against the counter, facing her. Sleeves rolled up. Concerned expression firmly in place. Soft voice. "Are you?"

She stopped splashing around in the soapy water. "I assume you're asking me that for a specific reason."

"The school called again."

No hint of emotion in his voice. She knew because she strained to listen for it.

"Do they have a new tattle policy where they pit parents against each other?" She dried her hands and waited for whatever came next.

"So, something did happen at school?" Harris had switched into Dad Mode. Active listening, or whatever it was called. "Something with Nathan's pickup, maybe?"

She hated when he looked at her with pity. The *my wife is not okay* stare made her want to throw things. "It went fine."

His eyes narrowed. "Are you using some sort of semantic loophole to answer me? Because it's not like you to lie."

She spoke the truth, but it was clear he'd lost the ability to recognize it. She blamed Josh for that, too. "I was at the school on time but your brother had already picked Nathan up."

"Why?"

That was the exact voice Harris used with Nathan. The one aimed at helping Nathan learn a lesson and understand the importance of being honest and taking responsibility for his actions. The fact Harris used it on her right now pushed out her headache and filled the open space with fury. "Ask your brother."

"He already told me you texted and asked him to step in."

This whole thing felt like high school to her. Everyone ran around behind her back, scurrying here and there, talking about her. Whispering. Pretending to be concerned.

She. Was. Fine.

She swallowed back the rage and internal screaming and delivered her answer in a clear, *not losing it* voice. "I didn't ask for his help."

"I saw the text, Elisa."

She couldn't stand there and take it. Not one more second. She needed to move, to burn off some of the excess energy raging through her. The pantry. She walked over to it, trying to think of ways to busy her hands and her mind so she could survive this conversation. "I didn't send him a text."

"Elisa, come on."

She heard him say her name but all she could see was the medicine bottle. The pain pills again. The same bottle Harris took the last time it suddenly appeared in the kitchen and she hadn't seen since. It sat on the pantry shelf, next to the bin with Nathan's snacks. Breakfast bars and medicine. The worst mix possible.

How the hell did that get in there? When . . . ?

She remembered locking the medicine safe this morning. Her anxiety medicine was in there. She'd even looked in the bottle and saw how few pills were left, which meant she needed a refill. Which meant going back to the doctor. There was no way the doc was going to sign a prescription without a visit. But that bottle was in there. One bottle. Not this bottle.

She was sparring with lucidity and didn't know how to stop.

"Elisa?" Harris's voice grew closer.

She couldn't let him see the bottle. He'd go off and probably never trust her again. She'd accuse him of being the last one who had it. They'd circle around, argue, and she would be the one to lose. She could feel it.

In a panic, she grabbed the bottle and slipped it in her cardigan pocket. Kept her hand over it as she turned around. "No lectures. Please."

"Are there any words I'm allowed to use?" His gaze stayed locked on her face. It didn't wander to her hand or her pocket.

She tried to concentrate on what he was saying but her mind got stuck on the new problem. *Bottle. Bottle. Bottle.*

"I'm worried about you," he said.

He'd been saying that almost every day since the shooting. Her answer never changed. "I'm fine."

He shook his head. "Oh, okay."

Sarcasm did not make this better. "Harris, say it. Whatever is in your head that you're afraid to give voice to, just tell me."

"I think Rachel has triggered you somehow."

Oh, definitely. Not the way he thought but she was very wary of Rachel now. "Meaning?"

She hated being out of control, under constant threat in her own home. Her fingers tightened around the bottle. She tried to ignore that she held a piece of evidence that proved Harris's case and might make him right about all of his worries.

Was someone playing hide-and-seek with her meds? She knew the safe combination. So did Harris. That was the entire universe of people who could easily mess with the medicine. But there was no way Harris could . . . no. Right?

"I'm not saying you don't like her." Harris started moving again and didn't stop until he stood right in front of her with his hands rubbing her tense shoulders. "But she came into the family and you've been spinning ever since. Leaving your medicine out."

Oh, God. "One time."

Lie. Lie. Lie.

"It only takes one time." He kept touching her. Caressing her. Acting like he was trying to soothe her.

"Right." This felt like a test. If he put the bottle there for some reason, he *wanted* her to stumble over it and doubt herself. He wanted a gotcha moment . . . and she refused to give it to him.

"But that's not the only thing." He continued the gentle massage. "You're obsessed about Abby. Angry at Josh. Forgetting things. Not picking up Nathan."

That list. It included random, unrelated things. Normal things. *Life gets in the way* things.

"You never pick up your clothes. You frequently forget to call when you've got an emergency and will be late. You defend Josh and believe him over me." She put her free hand against his chest, connecting them in the way that had always given her comfort. "See how when you take regular things and combine them together in a list it sounds terrible, but taken individually, there's an explanation for all of it?"

He hesitated before answering. "Fair point."

"Look, I don't want to fight." She never wanted to fight. She had this life, the one she'd dreamed about as a kid. Stable and happy, lucky and loving. The idea of upending it, even with all the confusion rushing around her head, made her physically ill. "But I can't just pretend Abby disappearing without a word is okay."

"I admit the circumstances surrounding Abby's leaving are upsetting."

Leaving. He insisted on using words that sounded tame. "Then please support me."

"I do, Elisa. I love you, but I also know you've had a shitty year. You want to ignore that, but I can't."

What happened to her at work made up so little of who she was and what mattered to her. It impacted her—still did—but he acted like there was nothing else left of her but the trauma. She couldn't let that be true. "You think I'm losing it."

"Hell, I'm losing it!"

"You are?" That was inconceivable to her. He'd never been anything but rock solid.

"The idea that you were in the middle of a shooting, that I wasn't there and what could have happened to you, stops my breathing sometimes. It makes me feel sick and guilty and furious." The pleading in his eyes matched the pleading in his voice. "I worry that when you feel those same feelings you think you need to hide them because they make you weak rather than normal."

Normal, random words he used jumped out at her and stayed there, lingering between them. On the surface he was talking about loving her and feeling like he didn't protect her. The layer underneath reeked of judgment and put her on the defensive. "I've had therapy."

"You stopped it early." His gaze searched her face. "I'd like you to restart. Just until you get through this rough patch."

Or until another one of the women in Josh's life died or disappeared, but fine. If that's what he needed—fine. "I'll think about going back. I'm saying maybe because nothing about it made me feel better last time."

He shrugged. "We can find a different doctor."

"I'm still a maybe."

"My amazing survivor." He wrapped his arms around her and pulled her close. Lips skimmed over her hair as he whispered, "I love you."

She kept a death grip on that bottle, not moving her arm even though her position made the hug awkward. After a few minutes she stepped back, putting a bit of air between them. "Let me finish down here, and I'll meet you upstairs."

He smiled and for the first time in days it looked genuine. "I won't say no to that."

He took off, going upstairs and acting like they'd settled the issues between them, but they hadn't. She watched him go, wondering what he'd say if she asked him to choose be-tween her and Josh. What would he do if he had to pick who he believed? She didn't ask because she knew the answer. Hearing him say *Josh* out loud would kill her.

She slipped the bottle out of her pocket and studied it. Her name and her prescription. The pills were all there and the cap lock worked.

The battle had entered into a new and dangerous phase. This time she got lucky.

Chapter Thirty-Six

Elisa woke up sick the next day. Every time she tried to get up a wave of nausea would knock her back down. Her head ached, as if someone had pounded on her skull, leaving it battered and bruised. Every part of her, from her muscles to her teeth, hurt.

Harris drove Nathan to school and she stayed in bed. It took her until noon to crawl downstairs to make some tea and find some crackers to nibble on. The journey back up the steps struck her as somewhere between daunting and impossible, so she opted for an afternoon of sleeping on the couch.

She laid there, cuddled in a blanket and exhausted just from walking from one room to another. Her head hit the pillow and she drifted off.

She woke up to the smell of chicken.

Groggy and off, she tried to move her head, but that didn't work. Lifting, shifting—both set off a riot of tumbling in her stomach.

But the chicken . . . "Harris?"

"Not quite." Rachel came into view as she spoke. She stood over the couch wearing dress pants and a silk blouse with a mug in her hand. "Don't move."

"What are you doing here?" Understanding now how little she really knew about Rachel made Elisa skip over logical questions like *How did you get in?* and *Did you bother to knock?* and head right to being tense and on edge.

"Medical recon."

Elisa heard the amusement in Rachel's voice, but she still didn't understand the answer. "What?"

"Harris wanted to come home early, but he had an emergency."

Elisa tried to imagine Rachel and Harris having informal conversations about her health, and couldn't. Mostly, she didn't want them near each other unless she knew Rachel wasn't part of the problem. Harris hated the phone and they both had jobs, though she wasn't convinced Rachel did, which led to a lot of questions about when and how they got together for this conversation.

"Wait . . . what time is it?" Elisa pushed up on her elbows and fell back against the pillows again. "The room keeps dancing."

"See? You should listen to me. No sudden moves." Rachel helped Elisa sit up a bit. Tucked the pillows behind her to keep her in a somewhat steady position.

"Nathan." Elisa could not mess up the pickup for a third time. Two calls from the school in one week were enough.

"Harris arranged for him to go to a friend's house after

school and . . . okay, I swear Harris said the kid's name was Titan." Rachel snorted. "I misunderstood, right? That's not his real name, is it?"

Elisa could do this. She could bat back mindless conversation. Play the game and try to lure Rachel in a bit and get her to talk. "Titan and his younger sister Lulubelle."

"Wow, that's something." Rachel sat down on the large round ottoman that served as a coffee table and handed Elisa a mug. "Here. Can you sip on this?"

Elisa held the mug, letting the warmth seep into her skin, but no way was she drinking that. She fought to keep her fractured focus on Nathan. "What time is it?" she asked again.

"Almost three."

"What?" Elisa tried to do the math but her brain rebelled. "I haven't done anything all day."

She tried to sit up higher a second time and failed just as quickly as she'd done the first time. Moving needed to be optional today.

"Do you want to projectile vomit?" Rachel snorted. "Yeah, I thought not."

Elisa leaned back, resting her sore and tired body on the pillows. "I don't understand how you got stuck taking care of me, which I don't need you to do, by the way."

"Your skin tone is green."

Elisa didn't think she was kidding. "Really?"

Rachel curled her leg under her. "I mean this in the nicest way possible . . . you don't look great."

Since she winced as she said it, Elisa assumed it was true.

Rachel was probably more complimentary than she should have been.

"I feel terrible." Elisa wrapped her fingers around the mug and held on. She was too out of it, and her muscles were too weak, for her to tell if she was managing a tight hold or not.

"There's a twenty-four-hour thing going around."

"Please, no." Elisa closed her eyes. "That's me begging the universe not to let Nathan get it."

"Yeah, that would suck. Should I move those?"

Elisa reluctantly opened her eyes and saw Rachel frowning at the cats curled together between her legs. "Fuzz and Buzz? No, they're fine." Rachel's skeptical expression said a lot. "You don't like cats?"

"I don't really understand the whole pet thing." Rachel looked at the cats as if they were on fire. "I've been trying to hide my anti-pet bias until you and Harris decide I'm not so bad. Some people are rabid about their pets. It's weird."

Elisa laughed and immediately regretted the jostling. "We like you just fine."

Well, sort of. Not really. For the most part, Elisa didn't trust Rachel. Not after the fake name and the conversation she'd overheard between Rachel and Josh. She might pretend to be friendly and step in and act like a good nurse, but she slept with Josh, and that ruined everything else.

"You still look green." Rachel eyed the mug. "Sip only."

Elisa continued to hold the mug. "I couldn't chew a noddle if I had to."

The next fifteen minutes continued with Elisa resting and

Rachel watching over her. Elisa opened her eyes at one point and drank without thinking. The broth revived her. The gnawing in her stomach eased and the room flipped at a much slower pace.

Maybe Rachel wasn't as bad as Josh. Elisa really couldn't come up with a coherent question to ask to check. *Why are you staying in a dingy motel?* didn't seem like the right way to go. Every idea that came into her head sounded offensive. Nasty. She'd heard what she'd heard in Josh's kitchen . . . right? . . . but that didn't mean Rachel was safe with him, or just in general, and all those unknowns left Elisa more confused than ever.

"Should I thank your boss for the day off?" Elisa cringed on the inside at her lame fishing question.

"What?"

Now that she'd traveled down this road, Elisa felt obligated to see it through. It wasn't unusual to want to know some more information about Rachel. At least Elisa hoped not.

"You're here in the middle of the day," Elisa said.

"Thanks to all the travel I do, my non-travel hours are pretty flexible."

That sounded vague and didn't give a hint about the motel, so Elisa tried again. "Since I'm sick and you feel bad for me—"

Rachel nodded. "I do."

"—I'm going to ask you some questions I should already know the answer to."

Rachel slipped the mug out of Elisa's fingers and tucked the blanket around her. "Shoot."

Getting all this attention was a nice change. Being a mom

she fell into the role of caregiver and usually didn't regret it . . . except for that time a year ago when Harris and Nathan had the stomach flu at the same time and she seriously considered hiding in a hotel.

Okay, here came the awkward question. "Your last name."

Rachel froze. "You don't know it? You're kidding."

Elisa searched through every memory since they'd met and couldn't think of a single time anyone had said it. "I have no clue."

"Josh is such an idiot." Rachel looked like she was on the verge of laughing. "Dunne."

Yeah, that was new. Elisa never heard that before. Not Dickson. No sign of Jane. Okay, then. "Do you have a work phone? I feel like we should have emergency contact numbers for each other."

Rachel waved off the suggestion. "Just use my cell. The human resources company I work for has office space but it's communal. I go in for meetings and some other things. Otherwise, I work from home or at the office of the business where I'm giving a workshop."

"What a fascinating job." Still no talk about the motel. Still vague on work.

Rachel made a face. "Is it?"

"Do you own a house or a condo or . . ." Elisa had to admit that wasn't her best work, but she was sick. She had limits.

"I rent a condo, but I've had issues thanks to a neighbor's plumbing causing a leak in my place so I'm in a crappy motel for now. It's temporary but her insurance is paying."

Oh . . . That sounded plausible and Rachel delivered the words with ease. No signs of lying.

Elisa knew people who had to move out due to flooding. One family they knew had a fire. None registered under a fake name . . . unless the woman at the motel had made it all up. She wouldn't be the first person to tell a tale to make a quick hundred bucks.

Elisa's emotions bounced back and forth. One second up, next down. So much tension and not knowing. She was back to feeling lost again. She thought she'd found enough, nothing specific, but enough questions to put Rachel in the enemy camp. Now she didn't know. She could just care about Josh and be stuck in the middle.

Not sure what to do or say, Elisa went with babble. "I work with numbers all day." And right that second she missed the certainty of playing with numbers and the simple consistency of checking and rechecking. The audits were her favorite. She'd sit for hours, matching up documents and seeing how a business ran.

"Josh told me you love your job . . . or did." Rachel shifted on the ottoman, crossing one leg over the other and looking as comfortable as someone sitting on an ottoman could look. "Sorry."

The desperate need to be okay clawed at Elisa. "You don't need to tiptoe around me. The shooting was months ago."

But, if she were being truthful, she really hoped they were done with this topic. Saying she was fine was one thing. *Being* fine was another, and she wasn't there yet.

Rachel snorted. "I carry grudges and wear the scars of

things that happened years ago, so no. I don't believe in a time limit on these things. You get to struggle with what happened for as long as you need to. No judgment here."

Permission. Deep down Elisa knew she didn't need to ask for room to grieve, but having someone tell her to just let her emotions be what they were felt freeing. "I thought I was getting better. For a few months I felt more grounded and sure, and then Abby didn't come back and days turned to weeks, and everything fell apart again."

Rachel nodded. "You miss her."

"We met in book club and shared a lot of the same interests, like movies and going to museums. We spent a lot of time together, especially on the weekends." Abby would come to the hospital and they'd go out for lunch during the week. They did family things together on the weekends. "She was really close to Nathan. She never balked at the idea of taking him to do some crafty thing, like painting pottery or drawing pictures. She really wanted to have kids."

"That's not my thing at all, but Nathan is pretty cool."

Thinking about him always made Elisa smile. "Except when he doesn't get his way."

"But about Abby. You don't deserve that kind of uncertainty." Rachel reached out and rested a hand on the part of Elisa's arm that peeked out from under the blanket. "I'm sorry. I really am."

"I want to know she's safe." Elisa broke off before going any further. "Is it weird when I say stuff like that? It clearly upsets Josh."

"I'm not all that worried about how upset men get about

specific topics." She eyed Elisa. "You should try not caring either."

Elisa wished. If only she wasn't so terrified of losing everything. "The situation isn't as easy for me. They're family."

"I guess."

Elisa didn't know what that response meant, so she continued to step carefully. "But if you and Josh are serious then . . ."

Rachel put a hand behind her ear, as if pretending she couldn't hear. "You faded a bit near the end."

Yeah, on purpose. "Because I wasn't sure what to say next."

Rachel started shifting again on the ottoman. Her foot fell to the floor and she sat up a bit straighter. "We're in the testing phase. Not serious."

But that's . . . Josh made it seem . . . Elisa didn't say any of the hundred ideas bouncing around in her head. She went with a noncommittal response. "Oh."

"That's a surprise?" Rachel asked.

"A little. I mean, you've been together a year." A little more digging, but Elisa thought she hid that try pretty well.

"The sex came later, but I understand what you're saying." Rachel sighed. "We're dating, and for a lot of people that means thinking about the next steps."

"You've been working with him to make me doubt myself." That's not how Elisa intended to broach the subject, but the words were out there now.

"That's not what . . . I was trying to shore up his ego and get him to leave you alone. I thought I could be the bad guy and he'd ease up." Rachel rolled her eyes. "It sounds ridiculous, I know."

Elisa blamed the slight fever and dragging illness, but she struggled to keep up with whatever point Rachel was trying to make. The conversation turned everything she believed to be true about Josh and Rachel's relationship upside down. "Are you thinking about a future with Josh?"

"No."

HOURS LATER ELISA'S health bounced back a bit. She sat on the couch with Harris after dinner while Nathan built and destroyed a block tower with an airplane over and over again.

She'd stretched her legs out across Harris's lap. He wore his glasses and watched television as he absently rubbed his hand over her calf through the blanket. The night was quiet and comfortable and she didn't intend to destroy it, but the curiosity was killing her.

She leaned her head against the couch cushion and watched to see his response. "If I told you that Rachel sees her relationship with Josh as informal and possibly temporary only, would that be a surprise?"

His eyes widened. "I think it would be to Josh. He told me he thinks she's the one."

"Well, to be fair she wouldn't be the first 'the one' for Josh."

Harris glanced at Nathan, who seemed oblivious to his parents' boring conversation. "I'm ignoring that shot because I don't want to fight when you're sick."

"Fine. We'll reschedule the fight portion of the conversation for later."

Harris smiled. "See, was that so hard?"

She slipped her hand over his.

"Did she really say they were only temporary?" he asked a few seconds later.

Elisa kept her voice low, almost at a whisper, to avoid the million questions Nathan would ask if he figured out they were talking about Rachel and Josh. "She said they were testing and not really serious."

"What the hell?" Harris snorted. "He told me she basically lives at his house."

"She's staying at a motel because of some plumbing problem." Rachel commented on it, so Elisa felt comfortable passing the information on.

"What? Why wouldn't Josh have her stay with him?"

Elisa had no idea. "Maybe we're too old and married to understand their relationship."

"I'm ignoring the 'old' reference," Harris said in fake-serious voice. "But there is a bit of an age gap between them. Maybe the problem is they're not on the same page yet."

"'Bit'? Isn't Rachel in her early twenties?"

"Josh told me she's thirty. I asked, which isn't like me because I usually don't care about other people's personal stuff, but I was curious."

"You do generally forget to ask the important gossipy questions, which is annoying." But Elisa could have sworn Rachel was twenty-something. Didn't Josh tell her that . . . or maybe she assumed? She'd lost all ability to ferret out what was true and what wasn't these days. Especially about Josh. "I wonder if Josh knows she's not ready to be his replacement wife. Technically, his second replacement wife."

Harris let out a long, dramatic exhale. "I'll go ahead and ignore that, too."

"But I'm not wrong." Elisa thought she should be congratulated for not outright calling Josh a killer. She thought it but tucked the word inside . . . for now.

Harris shook his head. "Still ignoring."

Yeah, that was the problem. "Okay, but I'm telling you, those two are headed for trouble."

"How bad can it be?"

Only a man would ask that. "Just wait."

Chapter Thirty-Seven

Rachel was right. The main thrust of the illness lasted about a day. Elisa spent two full afternoons doing nothing but sleeping on the couch. So, tonight, she wasn't tired. Not even a little.

She was hungry and maybe a little bored from not doing much, but everyone had gone to bed. Right around midnight she gave up on rest and decided to go in search of something to eat. In that moment even Nathan's favorite peanut butter crackers sounded delicious.

She slipped out of the covers and reached for her robe. A few seconds later, she stepped into the hall. A quick stop in Nathan's room found him curled on his side, hugging his stuffed tiger. The toy no longer traveled on day trips with them because he'd declared that *baby stuff*, but it did need to be somewhere on his bed when he went to sleep to avoid a tantrum. Elisa kind of wished she had some sort of security blanket. A lot of grown-ups she knew would benefit from having one.

Fuzz and Buzz slept at Nathan's feet and everything seemed fine. She checked the window lock, because she did that now. Checked his and the one in the hallway every night before bed. As if she needed one more thing to add to her routine, but touching the metal and knowing it held secure gave her some peace, so she did it.

After kissing him on the cheek she stepped back into the hallway and headed for the stairs. No breeze. No open windows. No noises. All good so far. She almost made it to the bottom of the stairs before she heard it.

The soft thud of footsteps. Practiced and purposeful in trying to hide any noise.

She froze on the second-to-last step and balanced her back against the wall. Her breathing echoed through her. She fought to slow it down. To remain as quiet as possible.

Next came a scratching noise then the slight clank of metal, as if someone were rummaging through the silverware drawer.

She concentrated on the sounds ringing in her head. She singled them out, magnifying them until she identified each one. The brush of her robe against the wall. The scrape of that one too-long branch as the wind moved it against the window in the family room.

Footsteps. They meant someone had gotten into the house. She debated screaming or running upstairs to wake Harris, but neither of those guaranteed they'd all be protected. She needed Nathan asleep and unharmed.

She thought about the open window the other night. About Josh. About how sick she'd been. For a minute she hoped she was dreaming, that the medicine had worked and she'd drifted off and was now locked in a nightmare.

Cool air hit her bare feet. Her body shook from the sudden chill. She thought about chalking the sensation up to fear, but it felt so real.

Risking everything, she inched down one more step. The wood creaked under her and she shut her eyes.

No, no, no.

Her heartbeat hammered against her chest and she could barely swallow. Every muscle tensed and strained as she waited for an attack. When it didn't come, she slowly lifted her head from the wall and peeked around it.

She couldn't see much in the shadowed downstairs. Nothing looked out of place. A light was on over the sink, as usual . . . and the back door stood wide open.

She ducked a bit and looked out into the backyard. She couldn't see any movement from her safe position smashed against the stairway wall, but the sensor lights had flipped on.

"Now what?" she whispered to the quiet floor.

Another step. She half expected someone to jump out or swing at her. But the menacing footsteps were gone. She couldn't see or hear anyone. They could be hiding, but she guessed the outside lights flashing on meant the person had left.

"Hello?" Yeah, that was silly, but she couldn't think of any good options.

After a quick mental countdown, she ran through the family room and into the kitchen. She slammed the back door shut and locked it. Threw the bolt.

"Elisa?"

The scream escaped before she could stop it. She also

jumped and fell into the door. When she spun around she saw Harris standing there in his boxers.

"Were you outside?" he asked.

What the hell? The pounding in her temples made it difficult to concentrate.

He stood there with his hands on his hips, looking confused and sleepy. His hair was pushed up on one side. "What's going on?"

She had no idea. "The door was open."

"Not possible." He shook his head. "I locked it."

She was about to make a snide comment about how it must suck for him to be accused of not taking care of the house when the scent hit her. Floral and strong. Cloying, really. Too strong for a candle and definitely not food. "Do you smell that?"

"No, I . . ." He made a face. "Is that new shampoo?"

Not shampoo. More like a strong bath gel or perfume. Feminine and unfamiliar. "Not mine."

He frowned. "Meaning?"

Someone had been in the house, but it was too scary to admit that out loud. "I'm not sure."

Chapter Thirty-Eight

Two days later Elisa pretended to enjoy some family time. Nathan ran around the backyard while Harris and Josh investigated alarm systems on their cell phones. When she'd said, "We need an alarm," she meant one installed by a reputable company. Not one put together with the help of the one man she wanted to keep out of her house.

She planned to schedule with a company as soon as possible. Harris seemed to think some sort of makeshift, do-it-yourself kit made more sense. She'd humor him then overrule him. She knew she'd be able to convince him to see things her way. It's not as if she had to fake being scared. With the window, the break-in, and her potential killer of a brother-in-law she spent most of her days terrified and on edge.

But she wouldn't need to have a fit or demand Harris listen to her. They'd talk later, after everyone left. After she sat there on the picnic table bound up in a jacket, sipping her tea and acting like she didn't spend every minute obsessing over Josh's love life and all the mishaps and strange occurrences that had happened over the last couple of weeks.

When Nathan grabbed onto a tree limb and started climbing, she bit her tongue. She had a propensity for hovering. Harris believed Nathan needed to fail at things, fall, get a little roughed up and learn. She wanted Nathan wrapped in plastic and protected at all times, which she knew was unrealistic and not even a little good for him.

She already felt judged and persecuted. She didn't need to add another reason for anyone in this family to question her sanity or her parenting, so she tried to not notice. It scared her that she was getting so good at pretending.

She glanced around and noticed Rachel had gone inside. Smart woman. Being away from the men and the alarm talk sounded like a good choice. "Anyone need anything?"

"Nope," Josh said.

Harris didn't even raise his head from his phone. "We're good."

She made one last try. "Nathan?"

"Later!"

Elisa almost shouted when she saw Nathan gripping the tree bark and pulling one leg up the tree trunk. He couldn't get far but those palms would hurt later. If he didn't look so happy she might have told him to come down. She just didn't have the energy to disappoint one more person in this household.

She stepped into the kitchen, expecting to see Rachel, but she wasn't there. Elisa was about to call out when she heard one of the cats meowing. Not the friendly welcoming kind. This was the noise Buzz made to punish humans and demand food.

"Probably got locked in a closet by accident again." She smiled, knowing the retaliation would be steep. Things knocked off counters. Those tiny mouse toys scattered everywhere. Nighttime prowling.

She headed for the stairs but stopped when she realized the sound came from the hallway to Harris's office. One turn and she could see Buzz sitting in the doorway.

"Get lost."

Rachel's voice. Then she pushed Buzz away with the side of her foot. Didn't touch him, but scared him off. He ran toward Elisa and she picked him up. Petted him. He seemed out of sorts . . . or as much as she could tell with a cat. Both of theirs enjoyed roaming around the house and were usually fine with visitors, but not today.

One kiss and she put him on the floor with an unspoken promise that she'd take over now. She tiptoed down the hall and really hoped no one saw her. It was a ridiculous thing to do in her own house, but Rachel being in Harris's private office space seemed pretty ridiculous, too. Stepping into the doorway, Elisa found Rachel immediately.

"What are you doing?" Elisa asked but she could see. Rachel had Harris's emergency vet bag on his desk and was looking through it.

"Shit!" Rachel jumped back. "You scared me."

That was the point. "Why are you in here?"

Rachel nodded at the open door across from her. "I needed to use the bathroom."

The one attached to the office and not the hall bathroom? That didn't make much sense to Elisa. "How did you even know there was a bathroom in here?"

Rachel's mouth opened then closed again. She smiled. "You caught me."

"Doing what exactly?"

"Your house is stunning. Historic properties aren't really my thing, but I got curious and went snooping. That's so rude, I know, but I wanted to see what all the rooms on this floor were used for."

The tone of her voice sounded right. A mix of amused and a bit guilty. Color even rose in her cheeks.

Elisa didn't buy any of it. Every time she thought she "got" Rachel, something new happened.

"And the bag?" Elisa stared at it and at the bottle on the desk.

"More nosiness, I'm afraid." Rachel shrugged. "Sorry about that, but I've seen these sorts of bags on television. Never in real life, so I wanted to see what's inside."

Before Elisa could come up with a line of questions that might get them closer to the truth, Josh walked up behind her. Because of course he did.

"What's going on in here?" he asked.

Elisa didn't try to sugarcoat it. Mostly she wanted to see if Josh would have a reaction. "Rachel is digging through Harris's bag."

He looked confused. "What?"

"No." Rachel laughed. "She's kidding."

No, not really. "Actually . . ."

Rachel ignored Elisa's comment and reached out a hand to Josh. "I'm afraid I was being nosy and looking around the house. I know I should have asked first."

"And looking in the bag," Elisa added because that was the part that really mattered to her.

Josh took Rachel's hand. "I can take you on another tour. The one I did when you first came here was abbreviated."

They continued to act like they had free rein in her house, as if Elisa weren't standing right there. "If she wants to see all of the rooms I can take her. This being my house and all."

If Josh heard the sarcasm, he ignored it. "There. It's settled."

Nothing was settled and Elisa needed that to be clear. "My bigger concern is about Harris's bag."

Rachel looked stumped. "What about it?"

Elisa wondered if these two had rehearsed this. Elisa's feelings about Rachel bounced all over the place. She showed up at the least helpful times and tended to just pop in, but at other times she came off as supportive and acted like she understood why Josh's actions might be problematic. Now . . . this.

Elisa tried the same question she'd asked earlier. "Why are you digging through the bag?"

"I wasn't."

Elisa was so sick of people lying to her. "You're saying it was on the desk?"

"Yep." Rachel nodded. "Sitting here when I came in to use the bathroom."

"Shame on Harris. I'm excited to give him shit about that." Josh looked at Rachel. "Hungry? We were going to start the grill."

"Sure." She repacked and shut the bag before glancing up at Elisa. "I'll take a rain check on the house tour for another time."

"Okay." Elisa doubted she had a choice since Rachel made the statement and walked out of the office.

Josh lingered by the desk. "Problem?"

"Have you ever known Harris to leave his bag out?" The one with the medicine and other items in there that he wouldn't want Nathan to touch. Elisa knew the answer and so did Josh.

"No, but he has a lot on his mind right now."

She wanted to ignore him but couldn't. "Like what?"

"You."

"Me?" But she knew that. Harris had made that perfectly clear. Her unraveling was an inconvenience to him.

"Let me guess." Josh's mocking voice dripped with condescension. "Now you think Rachel is trying to mess with you. You blame me. You blame her. Is anyone else trying to make you look bad?"

Elisa was also sick of Josh's dramatic outbursts. "I asked you a simple question about the bag."

Josh let out a long sigh. "Not everything is a conspiracy, Elisa."

Being around him used to be so easy. They joked and she found him annoying like a little brother might be, but harmless. Now every word carried a cut and she had to fight not to kick him out. "What question are you answering?"

"I'm just saying don't blow this out of proportion. Harris made a mistake. It's no big deal." Josh smiled. "You know what it's like to accidentally leave your medicine sitting around, don't you?"

He touched her pills. She didn't know how he knew about the safe combination, but she knew, down to her bones, that his fingers were all over this mess. But that didn't answer what Rachel was doing snooping around the house, and now Elisa would have to spend time trying to figure that out.

"I don't know, Josh. You're the expert on accidents, not me."

"What's that supposed to mean?"

The pompous jackass. "Ask either of your dead wives."

Chapter Thirty-Nine

Something about Shelby Tanaka made Elisa want to spill every thought zooming around in her head. Shelby possessed this sort of welcoming quality that had to benefit her as an investigator, but it wasn't as great for Elisa. The idea of opening up a vein and letting her entire life story pour out terrified her. She hadn't felt comfortable doing that with her therapist. She'd barely done that with Harris, and even now there were things he didn't know . . . like about how she'd hired Shelby.

Ten minutes after the receptionist ushered Elisa into the glassed-in conference room and handed her a cup of tea, Shelby walked in. Telephones rang in the distance. Elisa saw a younger man race down the hallway to the front door of the office then disappear.

Shelby sat down across from her with three folders in front of her, one thicker than the other two. She wore the same type of pantsuit as she had on the day they met, this one navy blue with a white tee. The juxtaposition of formal and informal intrigued Elisa.

"How are you doing?" Shelby asked.

I fear I'm slowly going insane, thanks. "Fine."

Shelby smiled. "That's not really believable, but we can pretend."

Elisa considered herself an expert in that skill by now. "Thank you."

"One question before we start."

Elisa felt every muscle in her body tense. She had her hands wrapped around the mug and had to concentrate on not squeezing it until it shattered. "Go ahead."

"Does your husband know you're here?" Before Elisa could answer, Shelby clarified. "That sounded annoyingly 'can I speak to the man of the house.' Sorry." She shook her head. "What I meant was, on the matter of the shooting, at some point the lawyers for Maxine's estate will want an official statement from you. The hospital might also want to enter an agreement to keep you from talking. You have rights, and I don't work for you on that case, so—"

"I already signed documents saying I waived any conflict of interest for your office." When Shelby called and asked her to come in for some final questions about the shooting, Elisa had hoped she'd be able to shift the meeting's focus to Josh's messed-up life.

"I get that. Just . . . I expect the lawyers representing Maxine's estate and family to start pressuring the hospital soon. There will be a lawsuit and discovery." Shelby took a paper off the top of her stack and slid it across the table to Elisa. "This is a letter explaining all of that and recommending you take certain steps to protect your rights."

Elisa understood Shelby had to do this to protect her business. She put the paper to the side without reading it. "Lawyer. I need one. I got it."

"Elisa . . ."

"I really hate talking about the shooting. It . . . I think about it and . . ." Elisa didn't know how to make anyone understand that just the mention of that day brought the pain and breath-stealing terror rushing back. She could smell the coffee cart. Hear the traffic nearby. See that look on Keith's face right before he fired the gun. All in slow motion. All in her head. All the time. "It never goes away."

The throwaway comment didn't come close to telling the whole story. She battled daily to keep from drowning in guilt and fear. Hell, most days she battled just to get out of bed in the morning.

Depression and anxiety. She'd read about the subjects, seen movies with characters who dealt with them, but none of it touched her or her life before the shooting. Her mother's death the year before she met Harris taught her how dark, how profound, grief could be. Nathan would never know the comforting warmth of a grandmother's hug or the fun of sleepovers at her house. He'd been denied that piece of childhood, and his loss magnified Elisa's.

She thought losing her mom would be the low point by which she measured all other low points, but the shooting reminded her how horrors waited and could jump out when you least expected them. Its aftermath taught her that fanciful notions about how smiling enough, being grateful enough, deciding to be happy, could chase away depression were insulting platitudes told by people who didn't know better.

Some days she backslid. Her mind scolded her and self-defeating beliefs about how she would be okay if she were stronger lingered. Ridiculous, but the ideas refused to stay banished.

"Learning to live with trauma and maneuver through it takes time," Shelby said.

Elisa's hands clenched against the mug. "I don't want to live with it. I want it to go away."

Shelby made a humming sound. "Trauma is—"

Elisa groaned. "I hate that word." Hearing it twice in a few sentences gave it power, and that's what scared her.

"Why?"

Elisa rubbed her arm. The soreness had eased a long time ago but sometimes she felt a phantom pain. She didn't need the reminder, but there it was.

"The shot and all that blood, those details . . . my memories." She didn't even know how to explain it without sounding clueless or harsh.

Shelby didn't jump in or move on. She seemed willing to sit in the resulting quiet.

Elisa longed to shut down and turn this conversation in a different direction, but the words kept spilling out. "It's this huge sucking hole and everything gets dragged into it. There isn't a part of me that it doesn't touch—the mother, the wife, the friend, the responsible professional. The roles and the anxiety get all warped and twisted, and I don't know how to separate it all out."

"I'm not sure you can."

Elisa refused to accept that answer. "But what happened

on that sidewalk is this one thing. Why does it taint every-thing?"

"That's how grief works. Grief, depression, trauma. They overwhelm. They're louder than the good things happening in your life. You can't compartmentalize the darker aspects and put them in a box and think they won't leach into the rest of your life."

Elisa heard voices in the hallway and leaned in closer to Shelby, dropping her voice. "I should be able to wall it off and—"

"Elisa." Shelby put her hand on the table but didn't move any closer. "I won't pretend to be a mental health professional, but I've been where you are and the one thing I learned is that you need to give yourself time. You're going to have terrible days and okay days, and you will not know which one you're getting until it's too late to duck."

Elisa sat back in her chair. She studied Shelby's concerned expression and thought about the words she said and how familiar they sounded. "You've been in my position."

"That story I didn't tell you about my business partner be-ing my ex-husband's uncle?" Shelby rolled her eyes. "Well, it's long and tedious, but it's about a shitty, brutal man who terrorized me. It took years for me to rediscover the person you see in front of you. Years of putting myself back together, learning how to trust, letting others help me."

This was most women's nightmare. Elisa couldn't imagine anything worse than finding out the one person who pledged to love you no matter what had no intention of keeping that vow.

"I've been divorced for seven years," Shelby said. "Been taking self-defense classes ever since."

"Oh my God." Elisa let her head fall back as she took in the horror of that statement. "I'm so sorry for everything you went through. I can't imagine doing this for years."

"You don't really get to decide. You can't just will all of this away, forget it and move on. The trauma is part of you now."

Elisa listened, knowing every word rang true, but that didn't mean she wanted to hear them. She needed to believe there was a light ahead of her and if she drove hard enough and fast enough, she could move on.

Shelby responded as if Elisa had said the words out loud. "The woman who avoided me for weeks can handle this. So can the woman who has been investigating her brother-in-law. The woman who drove here is raising a son, is holding it together—she's a survivor."

Laughter bubbled up out of nowhere and Elisa didn't fight it. "I'm exhausted."

"An exhausted survivor, then."

"Lucky me." Elisa finally drank the tea instead of just coddling it.

Shelby opened the top folder in front of her. "Well, at least you're not one of the women in your brother-in-law's life. They don't appear to be blessed with longevity."

"I know you just started looking into all of this, but . . . anything to report?"

"Candace. The first wife who turned out to really be the second wife."

Oh, God. "Yes?"

Shelby glanced at her notes. "The cause of death isn't as settled as you thought it was."

No. She'd been in the family during that time. She remembered the funeral. "What does that mean? The police cleared him and her family supported him."

"They signed over the house Josh and Candace lived in together only after he agreed to sign off on all of her other assets."

"I don't remember any of that." Elisa could see the funeral, hear the crying. But she had a vivid picture in her head of Candace's father wrapping his arm around Josh, consoling him.

"I wondered if you knew. Josh apparently fought for a piece of Candace's estate, or threatened to even though the vast majority of her assets were part of a family trust Josh couldn't touch. Apparently, he didn't like that at all."

Everything Elisa knew flipped upside down. "Wait, where was I while all of this was happening?"

"Doing your own grieving. You knew Candace. Her death impacted you as well."

"True, but still."

"Bottom line? Candace's family thinks Josh killed her and they've been trying for years to prove it."

Chapter Forty

The end.

Every story had a beginning, middle, and end, and the time had come to finish this one. All the planning had paid off. The meaty center had lasted for so long, increasing in danger and excitement. But the intrinsic need for closure could not be denied. Like it or not, want it or not, the theory applied here.

Of course, saying *the end* and actually ending were two different things. Stopping now might prove to be difficult. The bigger the web, the more tantalizing the game. It was so easy to get caught up in the thrill. To thrive off the intoxicating lure of intricate game play.

Days passed and the stakes increased. A chant, faint at first, took over. *Make it more compelling. Cause more desperation. Stack on details. Sow more doubt. Eliminate obstacles. Stir up trouble.*

All accomplished. All would be missed.

The work, the scheming, the attention to details, culminated in this. A simple but powerful ending. One predetermined. The steps had been fuzzy, but the goal never changed. Neither did the resolve to get there.

Winning this particular battle depended on a will to do the worse, forget sympathy, and ignore collateral damage. One woman, two women. None of that mattered. No wavering.

All the buildup, now this. A final week of putting the last pieces in place.

Five or so days of tending to the details. Mentally running through each step. Erasing the evidence. Playing the role.

Bottom line: don't screw up and lose allies.

Only one thing—one person—had the potential to derail it all. Elisa. Using her fragile mental state against her had been necessary. She'd been neutralized. Now she needed to stay out of the way.

Time for death.

One more.

Chapter Forty-One

The morning routine ran fine so long as everything and everyone followed the plan. If one of them woke up late—mess. If Nathan threw a fit—mess. If Harris had an emergency—mess. This morning when Elisa came downstairs Harris still lingered in the kitchen, sipping from his coffee mug on a day when he should be at the clinic early. That meant she should expect unforeseen incoming mess.

She wanted to stand at the sink and look out over the backyard as she did every morning to find balance and focus before moving through the day. She needed to get her hands on some coffee. He stood in the way of both, but she greeted him with a kiss anyway.

"Why are you still home?" She tried to sound interested rather than begrudging about him being in the way.

"My mistake." He glanced at his watch. "I forgot to tell you about the appointment I set for this morning."

She also had one a little later and since she scheduled most household appointments the comment got her attention. "With . . . ?"

"An alarm company."

"Really?" She gently shoved him to the side and reached into the cabinet behind him for a mug. She thought about tapping him with the door as a sign that he should move but decided to be nice.

"That thing the other night with the back door?" He shook his head. "I still don't get what happened, and I hate that."

Someone had opened the door and wandered through their house. She blamed Josh because she blamed him for everything, big or small, that went wrong these days. She had no idea why he'd run the risk of terrorizing them and getting caught by Harris, but it all related to him. That was Elisa's theory. The one she kept to herself.

Harris finally pushed away from the counter and headed for a seat at the breakfast bar. "I mean, this neighborhood isn't exactly known for break-ins."

"Especially by perfumed thieves who don't actually take anything." She still hadn't worked that part out. She didn't associate the scent with Rachel. She wore a fragrance that smelled like ginger.

"And we're sure about that, right?" he asked.

Elisa hadn't really been listening, so . . . "Which part?"

"I don't have every plate and piece of silver mentally inventoried and committed to memory, but I didn't notice anything obvious missing." He nodded toward the family room. "The television is still on the wall. I think my laptop was out and available for the taking, and the person ignored it."

Elisa poured her coffee and welcomed a sip before answering. "Maybe the visit wasn't about taking anything."

"I have no idea what that means."

Of course he didn't because she'd gotten into the habit of hiding things from him. Her feelings. Her uneasiness with certain people walking in the house without calling first. And the big one. "A few nights before the problem in the kitchen something else happened."

He slowly lowered his mug to the counter. "What?"

Before she could come up with a coherent way to talk about the open-window incident, Nathan bounded down the stairs and scrambled onto the stool next to Harris. "You're still here."

Harris grabbed for the box of granola and held it. "I had to quickly eat all the food before you got any."

"Really?" Nathan asked, clearly missing his father's wink.

She loved them but she needed more caffeine for this. "Daddy's kidding."

Nathan slipped the box out of Harris's grasp and poured some granola on the counter. He started eating it dry, like a snack. "Why are you home?"

"You know how to make your dad feel welcome." When Nathan smiled, Harris continued, "Someone is coming to do some house stuff."

Nathan screwed up his lips. "Boring."

"Very," Harris said in a faux serious voice.

Elisa felt a morning derailment coming and tried to head it off. "Nathan, feed the cats then get dressed, please."

"I want to eat with Daddy."

"I'll still be here." Harris pulled Nathan closer and kissed his hair. "Listen to your mom."

That got Nathan moving. He filled the cats' bowls, managing to spill very little. Then, after calling for the cats in a high-pitched voice and greeting them, he slid across the hardwood floor and headed for the stairs.

Elisa ignored all of it because she knew Nathan's performance was meant for Harris. Without Harris being there the morning included a lot more whining about wanting to play with his remote-controlled truck.

Harris watched it all then turned back to her as soon as Nathan left the room. "You were saying."

Of course Harris picked that moment to be very engaged in what she had to say. "When?"

Harris laughed. "Nice try, but I've learned how to mentally bookmark where we are in an adult conversation before Nathan cuts in. So, the incident before the kitchen . . . go."

There was no avoiding this topic now. Elisa didn't try. She put her hands on the edge of the breakfast bar and braced for Harris's grumpiness. "One night, maybe a week ago, I don't remember, I woke up and the hall window was open upstairs. No screen. No storm window."

"No." He shook his head. "We changed out all the screens, including that one."

"Yeah, I thought so, too. But since I had to go find the storm window—it was propped up against the house by the basement window well—and reinstall it, I can assure you I'm right."

"Maybe it fell."

"On the opposite side of the house?"

His eyes narrowed. "So, what are you saying?"

She was trying hard *not* to say it and get him all riled up because she didn't have a lot of extra time this morning. "Someone was in the house that night, too. I think."

"Wait." He shoved his mug to the side. "You thought someone was in the house, upstairs when we were sleeping, and you didn't wake me."

He sounded pissed. Any other time, if her world didn't feel shaken up and spun around, if Josh wasn't giving her a hundred new reasons every week not to trust him, she would have told Harris. She wouldn't have thought twice about it. She wasn't a martyr, but nothing ran normally these days. Telling him anything ran the risk of him worrying about her even more.

"At the time I didn't know what was happening." She still didn't, but didn't add that. "So, I looked around the house and everything seemed fine."

He shot her a *you've got to be kidding* look. "Elisa."

She winced. "I know. Next time."

"What the hell?" He stood up. "There better not be a next time."

It sounded like his anger was directed at the issue of safety, which she could handle. "That's why I'm happy you called about an alarm. I was going to do it, and you beat me to it."

"I'm furious you didn't wake me or tell me at any time since that night. What were you thinking?"

Or not . . . "I wasn't."

"What if something had happened to you or Nathan?"

"I know. You're right." He was . . . and he wasn't. "I promise we'll talk more about this when Nathan isn't hanging around."

"I still don't understand what's going on. You could have walked in on someone—"

"Harris, it's okay." She came around the counter to stand in front of him. With her hand on his chest, she flexed her fingers, caressing and soothing him. "Nothing happened."

"That's not my point." The grumbly sound to his voice eased a bit as he covered her hand with his. "But I'm thinking we need the cameras."

Now he'd flip into super-protector mode. She appreciated it and loved him for it, but she didn't want to live on display. "You mean outside, right?"

"The idea of someone getting inside this house makes me—"

More caressing. She'd learned that marital trick years ago. "You're handling it."

He exhaled. "I just wish I knew why someone would come in and not take anything. Then do it again. How and why are they doing it?"

Josh. That was the only answer Elisa could find. This, every strange occurrence and annoying detail, all related to him and his relentless drive to push her over the edge. She'd hinted at this answer before and Harris didn't take it well. Fine, she'd collect the evidence, pay Shelby—do whatever she had to do. But Josh's days of being a sick twist were almost over . . . and if Rachel was his accomplice and not a new victim, she'd go down, too.

Chapter Forty-Two

Elisa barely got Harris and the alarm system sales guy out of the house in time.

She had a doctor's appointment later that morning. She usually mentioned that sort of thing to Harris, but this time she kept the visit quiet. One of many secrets after a marriage of sharing everything with him.

With all the nausea and dizziness, she needed a checkup. Needed someone to tell her that her body was working fine. Her control might be faltering and her mind in free fall, but some part of her had to be on target.

Figuring she had plenty of time, she drove Nathan to school and came back thinking she could fit in a quick coffee run before her appointment, but the alarm company truck still took up most of the driveway. It was another twenty minutes of listening to talk of codes and motion detectors before the technician and Harris left. Now she'd have to settle for doctor's office waiting room coffee, one of the least appealing coffee options.

She grabbed the security company's literature and stuffed

it in her bag. Five minutes of *where the hell are my keys* floundering followed, then she was ready to go with a few minutes to spare. Possibly coffee-takeout minutes. It was the first bit of luck she'd experienced in days.

She stepped outside and . . . Rachel. Her car sat in the driveway and she was walking up to the door.

So much for the theory about luck.

They met on the path. Elisa didn't say anything because this was Rachel's show. She'd once again dropped in without calling. The way she could break away from work and drive around fascinated Elisa . . . and made her even more doubtful about Rachel's supposed work life.

"Sorry for the quick visit," Rachel said.

"I'm on my way out." Which Elisa thought would be obvious from the direction she was walking.

"Do you have a few minutes?"

"Nope." Elisa walked right past Rachel and headed for her car. "Not really."

"I'm sorry."

The blurted words had Elisa turning around to face Rachel. "For what?"

Elisa braced for the answer. Parts of her life had ruptured and unraveled. She blamed Josh, but the woman dating him stood in front of her. The same woman who she caught rummaging through Harris's vet bag. Elisa tried to write the incident in the office off as mere curiosity and couldn't.

Her life had been plunged into a never-ending series of strange happenings, scary events, and weird inconsistencies. She didn't trust anything or most people right now.

"The way you walked in and saw me in Harris's home office." Rachel stopped on the path. Usually steeped in self-control, she shifted her weight from one high heel to another.

Elisa noticed for the first time that Rachel wore a skirt. Part of a suit, in her usual monochromatic palate, but with a dressier look than what she tended to wear. The smooth hair, and cosmetics with that natural, makeup-free look, suggested she needed to be somewhere.

"Are you supposed to be at work right now?" Elisa asked.

Rachel waved a hand in front of her face. "I have a presentation on safety regulations in the workplace in an hour, but I couldn't let any more time pass without apologizing."

"I don't understand." Elisa wasn't really used to apologies being sent her way. She also hated that the mention of a work presentation made her waver about going to this very necessary doctor's appointment. She could follow Rachel one more time, maybe do a better job because Rachel's attention would be on the presentation and not on Elisa sneaking around, looking for business information.

"Josh."

Hearing his name set off an *ugh* reaction inside Elisa. She had to fight not to sneer. "What about him?"

"I didn't realize until later but . . ." Rachel watched a car drive by.

"Rachel? I need to go soon." Mostly, Elisa wanted to move this along. Whatever was coming, she just wanted to hear it.

"He told me I should check out Harris's office, that it was a cool part of the house. He mentioned a space behind the bookcase."

The hidden room. Small and intriguing to Harris when they bought the place. A nightmare to Elisa because she feared Nathan would get trapped in there, so they kept the bookcase closed and latched and hadn't told Nathan about the space. That allowed her to hide Christmas gifts in there. Once he was older, they'd tell him and teach him how to get in and out without trouble and everything would be fine, but not now.

But she had no idea what the peculiarities of their house's floor plan had to do with this conversation. "And? I'm still confused."

"He got me curious about the room and Harris's bag. He talked about the instruments Harris kept in there and I wanted to see . . ."

Elisa didn't buy the excuse. "You could have asked."

"I know." Rachel started a sentence then stopped before trying again. "Honestly, Josh tells stories. He was talking about Harris and this cow."

Elisa knew. As Harris's wife, she was very familiar with his work stories. "What does that have to do with the bag and roaming through my house uninvited?"

"Does Josh ever wind you up? It's like he says things and gets me thinking and I take on his lax boundaries. I can almost hear him in my mind, coaxing me on." Rachel shook her head. "Anyway, I had just gone in there and then you came in a second later. It was almost as if he'd set me up."

Elisa glanced at her watch. She'd eaten up most of her buffer time before getting to the doctor's office. But still, she wanted to hear Rachel out. "Explain the setup part."

"It sounds ridiculous, but I got the impression he wanted

you to find me." Rachel exhaled. "For you to think I was searching through your private things."

All of those thoughts had run through Elisa's mind. That day she'd made a vow to be more careful around Rachel and to push Shelby for more information on Rachel.

Elisa had half convinced herself Rachel and Josh were engaged in some sort of joint plan to make her think she was losing her sanity. The idea sounded a bit dramatic now that it ran through her mind with Rachel standing in front of her.

"Why not say that in front of him, call him out?" Elisa asked.

"I don't understand his endgame. It's almost as if Josh doesn't want the two of us to trust each other, and I want to know why." Rachel seemed to hesitate. "We both know he'll shut down if I poke around too much."

That sounded like the Josh Elisa knew. "How does any of this help him? He has to know we talk to each other."

"If I don't trust you then I won't trust what you're saying about him or your doubts about Abby voluntarily running away."

All those promises about being careful imploded. Enough of this. Elisa wanted Rachel to run. "If you think that, why are you with him?"

"I just—"

"What? Explain it to me." Elisa didn't understand the attraction. Maybe two dead wives ago, but not now. "You think he's manipulating me. You're doubting his story about Abby. There are dead women in his past, Rachel. Aren't you worried about becoming another one?"

"I know about Candace and the stairs. He's convincing

when he talks about the accident." Rachel let out a strangled noise. "He showed me the police report that cleared him."

That's not what police reports did, but Elisa ignored that part. "*Women.* Plural."

Rachel kept right on talking as if she hadn't heard Elisa's comment. "He's great at a lot of stuff."

What did she . . . oh. "I don't really need to hear about that."

Rachel smiled without any warmth. "That, too, but I mean the boyfriend stuff. He plans these great dates. He listens when I talk. He has this great relationship with his brother and, until recently, with you, which is pretty amazing. It all made him seem . . . I don't know, stable? Human. Grounded."

The idea of being one of Josh's dating props made Elisa want to heave. "But Rachel—"

"He's that guy. The redeemed bad boy with a haunted past. You hear about his parents and all the struggles and want to make things better for him."

Elisa couldn't deny that part. She'd been lured in by the story of the car accident and impressed that Josh had finally turned his life around.

"I didn't have a great upbringing." The words rushed out of Rachel now. "My sister was gone. My mom was absent and disinterested. My parents fought all the time, so there was little room for me. Then my dad got sick." She gulped in a big breath. "I travel for work, so I don't really have the time to make friends and cultivate relationships."

Hearing that made Elisa question her doubts about Rachel. She'd lumped her behavior in with Josh's, and with good reason, but now? "None of that sounds fair or healthy."

Rachel's mouth flattened into a thin line. Her expression looked strained. "I'm not asking for pity."

"I didn't mean—"

"I'm just trying to explain why all these women are attracted to Josh, why I was attracted." Frustration filled Rachel's voice. "He gives a lot of attention without being suffocating. He opens up and welcomes you in, but in a way that's hopeful, not clingy or needy. It's refreshing."

If the bar was that low, Elisa never wanted to be back in the dating pool. "But if you're not safe?"

"Until now I thought I was."

The words echoed through Elisa. "What changed?"

Rachel hesitated. She stared at the empty street then at her feet, everywhere except at Elisa. "I don't like how he talks about you. His anger at you for not believing in him about Abby is wild, almost uncontrolled. Whatever made you change your mind about his involvement has him flailing. He expects unconditional support and thinks you should pay for not giving it to him."

Elisa's mind went back to the conversation she overheard in Josh's kitchen. "And you've played along."

Rachel's head lifted again. "I admit I got sucked in at the beginning. I'm not proud of it. He starts talking and the way he talks makes you want to jump in."

"Rachel—"

"It's like being in high school. So juvenile, I know." Rachel sighed. "I know you need to be somewhere else."

Elisa no longer thought her appointment was the most important part of her day. "It's a doctor thing."

Rachel frowned. "Are you okay?"

"I haven't felt great. I'll have some bloodwork and get poked." But Elisa didn't want Rachel worrying about her. "I'm sure it's fine."

"Your health matters more." Rachel gestured toward the cars. "Go."

Elisa headed for her car then stopped. If Josh was desperate and thought he had nothing left to lose . . . if Rachel let her guard down . . . "Promise me one thing. Be careful."

Rachel let out a little laugh as she shook her head. "I've been taking care of myself for a long time."

That wouldn't stop a man hell-bent on killing her or making her disappear. "I'm serious."

"It's going to be fine, Elisa. We'll both be fine. You'll see."

Chapter Forty-Three

Harris was full of surprises today. He'd called Elisa as she left the lab, suggesting they pick up Nathan together and go for a trip to the park to run off Nathan's excess energy then out to an early dinner.

The suggestion sounded great and any other time Elisa would be celebrating an evening without cooking and cleaning dishes, but the conversation with Rachel had thrown her off stride. She'd tried to call Rachel twice to talk about Josh and her safety but both times got voicemail. Not a surprise since she said something about having a talk or workshop today. Elisa had meant to ask where and more about it, but then Rachel started talking and finding out more about exactly where she worked became less of a priority. Still, the lack of a response put Elisa on edge.

She met Harris at the office and as expected ended up chatting with everyone there, including the pet owners, while Harris finished up the *one more* client he tried to squeeze in before leaving.

Harris rarely cut his workday short. Today, he'd started

late and was leaving early. One of the technicians asked if it was Elisa's birthday or their anniversary, and Elisa had been so scattered and distracted that she had to stop and do a mental check. No, no special occasion, not that she could remember, anyway.

That raised the possibility Rachel had talked to Josh, who had talked to Harris, and now Harris wanted to fight or defend him, but Elisa doubted it. She got the impression Rachel was pondering leaving Josh but keeping those thoughts quiet for now.

Ten minutes later Harris finally pulled away from work and people and met her in the lobby. "Hello there."

"You promised me coffee," she said, still battling a headache from the lack of caffeine this morning.

He put his hand on her lower back as he guided them through the door and out onto the sidewalk. "We'll need coffee if we're going to survive post-school, full-energy Nathan."

"He gets that from you. I'd prefer to nap."

Harris wiggled his eyebrows at her. "If you'd rather go home and rest before grabbing him . . ."

The combination of nonstop, low-grade dizziness and a general feeling of nothingness meant afternoon sex was the last thing on her mind. Anytime sex, actually. When she'd lost interest in getting out of bed and getting through the day, sex became her lowest priority.

She snapped her fingers in front of his face. "Stay focused."

"Thought it was worth a try."

"Yeah, I—" She looked across the parking lot and came to a full stop.

The redhead.

His amusement faded. "Are you okay?"

Not again. Elisa thought she'd ended the *following her around* stuff at the school. "Yes, of course."

He tugged on her arm to start walking again, but she didn't move. The redhead—Meredith—wasn't facing them. She had her car's back door open and was dumping a bag inside.

Elisa glanced around, trying to figure out where she'd come from and if the shopping bag looked familiar. Not the pet store or the vet clinic. The only other options in the strip mall that made sense were a doughnut shop and a taco place.

But what were the odds? Here, in this line of shops. In this town.

Harris stepped in front of her. "Elisa, what is it?"

Right. Keep pretending. She forced a smile. "It's nothing."

"If you're worried we're going to talk about the open window and you playing house security guard, well, you should be."

That she could handle. Having a stalker she couldn't. "It's not—"

"Who are you looking at?" Harris turned away from her and scanned the parking lot. After a few seconds his shoulders tensed. "Is that the redhead you had it out with at the school?"

The redhead. "Don't worry. I'm not going to cause a scene."

"I am." Harris took off walking.

"Harris, no!" She tried to do a shout-whisper combination and only succeeded in ticking off a car that didn't want to yield as she ran across the lane. The driver threw up his hands at her and started saying something, but she couldn't hear him. She had to get to Harris.

"Excuse me," Harris said from a few feet behind the redhead. "Meredith Grange?"

"Yes?" Meredith glanced up with a smile on her face. It froze when she looked at Harris. It disappeared completely when she looked over his shoulder at Elisa.

"I thought we should meet." Harris held out his hand. "You're supposedly dating my brother, or did. I'm not clear on the timing."

Her expression went blank as she stared at his outstretched arm. "Who are you?"

He dropped his hand. "Harris, Josh's brother."

"Okay, I'm confused." Meredith shut the car door. "Who?"

As performances went, this one was pretty good. She looked confused and cornered. She shifted back until she rested against her car.

Elisa knew none of it was real. "Oh, come on. He knows. I told him about you."

Meredith reached for the driver's side door handle. "You'll have to excuse me."

"The school. Outside Josh's office building. This parking lot." Elisa refused to slither away. She'd run into Meredith over and over. It was time Harris heard the truth about what this woman meant to Josh. Then maybe they could figure out why she kept appearing.

Meredith shrugged. "You've lost me."

Before Elisa could go off, Harris started talking. "Are you saying you don't know Josh Wright?"

"I'm sorry, no." Meredith held her key fob in a tight squeeze. Her gaze darted around the lot as she inched closer to the front door of her car.

Harris hitched his thumb in Elisa's general direction. "And you never told her the two of you were dating."

Meredith's fingers kept clenching that fob. "That's ridiculous."

Elisa felt a desperate churning in her stomach as her control slipped away. A need to shout and scream until Harris believed her. That was the worry here. That he would hear the denials and stack them with all the other evidence he'd been collecting to question her.

Elisa vowed to fight. "No, lying about this doesn't make sense. We talked about this in the school parking lot."

"I don't have children and don't hang out at schools. You have the wrong person." Meredith opened her car door. "Now, if you'll excuse me."

Elisa used her hip to bump the door shut again. "You've followed me all over the area."

"You have me confused with someone else." Anger floated through Meredith's voice. She'd gone from welcoming to blank to indignant in a short span of time. She slipped her cell out of her jacket pocket. "I've tried to be nice about this, but if you don't leave me alone I'll call the police."

"Do it." Elisa figured they'd been headed for this showdown. They might as well have it out. "Go ahead."

Harris put a hand on her arm. "Elisa."

"Let her." She shook off his touch and reached into her bag, searching for her phone. "Then she can explain why she's been following me, hanging around Nathan's school. You forget that I have a photo of you on my phone."

Meredith threw the door open again and shifted until she stood in the space between it and her seat. "You're insane. I'm in a parking lot and you're attacking me."

Not insane. Not crazy. Not losing it. Elisa repeated those words until she almost believed them. She could not fall apart.

This time Harris pulled Elisa back and out of the way. He gestured for Meredith to leave. "Go ahead. We clearly made a mistake."

"No, Harris." Elisa tried to type in the cell's password but her hands were shaking too much.

Meredith jumped into her car and shut the door. A second later the lock clicked.

The sound ticked off something deep inside Elisa. Anxiety pumped through her until she could feel a flutter around her heart. She put her hand against the car window because they needed to have this conversation. There had been so much lying. She couldn't let Meredith get away with one more lie.

"Elisa, stop." Harris moved her away from the car.

No, no, no. She needed everyone to listen. For people to stop pushing her and insisting a serious flaw existed inside of her.

"Wait, I have it." She scrolled through the fifteen photos Nathan took of the cats this morning. Past the blurry ones and a shot of the kitchen floor.

It was too late. The car jerked and Meredith backed out of her parking spot. Tires squealed and horns honked as she pulled right in front of another car and sped away.

Now the pitying looks would start. The talk about medications and doctors.

Elisa grabbed onto Harris's jacket sleeve, begging him with every part of her to listen. "Harris, you have to believe me. I can show you. She's lying."

"I know."

Chapter Forty-Four

You . . ." That's as far as Elisa could go. Her arm fell to her side. She almost dropped the phone.

Wrapping her mind around Meredith's blatant lies and the way she pushed the whole thing back as some sort of mistaken-identity issue made Elisa want to scream. But if she lost control—started yelling and slamming her hand against the roof of a car—like she'd wanted to, then all those accusations about how she'd lost it and needed help might ring true.

The bitch. Until now Elisa had a bit of compassion for her. She'd gotten tangled up in Josh's life, and few women Elisa knew had survived that yet. But Meredith had gone the extra step today. Made Elisa look like a fool in front of Harris. Tried to make her question her memory and her sanity.

She realized Harris stood in the middle of the lot, watching Meredith's car pull away. "Harris?"

"I know that woman was lying," he said in a flat voice.

Elisa honestly had no idea how to respond. She didn't expect support, not on this. Ever since the strain with Josh started, she felt like Harris had picked sides. Not hers.

"You believe me?" She still couldn't process that. The weight of it was so profound that she feared believing.

He spun around and faced her. "Of course."

No *of course*. Nothing about their recent conversations fit in with an easy *of course* response. "Why?"

He scoffed. "Are you serious?"

She'd never been more serious.

"You knew her name," he said. "She answered to it when I called out to her. She turned around, then did you see her face?"

"Sort of." She'd been too busy running to catch up to Harris's long strides and hunting for the right thing to say to the woman.

A car passed by them, Then another. It looked like they were circling for spaces in the busy lot, so when Harris guided her to a grassy island in the middle of all the concrete, she went willingly.

"She had that 'shot out of a cannon' look, like she had to hurry up and lie," Harris said.

Elisa picked up on the rough edge to his voice and the scowl that had tension lines pulling at the corners of his mouth. "Okay."

"Her eyes got huge and she looked hunted. Like she'd been tracked down and found out." Harris glanced in the direction her car had driven. "Unbelievable."

"And that convinced you?" Elisa continued to be careful. The wrong word could send this whole talk spinning against her.

"I somehow doubt you randomly selected her name out of

a phone directory then we happened to see her, or that you're stalking her. And you have a photo. Why would you lie about that?"

Solid common sense arguments. Just like she'd expect from Harris, though she would have preferred a simple *it's her because you said so*, but that level of trust might be asking for too much right now.

"Here." She finally found the photo and showed it to him.

He glanced at it and nodded. "There. More proof." Some of the tension drained from his face. "And I talked with people at the school, remember? They called to ask about a woman who looked exactly like Meredith, or whatever name she's using."

Pretending. The thought sparked in Elisa's mind. Maybe Meredith was really someone else or knew Abby. She could be one of Josh's girlfriends, but why would he start dating Rachel if he already had a girlfriend he was seeing behind Abby's back?

She needed a scorecard to keep up with the names of the women Josh had screwed over.

"That was her. She told me her name—Meredith Grange—and told me she dated Josh while he was with Abby, and maybe even Rachel. I couldn't get a handle on the amount of overlap," she said, eager to explain the pieces she did know to Harris.

He sighed.

That response could mean anything, and her defenses were up. "You need to tell me what you're thinking," she said.

"I'm guessing Josh screwed up."

Agreed. A hundred percent agreed. "How exactly?"

Harris folded his arms across his chest. "He was cheating and I'm thinking the woman he was cheating with—"

"Meredith?"

"Yeah. I think he dumped her and she got pissed, or she wanted more and is now upset he's with Rachel." He shook his head. "Either way, I think Josh acted like a shit and now his former . . . girlfriend, I guess, is running around trying to catch a glimpse of him."

Elisa followed the whole line of thinking right until that last part. The part that absolved Josh to some degree and made Meredith out to be a crazed stalker. Nothing about her affect struck Elisa that way. She saw cool and detached. A woman on a mission.

That mission might be to destroy Josh, and Elisa could appreciate that, in part, but she wouldn't let that happen. He would get what he deserved, but not by someone sneaking up on him in a parking lot.

"There's one more thing. Her smell." And this was the part that scared the crap out of Elisa. Even broaching this subject sent panic running through her because she had no idea what it meant.

"What?"

"The scent in the kitchen that night. With the open door." She saw the light go on and his expression change. "The scent was a lot softer today, probably because we're outside, but that's the same out-of-place smell from the kitchen."

Harris froze. "Her perfume?"

"At a much more manageable level, but yes." She didn't notice until Meredith got in the car. Once the direct line to the scent cut off, the connection hit Elisa. She'd smelled it before and she knew exactly when.

"Does that mean she got a key to our house from Josh?"

Elisa tried to hide the shiver that ran through her. It shook her from head to foot. "She could have taken it without him knowing, though I know he has a new key."

Harris nodded. "He asked me for a second one."

Interesting he never mentioned that until now. "Why?"

"He gave me what I thought was a reasonable answer, but now I see it as a half-assed explanation about leaving his at work one day. He said it dawned on him it made sense to have two. Just in case."

That new alarm system better have an anti-Josh program. "When?"

"I can't remember. Before we met Rachel." Harris swore under his breath. "I'm going to kill him for lying to me."

They finally agreed on something about Josh.

Chapter Forty-Five

Perpetual play had to get dull at some point. Not yet, but the sensation rumbled in the background. No matter how tempting it was to rage on, if only for a bit longer, the downsides began to pile up. The opportunity for mistakes increased. The joy of savoring might become obvious.

The solution? Action. As immediate as possible.

With the final piece accomplished—put into motion but not yet triggered—there was no valid reason to wait other than the game had become addictive. A habit. That was the biggest clue that the time had come for a big finish.

No more acting. No more tolerating.

All of the planning and waiting came down to this. One last punishing blow. A final slice that would leave blood pooling on the floor.

Literally.

This wouldn't be quick. No, this demanded the slow drip as a life sputtered out of existence. A show. An ending fitting in size and scope to all the work and sacrifice that had gone into creating the moment.

It would get wild before the end. A full-blown, crazy-ass, *no one was safe* affair.

Accusations. Worries. Pain.

But was there ever enough pain? If everything went as predicted, yes. This time there would be enough to make all the work worth it.

Chapter Forty-Six

Elisa almost celebrated Harris getting back on his regular work schedule the next day. He'd tried to call Josh last night and talk about Meredith. Even asked to come over but Josh said he had something special planned with Rachel and they'd talk later.

That answer satisfied Harris, for now, but it had the opposite effect on Elisa. It touched off mind-numbing panic that had her up and pacing the downstairs long after the rest of the household had gone to sleep. She tried several times to reach Rachel. Elisa didn't relax until Rachel finally texted back to say everything was fine and offered to stop by with Josh tomorrow. It was the one time Elisa welcomed a visit.

The confrontation with Meredith, all the lying, and Rachel's doubts set off a countdown inside Elisa. She couldn't fight the sensation of a timer going off. She knew things were about to explode in some destructive way, and she needed to get ahead of it.

Still dizzy and exhausted, she set up a meeting with Shelby. Maybe if they talked through strategy and whatever Shelby had discovered about the line of women in Josh's life, Elisa could have some peace. Some sense that Rachel was safe for at least a little while longer.

She made Shelby promise there'd be no talk about the shooting. Elisa couldn't handle one more stressful topic. She felt stomped on and empty. She also needed more time to talk with Harris about lawyers and lawsuits. More time to explain why she was using their money to investigate his brother.

An hour after Harris and Nathan left the house, Elisa sat in Shelby's familiar conference room. Elisa sipped on a cup of tea. She'd taken a pill this morning for anxiety and felt a jolt of panic when she saw how close she was to the bottom of the bottle.

Getting back to the therapist so she could get a new prescription amounted to the *one more thing* her mind refused to deal with right now.

Shelby came into the room and slid into the seat across from Elisa. "Good morning."

"Sorry for the emergency call."

Shelby smiled as she separated the folders in front of her into neat stacks but didn't open any of them. "No worries. It comes with the job."

True, but even Elisa could admit she'd called sounding breathless, almost panting, as the winding sensation inside her pulled taut. "Yeah, but—"

"Elisa, stop apologizing."

That's all she did these days and was getting pretty good at it. "Okay."

Shelby balanced her elbows on the edge of the table,

managing to look both serene and in control. "You're allowed to take up my time. In fact, you get to take up time and space, and screw anyone who thinks otherwise."

Something about the way she said the words flicked a switch in Elisa. She tried so hard lately not to attract attention or take up too much room. She not only went along, she ran ahead of issues and smoothed out problems for everyone else. All while ignoring her own needs.

It was an odd time for a wake-up call, but Shelby's straightforward comment lingered. Elisa silently promised to think it all through—what it meant and how she could take back space for her concerns and her life. But later. Now was, as always these days, connected to Josh.

"Did something happen?" Shelby asked.

Unexpected laughter bubbled up inside of Elisa. The first thought in her head sounded so wrong and not even a little amusing, but she said it anyway. "Are you asking if I found another one of Josh's secret wives?"

"That's actually my job, and no. Two wives. One missing fiancée." Shelby lifted two, then three, fingers. "A few girlfriends."

"Meredith Grange." That woman was one of the reasons Elisa showed up today. Not the only, but a big part. Meredith registered as such a huge question mark. Her sudden presence in their lives didn't make any sense. Her lies were obvious. And the possibility that she'd been letting herself into their house . . . horrifying no matter the reason behind it.

Shelby shifted a folder to the side and started making notes on a lined yellow legal-size pad. "I did come across that name while doing some initial checks on Josh."

"Where?" When Elisa initially struck the deal with Shelby for her services, she'd mentioned Lauren, Candace, and Abby. She'd sent over some notes on each and listed her concerns. She talked about Rachel but at the time didn't know much more than her name . . . still didn't.

She'd left Meredith off the list because explaining about her meant opening the door to an accusation of paranoia. Elisa knew what she saw and what Meredith had claimed, but the fear of being branded out of her mind made her hold back from spilling more about the mysterious redhead. Good thing, too, since Meredith proved she intended to pretend the school incident never happened.

"One of Josh's former coworkers mentioned her," Shelby said.

Elisa relaxed into her seat. Up until that moment she hadn't realized she'd tensed up, trapping a bunch of pent-up energy inside. "She told me they were dating. I ran into her with Harris and she denied everything. Made it sound like I was making up her relationship with Josh and our conversation about it."

Shelby whistled. "That's a lot. Makes me wonder why she thinks she needs to lie."

The automatic acceptance that what she said was true and accurate stunned Elisa for a second. She carefully crafted what she said and how she said it to keep from causing explosions or being questioned. Having someone take what she said at face value was a nice reminder of how things used to be back when Harris didn't question her. When she didn't question her own mind.

"All I know so far is that she works in high-end condo sales in and around Philadelphia, or she did," Shelby said. "And I can tell from the frown that you were hoping for a different answer."

"It's just . . ." The stuff with the open window and the perfume. Elisa had no idea how to talk about any of that and still sound rational. "We've had these house break-ins and now Josh's current girlfriend is saying . . . I'm not sure what she's saying, exactly. She just sounded like being with Josh was getting uncomfortable."

Shelby sat up a little straighter. "Are these things related?"

"I have no idea."

"I went to Rachel's motel this morning. They didn't have any license or personal information on her, and she's checked out. The woman at the desk also talked about another woman who came and offered money for information."

Elisa could admit that wasn't her finest covert work. "Me."

"You, and I will skip the lecture about how dangerous that was. But this woman had an outstanding deal with Rachel that if anyone asked about her, the woman would get paid two hundred dollars to let Rachel know."

"That's quite a moneymaking scheme."

"Everybody has to make a living." Shelby made some notes. "Do you think Rachel is going to leave Josh?"

"Would he let her?" History suggested not.

"About that." Shelby picked up another folder and scanned

the note clipped to the outside. "The evidence does support Candace's death being an accident."

The words hit Elisa like a body blow. The wind ran right out of her. That resolution wasn't what Elisa expected to hear. Not after their initial meeting. "You said her family didn't agree with the listed cause of death."

"They don't, and I get why. Everyone, including law enforcement, thinks Josh was a bit too interested in Candace's estate and how to get a piece of it, even though most of it was out of his reach."

"Does he need the money? He's creeping me out lately, but I never thought he was after a fortune from the women he dated and married."

"First, everyone likes money. Never forget that." Shelby shot her a look that said *you know I'm right*. "Second, one very disturbing thing I've noticed in this job is that when there's a lot of money at stake, like piles of it and the bigger the better, principles can weaken. People who *would never*, do."

"That's disturbing."

"Very. But money or not, there's one piece of evidence that is likely to prevent any case against Josh about Candace from going anywhere." Shelby hesitated a few seconds, as if to purposely ratchet up the curiosity. "Neighbors."

Uh . . . "Excuse me?"

"I'm not sure if you remember the neighborhood where Josh and Candace lived."

"Sure. Pretty. Rolling hills." Elisa had been jealous of the neighborhood and its amenities once upon a time.

Shelby took a photo out of her file. It showed two houses

where their backyards met. She pointed as she talked. "This blue house belonged to Josh and Candace. This one behind their old house sits on an incline. The back is terraced and on two of those terraces are outdoor living areas—this one includes a gazebo—all looking down on Josh and Candace's property."

The peepers. That's how Candace had referred to them. Said they were nice but intrusive. "Candace complained because even with the fence and the hedges the older couple who lived on this higher lot could see right into the backyard. She said she felt like she was on display. She'd go swimming, and they watched from their patio."

"Lucky for Josh they were outside on the day Candace died." Shelby slid the photo back into her file. "They describe Josh and Candace hanging around the pool, seemingly having a good time. Laughing and joking. They were drinking and the music was on. Candace went inside and a short time later screamed. They described it as blood-chilling. A horrible sound that cut off abruptly."

Elisa closed her eyes, trying hard not to hear it.

"Josh ran inside as soon as Candace's scream ended. They could hear him yelling."

"The fall." Elisa had refused to look at the crime scene photos. She'd wanted to remember Candace as strong and stunning, fully in control and walking around.

Shelby nodded. "The husband rushed down to the house but couldn't get inside because of the property's fence and gate lock. But, and here's where Candace's family's theory gets derailed, the man did see Josh through the double set of

French doors at the back of the house. He was giving Candace CPR. The neighbor's wife called 911 about the same time Josh did, and the first responders showed up almost immediately."

"I'm not sure what to ask." But Elisa understood the bottom line—Candace's death likely was an accident. Either that or a brilliantly designed sham that depended on neighbors lying, which seemed unlikely. She wasn't sure that changed anything, except maybe lowering Josh's body count.

"The couple insists there wasn't any time lapse. That they saw the sequence of events in real time and that sequence only fits the theory of an accidental fall," Shelby explained. "I talked to the prosecutor and he can't figure out when or how Josh would have killed Candace."

Elisa's mind focused on that message from Concerned to Abby about the accident Concerned insisted was anything but. "Why did Candace go up those back stairs she feared so much? There was the main staircase and another bathroom."

"She'd been drinking. They were playing around." Shelby sighed. "It all fits, down to the one blow to the head and the blood evidence."

"That's good." No, it was, but Elisa didn't feel one ounce of relief. "What does it mean for the other women?"

"I'm only talking about Candace. I've had some trouble getting anyone in the police department to talk to me about Abby. Not sure what that means, but I'll push harder."

"They told me the case was closed." That's when Elisa could get them to return a call.

"Let me do some digging. I have contacts in the office."

That's why Elisa hired Shelby—to do the things and talk to the people she couldn't. Still, it killed her not to be in the middle, looking around and asking questions. "And Lauren?"

"I'm still gathering information on Lauren. That file has been closed for a while, so it's taking more time, but—and don't get too excited—"

"Too late."

"I did talk to my contact in the police about Lauren and why her case hadn't played a bigger role in the investigations into Candace and now Abby. As you suspected, the detective—"

"Detective Burroughs."

"Right. A contact of mine who used to work with Burroughs admitted two dead wives was a problem and would have gotten more attention if the detective there hadn't been looking out for Josh. He's a big 'but this will ruin his future' kind of guy. Word is he retired early because he used that phrase one too many times when dealing with sexual assault cases."

"He sounds like garbage."

"He's old-school and we should all be happy he's gone, but he did play interference for Josh," Shelby said. "I'm not sure anyone will admit that out loud, but those are the whispers."

"Lucky Josh. Must be nice to be connected."

Shelby nodded. "That sort of thing always helps people like Josh. They get to play by different rules than the rest of us."

Elisa thought about the women in Josh's life. "I'm not sure where Meredith fits in. I've tried to figure out if she is connected in some other way, but neither Candace or Lauren had a sister."

"You think this Meredith is more than another girlfriend?"

Elisa had no idea. The scrambled pieces refused to fit together.

"I think Josh did something terrible and is trying to hide it." Elisa couldn't come up with any other explanation. To make things worse, he didn't care if he had to ruin her or use Rachel to protect himself. "His relationships suggest a serious problem, and I can't help but feel more death is coming. There is this air of danger over everything right now."

"Then I'll keep looking." Shelby started to gather up her folders.

Elisa put a hand on the table. "Nothing else on Abby?"

All of the lightness left Shelby's face. "No use of her phone, bank accounts, or credit cards."

"And the messages I gave you?" Elisa had handed over the laptop. She figured with someone coming in and out of her house it was safer in Shelby's office than at home anyway.

"It's a file copied from the original direct messages sent back and forth between Abby and someone else, likely through social media. We have time stamps but no IP addresses or source information. It's in a Word document, so there's no way to trace them except that we know the document was created before Abby disappeared. About a month before and added to over time."

Elisa wasn't sure how that helped. "But Abby definitely created it?"

"We can't say for sure, but it's possible," Shelby said. "We've searched the laptop to try to match up the messages to another program on the computer or social media account Abby used, but nothing so far. The laptop doesn't have much else on it. It's almost like it was a backup computer."

That left one uncomfortable issue. "One more thing. I know I've gone back and forth about Rachel and that fake name she used at the motel."

"You should listen to your instincts."

Well, those instincts had her all over the place, and Elisa was taking that as a sign. "I am, which is why I'd like you to check her out. I mean, really dig in and figure out who Rachel Dunne is and what the name Jane Dickson relates to."

Shelby made a humming sound. "You don't trust that Rachel is really Rachel?"

"I once trusted Josh. I don't want to be wrong twice."

Chapter Forty-Seven

Meltdown. That was the best way to describe the evening. Nathan came home from school in a sour mood. The unwinding, complete with stomping feet and yelling, had to do with a school assignment. He wanted to give his presentation on robots but someone else picked that topic.

Nathan handled the setback with the grace of a tiny dictator. After he grumbled about starving and hating the lunch she packed for him today, all while refusing to eat a snack, Elisa told him to go outside. She'd hoped running around would burn off his frustration. He clearly thought kicking a ball against the side of the house repeatedly would be better use of his time.

Thump. Thump.

Relentless, annoying noise. It vibrated through her until she had to bite back a scream. When he missed the wall and hit a window or anything else out there, he'd roar in anger.

Thump.

The cats ran upstairs to hide. Elisa envied them.

For once she welcomed the bout of late afternoon dizziness because the sickness gave her a reason to lie down. Two seconds after her head hit the couch throw pillow she heard the thud of footsteps. Harris jogged down the stairs, making enough noise to rival the sound coming from outside.

"What the hell is he doing out there?" Harris asked as he stepped into the family room.

Elisa kept her arm thrown over her closed eyes. "Being pissed off."

"He's barely seven."

As if age was relevant here. "Which explains why he sucks at not getting his way."

Harris stood behind the couch, hovering over her with his hands pushing down the cushions and messing up the nest she'd made. "Did you ask him to stop?"

She lifted her arm and stared at him. "No, Harris. I find the noise delightful and never want it to end." She sent him a glare in case he didn't pick up on the sarcasm. "Of course I told him."

"My turn." Harris stomped off, demonstrating without saying a word exactly where Nathan's dislike of not getting his way came from.

Even if he couldn't see her, she couldn't help but roll her eyes. "Remember we're teaching him to get his emotions under control."

He said something she couldn't hear then something she did. "If so, we suck at teaching this lesson."

"Speak for yourself," she mumbled as she closed her eyes again.

Not three seconds later a sharp knock at the front door had

her jackknifing into a sitting position. She looked up in time to see Rachel and Josh walk in. They were dressed in work clothes and smiling. Holding hands.

Clearly not broken up.

"Hello!" Josh sounded overly excited. He practically bounced as he stood there.

As Elisa got up, he walked into the room. Kept going until he stood in front of her. Without warning, he gathered her into a suffocating hug.

Her stomach plummeted and she had to fight the urge to jerk back. Instead, she stood there and tolerated it. Even clapped him on the back in response. It seemed like the safest route since she had no idea what was behind the sudden show of affection.

The hug went on for what felt like an hour but probably lasted only a second or two. She pulled back once she thought a reasonable amount of familial touching time had passed. "I forgot you were coming tonight."

Elisa was impressed with her ability to issue the greeting of sorts when what she wanted to do was shout *why are you always here?*

Josh went back to Rachel. Back to holding hands.

Their matching smiles freaked Elisa out.

"Harris had something he wanted to ask me. I promised I'd stop by for a quick chat, so he'd stop calling me," Josh said.

That explained Harris's crummy mood. He'd come home from work after an early morning shift, given her a quick kiss then went for a run. That usually meant something was bothering him; in this case that something likely had to do with Meredith and Josh's lies about her. He'd been frustrated at not being able to talk the subject out with Josh last night.

Elisa tried to think of a good way to tell Josh bringing his current girlfriend along to talk about the woman he dated when he cheated on his last girlfriend was not a great move.

Harris picked that moment to come back in the house. "That kid is going to be the death of me."

Rachel laughed. "Isn't he only in second grade?"

"Don't let his little size fool you. His anger is mighty," Harris said as he looked back and forth between Rachel and Josh. "What's going on?"

"You wanted to talk to me." Josh shook his head. "I tried to reach you at work but you were in surgery."

Thump. Thump.

"What's that banging?" Rachel asked.

The swirl of conversation and noise ticked off something inside Elisa. She had to close her eyes as the dizziness ramped up.

"Nathan! Knock it off!" Harris's voice boomed through the downstairs. "He is on fire out there."

Josh whistled "Bad time to stop in?"

The brothers needed to have the conversation, and sooner rather than later made sense, but Elisa didn't sugarcoat her frustration at the choice of visiting now. "Well, it's not great."

Rachel tugged on Josh's hand, pulling him toward the front door. "We can come back when—"

"No. It's fine." Harris stared at Josh. "I just need to talk with you for a few minutes then you can run away from the house and we'll totally understand your choice to save your-selves from Nathan's bad mood." He gestured toward the back of the house. "Outside."

"That sounds like an order," Josh said with an awkward laugh.

Harris was already walking toward the back door. "Feel free to take it that way."

Rachel waited until the door shut and the men were outside to talk. "Is everything okay?"

Elisa noticed she didn't seem as happy as Josh. She wore an unreadable expression and kept fidgeting. Rubbing her hands together then shoving them in her pockets.

"Nathan's having a bit of a day." An understatement, but this was nowhere near their worst day.

They were lucky. Nathan rarely had tantrums. He was a happy kid. As he started to do more on his own, he was learn-ing how to self-calm. That skill apparently abandoned him today, but learning how best to express his concerns was a process. Elisa still preferred this to the moody teen years she knew loomed ahead.

She also preferred the thumping to the foul mood Josh might be in after a talk with Harris. She decided to prepare Rachel. "Come into the kitchen and we can—"

The back door slammed open and Nathan ran inside. He sang at the top of his lungs as he raced around the kitchen stools and the table, "'Because I'm happy . . . !'"

Rachel's eyes widened. "What's happening?"

Elisa took pity. As an only child she wasn't really raised

with much noise and assumed Rachel had a similar experience, especially since her upbringing sounded a bit sad. "This is what too much energy looks like."

Nathan started clapping to the song he changed in his head. "Happy, happy happy!"

"I don't get it," Rachel said.

"Because you haven't heard this song nine thousand times. It's from a movie, but he makes up his own lyrics." She raised her voice over the singing. "Nathan, that's enough."

He ran in circles and sang, "We should all be happy!"

Elisa's headache had kicked up to big band levels now. "Nathan, stop."

Rachel looked concerned. "I've never seen him like this."

"Sometimes he gets upset and he's not old enough to know how to control it or harness it for good use." This time Elisa caught his arm as he ran by. "Hey, I said no."

The song cut off. "You can't tell me what to do."

It was going to be one of those nights. "Nathan. You're done."

Harris and Josh walked back into the house. Elisa didn't see or hear them until Harris was practically on top of her.

He looked down at Nathan. "What's going on in here?"

Rachel was the one who answered. "A sing-along."

Just as Nathan started singing again, Harris cut him off. "Nathan."

Elisa had had enough. More than enough. The rounds of activity had her head spinning. She pointed to the kitchen chair. "Sit. Now."

"I don't like you," Nathan said in a soft voice. But he did sit.

"Come on, buddy." Josh sounded surprised by his nephew's behavior.

Elisa wasn't in the mood for either of them right now. She looked at Nathan. "I love you, but your behavior is terrible."

Nathan folded his arms across his chest. "I don't like zebras."

"Uh . . ." Josh glanced at Harris with what looked like a request for help. "I'm confused."

"School projects." Harris shook his head. "Don't ask."

Josh laughed. "Okay, clearly now isn't a good time."

"For what?" Elisa could sense they wanted to say something. Josh had come back in from the talk with Harris seemingly fine, so infidelity likely wasn't the topic.

"No." Rachel took a step toward the front door and motioned for Josh to come with her. "We should wait until we can sit down and have dinner."

Josh frowned at Rachel. "It doesn't need to be formal."

"They're busy," she said, continuing their private conversation out in the open.

Finally, Harris sighed at them. "What are you two talking about?"

Elisa couldn't think over her headache, so she wanted them to spill whatever inside joke they kept passing between them. "Yeah, just say it."

Rachel held up her left hand, showing off a sizable diamond.

Josh filled in the rest. "We're engaged."

Chapter Forty-Eight

Y ou said Rachel wasn't serious about the relationship." Harris's comment came out more as an accusation than a question. He paced around the kitchen, holding his cell phone. He was supposed to be picking a place for takeout for dinner, but who could concentrate?

Josh and Rachel dropped their news then left while Nathan was still wound up. The adults agreed to meet in the morning, after they dropped Nathan off at a preplanned playdate down the street. Now he sat on the family room couch behind them, snuggled down and humming to whatever he was watching on his tablet.

Elisa had been stunned then speechless by the engagement news and now, less than an hour after hearing it, was just downright confused. "Yeah, I know."

She sat at the breakfast bar and ran through her last conversation with Rachel over and over in her mind. She hadn't imagined it. Rachel looked . . . scared. At the least, unsure. She'd made it sound like the relationship—though she didn't even use that word—was chugging to a conclusion, not leading to the altar.

"Did she change her mind?"

Harris directed the question to the room and not her specifically, but she answered. "Don't ask me. Clearly I can't read Rachel very well."

That part stopped Elisa cold. Rachel listened. She was supportive and said the right things. She also lied her ass off when it came to her feelings for Josh. Forget love, Rachel had made it sound like she barely liked him and certainly didn't trust him. Now . . . engaged. Elisa had no idea what that meant about the veracity or genuineness of any other topic Rachel talked about.

"He bought a ring." Harris stopped and stared out the window above the sink. "When did he buy a ring?"

She had gone with Josh to pick out the ring for Abby. Not a word from him about a jewelry errand this time around. That didn't surprise her in light of the current state of their relationship, but it wasn't like him to handle this sort of thing alone. Like Harris, Josh didn't know a thing about jewelry.

Elisa stopped fiddling with the handle on her coffee mug. She hadn't gotten a good look at the ring, but it had to be a new one . . . right? He wouldn't be crass enough to give Abby's old ring to Rachel. No, of course not because then he would have to admit that Abby didn't take her ring with her when she left.

"The timing is . . . fast." *Suspicious. Alarming. Terrifying.* She could come up with a lot of words that fit the moment but stuck with *fast*.

"He didn't say anything." Harris turned around to face her. "I mean, I knew he really liked her. When he talked about Rachel, he called her 'the one,' but engaged? That's a big step."

Not as big for Josh as for other people, but yes. "He didn't hint to you?"

"What?" Harris seemed too lost in his own thoughts to carry on his side of the conversation. It took him a few seconds to catch up. "No. I would have picked up on that."

Men. "Would you?"

"Come on. I'm not that clueless."

Most days, but not all. Harris fell into his work. She forgave the tendency, but it either happened more now or she noticed it more. Either way, he could miss signs. Obvious signs of strain and trouble. "Maybe he was being more subtle."

"He's not a subtle guy."

No, but Josh did hide things. Big things, like an extra wife. Between the lying and the hiding, Elisa no longer trusted Josh to act like he should, like anyone else would, in a situation.

"Call him and ask." To Elisa, that sounded like a reasonable way to handle the fallout.

Harris flipped his cell around in his hand but didn't hit any buttons. "He just got engaged. My guess is that he had other plans this evening, like celebrating."

Ugh. "Right."

"I'm not sure when he got so secretive."

That stopped Elisa. "Really?"

Harris shrugged. "I'm serious."

His brain had to be misfiring. She tried to give him a little help. "He's been known to keep secrets, especially about his private life."

"What?" His frown slid away and his expression turned unreadable. "Oh, yeah."

She tried to ignore that her husband just used *oh, yeah* to excuse a communications blackout about a dead wife. She was beginning to think the way he just moved on, expecting no fallout, would haunt her forever.

"But he'd tell me. He always tells me things. Even things he doesn't tell other people." Harris sounded a little lost at the thought of being cut out.

The words punched into her. She really hoped Harris was wrong. Harris knowing about Josh's real first wife and not talking was bad enough, and they still hadn't had it out about that. Not the way they needed to. But the idea of him lying about Abby's whereabouts . . . she couldn't think about that horrifying possibility. If true, that would make him a different man from the one she married. A despicable one.

"So your problem with all of this"—knowing her use of *all* likely was broader than his—"is that he failed to confide in his big brother?"

Harris stopped fiddling around and looked at her straight on. "You're saying that in a way that suggests you think I'm being a jerk."

She decided not to push him now. "You're in shock. We both are."

They'd held it together in front of Nathan, but now Harris seemed to be the one unraveling. She didn't feel much better.

Rattled. That was the right word. In a few seconds, just by showing off her hand, Rachel had shaken everything Elisa thought she'd known.

Josh. Women. She didn't understand the appeal. Rachel had tried to explain it, but for Elisa, his deadly track record with women far outweighed the fact he'd likely remember Valentine's Day with a bouquet of flowers.

"Maybe I will call him." Harris's finger hovered over the cell phone until he put it down on the counter. "Forget it. We'll talk tomorrow."

His insistence that Josh confided in him brought back the one topic they'd skipped over in all the excitement. "What did he say about Meredith?" she asked.

Harris hesitated, glancing over Elisa's head into the family room where Nathan sat with his earphones on as he played some video game that involved smashing things. "He said the 'Meredith issue'—his words—was a misunderstanding."

"Does he know what the word 'misunderstanding' means?"

"Elisa."

"Harris."

Harris shrugged. "Josh said there was some confusion, but he had other stuff going on and something he wanted to tell us, then he'd catch me up on the Meredith situation later."

That was a lot to unpack but she was in the mood to do it. "So, and forgive me if I get the details mixed up, he told you he couldn't talk about the former girlfriend he lied about, the one who he may or may not still be seeing, because he had to tell us that he was engaged to his current girlfriend?"

"It's like you're looking for things to be pissed off about when it comes to Josh."

Harris's entrenched denial ticked her off. "Or, and hear me out here, what he says is a moving target and no one could be expected to keep up."

"I'm not taking the bait."

"You think I'm trying to trip you up? The woman specifically told you she'd never met me. Lied to your face with me standing there." Elisa still didn't understand the motive behind the lie or how it helped any plans, those of Meredith or Josh.

Harris sighed at her. "I don't want to fight with you."

"You don't really have a choice." She was done putting off conversations and tough talk. And she was about to tell him that when her cell buzzed on the counter.

The doctor's office.

He nodded at her phone. "Who's that?"

"It's a text." She looked at the clock and tried to figure out if the doctor's office was still open.

"I can see that." He stepped closer to the kitchen island. "I'm trying to figure out why you look pale."

"My doctor wants to see me on Monday. I'm supposed to call first thing." In the history of time that never meant good news.

"Which doctor?"

Okay, that was annoying. "I had some tests done. Blood, urine. You know, an annual physical sort of thing."

Harris frowned. "When?"

"Doesn't matter." When he started to say something, she

talked over him. "He says he wants to have a follow-up appointment and that I should check the notes in my client file."

"I have no idea what you're talking about." Harris's voice rose loud enough for Nathan to turn around and look at him for a few seconds before going back to his game.

"Our medical files. We each have an account. You sign in and can get test and billing information." She went to the app and put in her security code. "I handle all of this, so you're excused from knowing."

"Why did you go in for the tests?"

She thought about lying and saying this was a routine thing, but it wasn't and the weight of the lies wore on her over time. She didn't need one more thing to feel crappy about. "Because of the dizziness and nausea."

"You said that was a twenty-four-hour bug. Are you really sick?" He came around the island to stand next to her. "What are you doing now? I'm trying to talk to you about your health."

"Reading the doctor's note." She read it a second time because the concerns raised by the doctor didn't make any sense. "My tests suggest I'm taking high blood pressure medicine and he wants me to immediately stop."

"You have low pressure."

"He asks if I took your medicine by accident." They had so few pills in the house, and none for Harris.

He shook his head. "I only take a vitamin."

"Yeah." She started reading out loud from the doctor's note. "'The medicine, especially when mixed with your anxiety medicine, can drop your blood pressure. With your blood pressure already being extremely low, this likely caused the complained about dizziness and headaches." There were a few other comments about not taking other people's medication, as if she would ever do that. "He wants to discuss all of this as soon as possible."

She thought about the last few weeks and the mysterious moving pill bottle. It appeared in the kitchen twice despite it being kept in the locked safe in her bedroom drawer. She couldn't connect the dots.

"Did you get the wrong pills? Do we need to speak with the pharmacist?" Harris asked.

All valid questions. "I haven't gotten a refill recently. The ones I do have look exactly the same as always."

She knew because she stared at the pills every morning. For so long taking them felt as if her body had let her down. Other people survived terrible things and moved on. Why was she one of the unlucky ones who got stuck, whose life quietly unspooled as she sat there defenseless to stop it?

Those were the questions she wanted to ask a new therapist. She hadn't dared before, but listening to Shelby talk so clearly about trauma and knowing she didn't do anything to invite it made Elisa wonder if maybe, just maybe, she could try again. She'd viewed the anxiety and panic attacks as punishment. To Shelby they were livable illnesses that so many battled with daily. Nothing to be ashamed of or to fight against with rabid denial.

Elisa wanted to believe.

"How would the pills get in your system?" Harris shook his head. "I really don't understand what's going on."

"Me either." Her mind shut out the possible horrors but a few got through. Someone mixing up her pills or giving the wrong pills to her without her knowing. That kind of coldness, the idea of being medicated against her will, made her stomach heave. It could be a mistake, sure.

A person out there hated her enough to hurt her. She wasn't sure how to live with that.

Chapter Forty-Nine

They had fifteen minutes the next morning before Nathan needed to be at his friend's house then they'd head over to see Rachel and Josh. A thousand questions ran through Elisa's mind. She wanted to take Rachel aside and ask them all, starting with *what the hell?*

Despite the weekend morning, the house was in its usual uproar. Nathan tormented the cats by trying to hug them. The cats, being cats, hid where kid arms couldn't reach—under the couch. Harris walked around, spouting everything he knew about blood pressure medicine, not something he regularly dealt with as a vet. When he started talking about how a similar diagnosis of high blood pressure in animals meant something else was very wrong, she stopped listening. She didn't need an additional reason to be anxious. The pills weren't hers. End of story.

Wrong meds. Dizziness. Unexpected engagement. Secrets. Possible killer brother. Nope, she had enough to deal with right now.

The doorbell rang just as the front door opened. Rachel

and Josh popped into the opening, all smiles and still holding hands. Unexpected and, for Elisa, unwelcome.

"I'm not sure the alarm install can wait," she mumbled under her breath.

Harris frowned at her. "Not funny."

"Who's kidding?"

"Uncle Josh!" Nathan abandoned the cats under the couch and went running to greet Josh.

Josh managed to hug Nathan despite holding on to Rachel and balancing what looked like a box of food. Nathan stopped short of hugging Rachel, and she looked pretty happy about his decision. She patted him on the head. Not the most natural greeting.

"Hey, we decided to bring breakfast to you," Josh said. Carrying the box, he walked through the family room to the kitchen, guiding Rachel to go in front of him.

"We brought doughnuts and other sugar-filled options," Rachel said.

Nathan ran in front of them and climbed up on the barstool. "Let me see."

"You've eaten." Elisa wanted credit for sounding rational even as she kissed the morning timeline goodbye. Getting Nathan back on track would take coaxing. Possibly some bribery and yelling.

Nathan shrugged. "I can eat again."

Sugar in the morning would lead to the longest day of her life. Elisa silently cursed Rachel and Josh and their tendency to change plans without notice . . . and their lack of knowledge when it came to winding up Nathan.

To sidestep being a buzzkill, Elisa went for negotiation with Nathan. "We'll share one."

"I can eat six by myself." Nathan flipped open the box lid. "That one first," he said, pointing to a doughnut loaded with chocolate icing.

When he lifted it out, Elisa tried again. "Half!"

"Oh, sh—shoot." Realization dawned on Rachel's face. "I didn't think about the sugar. We should have asked first."

"About?" Josh asked.

The world revolved around him. A little boy stared at him, all smiles and sunshine, and Josh only saw the hero worship, not the morning routine or planned day with a friend. Josh wanted to come over, so he did. No one else's responsibilities mattered. The whole scenario made Elisa want to shake him.

Harris took what little of the doughnut Nathan hadn't shoved in his mouth. "We were going to come over in about a half an hour."

"Well, about that." Josh smiled at Rachel. "You might have been too late."

Harris frowned. "For what?"

Elisa barely heard the conversation. She was too busy noticing how Josh crowded Rachel. Practically sat on top of her, had to be touching her. That sort of overzealous attention made Elisa squirm. It came off as a show . . . one that made her worry for Rachel's safety even more.

"We're packing up and going away for a few days." Josh picked up a doughnut and tore off a piece.

If he fed it to Rachel, Elisa would lose it. Enough with keeping the peace.

Josh continued to hold the piece between two fingers. "I asked for a few days off as a surprise for Rachel. She's basically her own boss, so her schedule is flexible."

What was happening? They acted like teens in love, not adults in an early stage of getting to know each other. Elisa felt the room shift. Not from the usual dizziness. No, this round grew out of a blinding case of confusion. None of this lovey-dovey crap matched what Rachel had told her.

The public affection didn't match Rachel at all. She was the cool one. Even and unruffled. Always put together and never giggly, which was the exact opposite of her now.

"Right. This week is about us." Josh finally stopped staring at Rachel and faced the rest of the room. "We're going to celebrate the engagement then we'll be back and we'll have a dinner."

Rachel did not stop smiling. "Nice."

"Huh?" Nathan stopped munching but didn't bother to swallow before talking. "What engagement?"

Elisa had hoped to keep him out of this for as long as possible. Explaining one of Uncle Josh's missing fiancées was tough enough. "Nathan—"

"Rachel and I are getting married."

"Oh, cool." Nathan sounded more excited about the doughnut.

Elisa wanted this topic to peter out. She didn't want to invite more questions, though she knew Nathan would remember this part of the conversation at some odd time in the future and then engage in a thousand questions about the wedding.

"Maybe the celebration dinner should be a party." Josh lifted their joined hands and kissed the back of Rachel's. "I have some friends I'd like you to meet."

Elisa tried to block most of the conversation, but she heard that. "Have you met any of each other's friends?"

"What?" Josh asked.

Before she could answer, Harris shot her the side eye and jumped in. "Where are you going on this trip?"

Josh's smile grew even wider. "That's a surprise, but I'll text you from the road."

The chitchat made Elisa's head pound. She needed answers. Now. "Rachel, could I—"

"These are so good." Nathan climbed up until all of his upper body pressed close to the doughnut box.

Harris shoved the box away from Nathan. "Your mom said half of one doughnut and you've already gone over that."

Elisa felt the day imploding. She'd stayed up for hours, running through every fact she knew and the million things she didn't. She'd worked out what to ask Rachel, and now none of that mattered. "I feel sorry for Titan's mom."

"Oh, right. Nathan is supposed to be at a friend's house." Rachel pulled Josh away from the kitchen island. "We should go and let them get moving."

Anxiety ramped up inside of Elisa. She needed Rachel here. Safe. "That's not necessary."

"I don't want to go to Titan's," Nathan whined.

Harris snorted. "You're going."

"But Mooom." Nathan's whining shifted to expert level as he shifted targets. "Please."

The one thing she and Harris still did well was provide a united front. Elisa fell back on that skill now. "You promised your friend."

"But Uncle Josh is here." Nathan managed to look sad despite having chocolate icing on his cheek.

"You visit your friend," Josh said as he dropped that piece of doughnut he'd been holding. "We have to go. We just wanted to stop by before we headed out."

"Are you coming back?" Elisa blurted out the question and ignored Harris's confused expression in response.

Rachel hesitated before answering. When she did, she used a tone that suggested she found all of this chaos amusing. "Of course."

Too soon. They were leaving, possibly the state, and Elisa hadn't gotten one answer to her many questions. Worse, she didn't understand Rachel's choices or if she'd even be safe.

"Rachel, let me make sure I have your contact numbers." Elisa gestured for Rachel to step into the family room with her. "Take pity on me. I'm a mom. I'll worry without it."

"Of course."

As soon as the men started joking with Nathan and she had a bit of breathing room between Rachel and Josh, Elisa asked in the simplest way she could. "What's going on?"

Rachel glanced at Josh as he joked with Nathan about how few doughnuts were left in the box. She smiled then looked at Elisa again. "What do you mean?"

"You told me—"

"Not now." Rachel shook her head, but her voice stayed steady. The low whisper barely registered.

"Okay, but the engagement."

Rachel held out her hand and studied her finger. "He did a good job with the ring."

"Rachel." Elisa knocked Rachel's hand away and stepped in closer. "You said the two of you weren't serious."

"Hi!" Nathan popped up next to them. "Could I have another doughnut half?"

No, no, no. Elisa needed a few minutes of peace. Even a second to catch her breath and work through all the conflicting feelings bombarding her.

Biting hard on the inside of her cheek, Elisa floundered, trying to find some control. She didn't want to yell at Nathan, but she was so close. "Honey, give us a few minutes."

He stopped bouncing around. "But they're leaving."

"Yes, we are." Josh zoomed in and picked up Nathan. The squeals of laughter were loud enough to send one of the cats out of her hiding place and streaking up the stairs. "We have a plane to catch."

Josh carried Nathan on his shoulder as he walked past them and headed for the front door. Elisa stood there, trying to process what this all meant.

"A plane?" Surely she heard that wrong. Josh couldn't be that spontaneous . . . right?

Rachel touched Elisa's arm. "It's okay."

This was anything but okay. Words screamed through Elisa's head and she fought to stay focused over the drumming in her ears. "I need to talk with—"

"There will be plenty of time for that later." Rachel gave Elisa's arm a final squeeze then let go. "We'll talk soon."

The room started to spin. Elisa had to close her eyes to drown out the riot of noise and rush of colors as they swirled by. "You don't understand."

"I love that the women get along." Josh's voice rose above Nathan's squeals and Harris's laughter as Josh pretended to drop Nathan.

Josh, Harris, and Nathan stood outside now. The men talked on the path. Nathan tumbled around on the grass. Elisa could see them but kept Rachel just inside the entry with her.

"Elisa, you two can talk wedding stuff later. They need to go," Harris called out.

Josh had put Nathan down but he tried to climb back onto his uncle's shoulders again. "Take me!"

It was all too much. Elisa grabbed onto Rachel's hand. "Please."

"Listen to me." Rachel held up one finger. "It's going to be fine."

"You don't know that." All the evidence said the opposite. Elisa fought for the right way to say those words without alienating Rachel or upsetting Josh, who stood less than ten feet away.

"But I do."

Rachel sounded so sure, which only added to Elisa's confusion. She fought to keep her voice steady, to not give her fear away. "How in the world could you?"

The car alarm chirped as Josh unlocked it. He and Harris walked over to the driveway and Josh opened the car door. "Let's go."

"One second." Rachel turned and gave Elisa an awkward, barely touching hug. "I promise everything will be okay."

Elisa didn't want to let go of her. She let desperation fill her as she whispered in Rachel's ear, "Let me stop this. I don't care if Josh gets angry with me. I'll take the blame."

Rachel stepped outside. "You've done enough to help."

She hadn't done anything. Not for Candace or Abby. She had vowed to save Rachel and was failing at that, too.

She wanted to grab Rachel and drag her back inside, but she was on the porch now. Getting too close to that car. Elisa's panic spiked.

Josh tapped his key fob on the roof of the car. "Rachel?"

Shut up. Shut up. Shut up. Elisa wanted to scream the words. Make it clear that she didn't want to hear one more thing from Josh.

"I have all of this under control," Rachel said, getting Elisa's attention again.

"But how?"

Rachel let out a sigh. "I'm concerned."

"What?" What kind of response was that? The words had no bearing on the conversation, on Elisa's trembling fear. "You're what?"

"You heard me. Think it through." Rachel jogged down the steps and reached for Josh's outstretched hand. She turned to wave right before she got in the car. "See you in a few days."

Harris waved back. Elisa couldn't move. Rachel's response had her reeling. She spoke nonsense there at the end. Like some kind of cry for help, except that she seemed fine. Happy, even.

I'm concerned.

Then it hit Elisa. *Concerned.*

Rachel was Concerned.

Chapter Fifty

Elisa spent the rest of the weekend trying to figure out if she'd manufactured the scene with Rachel in her head or if it really happened. The line between what was real and what was part of some anxiety-fueled haze blurred. Things she knew to be true—where she put her meds, the closeness she and Abby shared, snippets of conversations—didn't hold up to facts thrown in her face. She blamed Josh for undermining her, for taking away her stability, but holding on to that belief was getting harder and harder.

As soon as Josh and Rachel drove away a thick blanket of darkness settled over Elisa. She tried to punch through, but her muscles felt weighted down. She wanted to curl up in bed and not think. Thinking invited doubts and second-guesses and guilt. And, yes, paranoia.

She tried to block all of it. Just drift off to sleep and remember a time a year ago before all of this happened. Abby would be there. Maxine would be alive. Her life would be on track. She wouldn't be lost in this thick fog that filled her until she choked. Her marriage wouldn't feel so shaky and uncertain.

She'd be stable. Josh would be decent.

She wanted to stop worrying about Rachel and Abby and everything else. She wanted to be able to travel outside of a twenty-mile radius without being overtaken by this desperate clawing sensation inside of her.

But that wasn't her world now. Her life had become one she no longer recognized, centered around hiding things and telling half-truths. Investigating people she supposedly cared about. Not being one inch closer to finding Abby.

And now this . . . Concerned.

Elisa tried to make all the pieces fit and only got more confused. Rachel in secret, anonymous talks with Abby. Rachel issuing warnings to Abby about Josh . . . then getting engaged to him.

Elisa couldn't make sense of it. She'd run through the possibilities, some so ridiculous they couldn't possibly be true. Rachel as Josh's willing partner. Rachel as someone with a connection to the women in Josh's life. Rachel as some sociopath, a stalker who targeted the family.

Harris played with Nathan all weekend and sulked. Harris insisted he wasn't, but even as her life crumbled around her, she did still know him. He seemed to take the news of Josh getting quietly engaged as a personal attack. Harris hated being cut off from information. He'd played the pseudo father role for so long—despite Josh's marriages and engagements in the interim—that he had trouble letting go of the assigned role.

In an effort to pull back some control, she spent the weekend looking through the saved messages between Abby and Concerned. Shelby had Abby's laptop at her office, but Elisa kept a copy of those messages. She hadn't studied them for days, but now she couldn't stop. By the time Monday morning rolled around, she almost had the entire back-and-forth memorized.

With Nathan at school and Harris at work, she needed to call the doctor, but she took another deep dive in the messages, hoping to uncover something the first hundred read-throughs hadn't shown her.

ABBY: Do I know you?

CONCERNED: what matters is that I know josh and you're not safe

ABBY: Convenient. How am I supposed to doublecheck what you say? To trust you?

CONCERNED: i don't care if you trust me just don't trust him

ABBY: How do you know these things about him?

CONCERNED: i've spent a lifetime studying him

ABBY: Why? How do you know him?

CONCERNED: he's dangerous and someone needs to stop him

Lifetime? Elisa didn't know how that could be possible. That sentence pointed her away from Rachel being Concerned, but other snippets led her in the opposite direction.

CONCERNED: you like that he's attentive, brings gifts, says the right things

ABBY: Yeah, that sounds horrible . . .

CONCERNED: it's a con

Elisa thought back to her conversation with Rachel about Josh's strengths. They sounded a lot like Concerned's list.

But comparing and contrasting styles and word choice didn't clarify anything.

Elisa held on to Rachel's words—*I'm concerned*. No way was the use of *concerned* a coincidence. Elisa refused to believe she was drawing incorrect conclusions or twisting words to fit her new theory. No, Rachel dropped the truth then left town. That wasn't a coincidence or Elisa overreaching, but it was terrifying.

While she sat there, waiting for the alarm company to call back with a time for tomorrow's installation, she thought back to why they needed the protection. The break-ins where nothing went missing. The inexplicable window. The medicine . . . the piece that still sounded so unrelated yet how could it be?

She needed caffeine. She thought about eating that one stale doughnut they hadn't finished off over the weekend. It was supposed to be espresso flavored. Nathan declared that "disgusting," but she craved it.

She got halfway to the kitchen when her cell phone buzzed. She tapped on the screen and slammed to a halt. Stood there, boneless and blinking, because the first text from Josh made her brain shut down.

Las Vegas!

A photo popped up. Hands, likely those of Josh and Rachel. Then Elisa noticed the details. A bouquet and the banner at the bottom of the photo.

Just married.

Chapter Fifty-One

Life had become a series of painful family dinners. Even Nathan seemed to notice tonight. He kept his head down and played with his spaghetti. Neither Elisa nor Harris said anything negative, but the surprise wedding announcement, instead of filling the house with a celebratory mood, cast a pall.

After fifteen agonizing minutes filled with bursts of awkward conversation and long silences, Nathan asked to be excused. Elisa almost sighed in relief as he went to enjoy his allowed hour of game time in the other room.

As soon as Nathan disappeared around the corner, Harris shoved his plate to the side and rested his elbows on the table. "What's wrong with you?"

Hushed tone or not, she hadn't expected the immediate attack. "Me?"

"You told Nathan his uncle got married with the same enthusiasm you'd use to explain what a funeral is."

Probably because she was preoccupied with worrying

about another dead wife in Josh's life. "You're not exactly cheering the news either."

"It was a surprise." He shrugged. "It would have been nice to be there."

"Because you like to attend all of his weddings?" Okay, she could admit that was a bit of a cheap shot, but Harris's mood made her defensive. She wasn't the one who ran off and got married. She wasn't the one with a list of dead and missing spouses.

"What the fuck, Elisa?"

Harris's usual even mood abandoned him tonight. He seemed determined to be pissed and, for some reason, aimed all of his anger at her. "It was a joke."

"It wasn't funny."

"None of this is."

He let out a long sigh that telegraphed how frustrated he was with her. "'This'?"

"Do you want the list? The thing with Meredith. Rachel's sudden change of heart. *Abby is still missing.*"

"Enough." He dropped his hand and it slammed against the table. Dishes clanked and Nathan's empty water glass fell over.

Elisa wanted to come out fighting, but something inside her shriveled. He blamed her for Josh's choices. She had no idea why, but she could feel it. "What did I do to make you so pissed off?"

"You alienated my brother," he shot back. Didn't even take a second to think about the question.

"Oh, come on. How, exactly?"

"Why do you think they ran off to get married instead of having it here with friends and family?" Harris started gesturing. "Why do you think we weren't invited?"

The verbal hits had her gasping as her mind searched in vain for the right words to say in response. She went with the first thing in her head. The only thing. The thing that played nonstop. "He's been playing games with me and still you're siding with him."

He looked at her like she was talking gibberish. "Now what are you talking about?"

Every word he uttered contained a smack. She felt battered. Unable to defend herself. Before she could think of the right words to say she felt a prick on her palm and realized she'd been holding the butter knife in a tight grip. The edge pressed into her skin and made a dent. She rubbed the sore spot, but the pain only intensified.

"You could start with Josh's messing around with the storage unit and not telling me."

Harris made a strangled sound. "He put the unit in your name to make it easier on you."

Yeah, because he was such a great guy and all. "It was empty!" And only one game of many. "Then there's the nonsense with Meredith."

"He said he'll explain. That it was a misunderstanding."

Harris gave Josh break after break . . . and gave her none. "What could he possibly say to convince you?"

"Whatever happened with Meredith, it's over. He's clearly not with her now."

This was like listening to Josh's talking points. Forget personal responsibility. Josh made a mess and failed to show one ounce of remorse, but they were all required to move on.

She didn't understand how Harris couldn't see what was so obvious. "You have no idea if that's true because he's hidden Meredith and, for some reason, she's lying for him."

"Mom?" Nathan shuffled into the room and stood by her chair.

She had no idea how much or exactly what he'd heard. The entire argument had passed in whispered angry words, but he was a kid. Kids tended to hover and hide and overhear things.

This time, he popped up and she never saw him coming.

She tamped down on the energy sprinting through her. Putting on a fake smile, she tried to modulate her voice. Keep things normal. "What do you need, honey?"

"Are you guys fighting?" He carried a plastic robot that lit up and talked when it was turned on. It fell silent as it hung from his hand.

"We're having a discussion." Harris's tone didn't leave a lot of room for questions.

Nathan's gaze bounced between his parents. "Okay."

Those big eyes got to her. She hated to see him shut down when he usually brimmed with life and excitement. "Go back to your game."

"But I want to stay."

"You heard your mom." Harris sounded stern and unbending, not at all the usual tone he used with Nathan.

Nathan's little shoulders shrunk and his head bowed.

Elisa wanted to kick Harris. Instead, she focused on Nathan. "It's fine, honey. I promise. We just need a little adult talk time." She glared at Harris, daring him to disagree. "Daddy will be in to play with you in a few minutes."

Nathan shrugged and walked away.

"Happy?" Harris didn't give her a chance to fire back at his snide tone. "The mood of the house sucks."

He kept throwing new sins on her pile. She didn't notice him adding any to his own. "And that's my fault?"

"You stopped seeing your therapist—"

"That's what this is about?" There it was. The one thing Harris thought would resolve everything. If she could just get better and be faster doing it. He never said the words, but she heard them.

"Yes, Elisa." He glanced in the direction of the television room, as if waiting for Nathan to peek out. He dropped his voice even lower but the angry beat came through loud and clear. "You don't trust Josh. You're starting fights at Nathan's school with women you don't know."

"One woman."

"Your behavior has attracted attention. It's getting people talking and wondering if you're okay. Misplacing your pills. Taking the wrong medicine. Medicine no one in this house even takes, so where did you get it?"

The long list of her failures. He didn't even hesitate when reading through them.

She didn't know where to start, so she skipped to the end. "I have not taken the wrong medicine. Not willingly."

"Do you hear how paranoid you sound?" But he wasn't done. "And now there's Rachel."

Elisa froze. She had doubts she didn't dare share. There was no way to explain the part about Concerned without explaining it all, and Harris's pinched face and closed-off stance made it absolutely clear he was not willing to have a deeper discussion on anything related to Josh. "What about her?"

"You're raising concerns about her. You don't think I saw how antsy you were the last time they were here. You were nervous and odd, trying to take her aside to whisper things to her."

She had a reason. A good reason. One she refused to share because it would give him more ammunition against her. "You don't think her quick change of heart on the relationship is a problem?"

"I'm not convinced you understood what she said about her feelings in the first place."

Elisa sat back hard in her chair. "Excuse me?"

"You're seeing things and hearing things." He shook his head. "I don't know what the hell is happening with you. The shooting was awful, but it's been eleven months."

Get better faster. That's what she heard.

"I can't keep doing this with you." This time he stood up.

Divorce. The end.

She could feel the worst coming, the thing she feared more than anything else, and all she could think was that Josh had won. "What are you saying?"

"When Josh and Rachel come back . . ." Harris looked

everywhere but at her. "Maybe Nathan should spend some time with them." Then he faced her again. "Until you get yourself together."

Her world, already stretched at the seams, ripped apart. Shredded until she could feel every tiny tear. He'd tested everything about her—being a mother, being a good wife and friend, her home, her mental stability—and found her lacking.

"Absolutely not." It took all the strength she had left to get those words out.

"You are not okay, Elisa."

He was doing this to her. He and his brother. She'd never felt so vulnerable, so shaky and unsure, before.

"Maybe if you supported me." Her voice bobbled and she hated the sign of weakness.

"I've done nothing but listen and support you, and I can't keep doing either if you're not going to admit there's a problem." He stood there, all tense and clenched. "With you. Not with other people. I don't want to hear one more word about Josh, or Abby, or any negativity about the wedding."

A raw emptiness crept over her. A pain so overwhelming it hollowed her out. Being there, listening to him, took all of her concentration and will not to double over and cry out.

She'd never seen this side of Harris before . . . the side that seemed to hate everything about her. "You're telling me to shut up in my own house."

"I'm begging you to get help." The chair screeched across the floor as he knocked against it on the way out of the room.

Yeah, no doubt about it. Josh had won.

Chapter Fifty-Two

Elisa didn't get out of bed until after noon the next day. She'd moved the alarm company installation. She wanted to cry and scream, but she felt nothing. Just alone and sore. One big thumping ache.

After ignoring her doctor's office, she finally picked up. The doctor confirmed the pills left in her bottle were the right pills. Antianxiety meds. The same ones she'd been taking for months.

The doctor grilled her about the dangers of taking other people's medicine, which she wasn't doing. Suggested she might have picked up Harris's blood pressure pills until she made clear there weren't any pills like that in the house or shouldn't be. The whole mixed-up-meds thing stumped the doctor. That made two of them.

Moving on fumes, bumping from one destination to another, not seeing the road or remembering how she got there, she arrived at Shelby's office. She'd arranged a hasty meeting after the news of the surprise wedding and the fight with Harris.

The only control she possessed in the world centered on this conference room. With her life blown apart and her marriage in tatters, she could barely function. She hadn't said a word to Harris since last night. She spent breakfast listening to Nathan chatter and trying not to pull him into a fierce hug to keep Harris from taking him away.

A part of her wanted to give up. Apologize to Josh for being wrong and go back to the therapist and stay quiet. Be whatever they all wanted her to be. Do whatever others wanted her to do to prove that she was fine, as she unraveled even more. But this tiny part of her held on. Even if trauma did wash over everything, color it gray and dull the edges, she'd made a vow not to give up on Abby.

She'd write whatever check Shelby needed to get this done fast. If she was wrong and Josh had gotten wrapped up in an untidy string of complicated coincidences, fine. She'd beg for his forgiveness. But she had to know the truth. She'd risked so much—lost so much—and it all had to mean something.

Shelby walked in with a file tucked under her arm and two coffee mugs in her hands. "I hear you're not doing so hot."

"It's that obvious, huh?"

"You look sad." Shelby put a mug in front of Elisa. "Worse, you look defeated."

Elisa sipped on the tea but couldn't taste anything. "Amazing what you can see if you're looking for it."

"Uh-oh." Shelby slowly slid into the seat across from Elisa. "What happened?"

"Josh and Rachel got married."

Shelby frowned. "That's a surprise."

"A quickie wedding in Las Vegas." Elisa wrapped her fingers around the mug, mostly because she needed something to do with her hands. "Harris and I weren't invited."

"Ah, marriage for them and marriage trouble for you."

Elisa never imagined she'd use that description for her marriage. Sure, they'd experienced tough times and fought, but they emerged stronger. They were in sync. They wanted the same things. Had the same values. Now . . . they had anger.

"How did you guess?" Elisa asked.

"First, it's my job. I see a lot of marriage stuff and most of it, unlike yours, is horrible. You'd be amazed by the sick things people do to each other." Shelby put a notepad and pen down in front of her with all the other files sitting there. "Second, I'd bet marriage trouble is the one thing that could shake you."

"Haven't you heard? Everything shakes me." The blip of anger broke through the grief. Elisa welcomed the heat.

"That's not true, and anyone saying it isn't paying attention." Shelby picked up her pen and started tapping it against the notepad. "The strength that it takes to search for a friend when everyone insists she's fine? That's determination."

The tapping sound actually soothed Elisa. Gave her something to mentally grab on to. "My husband takes it as a sign there's something wrong with me."

"There's not." Shelby nodded to someone on the other side of the glass before glancing at the stacks spread out on the table. "You were right. There's no indication that Abby picked up her life anywhere. I quizzed an assistant I know in the police department until he got uncomfortable and rushed me off the phone."

That sounded familiar to Elisa. "Been there."

"Then a detective called me back this morning. Not Burroughs or anyone who had been affiliated with Josh or the case in the past." Shelby looked at her notes. "Rogers. He's new and runs a task force, looking into cold cases."

Elisa tried not to get excited. "Is Abby's case considered cold? I thought it was closed."

"Rogers didn't give away much." Shelby shot Elisa a satisfied smile. "But after my call he said he did a little digging and didn't like what he found."

"Like what?"

"I'm not sure, but he mentioned Josh's deceased wives and didn't sound like he believed Josh's stories about either."

Elisa set her mug down and sat up straighter. Shelby had her full attention now. "That's promising."

"It might be." Shelby's pen tapping grew louder. "It's better than my Rachel news."

The brief reprieve of excitement passed. Elisa could read Shelby's tone and it wasn't good. "What does that mean?"

"How well do you know her?"

"Barely." Enough to be confused. "I know it sounds insane—"

Shelby groaned. "Don't do that. You're not insane. No one should throw that word around. If someone is going to, don't let it be you."

"Sorry."

Shelby switched to laughing. "And stop apologizing."

The back-and-forth relaxed Elisa. She'd come in tense and scattered. Being there, listening to Shelby's soothing voice, helped to clear Elisa's head. "You ever think of becoming a therapist?"

"No, but I've had years of therapy, so it's possible I picked up a few tips." She reached into her pocket and pulled out a card. "By the way, in case you're in the market for a therapist you might like better than your old one, here's her card."

The way Shelby said it, so nonchalant—Elisa ached to have that style. But today wasn't about her mental health, well, not directly. "So, about Rachel, or maybe her name is Jane."

"I don't think either name is right." Before Elisa could jump in and ask a million questions, Shelby continued. "Let's walk through what we've uncovered. Here's my Lauren file." Shelby put her hand on a thick file. "And Candace." She touched the side of the box sitting next to her then she picked up a regular-size file, full but not bursting. "This one is for Abby."

"Okay . . ."

"See this one?" Shelby held up a file that looked like it had a few pages in it but not much more. "It's Rachel's. It's thin because there is nothing to find."

The visual was interesting but Elisa didn't get whatever message Shelby was trying to deliver. "I don't get it."

"You don't have a photo of her, which makes searching tough but not impossible." Shelby flattened her hand on the nearly nonexistent file. "We've called in favors. We've looked in places we're not supposed to be able to look."

"And?" Elisa asked because with that buildup she had to know.

"Jane Dickson clearly was an alias. And Rachel Dunne? She doesn't exist."

Elisa had no idea what to say to that. The silence in the room suggested Shelby had the same problem.

Finally, Shelby started again. "I've called contacts and more than once pretended to be a potential client looking to hire her, and none of the human relations or staffing companies I spoke to have heard of her or employ her."

"She made it sound like she doesn't really have an office. It's possible she owns her own firm and works from home."

"If so, there's no business documents or tax returns filed for it." Shelby took out a loose page from the file she had on Rachel. It looked like a spreadsheet. "So, we took the long road around. We traced all of the conferences Josh has gone to for two years and cross-referenced those with other conferences in the same hotel or nearby, thinking we'd find her that way since you said that's how they met. And nothing."

"But . . . I mean . . . tell me what to ask." Elisa thought about all those afternoons Rachel just showed up. How she seemed not to have work hours. About how she was at the motel in the middle of the day and not at a conference, like she said she'd be.

"There are Rachel Dunne in the Philadelphia area, but not your Rachel Dunne. None of the women fit. Same problem with an extended search of the whole state," Shelby said.

"It's possible her company is located somewhere else. A lot of people freelance or work as independent contractors like that." Elisa looked for any angle that would offer a reasonable explanation, but she remembered Rachel saying she saw the shooting on the news. That made it more likely she lived close.

Shelby made a humming sound. "Sure, but she drives, right?"

Dread settled over Elisa. "Yes."

"No record of a license. No sign of a rental agreement. No tax or other identifying records we could find. When we didn't find her in Pennsylvania, we extended the search and nothing." Shelby threw up her hands. "As I said, she doesn't exist. I'm beginning to think she doesn't have a job at all. It's all smoke and mirrors."

Elisa's mind raced in a thousand directions. She had trouble catching on to one thought long enough to ask a coherent question. "Then who is she?"

"Excellent question." Shelby opened the file she brought into the room with her. "I have some photos I want you to look at. Since Josh seems to be the key, the photos are of women in Josh's life or people associated with those women."

Shelby flipped the file around, and Elisa started paging through it. Pretty women. Different races and a range of ages. Elisa recognized one of Josh's former neighbors and another she couldn't place but knew she'd seen before. "This photo looks older."

"It is. She's another former Josh girlfriend." Shelby held up a hand. "Before you ask, she's alive."

"Lucky her."

Elisa expected two or three photos, but there were more like twenty in the stack. Some women were in more than one photo. "Pretty."

Shelby looked at the photo that had Elisa's attention. "It looks like her time as girlfriend crossed over with Candace, wife number two. Clearly your brother-in-law is always looking to trade in."

Elisa got to the last page and stopped. One photo jumped out.

"That one?" Shelby whistled. "Interesting."

"That's Rachel. Much younger and with lighter hair. It's either her or someone who looks a lot like her." The resemblance was too close for the woman not to at least be a relative. "Who is she?"

"Lauren's sister."

Elisa let the words sit there for a few seconds, but they didn't make any sense. "That's not possible. You confirmed that Lauren was an only child, just like Josh said. It was one of the few things he didn't lie about when it came to Lauren."

Shelby flipped the photo over. On the back were a bunch of notes that looked to be in Shelby's handwriting. "From what I could piece together from records and former friends and neighbors, after Lauren died, Lauren's mom, Allyson, got married. The move surprised everyone who knew her. Most thought she was just lonely. She met and married Ben Robinson, who was a widower with a young daughter, so some people who knew Allyson thought the idea of having another daughter appealed to her."

Them. Elisa remembered Allyson's obituary and that note in the comments: *it was smart to leave* them *out. Them* meant the new family and *them* clearly didn't end well. "Lauren was an only child, but Rachel said she had a sister. Was she lying?"

"Depends on how you reference the family relationship, I

guess." Shelby flipped pages on her notebook to what looked like a handwritten timeline. "I worked this out and double-checked it. It's true Rachel and Lauren would have been stepsisters, but they never even knew each other. Lauren was already dead when her mom met Rachel's dad."

Rachel and Lauren. "Oh my God."

"Exactly." Shelby flipped the photo back over and pointed at the young girl. "This is Rachel Dunne, formerly known as Nina Robinson. She was about eleven when Ben and Allyson got married. Ben and Allyson stayed married for six miserable years. Nina would be almost twenty-five today."

"And Josh's third wife."

"The stepsister Lauren never knew." Shelby nodded. "Apparently the happy marriage part for Allyson and Ben only lasted a few months. The rest was a slog. They fought. Nina, now known as Rachel, and Allyson didn't get along. Friends say Allyson never stopped grieving for Lauren, and Nina was a tough kid. Not warm. Jealous in a rabid way. A school counselor said Nina's mother left when she was a toddler. Nina viewed Allyson's obsession with Lauren as rejection."

Elisa remembered Rachel's comments about her mom being in perpetual mourning, but she really meant stepmom. It all fit except for the emotional part. "If there wasn't a real connection between Rachel and Lauren, why hunt down Lauren's husband?"

Shelby shrugged. "Some sort of revenge? Maybe she's a person who likes chaos? I'm not sure yet, but Lauren is the key here."

"I don't understand." Elisa grabbed onto the edge of the

table as her stomach tumbled and churned. "But does this mean Josh is in danger?"

"Could be, or he might have found a partner with as many secrets as him."

All this time Elisa had seen him as the aggressor, and he might still be, but something else was at play here. It was possible he knew who Rachel really was, but Rachel being Concerned blew that theory apart. "When and why did Nina become Rachel?"

"Nina bounced around a couple different types of jobs since graduating from high school. She tried college for a semester but dropped out. She was a receptionist and worked in retail the longest of any of her jobs. Then her father got sick. She moved back in with him and basically acted as his nurse and full-time caretaker." Shelby flipped through her notes again. "It looks like Rachel came to life a few years ago, complete with an established fake backstory and false work history. We're still tracing that, but before then she was Nina."

Elisa traced a finger over Nina's photo. She wore a soccer uniform. Her hair had come out of her ponytail on one side. Her expression, too wise and without any excitement or amusement, ate at Elisa.

Elisa didn't think of Rachel as particularly great at showing affection. She couldn't imagine Rachel taking care of someone in such an intimate way. "Not the most enjoyable existence."

"Her father died less than two years ago and left her everything, which is probably how she's financing her current lifestyle or con or whatever this is." Shelby shuffled some papers around. "Heart condition."

Elisa almost missed the throwaway comment. Her head shot up. "What?"

Shelby studied her notes. "He had dangerously high blood pressure. Looks like the medication couldn't control it. He went blind and, eventually, died of heart failure."

Blood pressure medicine.

That was one coincidence too many.

Chapter Fifty-Three

Fall blew into their part of Pennsylvania two days later. The end of September brought high winds and cold rain. The chill settled deep inside Elisa, but she didn't blame the weather. Josh and Rachel were home from their whirlwind wedding vacation and announced they were coming over for dinner.

Elisa hated the idea of entertaining guests. But the arrival of *these* guests had every nerve ending pinging. Dizzy and aching, exhausted from her inability to sleep and grieving for the marriage she thought she had, she dragged her body downstairs after changing out of her lounge clothes. Every muscle rioted at the idea of pulling on less informal clothing, but she forced it.

From the second she stepped into the kitchen Harris watched her. He'd been watching her ever since their big fight. Since then he talked and she listened. She didn't say much; keeping her body moving took most of her energy. And what did she say? He spoke as if he knew what was happening with Rachel and Josh, but he didn't. She didn't either but she knew the truth—neither of them was who they pretended to be.

"Elisa?" Harris called out to her in a soft voice as if he sensed she might explode if he talked any louder.

She had no interest in conversation. He'd made his position clear. She didn't know how to respond, so she didn't. Staying quiet seemed safer. He wanted acquiescence and harmony, no matter the price. She understood that now.

A rush of tears hit her out of nowhere, and she stepped into the pantry to hide them, pretending to look for her tea.

"Elisa, I want to—"

"Where's Nathan?" Inhaling deep, she forced her emotions back into a mental cage. She stepped out of the pantry, tea bag in hand. "I want to make sure he changed his clothes."

"I think we should talk."

His timing sucked. She had no intention of engaging. "We talk all the time."

"You know what I'm saying." He sounded more desperate than angry.

She picked up on his emotion but couldn't call up any of her own. "I already know your position on my mental health and ability to parent. You don't need to repeat it."

"I didn't mean—"

"Nathan?" A second after she called out he popped up in the kitchen.

"Hi!" Nathan sounded a bit like his regular self. Happy, well-adjusted, and excited about things.

They'd all been kicking around the house, moving at half speed and not showing much enthusiasm for anything. Like any kid, Nathan picked up on his parents' moods. She could barely muster a civil hello to Harris when he came home these days. He studied her as if he thought she'd shatter into pieces at any minute . . . which only made her angrier.

The bouts of sadness gave way to rage. She bounced back and forth, and not gently. More like flung from one end of the scale to the other. Rustling up even the littlest interest in anything was beyond her reach.

She fell back on pretending. She answered what needed to be answered but otherwise stayed silent. That guaranteed she never said the wrong thing. She held on, sucked it up . . . melted down only when alone.

Now she had to survive this ridiculous evening with people she wanted to turn over to the police and never see again. A celebration dinner for a woman with a manufactured identity and a man who had likely killed at least one wife. It was the nightmare-party scenario.

Elisa forced a smile for Nathan. "Nice shirt. Good job picking it out."

Nathan beamed. "Am I allowed to call Rachel Aunt Rachel?"

Elisa fought to keep standing. Maintaining a smile took almost all the energy she possessed. "You'll need to ask her."

"Nathan, can you give me a minute alone with your mom?" Harris asked.

Nathan rolled his eyes. "Sure."

That was the last thing she wanted. "I need to check on the food."

She went over to the oven, but Harris caught her before she could open it. She tried to step away, put some needed distance between them, but he held on to her.

"Everything is fine, Elisa."

The words grated across her nerves. Only someone not paying a bit of attention would spout that nonsense. She clamped her mouth shut to keep from screaming at him. "What do you need?"

That seemed to stump him for a second. "To explain."

She could see the strain on his face. Any other time she'd rush to take care of him, to make him feel better. She couldn't call up the will.

"I don't know what that means." She pulled out of his hold and went to the sink. Needing to keep her hands busy and mind occupied, she started making tea.

"This dinner—"

"I'll behave." Now she got it. He could skip the lecture. Actually, he could shove all his lectures. She forced herself to look at him. "That's your concern, right?"

He frowned. "What? No. Of course not."

"I'm guessing you're worried that I'll say something to upset Josh and Rachel. Well, I won't. We'll have a nice dinner without any problems from me."

His mouth hung open. "Okay, this isn't what I want."

"Obedience?" Probably not fair but she didn't care. He'd struck out at her and now she'd returned the favor.

He glanced at Nathan, who was perched on a chair, staring out the family room window, then swore under his breath. "When did I ever ask for that?"

Every damn day. Maybe not in words, but if her disagreeing or questioning led to this, then they were on very different sides. She feared they'd never breach the gap again.

She called up a reservoir of control. "Forget I said anything."

"I don't want it—us—to be like this."

Tough shit. The words flew through her mind but she never got the chance to say them. The front door opened and chaos descended. There were welcomes and raves about the rings. Josh and Rachel talked about the wedding.

They slid from predinner talk to dinner to dessert with relative ease. Through it all, Elisa moved food around on her plate and smiled when anyone glanced in her direction. She'd even managed not to flinch when Josh stood up to get more drinks during dinner and stopped to give her a quick hug.

Elisa only made it through the two hours thanks to Nathan. He was nonstop chatter. He wanted to know about Las Vegas. He'd read about a show with tigers and had about a hundred questions on that topic.

After the meal everyone lounged in the family room. Elisa used the opportunity to sneak into the kitchen alone, thinking to get a few minutes of breathing room, but Rachel followed her. She hovered, not talking at first, then she joined Elisa at the sink.

"Are you okay?" Rachel sounded concerned.

Elisa had to concentrate on not calling her Nina. The name stuck in her mind and was right there on her lips, but she managed not to mess up . . . yet. "Sure. Why wouldn't I be?"

"Elisa, you're upset. It's noticeable," Rachel whispered as she snuck peeks into the family room where the men and Nathan sat. "Did you two fight?"

Over you! "Harris was upset he missed his brother's wedding."

Rachel swore under her breath. "I'm sorry. It happened so fast."

She sounded genuine and concerned. Nothing about her or how she looked had changed, except for the impressive diamond on her finger, but Elisa saw a different person. Someone who lied and schemed and fooled her. Until she knew Rachel's endgame she'd be careful.

"Why did it happen at all?" Elisa asked.

She'd stepped into a disturbing game of cat and mouse. Round and round they went. Rachel acting concerned while being Concerned. She had to know Elisa would react to the revelation, that she'd draw conclusions and go searching. Not that the real name of Nina Robinson had been all that easy for Shelby to find . . . yet it wasn't exactly hidden either.

Rachel's expression and demeanor stayed the same—unreadable. "You need to know I have all of this handled."

Now they'd entered the *does she know I know* phase of the game.

Every minute in a room with Rachel and Josh sapped Elisa's strength. She felt the energy drain out of her. There wasn't any tension at this point because Elisa couldn't feel anything but blank.

Elisa understood Rachel's code on one level but the parts that remained mysterious scared the hell out of her. "What are you talking about?"

Rachel's eyes widened. "You heard what I said before we left for vacation, right? About . . . Concerned."

The remaining doubts, small as they were, about whether she'd created that conversation disappeared from Elisa's mind. She'd heard correctly. She wasn't losing it. Rachel was not who she claimed to be, and she'd stopped the act between them.

Elisa turned on the water, hoping to drown out any sound of their conversation that might linger. "Tell me your plan. Help me understand your choices."

"Not now." Rachel looked into the family room and met Josh's gaze. She winked at him.

Elisa managed not to vomit. "When?"

"Just know I'm on your side." Rachel touched Elisa's arm. "We're in this together."

Elisa stared at Rachel's new ring. "It feels like we're working against each other."

"That's how it needs to be right now." Rachel rushed her words. "And before you ask, you know what it's safe for you to know."

The cryptic conversation circled and dove but didn't go anywhere. The whole whispered exchange gave Elisa a headache. "If you tell me, I can help. I have resources."

It was a risk. If Rachel said yes, she might ask for something Elisa could never deliver. But the not knowing, the confusion and planning, kept Elisa off-balance. She hated the sensation. She also needed something concrete to give to Shelby. She knew Shelby would run with it and call her contacts, possibly call the police in sooner rather than later, but right now they only had pieces.

And then there was Josh. Her former sisterly affection for Josh had been wiped out. If her suspicions were right, he'd done unspeakable things. Evil things. And she'd be the one responsible for pointing a spotlight at him.

"Give me a little more time." Rachel shifted from touching to squeezing Elisa's arm. "It's almost over."

It? Elisa did a quick glance around and saw Harris and Josh locked in a serious conversation with Nathan about robots. She abandoned caution and dipped into the topic that mattered the most.

"Do you know where Abby is?" Elisa asked in a voice barely above a breath.

"Yes."

A gasp escaped before Elisa could pull it back in. "Is she okay?"

Rachel leaned in even closer. "He'll pay, Elisa. I promise."

Chapter Fifty-Four

The next morning Elisa left an emergency message for Shelby, who was in a meeting outside of her office. Elisa kept her mind busy and off Abby while waiting for a return call and engaging in the mundane job of hunting for a cat. She hadn't seen Fuzz all morning. Nathan whined about not being able to feed him before going to school and insisted Fuzz would starve. Apparently no one in the household thought she was capable these days.

No matter what she said she couldn't totally console Nathan. She promised to hunt the little black fluff ball down by the time he got home from school. Now she had to deliver on that assurance. The problem was Fuzz could hide all day by stuffing his body into some small space. In a historic house small spaces existed in every room.

One floor down and no signs of the cat. She gave up on the upstairs and ventured to the first floor. Turning the corner at the bottom of the staircase, she caught sight of a shadow in the window of the front door. If the doorbell had rung she'd missed it.

She wasn't in the mood for company. She'd become so

isolated and people averse that no one she knew stopped by these days. Well, except for Josh and Rachel, and they barged in without bothering to call or ring the bell.

She took another few steps and the shadow didn't move. A person stood out there. The realization probably should have scared her in light of everything else going on, but she felt more annoyed at being bothered than anything else.

Curiosity pulled at her. She peeked out the window on the side of the door. A woman in a raincoat, facing away from the front door. Not just any woman. Meredith.

The redhead.

Talk about nerve. Elisa threw open the door. "What do you want?"

Meredith jumped and let out a faint panicked sound. "I didn't mean . . . I've been standing . . ."

Meredith shuffled around, stammering. Hardly the same confident woman who spouted the *I've never heard of Josh* bullshit to Harris. But the pathetic act didn't work.

Elisa was done with this woman. "Let me guess, you're here by accident, and you still don't know who Josh is."

"I'm here because of him."

"Ah, so you changed your mind again." *Whatever.* "What do you want?"

Meredith twisted the belt of her raincoat in her hands. "May I come in?"

"No." Elisa had been forced to welcome too many liars into her house already.

Meredith glanced out at the empty street before answering. "Please. I don't feel safe standing out here."

"Your 'poor me' act needs work." Elisa held onto the edge of the door, keeping her body wedged in the opening in case Meredith got any ideas about storming the house.

"If you would just listen."

Elisa had run out of patience for this nonsense. "What game are you playing today? I'm having a hard time keeping up."

Meredith held the belt like a tourniquet, and the skin on her fingers turned chalky white. "I want to explain."

"When no one else is here? Convenient." Elisa stepped back and started to close the door. She intended to slam it, but Meredith slipped in too close.

"Elisa, please."

Through the angry haze filling her head, Elisa heard the pleading in Meredith's voice. She didn't understand it or the fidgeting. None of Meredith's uncertain behavior today fit with the woman she'd sparred with at the school or who had openly lied to Harris.

"Why in the world should I trust you in my house?" This was her last bit of sanctuary in the world, and even that only lasted until Harris got home.

"I know I haven't given you a reason to believe me, but I can't play this role any longer." Meredith put her hand on the door. "Please let me in."

Elisa glanced into the street behind Meredith and then to the driveaway. Only her car was parked there. "How did you get here?"

"I had a ride share drop me off a block away."

The answer didn't exactly earn Elisa's trust. "How do you know where I live?"

"I know everything about Josh. I've been . . ." She exhaled. "If you give me five minutes. That's all I need to explain."

A mental battle waged inside Elisa. Letting this stranger in wouldn't be smart. Meredith could be dangerous. She'd already shown that she didn't deserve the benefit of the doubt.

But . . . why was there always a *but*? Elisa's mind had shut down after the fight with Harris. She just wanted to be left alone to sleep. Then Meredith arrived.

Elisa studied her, looking for any sign to direct her about the right thing to do. She watched true crime shows. She knew how this scenario ended in those. She'd yelled at the television more than once as she watched someone willingly invite a killer into their home.

Now, being on this side, it felt different. She'd worked with Keith, the man who killed Maxine, and had known he was not okay. The hospital tried to hide the facts and all the warning signs, but he'd made threats. He did nothing to hide his rage and disgust. He failed in his position and blamed Marian. The situation here wasn't the same, but Elisa wanted to believe she'd recognize evil when it stood right in front of her.

As her mind rebelled, she stepped back and gestured for Meredith to come inside. "You have five minutes, and I can revoke those at any time."

Meredith dropped her belt and shoved her hands in her coat pockets as she walked inside the house. "Okay . . . I . . . what are you doing?"

Elisa snapped two photos of Meredith with her cell phone and sent them to Shelby with a quick note of explanation.

"Texting people to let them know you're here. Not Josh, but people who will know what to do."

"Why?"

"Why do you think?" Elisa made a show of checking the clock on her phone. "Four minutes."

"Okay, you were right. I didn't lie before. Josh and I . . . we were together while he was with Abby. It started as sex on the side. No commitment. Fun without ties." She let out a long sigh. "He said Abby withheld sex whenever she got angry. He hated that. Said it was like making him beg for it."

This was far more insight than Elisa ever wanted into Josh's practiced lines and dating skills. "And for some reason that juvenile reaction made you want more?"

"She was this artist type and not really supportive of his goals." Meredith moved around, not pacing but not standing still. Very jumpy and uncomfortable. "He said they were too different and she didn't really understand him. They were both unhappy."

Elisa rolled her eyes. She couldn't help it. Men had been delivering that lame line forever. "Please tell me you didn't fall for that nonsense."

"He had this thing. Like, a vulnerability. I went from wanting sex to wanting to comfort him."

Except for the sex part, Elisa could relate. She'd met Josh and felt a protective surge.

"The way Josh talked about his parents and losing them. How much he missed them and how his life fell apart." Meredith stopped to take a deep breath. "I can't really explain it except to say, he makes you want to be with him. He's been through awful things and was really empathetic. He's also really attentive and listens. Even in the beginning, when it was just sex, he didn't forget things that were important to me."

"But he did forget he had a fiancée." Fidelity mattered to Elisa and it made her antsy when it didn't matter to other people. They could do whatever they wanted in their relationships but she had a line that couldn't be crossed.

"Even when he talked about Abby . . . it's just . . . " Meredith sighed. "He would say he made a mistake and jumped too fast. He'd been lonely. Missed being in a relationship. Talked about his wife's awful accident."

"Which wife?"

Meredith stopped shifting her weight around. "What?"

So, he hid Lauren from Meredith, too. Seemed he spent a lifetime forgetting Lauren, which made Elisa ache for justice for Lauren, too. "Nothing. Go ahead."

"You're married so you might not understand this, but it's rough out there. Dating is just . . . awful. You see this guy who has his life together and loves his brother and you. He talks about his nephew and doing things together. It's refreshing. It's easy to be drawn to that."

"He used my son as a dating tool?" *Of course he did. The asshole.*

"The point is we had something, or I thought we did." Meredith rubbed her forehead, her expression looking just as pained as it had when she'd started this story. "Then Abby left. He had all these excuses and said that's the type of person she was, which made sense at first . . ."

"But then?"

"He immediately stopped talking about her. It was like he was . . ." Meredith shrugged. "I don't know the right word. Relieved she was gone?"

The words sat there, confirming every doubt and fear that had been percolating inside Elisa since Abby disappeared.

"I thought we'd be together then, but he said it would look suspect. People would think he did something to Abby if they knew he was cheating on her."

Elisa had the exact thought as Meredith said it. "Uh, yeah."

Buzz, the tabby cat, wound its way around Elisa's feet. It meowed and rubbed and generally begged for attention. Not the usual cat behavior for Buzz but Elisa ignored it.

"We were still together then he started canceling dates. I followed him and saw the new woman. It was obvious he was dating—"

"Rachel?" Elisa moved her legs apart so it was easier for Buzz to walk in between them.

"Yes. The relationship came out of nowhere and he was showing her off to you guys. Acting like moving on and dating someone new wasn't a big deal, despite what he'd told me. I confronted him and he denied it at first, but he stopped calling. Stopped . . . wanting anything from me." The anger rose in Meredith's voice the longer she talked about the new relationship.

"You've been following him."

"I didn't know what went wrong." Meredith stopped to take a deep breath. "I admit, at first I was going to tell everyone about us. Ruin him by getting the police's attention. I didn't care, but then I started to think about Abby and his behavior. I became convinced something terrible happened to her and worried he'd somehow blame me."

Elisa couldn't process the *how* behind that last part right now. Letting thoughts about Abby into her head would derail her, and she needed to be on her game until she ushered Meredith out of the house. "Why stalk me? Why lie about everything to Harris?"

"Josh can't stand to disappoint Harris."

Buzz's meowing grew louder at Elisa's feet. "I'm aware."

"He will lie and twist things, lash out and—" Meredith came to an abrupt stop then started again. "I was following the two of you, you and your husband, to try to figure out what you knew about Abby and the new girlfriend. When Josh found out about our run-in at the school, he was livid. I'd never seen him like that. He said awful things. So personal and untrue. He told me to fix the mess and act as if you'd made it all up."

Elisa gave up and picked up the cat. She didn't break eye contact with Meredith but rubbed her hand over Buzz to make sure he wasn't injured. "Why?"

Meredith stared at the cat for a few seconds before answering. "He said he needed to discredit you. He thinks you're looking into Abby's disappearance. He's convinced you'll mess up his life and get the police looking closer at him. If you start talking, he wants to be able to tell people you need help."

That fit with every one of Elisa's theories about Josh's recent behavior. "Why are you really here today?"

"I kept thinking about your husband and what I said in the parking lot. Your expression . . ." Meredith's own stark expression mirrored the roughness of her voice. "Well, I couldn't do it. Not for Josh. He doesn't deserve that kind of help from me."

"Okay." Elisa didn't believe Meredith had a burst of conscience, but fine.

Meredith's information was shocking but not surprising. Horrible but not hard to imagine. Every word she said about Josh made sense. He'd morphed from surviving a tragedy to using the telling of it to lure women. So many smart women got sucked in, wanted to save him. And he destroyed them.

"What else do I need to know?" It took all of the energy Elisa possessed to ask the question. She appreciated the validation, but she really didn't think she could take much more.

Meredith shook her head. "I shouldn't have played along. Hell, I should never have gotten involved with him."

Elisa shook her head at the understatement. "You're clearly not alone. He must sell his sad tale pretty well."

"Well, now you know all of it."

But what did that get her other than the confirmation that she needed to be careful? "Lucky me."

"One more thing." Meredith moved in a little closer. "I really do think he killed Abby. He never said it, but he implied it when he got angry. Told me to be careful because I wouldn't like to see him furious."

Elisa showed Meredith out and checked her phone. She noticed Shelby had texted back. Seven times, growing increasingly more concerned with each one.

Elisa was about to reply, reassuring Shelby, but stopped to

look down at Buzz. "What is wrong with you? It's like you're a guard cat."

Buzz took off running down the hall. He still made noises, and a terrible thought hit Elisa. Fuzz could be hurt. She knew it was ridiculous, but she could not handle anything terrible happening to the cats. Not today on top of everything else.

She forced her legs to move and went in the direction Buzz ran. The scratching noise gave him away. He was in Harris's office, rubbing back and forth against the bookcase. Specifically, the movable section that led to the secret room.

She heard a faint meowing sound, and not from Buzz.

"What the hell?" Without thinking, she rushed over and pulled on the tiny lever hidden behind the second book.

With a click the door unlocked. She pulled it open and Fuzz darted out of the secret room. Ran right into her. She picked him up and tried to calm the furball down. "How did you get in there?"

Another voice boomed through the room. "I'm afraid that was my fault."

Elisa spun around. "Rachel?"

"Thanks for not installing that alarm system while we were in Las Vegas. That would have made this very difficult."

Chapter Fifty-Five

Elisa slowly set the cat down. Everything about this situation screamed *danger*. She tried to fake her way through it until her groggy mind could come up with a better tactic. "I didn't know you were coming over today."

"I thought Josh's ex would never leave." Rachel stood at the doorway to the hall. "She's something else, isn't she? Totally committed to him even though he treated her like crap."

All Elisa could see was the knife in Rachel's hand. It looked like one from the kitchen butcher block. That made keeping her voice steady even harder. "You know about Meredith?"

"Of course. I've studied Josh for a long time." Rachel tapped the side of the knife against her dress pants. "The poor thing actually thought he loved her."

"It sounds like they dated." Elisa was just saying nonsense now. Anything to stall.

Rachel scoffed. "That's an overly romantic and childish way of putting it. They had sex. He moved on. She stalked him. Period. It's a shame she involved you."

Elisa thought the same thing. "Meredith thinks he did something to Abby."

"Yet, she would take him back if he snapped his fingers." Rachel shook her head. "So weak."

That knife still was right there. Elisa shifted, thinking if she could get to the desk there might be a pen or a stapler— anything she could use as a makeshift weapon. "Why are you here?"

"I mirrored Josh's phone. Meredith texted him and told him she was coming clean with you. I was already at your house, thank goodness. I can run interference." Rachel shrugged, as if she was having a conversation with herself. "The timing is a bit fast. My plan was not to do this for another few weeks. Let some time pass between the wedding and the big finish, but I can make it work."

This was new. Since they met Elisa had never known Rachel to ramble. That's where they were now. On some meandering thread that Elisa didn't understand. "You lost me."

Rachel rolled her eyes. "It's a convoluted mess. Blame your homicidal brother-in-law."

"Happy to." Elisa thought of Josh as a killer. Hearing that he was from someone else should have been validating, but not under these circumstances.

Rachel leaned against the doorway, looking all casual but still keeping a firm hold on that knife. "Basically, because of Meredith's flare-up of morality, Josh will now feel obligated to come here. Or mess with you. Or do something to you, and I can't have that."

Elisa barely heard the words. She was too busy fighting through the darkness that threatened to envelop her and shut down her body. The anxiety flowing through her clouded her vision. Made it hard for her to read clues and think clearly, but she pushed on.

Through the emotional battering and blinding fear, she continued to look around for something that might have a chance against that knife, sneaking glances here and there, all while trying to drag Rachel's attention to any other topic. "You're protecting me?"

"Nothing so altruistic, I'm afraid. But I think what you really should be asking is why your cat was in the secret room."

That was only one of about a million questions floating in and out of Elisa's brain. "Fine. Answer that."

"Your snooping started all this." Rachel let out a harsh laugh. "You just had to dig around in Josh's closet and find the duffel and create a mess. Until then you were quiet. At home healing and out of my way. Taking your meds and not causing a problem, except for an occasional call to the police to ask about the investigation."

"You know about that?" That surprised Elisa.

Rachel shrugged. "I studied all of you. Looked at your phones. Called the police and pretended to be you."

Damn. "What?"

"I figured if I called and was annoying they'd stop taking your calls and leave you in voicemail." Rachel's eyebrow lifted as if to say her plan had worked. "But the bag and all those other items? I planted those for the police to find at the end, not you."

Elisa saw it now. The long-term planning. The checking and double-checking. She didn't understand why or how, but this was all aimed at Josh and she'd gotten in the way. "The end?"

Rachel droned on as if Elisa hadn't asked the question. "The sweatshirt. The books. The laptop. All that searching through Abby's social media to find the right pieces. It took me forever and I only needed one more thing. Something personal, like a nightgown, that I could tear. Show the violence. Plant more doubts about Josh."

Despite the waves of fear smashing into her, Elisa kept up with her end of the conversation just fine. "Why not buy one?"

"DNA." Rachel shot Elisa a look that basically said *come on*. "I wanted the obvious hook to Abby, but Josh got rid of all of her things. Then you took what I collected, so I had to hunt it all down. I've been coming to your house at night, trying to figure out where you put it all. The secret room made sense."

Elisa shifted her feet, not making any noise. "You broke in and staged it to look like Meredith."

"Her stalking made her an easy target. I knew you'd fall for it."

Elisa picked up on the change in Rachel's voice. It had taken on a darker, more sarcastic tone. "Right. That sounds like me."

"I made a copy of Josh's key. Hell, sometimes I just took his." Rachel shook her head. "He can be oblivious."

Desperate to keep Rachel's attention focused on her, Elisa rushed out a response. "That's the Josh I know."

"Stop moving, Elisa. We're not going to do battle." Rachel dropped her arm to her side again, no longer holding the knife as if she intended to lunge. "Not the two of us."

That response didn't make Elisa feel one bit surer she'd survive whatever came next. Her knees buckled and she grabbed onto the edge of the desk to stay on her feet.

Rachel frowned. "What's wrong with you?"

"If you want to hurt Josh so much, why try to make me look unhinged?" Elisa asked.

"I needed to make Josh think I believed him."

It was an all-out assault, coming at her from all sides. That explained why Elisa felt so hunted and overwhelmed. "You worked with him against me."

She took a mental inventory. *Lamp. Desk phone. A few heavy books.* She had no qualms about throwing one or all of them at Rachel now.

"I admit I stoked his hatred of you. Told him you were talking about him and talking with the police. Hiring an investigator." Rachel sighed. "Problem was, you were poking around. Going to his work, following me, checking his story. That attack on Meredith at the school? I didn't see that coming. Also never thought you'd hire an investigator against your own family."

Elisa estimated the number of steps she'd need to pounce. "Me either."

"I couldn't afford to let you mess up my plan. I've been working on this for a year. But you going against Josh, taking a run at him face-to-face did end up helping me, so thank you." Rachel smiled, looking like the old supportive Rachel she'd pretended to be. "He was too focused on you to realize I was the one he should be afraid of."

Elisa fought for breath. Her airways shut down and her lungs ached.

"The trick with the storage unit?" Rachel made a *tsk-tsk*ing sound. "So easy. He lapped that up. Anything to make people question you."

Elisa needed Rachel engaged and talking but part of her wanted to yell *shut up!*

"And you played right along in demeaning me," Elisa said, fully understanding the role she'd been duped into playing.

"Only to the extent his schemes helped me."

Josh tried to dismantle her life. Take away her security and stability. Twist and turn until she didn't trust her own mind. And Rachel handed him the ammunition to do it.

Elisa hated both of them. They hadn't just rattled her. They'd destroyed the foundations of her life. Took away what mattered and made her question everything, including her own eyes. Worse, they weren't done. They were still hanging around, threatening her in her own home.

"What is your plan here, Nina? That's your real name, right? Nina Robinson."

Rachel's satisfied expression disappeared. "You've been busy."

"I've had some extra time."

"I like you," Rachel said as her gaze traveled around the room before landing back on Elisa. "The men in this family underestimate you. Josh thinks he can rip you apart and then put you back together once he's sure you won't cause him trouble. And your husband? He doesn't appreciate you."

Elisa balled her hands into fists and dug her fingernails into her palms. The sting gave her mind something to focus on other than fear and anger.

It sounded like Rachel wanted an argument and Elisa refused to give it. "Let me worry about Harris."

"It's better you know now. I gotta say, it's painful to hear you talk about him. The things you said, how you praised him, bordered on hero worship. Realizing he takes you for granted, puts you second to Josh, this was the wake-up call you needed." Rachel gave a little fake bow. "You're welcome."

Elisa had never wanted to punch another human being as much as she did right now. "No offense but you're probably not the person I'd go to for marriage advice."

"You know I'm right."

"Elisa?" Josh's voice echoed through the otherwise quiet house.

"Look who's here." Rachel rolled her eyes. "He's so predictable."

Now Elisa had to battle two of them. She didn't love those odds. "What now?"

"Now we end this." Rachel kept the knife by her side and gestured with her other arm for Elisa to step into the hallway. "Go."

She went, dragging her feet, trying to think of a way out of this disaster while also hoping whatever Josh had planned wouldn't happen here. The idea of Nathan finding her—seeing her dead and bleeding—made her physically sick.

Elisa walked into the kitchen. "I didn't know you were coming today."

Josh stood by the sink, helping himself to a drink of water. He turned to face her then his gaze slipped behind her. "Rachel?"

"Hey, honey." Rachel moved beside Elisa with the knife still in her hand. "It's time."

Chapter Fifty-Six

Rachel planned all of this. Befriended her, claimed to be an ally, played with her emotions. The realization hit Elisa like a slap.

"What are you doing here?" Josh asked, still looking directly at Rachel.

Rachel smiled. "Surprise."

The tension ratcheted up in the room. The walls pressed in and the air grew thin. The choking sensation filled Elisa. *Backstabbing. Double-crossing. Lying.*

"What's going on?" Josh looked from Rachel to Elisa. "I'm confused."

Elisa couldn't stand his smug face. "You already know Meredith came to see me. The ex you claim isn't an ex."

His gaze shot to Rachel. "I know that looks bad, but I can explain."

Always looking for an angle, searching for a way to duck responsibility. He'd lied and convinced Meredith to lie, and his only thought was to bury his behavior so Rachel didn't see it. He was pathetic and clueless.

Elisa didn't know if he'd missed the knife in Rachel's hand, but he clearly didn't understand what was happening here. Still, Elisa couldn't muster any sympathy for him. "You always have an excuse ready."

Josh started walking around the kitchen island toward them. "What's wrong with you?"

"You should have seen how excited he was to make your life miserable, Elisa. He jumped at the chance. Kept coming up with new ways to break you down," Rachel said. "He never said it, but it all came from fear. If you were believable, if you got stronger and threw doubts on Abby leaving on her own, then people might listen to you. You could make life difficult for him. Uncover his secrets."

Josh froze.

Elisa understood. "Because if people believed me, they might do their jobs and look closer at his past."

"Exactly." Energy thrummed off Rachel. She sounded wound up and ready. "They could find the trail of dead women. He couldn't let you get there, couldn't let his precious brother, Harris, lose faith in him. Couldn't lose everything. After all, he'd killed to get what he had."

Some of the color left Josh's face. "What are you doing?"

Elisa could see Rachel moving. Slow and with small steps, she inched closer to Josh. Elisa was about to call out when Rachel answered him.

"Ending this."

"Okay, wait a second." Josh shook the glass in his hand in what looked like a nervous gesture. "I clearly walked in on something strange. Like, a really bad joke."

He still wasn't getting it, and Elisa couldn't take his not knowing for one more second. "Open your eyes and see that your newest wife is holding a knife."

"I am." Rachel brought it up just high enough for everyone to see. "Put the glass down."

Rachel's rhythmic voice echoed through Elisa. She tried to block it out, find something else to focus on.

The other knives.

Elisa looked at the empty slot in the block and the ones still there. They were near the stove and not anywhere near her. She'd have to get around Rachel or vault over the kitchen island to get to them. Josh was closer but him grabbing them wouldn't help her.

Josh set the glass down. He kept going and took off his suit jacket. "This isn't funny, Rachel."

"It's hysterical, actually." Rachel held the knife perfectly still, as if she'd been waiting for this moment her entire life and would take care not to mess it up. "You, thinking you can destroy people's lives and walk away from them without even a scar? That's not happening. Not this time."

Elisa needed Josh and Rachel to focus on each other and leave her out of it, but she knew she'd be collateral damage in whatever battle fallout happened next. She tried to draw their attention as she conducted a mental inventory of the drawers closest to her. There should be scissors.

"Does he know who you really are?" Elisa asked Rachel as she thought through where she dumped the scissors the last time she used them to open a box.

Rachel didn't even look at her. "Don't help."

"Wait." For the first time Josh looked like he understood his plan had flipped upside down. "Who is she?"

"Lauren's sister." Elisa hoped that bit of information would keep them preoccupied. She fought through wave after wave of dizziness as her mind jumped around, looking for a solution. A heavy pan. She needed the one that would cause the most damage.

"She didn't have . . ." Josh blinked a few times as his attention centered on Rachel. "You know about Lauren?"

"Everybody knows Lauren. Lauren's perfect." Rachel practically spit out the words. "I heard about her every damn day of my life from the time I turned eleven. Lauren was so smart. Lauren was beautiful. She was the talented one. The one with potential." Rachel said the words in a singsong voice. "The only one *she* cared about."

Josh flinched. "'She'?"

Cast iron. Elisa knew that would give her the best chance. Now she just had to remember where she stored it. Until then, she'd stall by pitting Josh against Rachel. A perfect match.

"I believe she's referring to Lauren's mom, Allyson." Elisa gestured toward Rachel. "Meet Nina Robinson. The daughter of the man Lauren's mom married."

"She was supposed to love me, but she didn't have room. Just like my mom, Allyson ignored me. Abandoned me. I was in the same house and she looked at me with disgust. Locked the door to my room and said I was uncontrollable." Rachel shook her head as if trying to block out the images playing in there. "My father blamed me. He said I made my mom leave. That I wasn't lovable, but I had a second chance with Allyson.

Then she . . . I was never good enough. I didn't like the same things as Lauren. I didn't look like her, enjoy the outdoors and animals like her."

Elisa felt this going sideways, into danger territory. "Rachel—"

"As if any of that was my fault." Rachel lifted her hands to her ears. The knife sliced through the air. "So much pain and none of it would have happened if you hadn't killed Lauren."

Josh's eyes widened and his face drained of all color. "How the hell is your upbringing my fault?"

"If Lauren had been there we would have been a family. I would have had a sister to love me and protect me. But you destroyed that. You killed her and stole my one chance at having a family." Rachel seemed lost, locked in memories that only she could see. "And then I had to take care of him. Allyson was long gone and no one else wanted him. He hated me, told me the end to both of his marriages was my fault, and I had to feed him. Watch after him."

Josh swore under his breath. "What the hell is going on here?"

The question seemed to snap Rachel out of her emotional windstorm. A calmness washed over her. Elisa found this scarier than the ranting.

"This, Josh, is your life unraveling." Rachel stepped closer to him. "Not Elisa's, yours."

Josh lifted both hands. "Okay, we can work this out."

"Do you think that usually works for him? That soothing, let's-be-rational voice?" Rachel asked Elisa without breaking eye contact with Josh.

Elisa didn't see any harm in answering. "Apparently." More like *always*, but who was counting.

Josh turned to Elisa. "Sis, come on. You know me."

The begging. Elisa knew they'd get there. Josh would rationalize and plead, try to win Elisa over despite all he'd done to ruin her life. They'd come full circle in their relationship. Back to the point where Josh pretended to need her and tried to win her over. All thanks to the knife in Rachel's hand.

"You literally attempted to drive her to the point where Harris would commit her," Rachel said. "We joked about it."

Josh shook his head. "That's not true."

But Elisa knew it was. The words threw her off stride for a second.

Josh and Rachel stood on opposite sides of the kitchen island. Rachel, unblinking and in full control. She sounded at ease and ready. Josh kept scanning the room. More than once he looked at the glass he'd set down.

He better not throw it. Elisa doubted that would end well. "You let her in my house to poison me with someone else's medicine." She looked at Rachel. "Your father's pills, I assume."

Rachel shrugged. "I think I misjudged the amount, but it helped that you were a tea drinker. Just throw that box in the pantry away or you'll continue to get sick."

"Stop talking." Josh slammed a hand against the counter. "You poisoned Elisa?"

"Admittedly, my mistake. I needed her docile and unaware so I could search the house, but I didn't know how it would affect her."

That explained at least some of the dizziness and dragging exhaustion. Elisa knew her mental state had provided a path that made all of this easier, sped up her downfall. At least she had confirmation she'd been drugged. She hadn't forgotten medicine or taken the wrong pills, or whatever Harris thought. She'd been attacked in an intimate and horrifying way.

"Enough of this." Josh slipped his cell out of his pocket. "I'm calling—"

"Really?" Elisa couldn't believe he thought that would work. Rachel *held a knife*.

"Do. Not. Move." Rachel shifted around the side of the island and stood next to Elisa again. So close to Josh. To doing more than wielding that knife.

Josh's mouth dropped open. "You're insane."

"Stop throwing that word around." Rachel grabbed Elisa's right arm and held her steady. "You have two seconds to tell the truth about Lauren."

He shook his head. "There's nothing to tell."

Liar. Elisa knew for sure in that moment. Oh, he tried to hide it and continue playing the game, but his reaction when talking about Lauren came off as shaky. His body hinted that whatever was happening in his head was messy.

"Josh, she's serious." Elisa's arm ached from Rachel's tight grip. "Just tell the truth."

He continued to shake his head but his voice bobbled this time. "It was an accident. There's a police report."

"Did your detective friend cover Lauren's death up for you, too?" Elisa felt a surge of satisfaction when Josh froze. All of his secrets were coming out now.

Rachel dragged Elisa closer to Josh. Pinned him with his back against the counter with the sink. "You killed her."

"That's not true." He swallowed.

"I've seen the evidence." Rachel's voice kept up a steady drumbeat. "You are a liar."

"Let's sit down and talk about this." Elisa forgot about stalling and weapons. She wanted to survive and that meant tamping down the heat flowing between Josh and Rachel. They volleyed comments back and forth, talking past each other, and with each turn, every step, the energy vibrating off Rachel turned darker.

Rachel shook Elisa's arm. "Stop protecting the mediocre men in this family."

Rachel was going to do it. Stab him.

Elisa didn't think, she just shifted until her body shielded Josh's. "Don't do this."

Josh tried to push her away. "Elisa, get back."

It was too late. The blade sliced into Elisa's left arm. The same arm that had been injured in the shooting.

She saw the tip and watched it sink into her flesh, cutting her from elbow to wrist. At first she felt numb. Shock radiated through her right before the screaming pain hit. Her skin had been flayed open until she thought she saw bone.

Her stomach heaved and she saw red everywhere she looked. Her legs gave out. Josh caught her as she stumbled, pulling her body against his and holding her up.

"Oh, shit." He repeated the phrase over and over.

"Look what you made me do!" Rachel's scream bounced off every wall.

Elisa didn't have time for blame. Blood gushed from her arm and a sudden light-headedness made the room spin. If Rachel meant to deliver a shallow slice, she'd failed.

"Towel." Elisa forced the word out as bile rushed up her throat. "Get a towel."

Josh jostled her as he tried to hold her steady and grab for a towel. The room shifted and a sudden booming headache had Elisa's vision blinking out.

"Tell the truth!" Rachel kept screaming. "She'll bleed out, or do you not care at all?"

Josh lost his balance and their bodies shifted. Elisa was sure they'd fall to the floor but he caught them in time.

Blood soaked the towel. A choking sensation clawed at Elisa's throat. She'd never been good with blood but the sudden pressure drop made it feel as if every bit of energy was draining from her limp body. "Josh, please. Just tell Rachel about what happened to Lauren."

He shook his head as he fumbled with the towel on her arm. "It was an accident."

"Get out of the way, Elisa." Rachel grabbed Elisa's uninjured arm and tried to tug her loose from Josh's grip.

Elisa felt the pull through her entire body. It was as if something inside her broke and snapped off. "Josh, tell her!"

She was going to throw up. She counted and closed her eyes—anything to keep from falling or fainting.

Rachel smiled. "I will kill you both and not care."

Elisa barely heard Rachel's new threat. She hoped Josh did. "Tell her before she does it."

Rachel nodded. "Listen to your sister-in-law."

Panic rose through the chaos. Elisa couldn't force another word out. Her body betrayed her and her muddled mind refused to focus. Blood made the floor slick and covered Josh's hands.

Still, he whined and denied. "I can't."

"Then she's dead." Rachel looked ready to lunge again, this time aiming for Elisa's stomach.

"Stop!" He braced an elbow against the counter and held them both upright.

Elisa could feel Josh's body shake behind her. His gasping rattled in her ears. Her whole body seemed to melt.

His voice rang out loud and clear. "I killed Lauren."

Chapter Fifty-Seven

Elisa couldn't breathe. Couldn't think. Josh's words didn't offer apology and didn't deliver relief. She still stood there, half off her feet and slipping into unconsciousness, bleeding out in the middle of her kitchen.

"Say all of it." Elisa wanted this over.

"It really was an accident," Josh said in a voice that had lost all emotion.

Rachel's jaw clenched. "Stop using that word."

"We were camping and we'd been . . . we were . . . fighting." Josh stumbled through his words, racing through some and hesitating on others. "We wanted different things. We'd gotten married so young."

"Keep going." Rachel grabbed a clean towel and held it out to Josh.

He wrapped this towel around the blood-soaked one on Elisa's arm as he spoke. "It was late and we fought. She stormed out of the tent and I followed her."

He kept drawing this out. Elisa didn't have much strength left. She needed for him to make his admission, then they'd deal with whatever price Rachel thought he should pay. "Tell her. She deserves to know."

"We were yelling . . . because . . . well, that's how we were. Passionate."

Rachel made a furious groaning sound. "Spare me."

"She tripped and—"

"No, don't." Elisa knew that was wrong. Knew with every damaged and depleted part of her. "Josh, do not try to make this better. The truth."

"I thought . . . I didn't . . ." He nodded as he tightened his hold on her wound. "I pushed her and she fell back. Her head slammed into a tree." A new surge of red seeped through his fingers and he seemed lost as he looked at it. "There was blood everywhere. I panicked."

"Because you're weak." Rachel almost spit the words at him.

"I loved her."

Rachel held the point of the knife in front of his face. "Do not ever say that again."

His fingers dug into Elisa's arm, likely trying to stem the bleeding. Her whole body ached. Every time she moved her head a new shot of pain seared through her. Her mind got more muddled the longer Josh held her there.

"How did Lauren end up in the water?" Elisa asked when she could no longer support her own weight and his hold eased. She was sure she'd fall on the floor soon. "Josh?"

"I . . . I . . . just . . . put her in the water."

"Josh. Oh my God." Elisa didn't know she'd said the words out loud until she felt Josh brace behind her.

"She was dead." Josh looked at Elisa then at Rachel, as if willing them to believe him.

"She wasn't." Through all the pain and fear Elisa knew that statement was a lie. She didn't need a confession because she could *feel* it. "The proof is in the report. There was water in her lungs. She was alive when she went into the water."

"No . . . that can't . . . I didn't feel a pulse."

Elisa could almost see the events as they happened. "You held her under. You hit her and wanted to make sure she was dead . . . you hid the evidence in the water."

"I . . . I didn't expect . . ." He was swallowing and fidgety, his whole body one nervous ball of unspent energy. "I wanted to make it look like she fell in but then she opened her eyes and started kicking."

Elisa felt a rush of heat through her body. She fought not to throw up. "You drowned her because you didn't want her to wake up and accuse you."

"And you still had the presence of mind to make it look like an accident and save yourself because you are a lying piece of shit," Rachel said in a flat tone.

Elisa wanted to push away, not let him touch her, but she needed him right now. "You didn't call for help after you pushed her, when she was still alive, even though Harris was right there."

Josh shook his head. "I couldn't let him know. He thought we got married too soon and . . ."

"You killed her," Rachel said. "And ruined my life."

He was sobbing now. Half pleading and half crying. His

body trembled as he shook his head. "I never meant . . . please . . . I loved—"

The word sent a new shock of panic through Elisa. It was almost as if he was daring Rachel to kill him. "Rachel, Nina—whatever you want me to call you—he admitted it. You got what you wanted."

Rachel shook her head. "I want to destroy him. Dismantle his life. Ruin his reputation. Take everything."

Elisa blinked, trying to hold on as her body started to shut down. "He'll confess to the police. This will change everything. I'll make sure. Josh, tell her you will say it to the police and then tell them where Abby is."

"Not good enough." Pure rage showed on Rachel's face. "He's going to keep screwing women. Killing them. Rampaging their lives and destroying their confidence and will."

Elisa lost control of her head. It lolled back, rolling against his shoulder. She fought to stay coherent. "No, that's not true."

"After what he just said you still defend him?" Rachel shouted the question.

"There's been enough damage." Elisa could hear her words slur. "Please. I need to get to a hospital."

It happened in one step. Rachel moved in, pushing Elisa to the side, and stabbed Josh. One slice to his stomach. Elisa knew the second it happened because his arms dropped and her body slid.

"No!" The scream echoed in her head. Elisa had no idea if she'd said it out loud.

She was on the floor now. She fell and landed on her injured arm. Tears ran down her face as the throbbing morphed into a pain that had her gasping. She shifted but couldn't go anywhere because Josh sprawled next to her on the floor, bleeding with his body moving in time with his short panting breaths.

Rachel crouched down. "If you live, you go to jail. If you die, you die. And as a bonus, I took everything. I married you and took every dime. I had planned to take your house, too, but I had to rush the ending."

"Rachel . . ." Elisa whispered the name as the room tilted. "He needs an ambulance."

"So?" Rachel scoffed. "He's no longer my problem."

Elisa closed her eyes. When she opened them again, she tried to look up but couldn't. Rachel's shoes tapped against the floor as she walked around their still bodies toward the back door. It opened and she was gone.

They were going to die there.

"Elisa." Josh's arms were stretched out in front of him. His bloody palms were open toward the ceiling.

Phone . . . something about a phone. Elisa strained to remember. "Don't say anything. Just breathe."

He'd had a cell. Did she?

"I didn't mean . . ." His breathing sounded more like a gurgle now.

"You did. You totally meant it."

"Elisa!"

"Where are you?"

Elisa was pretty sure she was hallucinating. She tried to separate out the voices yelling in her head. The first, Harris.

Strong but panicked. The second . . . Shelby. But that couldn't be right. She wouldn't be with Harris. They didn't know each other.

Footsteps. Running. Then Harris's voice again. "Call an ambulance."

"Already did," Shelby said as she kneeled in front of Elisa.

Elisa had the sensation of being lifted off Josh. She cried out from the pain.

"I'm so sorry. Are you okay?" Harris's panicked voice.

"No." Elisa gave in to the adrenaline crash and the dizziness, the spinning and the nausea, and passed out.

Chapter Fifty-Eight

Elisa bounced in and out of consciousness. When she finally woke up even her bones ached. She felt drained and thirsty. Machines beeped around her. The scent of cleaning fluid made her cough.

She felt a hand in her good one and looked over to see Harris. He sat at her bedside with a pained expression. His features pulled tight as he rubbed his thumb over the back of her hand. The gesture made her smile. After everything, all the loss, it still brought comfort.

She drifted back out without saying a word.

She woke again, this time to the sound of talking. She opened her eyes and saw Harris standing across the room, talking to a man she didn't recognize. Shelby was there, animated and arguing about something.

Elisa's arm ached. It hurt to shift and wiggle her fingers. She tried to move her head, to call out and get the attention of the people less than ten feet away, but her body gave out. She wanted to say something . . . something about Josh and Rachel, but her mind went black and she fell back asleep.

The next time she woke up a nurse was fussing over her. Her head wasn't as fuzzy. The dizziness, after what seemed like weeks, finally had eased. She could move her head without wanting to throw up and the light no longer made her squint.

She glanced down at her arm. It was wrapped in a thick bandage. She tried to move her fingers and sighed in relief when that worked.

"You're awake."

Elisa didn't recognize the voice but glanced up and saw the nurse. Watched her smile. "My husband?"

"Ran down to get coffee." The nurse winked. "We had to force him. That man has been plastered to your side."

She couldn't think about that. "My son?"

"He hasn't been in, but we've heard about him." She pointed at a piece of paper taped to the wall with a lopsided crayon-drawn picture of a dinosaur on it. "He did that for you."

Some things never changed. He might be growing and getting older, but he was still her little boy. Knowing his life ticked on as usual made her smile.

The nurse took her temperature and promised to call in the doctor. It was another five minutes before the woman stopped fussing.

Elisa asked the question she dreaded to know the answer to. "How's my brother-in-law?"

"He's in the room next door. We shifted things around to make it easier for your husband to visit both of you."

Of course. Harris had to be with Josh. Some things changed and others never did. Elisa couldn't even call up tears. She just wanted to go home and hug Nathan. Sleep and sit in her yard, enjoying the last bits of warmth before late fall and cold settled in.

Harris slipped into the room without saying a word. He waited until the nurse left to approach the bed. His steps looked careful and a bit wary. "How are you feeling?"

She'd been there two days. She knew because she got a peek at the nurse's chart.

"I want to go home." She blocked out visions of the kitchen and the blood. Tried not to think about how awful the cleanup must have been.

Harris stood there, holding his takeout coffee cup. "The doctor said tomorrow."

"Really?" She feared it would be a long, drawn-out process.

"You have physical therapy ahead of you, but as long as your blood pressure stays steady the doctor thought you'd be happier at home."

A horrible reminder. Pills. Rachel. Being drugged. "How much do you know about what happened?"

Harris set the cup on the tray next to her bed. "Shelby filled me in about how you'd hired her and what she found. The police filled in the rest."

The memory of the two of them running into the kitchen floated through Elisa's head. Shelby had looked so out of place in the house. Elisa truly thought she'd dreamed that part. "I didn't tell you about Shelby."

"She called me after she got your text with that photo of Meredith. We raced to the house. Called the police and an ambulance." He stopped and took a deep breath. "Seeing you on the kitchen floor. Elisa . . ."

She didn't want to talk about what happened. Not yet. "How bad is Josh?"

"He's okay. She stabbed him in the stomach, but they stopped the bleeding and he's infection free so far." Harris shrugged. "He got lucky."

"Of course he did." Elisa sat up. When the usual dizziness didn't come, she kept moving. "Can I see him?"

"I thought you wouldn't . . . " Harris shook his head. "Sure. Let me help."

With gentle care, he helped her out of bed and closed the back of her gown. She held on to the IV pole. A nurse stopped her only long enough to look her over then nod for her to continue.

The first few steps sapped all her strength. She wanted to close her eyes and curl up on the floor. Leaning on Harris helped. So did the shortness of the walk.

She stepped into Josh's hospital room expecting a riot of machines and buzzing and medicine and doctors. But the room stayed quiet. He laid in bed, staring at her. His color looked good. Most important, he was alive.

"Thank you," Josh said when she stopped at the side of his bed.

She didn't understand the comment. "What?"

"You put your body in front of mine . . . I'm . . . I didn't know who Rachel really was or what she was capable of. I just wanted what you and Harris have."

He probably expected sympathy. Elisa didn't give it to him. "You killed Lauren."

Harris jerked back. "What?"

"You didn't tell Harris that part, did you?" Of course. Why was she surprised? "That makes me wonder how you explained why Rachel did what she did."

Josh's gaze slipped to Harris then back to her. "We need to talk—"

"No." She tightened her hold on the IV pole. "You're going to tell Harris the truth about what you did to Lauren, how you were gaslighting me, and then you're going to tell the police."

Josh rubbed a hand over his stomach, gently touching the bandage over his wound. "Elisa. I could go to prison."

"You told everyone it was an accident. You always insisted." Harris rested his hands on her hips in a gentle touch that didn't match the anger moving through his voice.

She wanted to be strong and confident, but her body faltered. Exhaustion swept through her. She leaned back into Harris, letting him take on most of her weight.

Josh kept that hand on his stomach. "You have to understand. You're asking me to implicate myself."

He actually thought she would support him, let him get away with killing a woman. Even if he hadn't set off a bomb in the middle of her life the answer would be no. "I'm going to tell them what you said, how you did it and why. I saw officers in the hallway, so I'm sure I'll be questioned about the stabbing and Rachel."

"Rachel got away." Josh looked at his finger where his wedding band should be. "They're looking for her."

Elisa sighed. He still wasn't getting that she was done. Totally done. No more protecting him. He'd have to earn her trust back, and she couldn't imagine him being able to do that. "Listen to me, Josh. I will tell your sick secrets. I will do whatever it takes to get justice for Lauren and to find Abby."

He fell back on his usual it-will-be-fine, relaxed tone. "The three of us can talk about this, maybe find a good way—"

"You heard her." Harris's voice suggested he was done, too.

All of the emotion left Josh's face. "You can't expect me—"

She waited for Harris to back up Josh, to give some sort of twisted explanation, but he didn't. He stood there, siding with her. Doing what was right. Being the man she believed she married.

"What was the gaslighting part?" Harris asked.

"He not only killed Lauren. He told Meredith to lie to you. He tried to make me think I was losing my mind so I'd stop investigating Abby's disappearance. Planted those medicine bottles." Fury rose in Elisa and she struggled to push it back down.

"Shit." Harris sounded lost. "I gave him the pain pills after we found them in the kitchen."

Elisa noticed he changed how he talked about the pill bottle now. "And then Josh planted the bottle back in the house to incriminate me, or had Rachel sneak in and do it."

Josh wore a pleading look. "Elisa—"

Her fingers clenched on that pole. "Where's Abby?"

"I really don't know. I never hurt her or Candace. I swear." He held up his hands as he tried to convince them. "Lauren was an accident. I pushed her and—"

She was not going to let him squirm out of this. "When she survived that, you drowned her."

Harris stared at his brother. "Son of a bitch."

"I know you think you're the victim here, that Rachel lied to you. She did, but you invited all of it." Elisa took a deep breath. "You're not a good man, Josh. You've convinced yourself you are, that you've had bad luck and deserve everyone's trust, but you don't. You're weak and angry. You need to grow up and take responsibility."

Panic thrummed off of Josh. "I didn't mean—"

"Shut up." Harris's voice didn't invite any argument.

Elisa had never been so happy to hear those words. Maybe she and Harris did have a shot after all. She'd have to figure that out later because right now she needed to sit down and not think. With so many unanswered questions and Abby still missing, she couldn't rest easy but she hoped someone else—someone in law enforcement—would take over.

"I'm going back to my room and see what I need to do to get out of here. Talk with the police and give whatever statement they need." She looked at Harris, the man she still believed was the love of her life. "If you're thinking about helping Josh avoid responsibility don't bother coming home."

Chapter Fifty-Nine

The next day Elisa plunked down on the bottom of the staircase at her house. She thought about going up to her bedroom and delayed walking back into her kitchen. Not sure what to do and exhausted from the walk in from where the car service had dropped her in the driveway, she decided this seemed like a good place to stop and think. When the doorbell rang twenty minutes later she was able to reach over and open the door and sit right back down.

Shelby stepped inside. "You look good, especially compared to the last time I saw you."

Elisa remembered Shelby visiting in the hospital. She also ran interference with the police and filled them in on what she knew. Basically, she made Elisa's life easier and she appreciated that more than she could say. "Thanks for coming to the house."

"Now or before?"

Shelby had saved her life. She'd probably broken rules and had to convince Harris, but she did it. One more thing Elisa owed her for. "Both. I haven't found the right thank-you-for-rescuing-me flower or bagel arrangement to send to your office, but I will."

"I love bagels." Shelby's smile faded a bit as she continued, "I made sure the police know what I know. I also told Harris, as you asked."

Elisa tried to imagine that conversation. Harris had no idea she'd been working with an investigator. "How did he take it?"

"He was terrified for you." Shelby shrugged. "He thanked me at the hospital."

"I wonder what he'll do now." Elisa meant to think the words and not say them, but they came out.

"What do you want him to do?"

That depended on Harris, and Elisa couldn't think about that right now. It was easier to concentrate on her anger and disappointment. "What will happen to Josh?"

"I'm not an expert on this, but he might get lucky. The detective I talked with, the new one and not Burroughs, talked about how much time has passed. He mentioned degraded evidence and questionable memories. He also thinks Josh will insist he made the confession under duress, and it's not real."

"Unbelievable." Only it wasn't. That's how Josh's life worked. Totally charmed so that he never paid the price.

"He told you Lauren woke up. It probably depends on how he spins the story when he tells it again." Shelby whistled. "With the right defense lawyer, who knows?"

Once again, avoiding what he truly deserved. Elisa had to take a few breaths to keep from getting fired up and furious again. "His luck is amazing."

Shelby sat down on the step next to Elisa. "I think he'll pay in other ways. I found out the reason the real police avoided your calls lately, and mine, is that Abby's case is open and active. They have that new task force on it and they've been digging. They're even reopening Candace's fall to give it a second look."

"They think he did something to Abby?" Elisa felt a surge of relief. Abby was the reason she started all of this.

"The police are going back to the beginning but agree it's likely that something bad happened to her."

Elisa knew the truth was so much worse. "That she's dead."

"Yeah. I'm sorry, but yes." Shelby rubbed her hands together as she sat there. "Abby vanished. There's no body, but there's no evidence she's still alive."

"That makes me sick."

"Josh had a pattern of hurting women. That will work against him now. The story is on the news. He's expected to lose his job and along with that any reputation he may have. I don't think this will end as well as he hopes."

It wasn't enough, but it was movement, and Elisa had to settle for that. "Good."

"I can stay if you want. Make some tea and keep you company," Shelby said.

"Tea?" Elisa winced. She might never be able to drink tea again. "Thanks, but Harris is on his way home."

"Do you know what you're going to say to him?"

"Yeah." She would give him a chance. Exactly one.

Shelby stood up. "Oh, I do have some good news."

"That would be nice."

"It looks like the hospital is going to settle with Maxine's family. The family wants an admission of fault, which is going to be a fight, but I doubt you'll need to testify. I suspect once your lawyer is contacted, you'll get an offer as well."

"At least I can put that behind me." Not the memories, but the ongoing anxiety about having to tell the story over and over and relive it each time. Elisa looked forward to that.

Shelby smiled. "So, next week. Why don't we meet for coffee?"

"To discuss the settlement?" Elisa's stomach turned over in response.

Shelby laughed. "No. No work at all."

Right. Coffee. Like people did. Like she used to do with friends. "I'd love that," Elisa said.

The front door opened and just missed hitting Shelby in the back. Harris jumped when he saw her then apologized.

"It's fine. I was just leaving." Shelby winked at Elisa. "Text me if you need me."

Elisa knew that amounted to a promise, and not just about the case.

Harris closed the door behind Shelby. When he turned to Elisa, pain and remorse showed on his face. He looked exhausted, weary enough to drop. The half-untucked dress shirt and ruffled hair were a stark contrast to his usual put-together self.

"Elisa, I . . . I'm sorry."

"For what?" It was a test of sorts but everything depended on his answer.

"Not listening to you. Not believing you. For making you

think you had to hide things from me. That you had to walk into danger without me." He shook his head as his expression turned bleaker. "But mostly for putting you in danger."

"You didn't do the last one." He had a lot to answer for, but not that.

"I did."

She sighed, letting him know she didn't agree. "I'm not interested in being married to a martyr. Let your brother take the blame since this was his mess."

He gestured to the stair next to her and she nodded for him to sit down. It was a tight squeeze on the step with their arms touching, but the closeness gave her comfort.

He stared at his hands. "I didn't know about what really happened to Lauren."

"I know. I would have changed the locks by now if I thought you did." She switched the subject because she needed to and because she was desperate to hold her son. "Where's Nathan?"

"Titan's house. He stayed over last night and his mom said he could hang out there as long as we needed." Harris looked at the door and the floor, anywhere but at her. "I thought we should talk before he comes home."

"Go ahead."

"I messed up. The things I said to you during that last fight . . ." He finally looked at her. "I'm sure you hate me."

"Never." That was the hard truth. Their lives were bound up together and she did not want Josh's actions to rip them apart.

"I'll make this up to you. I'm not sure how, but—"

"Therapy."

His eyes widened. "Okay, sure."

It surprised her, too, but she'd learned so much. Shelby was right about trauma, or at least made Elisa think she needed to stop beating herself up for not being okay.

"I'm going to go back for me, too. Separate from us." For the first time, talking about therapy and getting some help sounded right and not like an admission of defeat. "I want to feel better and now I have to figure out how to deal with multiple traumas."

"Elisa—"

She couldn't deal with the pleading look on his face one more second, so she skipped to the question she had to ask. "What are you going to do about Josh?"

"Help him get a lawyer." There were a few seconds of tense silence while they stared at each other. "That's it. He has to take responsibility and your statement to the police, whether he realizes it now or not, will force him to do that."

She didn't care how Josh got there as long as he did. "I won't apologize."

"Don't. I love him but the things he did are unforgivable. I mean, damn. I can't help but think if I'd done something different after our parents died none of this would have happened."

She knew his mind would go there. It's one of the reasons they needed to get some help together. "He did this, not you. He brought all of this on."

"You're my concern. You and Nathan." He turned his hand over, palm up.

"Good, because we're going to try to put this back together. It won't be easy and we'll be different. I'll be different." She slipped her hand into his. "You *are* a good man, Harris, but our marriage can't be about me idolizing you and you worrying about me. That's no way to live."

"I don't want that either." He gave her fingers a gentle squeeze. "But you're willing to give us a chance?"

"I am, but not tonight." She dropped his hand and stood up, towering over him. "Go get Nathan and we'll have some dinner."

"Really?"

"After, I'm going to take a long bath. Probably have some wine while you take care of Nathan."

He stood up, one step below her, which made them about the same height. "We'll need to figure out how to tell him about Josh."

She couldn't imagine what they would say. There was no manual, no easy words, for this kind of thing. For all the reasons she hated Josh, this was the biggest. He was going to break Nathan's heart.

"Yeah, and then we'll learn how to be a family without Josh's influence." She couldn't think of a better ending. "One day at a time."

Chapter Sixty

Not everything had gone according to plan. She'd cleaned out Josh's bank accounts but had also intended to steal the house from under him. Kill him and claim self-defense. Destroy his reputation. Plant evidence that tied him to Abby's disappearance and wipe out any life he had.

Rachel hadn't counted on Elisa stepping in to take the stabbing meant for him. That was a miscalculation. She should have known. Loyalty was an integral part of who Elisa was. It was in her blood.

If things had been different, if she were different, she and Elisa might have been friends. They could have met and formed a bond. Had coffee together. Gone out to lunch. Done all the things normal people did, but she knew she wasn't normal. Emotions had been ground out of her. She long ago lost the ability to care about how people felt and reacted.

If only *Lauren's mom* could have stopped being Lauren's mom and tried being hers this might have had a very different ending. But she'd been taught, through inattention and a lack of concern, not to attach. Groomed to believe she didn't deserve a family.

Josh took everything from her when he killed Lauren. Took her sister away before they could know each other. Lauren would have loved her, but Josh stole that one chance she had of a family connection, of living without the unending fights and yelling.

Good thing she'd planned this out. Took more than a year while she watched the life seep out of her father. His slow death fueled her. Someone had to pay and the logical target had been Josh. He used and discarded. Made women care about him then sucked the life from them.

She'd solved that, at least. She gave Elisa the truth. Elisa would see that Josh paid for Lauren.

Now she would disappear. Become a new person. Be somebody without having to plot and scheme. Find a new state and a new name. Start over. But she needed to tie up one loose end first. Josh didn't get to win. He needed to be haunted and shamed. To have his precious safe life taken from him.

CONCERNED: are you there?

ABBY: Finally! I've been trying to reach you.

CONCERNED: it's been wild

ABBY: I saw the news. I can't believe Josh finally admitted to killing Lauren. You were right about him. I'm sure he killed Candace, too.

CONCERNED: the important thing is he's finally been caught like I promised

ABBY: Is Elisa okay? I really want to tell her the truth.

CONCERNED: we've talked about this, you need to stay hidden

ABBY: But if Josh goes to prison?

CONCERNED: he can't know you're alive or you could lose everything, the thing that's most important to you

ABBY: Xia. The baby. That's her name.

CONCERNED: you and your daughter stay where you are and never tell anyone who you used to be

ABBY: Will we talk again?

CONCERNED: I'm here if you need me

ABBY: thank you for saving us

CONCERNED: goodbye abby

She had his life savings, some of which originally belonged to Candace. That counted as a justice of sorts. She'd convinced Abby to leave him. Stole his family like he stole hers. Now they were even.

Acknowledgments

Writing thrillers might be a solitary pursuit, but editing, producing, and promoting them is a team effort. Honestly, I have the best team. A huge thank you to my editor, May Chen, for all of the support, and to everyone at William Morrow for bringing *The Replacement Wife* to life. I don't have adequate words to express my gratitude, which is a little sad since I write for a living. I'll just say thank you, and please know it's heartfelt.

Thank you to all the readers, reviewers, podcasters, librarians, booksellers, and bookstagrammers out there who were so supportive of my first thriller, *Pretty Little Wife*. The success of that book makes the rest of this possible, and that success is due to word of mouth by all of you. I am so grateful. I'd also like to give a special mention to the Book of the Month readers, readers who write reviews on Goodreads, and readers who post book photos on social media, like Instagram. I want to hug you all.

I couldn't survive this career without an amazing group of women who listen to my daily whining on our Slack chat. I love and admire all of you. That is true of my agent, Laura Bradford, who somehow manages to sell my ideas based on a few paragraphs of babble. You are a superstar.

As always, big love to my husband, James. You make all of this possible. And this one is also for my parents and amazing family. Losing my dad in the months between turning this book in and having it release was heartbreaking, but I know he's watching . . . and trying to get anyone who will listen to buy a copy. Love you, Dad.

About the Author

DARBY KANE is a former trial attorney and #1 international bestseller of domestic suspense. Her debut book, *Pretty Little Wife*, was featured in numerous venues, including *Cosmopolitan*, the *Washington Post*, the *Toronto Star*, Popsugar, Refinery29, Goodreads, The Skimm, and Huffington Post. A native of Pennsylvania, Darby now lives in California and runs from the cold. When she's not writing suspense, she can be found watching suspense, thrillers, and mysteries. You can find out more at darbykane.com.

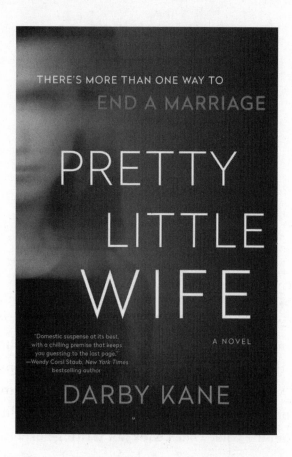

THERE'S MORE THAN ONE WAY TO
END A MARRIAGE

PRETTY
LITTLE
WIFE

A NOVEL

"Domestic suspense at its best,
with a chilling premise that keeps
you guessing to the last page."
—Wendy Corsi Staub, *New York Times*
bestselling author

DARBY KANE

#1 international bestseller Darby Kane thrills with this twisty domestic suspense novel that asks one central question: shouldn't a dead husband stay dead?

Lila Ridgefield lives in an idyllic college town, but not everything is what it seems. Lila isn't what she seems.

A student vanished months ago. Now, Lila's husband, Aaron, is also missing. At first these cases are treated as horrible coincidences until it's discovered the student is really the third of three unexplained disappearances over the last few years. The police are desperate to find the connection, if there even is one. Little do they know they might be stumbling over only part of the truth....

With the small town in an uproar, everyone is worried about the whereabouts of their beloved high school teacher. Everyone except Lila, his wife. She's definitely confused about her missing husband but only because she was the last person to see his body, and now it's gone.